The Touch of Her Hand

Highlander Heroes, Volume 1

Rebecca Ruger

Published by Rebecca Ruger, 2019.

To Every Girl,

Who has ever discovered a love of reading in a long-forgotten book pilfered from her own mother or sister, who dreamed to be that heroine, and to meet that hero, and to live that romance.

Cheers, Sister and Happy Reading!

PROLOGUE

Scotland 1293

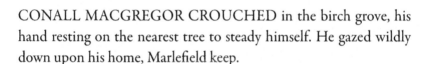

CONALL MACGREGOR CROUCHED in the birch grove, his hand resting on the nearest tree to steady himself. He gazed wildly down upon his home, Marlefield keep.

His home no more.

In the distance, Conall saw the flickering torches, hung from iron rings mounted on the stone walls. Soldiers, whose names he would never know, strolled watchfully along the ramparts. Others, in the bailey below, hauled bodies across the yard, the lifeless arms or legs leaving grooves in the mud, and heaved them into a large and rising pile of dead. More dead were brought from within the keep, as Arthur Munro's army attempted to conceal the evidence of this slaughter of a large part of the MacGregor clan. Conall watched the surreal tableau, still reeling from Munro's treachery. His father and dozens of other MacGregor men lie dead inside those walls. Conall, himself, had barely escaped.

When all the dead had been dragged onto the pile, torches were struck at, and in between, the bodies. Fabric caught quickly, holding a flame long enough to burn hair and skin until all the flames joined, creating one grotesque pyre, sending light and shadows to every corner of the yard.

At this time tomorrow, there would only be ashes.

Conall tightened his hand on the bark of the tree. His chest burned with sorrow and rage. His father was gone. He was still trying to comprehend this.

"C'mon then, boy!" John Cardmore, his father's captain, urged in a forceful whisper.

Conall swiped angrily at the tears upon his cheeks, the wetness brightened by moonlight. None would see him cry; he would not dishonor his father in that fashion. He stood finally, his jaw, still angular and spare at only seventeen, spasming with the constant clench of the last thirty minutes. He passed one final glance over the castle, not allowing his eyes to rest upon the mound of burning bodies.

He turned and followed John further up the hill.

"Where do we go?" He asked the captain.

John Cardmore strode with purpose before him, a hulking man older than even Conall's sire, with fists the size of a young lad's head, and a face as sorrowful and wretched as Conall had ever known.

Conall didn't know why he'd asked that question. He didn't care. All that he had ever known and loved was behind him now.

But how had it happened?

Over one hundred Munros had traveled the great distance between the two castles to negotiate the betrothal of the clan chieftains' only children—Conall to some mere Munro girl-child. He'd not complained even once to his sire, though he'd been sore displeased by the prospect. The Munros had borne game and fruit to celebrate, had shaken hands with old friends, and had shared ale to lighten the deliberations. They had eaten and drunk and diced, and they had flirted with bonny MacGregor lasses.

And while Douglas MacGregor and Arthur Munro began to seriously debate the wisdom of joining these two clans, the mighty Munro warriors had sipped ale with one hand and reached for their weapons with the other.

It had happened so fast—too fast.

Before Conall had even drawn his sword, his father was on the ground beside him, mortally wounded, and Arthur Munro was telling him, "Always, our faithfulness belongs to Edward." Munro had stepped on Douglas MacGregor's chest, using his booted foot as leverage to remove the sword. Munro had turned to engage a MacGregor soldier, giving John Cardmore the chance to pull Conall out of harm's reach.

Conall stumbled now across the black hills as they moved deeper into the thick trees. He thought of all those MacGregor souls lost this night.

"Where do we go?" He asked again, needing the answer now. "We must find survivors, call in armies loyal to—"

Suddenly John Cardmore towered in front of him in the darkness, so close that Conall could see the hate that lit his eyes, turning the blue to black. He could smell something primal and resolute about the larger man.

"I saw your mam die, and now your da," John Cardmore said, his voice scratchy and fierce. "I've buried my beautiful Belle and three sons in the last five years. All gone." He grabbed Conall up by the leather of his tunic and said, heat and spittle chasing his words, "Aye, and now we're done with death. I'll bear it no more, do you hear? You'll get your retribution, 'cause that's what's owed you, but first I'll be keeping my pledge to your mother and you can seek your vengeance when I'm gone."

CHAPTER 1

Scotland, 1304

TESS MUNRO STARED STEADILY into the pale gray eyes of the man she would very soon vow to honor and love above all others. She searched deeply—reaching into his soul she was sure— and waited, with the greatest of hopes, and saw...nothing. Nothing that inspired or impassioned her, nothing to hold her interest nor warm her heart. Nice eyes they were, but blank.

No, not blank. Detached, lacking any promise.

Alain Sinclair possessed nothing at all that would have ever inspired her to choose him as her mate. He was, however, hers. Or soon would be, if her father had anything to say about it. Alain Sinclair was her father's current pet. His rapid rise up the ranks from page to knight did much to recommend Sinclair to her father. And it didn't hurt that he was second son to the Earl of Caithness.

Tess found herself intrigued now only by his willingness to meet with her today. Surprised, too, for they were only recently betrothed and there were few who would dare to risk the wrath of her sire, Sir Arthur Munro—this she had learned rather quickly.

Truth be known, Tess Munro could hardly claim to know much else about her own sire. She'd spent the majority of her life in England, where her mother had been exiled as punishment for failing to produce a male heir. Set aside, as if only a pair of worn riding gloves for which you no longer had any use. When her dear mother had passed away last year, Tess had been summoned to Scotland.

What little her mother had ever said about her father and his severity during their short marriage had left Tess only with an impression of a cruel and imposing figure. Thus, when she'd been reunited with her sire after nearly seven years apart, the meeting had been coldly civil, and she knew that her mother had not exaggerated his unkindness. Any fanciful notion she'd had of a warm and loving welcome had been just that, no more than wishful thinking.

She was to serve a purpose. That was all.

"Families and fortunes and castles and coin," her mother had answered dully when Tess had, many years ago, asked, "Why did you marry father if you felt no love for him?"

Tess knew now that her years at the nunnery—where her father had discarded his wife and daughter, so that he might pursue another, younger, and hopefully more fertile wife—while idyllic, had not properly prepared her for life outside those cloistered and happy walls. Marlefield was not a happy place. Her home of the past year was cold and stark and unfriendly, exactly like her father.

This, then, had Tess feeling quite desperate and so very unsure, which had then prompted her to secretly send Alain an invitation to rendezvous with her outside the fortressed walls of Marlefield, away from the watchful eyes of her father, his warriors, and the serfs and servants of the hall.

She knew she hadn't a prayer of swaying her father. Sir Arthur had made up his mind about her marriage and there would be no further discussion about it. One neither disagreed with nor disobeyed Sir Arthur.

So be it.

But she could learn of Alain. She could discover if her present reality would also be her future reality. She'd prayed just this morning that this would not be the case. She'd prayed that she would find in

Alain someone she could confide in, trust, and whose company she enjoyed.

She'd used the postern gate of Marlefield to creep outside the walls of the keep and had waited for her betrothed in one of her favorite spots, a small glade of tall grass surrounded by a copse of trees, just off the lane, which led to the village down in the glen. She'd left a ribbon marking the spot where Alain should turn off into the trees, which he'd complained might have been a sign for any random passerby to find her.

"Once I am master of Marlefield," Alain said now as Tess leaned against the trunk of the lone tree in this small clearing, "I shall not allow you to traipse around the woods as you have." His diction was near perfect. She was aware that he had spent considerable time in England; he seemed to work very hard to betray none of the rough Scots sounds in his precise language.

"I thought we might get to know one another," she said, searching his face, offering a slight smile.

Thin brows lowered over his light gray eyes. "There will be plenty of time for that after we are wed."

"But aren't you curious about me? I am very curious about you."

The brows remained lowered. "What is there to know? King Edward and your father and the Scottish council have decreed that we marry. And so, we shall."

Pushing herself away from the tree, Tess gave a little laugh. "But do you like riding? Have you ever participated in a joust? What is your horse's name? Do you prefer rain or sun?"

Tess wanted only to know what Fate had dealt her. Would there be love? Respect? Affection? She guessed not, having spent several minutes now in conversation with Alain. He was an easy man to appreciate in a casual sort of way; he was handsome and educated and brave, and purportedly loyal beyond question. Yet he aroused in Tess no greater sentiment than one might feel for the hounds in the hall.

Sadly, she now knew her fate.

Loneliness.

"Lady Tess, I'm not sure what you are about here—why would my horse have a name? I think we should get back—"

"Kiss me, Alain," she said suddenly, cutting him off in mid-sentence.

"Excuse me?" He appeared nonplused, as if someone had ruffled his perfectly tailored garments for no reason at all.

"Kiss me." Tess needed hope and was desperate enough to want to believe the whispered confidences of her maid, who had declared with a red-faced giggle that a kiss could make you fall in love. She stepped closer to him.

Though disheartened by his brows crinkling yet more, Tess closed her eyes and lifted her face. She waited and listened to him clear his throat. She heard a rustling sound followed by a weak groan—preparations, she guessed—and then his lips touched hers.

Soft at first, with the newness of each other, lips gently glided over hers. She sighed and leaned into him, felt his hands settle high on her arms, larger and stronger than she would have imagined of Alain, pulling her closer.

He shifted his head and slanted his lips fully over hers, moving them slowly back and forth. He pulled back slightly and tasted the seam of her lips with his tongue. Tess gasped and felt his fingers tighten on her arms as his tongue pushed into her mouth, swirling around her own. Tess was undone. The feel of him was entirely delightful, the things his touch did to her insides was inexplicable. Suddenly she did not know her own body. She was cognizant of the butterflies—of which her maid had warned her—searching for flight in her belly. Her legs grew weak, making her vaguely grateful that he supported her so easily and allowed her hands to cling to him.

Odd that she truly hadn't put much stock in what her flirty maid had said, but now, in his arms, with this kiss, she believed it all. Believed him capable of wooing her successfully, making her a slave to his touch, and bringing her to her knees in awe of his power over her.

It lasted no more than a minute, this, her first kiss, but it seemed as if the sun had risen and set several times before he finally pulled his head away.

And she could not move. Indeed, she scarcely remembered how to draw breath.

Her eyes remained closed, invoking the wonder of this, caused merely by touching two mouths together.

A faint yelp, a child in distress perhaps, finally opened her eyes.

Arms held her still. Tess raised her eyes to Alain's and saw...

Not Alain at all.

In his place, a barbarian of extreme height with mesmerizing blue eyes, watched her with a mixture of restrained humor and what Tess, in her relative innocence, could only describe as hunger. He said nothing, only stared at her, waiting, Tess supposed, for outrage to evolve.

But she could garner no such emotion. Not now. Not yet.

As if in a dream, as if not really a participant of the drama unfolding, she turned her head. There was Alain, at the edge of the glade near the trees, held stiffly between the arms of two men similar in size to the giant before her. A gag was shoved in Alain's mouth and his eyes were widened in horror. They were surrounded by perhaps ten or twelve men, all watching as if the next move belonged to her. She turned back to the one holding her, staring in dumbfounded bewilderment at this man who had stolen a kiss, at his incredible blue eyes. She opened her mouth, though what she would have said she did not know; no sound came forth. Indeed, she must be dreaming—her body felt weighted and disconnected, as if trying to swim against the current.

"Now you are kissed," said the giant before her. "Let us leave."

Her first thought, upon hearing his voice, was that his Scots accent was so much thicker than what she'd grown accustomed to in these past many months in Scotland. Tess, having spent so much of her life living in a small cloister in the north of England, had only known the soft melodious words of her countrywomen. She had never heard sounds such as these.

But with his words, with that sound, also came reality.

Tess shook her head, slowly at first, not in refusal of his command for she had yet to grasp its meaning, but in denial of what was transpiring around her. She moved her head more wildly now as the horror of her circumstance became very real to her.

"Alain?" she called but was dragged away and now understood that the giant's request to leave included her, though for what purposes, she could not imagine. True, the beast's kiss had stirred her as she was certain a kiss from Alain never would, but she didn't want to be kidnapped by him!

Tess cast frantic eyes to Alain and watched with increasing terror as he was laid out by a blow from a thick and meaty paw. He collapsed like so much honey dripping from a ladle, oozing lower onto the ground. She screamed, loud and long, turning this way and that, avoiding the hand of her captor as he tried to silence her. Twisting in his steel-like grasp, she shrieked for quite a moment until finally the giant managed to wrap her in his arms and clamp one large hand, the hand which had touched her gently only moments ago, over her mouth, effectively muffling her screams.

"Perhaps now, we shall make haste," he said to his companions, sounding not at all put out by her resistance. He lifted her high up in his arms, tossing her over his shoulder like a sack of grain and strode through the tall grass as though a body slung over his shoulder was no impediment at all.

Completely horrorstruck, her fear choking her, Tess tried hopelessly to draw breath enough to scream again as they raced through the open field, away from Marlefield.

"Dinna make me kill you here." Tess's captor whacked her bottom hard, a sharp warning that any effort to save herself might well result in her death.

Now true panic closed in. Tess lifted her head and watched as the other brigands followed their leader, loping silently along the old northern trail as if they bore not the great mass of themselves.

It occurred to Tess that she had nothing to lose by giving voice to one last effort to save herself. Dead now or dead later was still dead. Drawing in a quick rush of breath, she shouted again. But it was not done nearly well enough to save herself, she knew, and she was dumped to the ground before the giant and held fast by one large paw as the other yanked at the sleeve of her left arm. Tess shrieked again as the fabric was torn clean away from the shoulder of her gown. The giant pulled the ripped piece down over her wrist, leaving her arm completely bare. He then covered her mouth with the fabric, tying it at the back of her neck. Tess fought this, her finger scratching at the sleeve as it was secured so tightly, she was forced to open her mouth.

When it was fastened to his liking, and so that Tess could not make a sound, he gripped her upper arms firmly and put his face very close to hers. "If you touch it, I will kill you."

CONALL MACGREGOR LED his small party over the last rise and into the green valley which would eventually take them back to Inesfree. They'd been riding hard for more than half a day. The lass's fear had long ago given way to exhaustion and she'd slept more than half this time. Their pace had slowed considerably in the last few hours as the threat of pursuit had never materialized. Obviously, none had heard her call for help.

Overall, Conall was pleased with this day's work. He'd expected much of Sir Arthur's defenses but had seen little of them. The girl had made his work childishly simple by traveling beyond the secure walls. Conall had only to listen to their wooing, determine the identity of her obviously ill-suited beau, ascertain that he was no threat, and make his move. That had been the fun part. He could not resist stepping in for that kiss. As he'd watched the rendezvous, he'd been struck first by her astonishing beauty and then by the other man's complete disinterest in her. She'd watched the man with something close to hopeful admiration; she was clearly not taken with the man, but she wanted to be.

He would not dwell on the feel of her in his arms, the taste of her on his lips. While clearly inexperienced, she had managed to swiftly raise within him a desire of alarming proportions.

He glanced down again at his captive. Her head was pressed into his shoulder, her hair a curtain of silk across her face. Not for the first time, he brushed aside that hair, so unusual a shade, he could not name it. 'Twas not brown or blonde, and neither was it red, but it was all of these and then, when they rode through a shaded copse of trees, it was none of these. It was long and waved as the loch should in a breeze, some tendrils lying in shorter curls around her shoulders. Once pushed aside, it revealed a face upon which men might dream, men of simple intelligence or not, perhaps men who believed that angels might be real.

Conall was acquainted with the delicate ladies of Edinburgh, polished beauties whose attributes were displayed to the best of intention, and whose liabilities, if any, were well concealed in artifice. And, too, he knew well the country lass, bred to chores, hopeful only to maintain a mouthful of teeth until two score years, aggrieved not at all by their robust figures and sometimes unkempt ways.

Tess of Marlefield, lately of England, was neither of these women. A slender beauty with no more artifice about her than God had given the stars, she showed a face of palest cream dotted not at all by any of God's little imperfections. Her hands, resting limp upon her own thigh, were as delicate as might appear a spider's web, so transparent the skin, so tiny the palm that held such long fingers.

But her eyes, Conall could not forget, soft, liquid green shining bright, large and round with so innocent a gaze. There had been a momentary pang of remorse—brief to be sure and extinguished without a thought—over his actions. Eyes as hers, with that untainted glow, were never meant to stare with such tremendous awe at someone like him.

Below, her nose was straight and small, and further, her mouth was still, parted slightly. It was too dark to see them now, but he recalled her lips were of a pinkish hue, full and temptingly curved, their taste and texture already met, and surely not to be forgotten.

Conall scowled and slowed his mount. Bringing the animal to a halt, he motioned for his men to close in around him and waited to resume his pace until they were in place. There were few dangers to a man of Conall's perceptions and instincts, but he was ever careful. These were the backroads, some of which belonged to warring clans, none of whom would welcome a band of night riders.

He was unperturbed when the girl roused from her slumber. He knew she was fully awake and aware of her predicament when she went completely rigid before him. He was not a man who laughed easily. If he were, he might have done so now at the time it took her to gather resolve enough to turn and face him. Her back stiffened as she attempted to glance up at him, using her wealth of hair now as a shield. When her eyes nearly reached his, he removed his gaze from her person, settling his features into a hard mask. His broad chest captured her reacting shiver, and Conall realized that he relished her fright. Fright was an easy-to-obtain impetus to acquiescence.

He did not look at her, but as she was trying to sit more upright in the saddle, Conall tightened his arm around her middle and drew her straight up against his chest. She stiffened but remained still. After another mile or so, when she did not struggle against him or the fabric that surely was most uncomfortable across her mouth, Conall reached into her hair and untied the knot at her nape.

With slow and careful movements, she pulled the sleeve away from her face.

"Dinna scream or you'll be dumped from the nearest crag," he warned.

She was silent for quite some time before she dared to ask, "Who are you?"

He said nothing,

"Why have you taken me?" she persisted.

Conall did not respond.

"I know of your intentions," she told him then.

No, he was quite sure she did not. "And what do you think they be?"

"To kill me, of course."

"For what purpose?"

"Why should I care? I shall be too dead to consider your mad reasoning."

Conall let another silence surround her until he was quite sure it gnawed at her.

"What plausible reason could you have to kill me, a complete stranger?"

"I have no intention of killing you. Not that I wouldn't if warranted."

He felt her consider this, felt the tension grip her and was both amazed and intrigued by the squaring of her thin shoulders.

"My father shall not ransom me. You must know that."

"'Tis no a ransom I seek."

"What then?"

"Marlefield."

"That is not mine to give."

"But it does become your mate's upon your marriage," he informed or reminded her, not at all sure to what the lass might have been privy.

She was silent, consuming this.

"You would kill me that Alain may not have Marlefield?"

"I mean to have it myself." He did not tell her that it was rightfully his.

Conall knew the moment the implication of this was understood, when a small sound, akin to a sob, escaped her.

Another long silence.

"I would kill myself before I would wed you."

"That, lass, I should never allow my betrothed to do."

CHAPTER 2

When Sir Arthur heard the news of his daughter's abduction, he roared with enough volume to be heard clear to Edinburgh. His huge paw of a hand sliced through the air to slash across Alain Sinclair's sheepish face with enough force to topple the chair upon which he sat, sending the young man sprawling onto the floor of the castle steward's room.

"You sniveling, belly-crawling coward! What in God's name was she doing outside the walls?"

"She requested a meeting, sir," Alain answered, shaking off the effects of the laird's assault though not yet rising to his feet. "I thought it unwise to leave her awaiting my presence alone. Of course, I answered her summons," this, defensively, shifting blame.

"*Of course you met her,*" Sir Arthur sneered, his dark eyes narrowed to slits of derision. "What you should have done, you priggish snob, was to come to me with news of her dereliction."

"I'd thought," Alain persisted, dabbing at his bloodied lip with a square of silk, "to advise my own betrothed of the perils of so foolish an endeavor. Forgive my impudence, Sir Arthur, but your daughter is willful and left too much to her own machinations, well in need of a yoke of control."

"Well, what is it, my good man?" Sir Arthur asked, placing his heavy hands upon the steward's desk, leaning down to where Alain still sat. "Is she *your* betrothed or *my* daughter? In your pitiful arguments, you cannot have it both ways!"

But Alain Sinclair, though wary of Sir Arthur's violent bent, did not fear his position; Sir Arthur was more desirous of a husband for Lady Tess than Alain was of his troublesome daughter's drafty Scottish castle.

"It is her stubbornness, her untoward willfulness which now has her lost," Alain observed and finally came to his feet, brushing off the effect of violence upon his fastidious person.

"Lost? Nay, Tess is not lost, you fool. She is merely in the hands of that ever present thorn in my side, MacGregor!" He was working himself—again—into another fine fury.

He glanced down at the rock in his hand. It had been found tossed into the castle yard and bore, on one side, the blood red wax and crest of the MacGregor.

Sir Arthur's lip curled upward. "I am well aware of the risks—indeed, the improbability—of regaining her by force. I need to know what the MacGregor's plans are for her. It is unlikely that he holds her simply to ruin her. A shamed daughter is a hindrance but would not break me. MacGregor must know this."

Sir Arthur paced thoughtfully back and forth behind the rough-hewn desk. "Murdering Tess, likewise, would gain him naught, as I'd not long mourn a child I barely know. So, what is it he seeks? Marlefield for Tess?" Sir Arthur laughed briefly but viciously. "Then the man has done little investigation. Not even for my daughter would I sacrifice Marlefield. Know your enemy," he lectured, shaking a finger at Alain. "Obviously, MacGregor knows me not at all."

"But then," Alain dared to interject, "Marlefield does become the property of her husband upon her marriage."

"That is *not* common knowledge," Sir Arthur informed him and waved a dismissive hand. "'Twas all an attempt to make my taking of Marlefield seem not so dastardly a deed after all. Hence Tess's betrothal to a fine son of Scotland such as yourself. The guardian of

Scotland and Edward himself proposed the match. Our English sovereign has ample respect for your sire."

"Which lined your purse and padded his army, no doubt," Alain guessed correctly. "I must ask, what if MacGregor *has* come by this knowledge? What if he has already married Tess?" A grimace contorted his pretty features as he recalled the way Tess had so innocently responded to the brute's kiss. It sustained Alain only to remember that she'd thought it was him she was kissing.

"I know my daughter," Sir Arthur proclaimed, thumping his chest, "and if there is one thing I have instilled in the silly chit, it is loyalty. She'll not betray me."

"But what if she has?" Alain raised a brow.

There was only a slight pause. "Then it is unfortunate that my daughter must die as well as MacGregor."

"And if she manages not to wed him?"

Sir Arthur chewed the inside of his cheek. "I begin to think that perhaps we should not hold to chance the strength of Tess's will, after all." He met Alain's eyes with his own cold ones. "I fear that so long as MacGregor holds Tess, Marlefield is at risk."

"Thus," Alain concluded, a hint of angry disbelief in his voice, "Tess must die in any case."

"Do not despair, Sinclair." Arthur smiled without emotion. "Surely, there are other heiresses available to suit your purposes, mayhap even one who will turn a blind eye to your proclivities, eh?"

IT WAS NEARLY MIDNIGHT when they finally reached Godit's Rise, the ridge overlooking Inesfree. In the flattering moonlight, Conall could appreciate that Inesfree was a beautiful castle. Modern and indestructible, it boasted a tower keep in each of the four corners, a bailey larger than even Marlefield's and peopled by survivors, their hardiness bred of a massacre. Inesfree and its village housed nearly three hundred souls, less than two score of these MacGregors, though Munro had done his best to wipe them out completely. It had taken Conall several years to reclaim his clan. The MacDonnell of Glengarry, Inesfree's previous chieftain, had taken pity on the horrified boy he'd been all those nights and years ago. But MacDonnell was old, his own clan small and ineffective for the war that Munro had begun. And so, the revenge he'd sought had been put aside.

Conall had learned much under the tutelage of the MacDonnell, had become invaluable enough to have become their chieftain upon the old MacDonnell's death two years ago, and had discovered new depths of forbearance. He'd waited nigh on a dozen years to reclaim what belonged to him. And there was more waiting to be done.

Many years ago, he'd returned to the home of his father and found that Munro had not abandoned the keep at all but had instead claimed it as his own. What few had survived the butchery had come to Inesfree in Glengarry with Conall, taking strength from a boy who'd seen his clan murdered and would one day, they knew, avenge them.

Gently nudging his steed's flank, Conall descended Godit's Rise, eager to finish tonight's business. The girl's fear had given way to exhaustion and she slept again in his arms, her head resting in a niche between his shoulder and chin.

At the gates of Inesfree, Conall's captain, John Cardmore, called up to the gatekeepers that their laird had returned and in short order they raised the portcullis and the party led their horses over the timber of the bridge.

John Cardmore had been a constant at Conall's side since the massacre at Marlefield. He had made it his solemn vow to support Conall's quest for the vengeance that was rightly his, requiring Conall to do it wisely, sparing all innocents. However, the intervening years had forced them to expend their energy instead on the war for Scotland's freedom, and personal revenges lost a bit of their consequence when compared to the grander picture.

Inside the bailey, Conall was glad for the late hour, with none about to question yet the presence of his guest. There would be time enough for that later. He dismounted in one smooth motion, holding her still in his arms. As she began to rouse, he set her down on her feet. Her small hands reached for and gripped tight his forearms as she steadied herself and woke completely.

Conall owed her no explanations and so offered none. He grabbed her wrist and, leaving his men to their duties, began pulling her along behind him, through the bailey and into the keep. All was quiet within, the household settled down for the night. Conall moved swiftly but stayed to the edges of the hall, avoiding the bodies sleeping audibly upon the floor, most near to the hearth at the far interior of the room.

"You cannot force me to marry you," the girl cried as they entered a long corridor at the back of the hall. He dragged her down a flight of damp stone steps, dimly lit with fading torches, and into the chapel at the eastern end of the castle, sparsely furnished with a crude altar and several pews.

Conall pushed Tess of Marlefield down onto the pew closest to the altar.

"Aye, but here we are, lass," he said, leaning over her, his face inches from hers. "Do you think I visit the chapel tonight to pray for my soul?"

"I am quite sure your soul is beyond the hope of prayers," she responded before she thought better of it.

But Conall only smiled, a glint in his eye. "Exactly."

Within minutes, a small, square man entered the room from a narrow door in the east wall, pushed inside by the hand of one of Conall's soldiers. "Ah, here is our good cleric now," Conall intoned.

"What is this about, my lord?" Asked the sleepy eyed priest, his untidy robes and mantle telling one and all that he'd been rudely jostled from his bed and into his clothes.

"A wedding, Father," crowed Conall. "You finally get to perform at my nuptials."

The priest was taken aback, his little rheumy eyes darting back and forth between Conall and Tess.

"But the license and the banns—and who *is* this girl?"

"Here are the papers," Conall supplied, pulling out a rolled sheaf from his tunic, splaying them out upon the altar. "Here," he said and pointed at the vellum, "is the signature of my good friend, the bishop. All is in order. And this is my bride, Tess Munro of Marlefield." He swept an arm wide to indicate his reluctant, scowling bride.

"Yes, yes. Everything seems to be in order. Let us proceed then. Come along, Lady Tess," the priest said and moved to a position at the front of the altar.

Conall went to Tess, took up her wrist, and pulled her to her feet. "Come, bride."

She followed, apparently meek, and Conall spared only a moment's thought for her lack of resistance. No sobs, no cries of outrage, no pleading with the good Father Ioan for salvation. Mutely, she stood at his side.

The little man began to drone on in Gaelic the beginning of the marriage ceremony. In his mind, Conall was already picturing his victorious return to Marlefield.

And the death of Arthur Munro.

"...and do you, Conall MacGregor, chief to the MacGregors and lord of Inesfree and all the MacDonnells, take this woman, Tess of Marlefield, to be your wife, to ..."

"Aye. Move on," clipped Conall. He was then aware—triumphantly, he admitted to himself—of her stiffening form. She now knew his identity and her response was as he'd expected. Any horror she might have previously felt was now enflamed as she realized she was about to wed MacGregor the Murderer.

The priest frowned but continued, asking for the same response from Tess.

"She does." Conall supplied curtly.

"My lord, I need to have her response."

Silence.

Conall squeezed her wrist.

Silence.

Squeezed harder. And still, silence.

Growling, Conall stalked away from the altar to the far corner of the chapel, pulling Tess once again behind him to the door from which they had earlier entered. He spun around, whipping her about to stand facing him.

"You will respond, woman." His voice was low and threatening.

"I will not." Tess raised her chin a notch.

"You will, I say, if you value that lovely white skin of yours," he ground out.

"No."

Conall clenched his teeth together with enough force for the motion to be audible.

"Let me make the choice very simple. Say 'I do' or die by my hand. Tonight."

"No."

"Goddamn you!" Quickly, before she could have guessed his exact intentions—she must have had a notion of what her resistance might bring—Conall seized her by the throat, his dagger appearing before her eyes, lowering then to press into her cheek. Not cutting, but dangerously close, the point visible even to widened eyes that only held his. Tess's hand clawed uselessly at the vice around her neck, scratching the skin of his own hand as she was lifted nearly off her feet, her toes barely touching the cold floor. Her fear was palpable, had its own scent, nearly engulfing the pair. The blade inched lower, scraping with its sharp edge the underside of her jaw, making even her short raspy breaths impossible for the moment, lest she be pricked.

After an endless moment, assuming he'd made his point, Conall removed the weapon and released her, watching dispassionately as she choked and gagged for breath, sputtering and coughing.

"Shall we proceed?" He asked pointedly and tucked his dagger back into its sheath on his belt. He prodded her along to the altar without waiting for a response. To the now heavily dismayed priest, Conall ordered, "Continue."

"Ahem. Yes, where was I? Oh, yes. Ahem...do you Lady Tess of Marlefield, take this man to be—"

"No. I refuse."

The priest's eyes widened at this, and then yet more so at the reaction of Conall.

Rage overtook him. He roared his fury, shaking the timbers above, stomping around before clutching Tess to him with his hands on her upper arms. This time, he lifted her fully off the ground, raising her to eye level.

"Are you dimwitted? Are you a witless fool to prefer death to a wedding?" He shook her back and forth, as easily and carelessly as one might a rag doll, the volume of his rage exploding in her ears and to all corners of the dank chapel.

"My Lord!" the priest objected frantically and watched in horror as Conall released her, just dropped her to the ground to roar above her head while the short cleric tried to install reason.

"Do you wish to die then?"

"My lord, cease!"

"Shall I spill your blood here and now?"

"This is highly inappropriate—"

"Do you care so little for your life then?

"You cannot threaten death merely because she refuses to wed you."

Tess finally raised her eyes but did not beseech the palpitating priest to save her. She stared firmly at Conall, while tremors shook her.

"I swore you would see me dead before wed to the likes of you. Get on with it, then."

It was just unnatural, Conall thought, stunned that she should defy him so. Grown men—seasoned warriors, able lords!—would have relented at less. But she, this woman-child, held out. Conall was speechless.

Shakily, she regained her feet and brushed her hands off on her skirts. "The answer will always be no. So be done with it."

It was impossible to control the grimaced wrath that contorted his features. His hands itched to strike her, and he would never know what prevented him from doing so. Standing in the house of God? The presence of the cleric? The shimmering tears that threatened to spill down her cheeks while she so steadfastly met his dark gaze?

"Death you prefer, death it shall be," Conall promised, his voice seething. With less care than the little he'd shown her thus far, he grabbed her up in a bruising grip and left the chapel with her in tow.

"My lord!" The priest tried to follow but Conall's bellow of "Silence!" and the door slamming in his face precluded a chase.

They retraced their steps and were soon back inside the main hall, Tess struggling to keep up with his angry pace. He hauled her across the hall, uncaring now of the bodies disturbed, and up a narrow and steep flight of steps in one corner of the room. They sped through a long and dark corridor before Conall mounted another flight of stairs and then kicked open a heavy wooden door at the top and shoved her inside.

He watched with cruel eyes as she sprawled onto the floor at his feet.

"You shall meet death here."

And he left, closing the thick wooden door behind him.

CHAPTER 3

On the third morning of her captivity, Tess was quite sure the beast meant to starve her to death. He would soon succeed, she deduced, for she'd not eaten since being brought here. Indeed, she had not seen another living soul since the beast had so unceremoniously deposited her here. He'd closed the door behind him and left her in total darkness. It had taken her a good half hour to command the strength of will to explore her prison. She had risen shakily on weak limbs to seek out clues as to her whereabouts, stumbling around the room in the unnerving darkness. It hadn't taken long to discover that she'd been locked in a tower room, a large square chamber, sparsely furnished, and with only one small window to the outside world.

To freedom.

Something she feared she might never know again.

Since then, she had spent most of her time sitting or lying upon a fur throw, which she had discovered was infested with bugs, but it offered the only warmth, inadequate though it were, in this damp place. She waited for her father or Alain to come for her. Surely Alain would have alerted her father and they would have gathered the men-at-arms. Surely by now they were almost here. Perhaps as she sat here, they were just beyond the trees she had spied out that lone window, strategizing. Perhaps tonight they would come.

She would be safe again.

But the night came and went, the sun rose behind idyllic puffy clouds and still they did not come for her.

It was on her fourth morning that Tess began to truly notice the ill but inevitable effects of hunger.

Gloomily, Tess cast her eyes once more around the room where the beast had proclaimed she would meet her death. It was truly a prison cell, with only a table and chair, and that one very dirty fur throw on the ground, which offered little warmth but several varieties of nits. But what did it matter if she herself were subsequently infested? Her jailer would not care, might even revel in the thought. Her coming death made such matters mere trifles.

Oh, how glad she was that her mother was gone. That she'd be not subjected to such fear over Tess's disappearance. That she'd not dream of what might have befallen her only daughter. That she would never know a fright such as this.

Hopelessly, Tess fell onto the fur throw, scratching automatically at her head.

For perhaps the thousandth time, she let her thoughts drift to her captor. MacGregor the Murderer. There were few in Scotland who'd not heard of him. Said to have been raised by forest beasts—this, the only part of the myth she'd yet to fully accept as truth—he purportedly preyed upon the weak and unarmed, murdering as he pleased, wreaking havoc as sport, raping and pillaging some said only to add kindling to his legend. Having looked into those ice blue eyes, having witnessed his rage, Tess was prepared now to believe it all.

At Marlefield, there was always talk of the MacGregor. Whatever his reasons, her father, Sir Arthur, had a special hatred of him and stoked that hatred in his soldiers at every opportunity. Tess was not sure of his exact reasons and knew her father to be no saint—indeed, he was the most difficult man at times—but she had wondered at this particular revulsion he nurtured for the MacGregor. But 'twas not only her father who spread the loathing. The entire clan shared Sir Arthur's passion for seeking justice against the MacGregor. Now recalling some particular atrocities attributed to him, Tess seized upon the notion that she had been correct in her resistance, that indeed she might rather die than endure what fate might befall her as his wife.

Wearily, wondering if she might be losing her mind, Tess considered her options. They were simple: marriage or death. But she had more to consider here than herself alone. The entire clan Munro, whether they knew it or not, might survive only because of her loyalty. For while it was true that her father, Sir Arthur, more Edward's vassal than a true son of Scotland, did have holdings in England, the clan's people would be unlikely to find welcome there. They would be left homeless should she be forced to marry this barbarian, and if he chose to put them out.

And yet... Tess considered the tenderness of the MacGregor's kiss and could then barely reconcile the rumors to the man. She wanted to believe that no man touched like that and murdered for diversion. To justify her own damning response to that kiss, she needed to believe this—that no man could entirely conceal his inner self at such an intimate moment.

The sudden sound of footsteps roused Tess from her reverie. The steps were steady and sharp, not familiar in the least, but Tess knew to whom they belonged. They were sure and solid, and no doubt carried the beast to her now.

Keys rattled. The door was pushed open.

Tess lifted her head and stared at her captor.

He filled the large doorway, shrinking it and the impressive size of the tower room. Taller surely than Goliath, he ducked and entered, stepping fully into the room. Tess did not rise, but neither did she cower nor reveal any expression. This was not intentional. It was all she could do to keep her head up and her eyes focused, her weak-

ness from three days unfed having sapped what little strength her
fright had not.

He was without doubt the largest person Tess had ever encountered. Shoulders nearly as wide as the portal tapered down to neatly
trim hips and thighs of powerful proportions, encased tightly in dirt
colored breeches. His hair was black as pitch, thick and untidy, curling just to the bottom of his neck. His plaid of green, brown, and
gold was draped across his chest, secured at his shoulder with an eagle's head brooch.

Tess met his gaze without shrinking away in fear for truly she saw
not his expression, only his eyes, as blue as she remembered them,
remarkably so. Neither small nor sunken, not narrowed or deep set,
they were curious eyes with, Tess understood immediately, a great
perception and intelligence. Beyond his eyes, his face was unremark-
able, she judged, save for the strength reflected in it. Not of physical
power, for that was measured easily in his immense size, but of inner
strength. There was about the sharp lines of his features—the square
jaw and straight, blunt nose, the contours and hollows of his cheeks,
the smooth, firm tightness of his mouth—a wisdom, a resilience that
could not be denied and Tess knew instinctively that her fears were
greatly justified. Here was a man not easily swayed. He would not be
deterred nor easily led wandering from his course. He would have his
way.

"Come," he said, and Tess could only stare at his hand, larger as
he stretched it out to beckon her, seemingly too large as it neared her,
flicking his fingers impatiently in a gesture suited to his command.
She imagined that hand might circle her whole, wrap her up in its
grasp and consume her, spirit and all.

"Move, woman. Now."

Tess ignored the outstretched hand and made to rise but felt her
knees crack from many hours upon the hard timbered floor of the
tower room. She stumbled as her feet gave way beneath her.

Immediately, his immense hand was upon her arm to bring her fully to her feet, supporting her as her own legs could not.

Without a word, he led her out of her prison, down the narrow steps and around a corner to another staircase. This was it, then. Now he would murder her. She considered agreeing to marry him but dismissed the idea. Aside from loyalty to her own kin, she suspected that even if she were to comply with his wishes, he might still murder her after laying claim to Marlefield.

Soon enough, they reached the main hall.

Tess glanced around the large stone and timbered room, which was capped by an arched ceiling and showed few windows. Tallow candles hung in iron rings at regular intervals about the east and west walls. People milled about; serving wenches tidied up the tables from the morning meal; several pages huddled in the far corner, surrounded by huge hounds, polishing shields and swords; two older knights sat at the nearest table, their hands wrapped around dull tankards, their voices low.

Upon spying their laird, all activity stopped. Many eyes turned her way, not bothering to disguise their dislike—nay, their hatred—of the Munro prisoner.

The beast was either obtuse or chose to ignore their loathsome glares.

"Eat," he then surprised her by ordering, pointing toward the nearest of the twelve trestle tables in the hall, where sat—to Tess's eyes—a feast. She shook free of his arm just as he released her and stumbled onto the roughhewn bench before the seeming banquet of hard cheese and bread and ale. She cared not that she ate as might an animal, shoving food ravenously into her mouth, chewing wildly as if this would be her last meal.

She cast timid eyes around the hall while she ate. The maids and pages had returned to their business. The knights continued to regard her with their calculating glares. She watched a young woman enter from the far end of the room. Dressed in fine velvets, her hair arranged prettily atop her head, it was obvious to Tess this woman was either immediate kin to the beast or very high in his favor. The woman sent inquiring glances their way but did not approach and Tess was revived enough now to notice that this woman showed no visible hatred toward her.

After a moment, Tess lowered her head and concentrated fully on the banquet before her. Already she had begun to feel strength return to her limbs. Her body felt heavy, her stomach pleasantly weighted for the first time in days.

And then the beast pulled the trencher of food out from under her.

With mouth full, she turned on him and cried out, her hand still holding the bread.

"Too much will make you sick," was all he said.

"Noo," she argued through the food, her eyes fixed on the removed portion. Swallowing what remained, she met his eyes. "I want that."

"No."

Tess raised her eyes to him, found his gaze still hard, and thought to hide the bit of bread that remained in her grasp.

"You may finish that," he said, nodding toward the hand she tried to tuck within the folds of her skirts.

Tess bit hungrily into the bread and closed her eyes while she savored what was left to her. "If you plan to kill me, why should you care if I am made sick by it?"

The bench shifted as he sat down beside her, his back to the table, his elbows atop the surface behind him.

"I have decided to allow you to change your mind."

"But I shan't," she said simply.

"Perhaps you need more time in the tower to convince you," said the beast with emphasis.

Tess opened her eyes, having swallowed the last of her feast. She licked her lips, finding a final crumb to savor. He was watching her, his eyes focused on her mouth, his countenance fierce. "As I shall not change my mind, I assume that was to be my last meal."

"It verra well may be."

"Then I should like to return to my room."

His laughter then stunned Tess. Not that he laughed, though she was somehow sure that this was certainly exceptional—and the gawking glances from the other witnesses bore this out. But that he laughed so beautifully. His voice, deep and rich, warmed her as she was sure fire never would, enveloping her in smooth and lush rhythms. Stunned, Tess could only stare at him, aware that he laughed *at* her, but unconcerned, watching as he moved his elbows to his knees and held his head in his hands while he continued to sound out his merriment.

Eventually he brought himself under control and turned to regard her, seeing, Tess was sure, someone gaping with absolute wonderment. That such a melodious sound, such a pure and enticing noise should come from such a beast.

There was a moment now when they simply stared at each other, she with open curiosity, he with some unreadable expression, though his eyes still were lined with laughter.

"You would like that I return you to your room?" He finally asked and his smile now was less ebullient but no less charming. "Do you see yourself as a pampered guest? An honored visitor? Lady, to the tower you will go but because I command it, no because you demand it."

"I care not for the reasons that remove me from your presence," Tess answered, her tone bristling. She had learned *some* things from Sir Arthur. "Only that the end meets my desires."

He stood then and offered her the bow of a chivalrous knight. "My great lady, after you."

Refusing to be baited, Tess rose and swept by him with all the arrogance her tattered gown and matted hair would allow. She felt him fall into step behind her and found her own way up to the tower, where presently, she decided, there was no other place she'd rather be.

CHAPTER 4

It was another full day before Tess's solitude was interrupted. The beast had abandoned her yet again in the tower room and had not returned. But now, a woman of indeterminate years was supervising several young boys as they trotted in a tub of graying wood and steaming buckets of hot water for what Tess hoped was not the cleansing before the torture.

Warily, she considered escape, as she had for all of the previous five days but deemed it near impossible. The woman clearly ran the household. She gave out orders with ease and stood tall and alert at the door as the boys completed their task. When the last boy had deposited his bucketful into the tub and departed, the woman finally looked Tess up and down.

"Off with your clothes, me fine lady," she commanded, doing little to hide her disdain.

Tess was unaffected by her hostility as the bath was the answer to at least one of her prayers. She wasted little time doffing her ruined garments and soon climbed wearily into the tub. She would have been happy then just to sit there against the padded cloth of the tub and soak, but the woman would have none of it.

"Sit up straight, stupid girl," she barked, and Tess obeyed immediately for lack of will to object. Summarily, Tess was scrubbed quickly and efficiently by a woman whose other job surely included kneading bread. Her hair was washed and rinsed no less than three times and Tess was confident this had something to do with the other occupants of the tower room.

When the heavy-handed woman finished, Tess thought to rest her head upon the back of the tub for a moment. She settled back and closed her eyes, thinking never again to take a bath for granted.

"Do you ken I've more to do than coddle you?" The woman said and Tess reluctantly opened her eyes to find the sour faced woman standing tubside with a large bath sheet.

Sighing, Tess rose and stepped out of the bath and into the towel just as another woman entered the room.

This one was younger, prettier, and offered Tess a shy, hesitant smile.

"Good day to you, my lady," she said and laid some garments upon the sole table within the room. "My name is Serena. The MacGregor had asked that I share some of my wardrobe with you." Tess then recognized her as the girl from the main hall yesterday morning.

"That is unnecessary," Tess responded coolly. "I have my own dress to wear, if I could have it laundered."

"'Tis not much to recommend laundering, my lady. I'm afraid it is much beyond hope," Serena answered lightly. "This will do." She shook out a soft blue velvet kirtle from the pile atop the table but first offered Tess a crisp white chemise. "Are you dry?"

"I can manage to dress myself, thank you."

"We know you've got your airs, me lady," the older woman said shortly with a brusque chortle. "You're used to having everyone do for you and were it up to me, you'd no see that here. If the MacGregor's temper tells me anything, it says I'm right about this and you'll no be having that style of life again."

"You may leave now," Tess informed the old witch with as much aplomb as she could muster.

"Oh, and here she be, still giving the orders," laughed the witch. "Not here, me fine lady. you'll no more be the one to say, but you will be the one to do."

"Dorcas, thank you," Serena said, her tone not sharp but Tess was happy to see the old witch depart. When she was gone, Serena smiled at Tess, "Dorcas is..."

"A witch?" Tess could not help but supply.

Serena laughed, a quiet little titter. "Sometimes," she agreed, "but she works hard and is loyal to the MacGregor." Serena then offered the chemise to Tess.

"Thank you," and she donned it hurriedly to ward off the chill, which had returned quickly since she stepped from the tub. She followed with the blue velvet and the tunic, which seemed to fit her rather well, save that they were a bit long, the velvet skirt pooling a few inches on the floor.

"You have beautiful hair," Serena said. "May I brush it for you?"

Tess only shrugged for her eyes were trained on the open and now empty doorway. Serena stood behind her, at the table, fishing a brush from inside a beaded bag. Without considering the consequences, Tess picked up the long skirt of her kirtle and darted through the doorway, down the flight of stairs and into a corridor, vaguely recalling she did not want to descend further, to the main hall. She turned left where the corridor split in two. Breathing heavily, she raced through the dimly lit passage and came upon only two options, both doors, before the corridor ended at an exterior wall. Frantically, hoping for an outlet, she pushed open the first door and felt her heart sink upon finding only a private solar with no escape. Undeterred, she opened the second door to find yet another private chamber and still no outlet.

Her shoulders fell as she pulled the door closed again and slumped her back against it, considering her options.

There were no options. The MacGregor stood at the far end of the corridor watching her, one shoulder propped casually against the wall, arms folded across his massive chest. There was, however, nothing casual about the expression on his face. While it did not exactly portray a man motivated to extreme anger, it showed a man very shy of patience. The lesser of two evils, Tess hoped.

"Had you a destination in mind?" His voice was deceptively calm.

"Home," she responded automatically, suddenly acutely aware of her exhaustion. She wanted only to lie down, to close her eyes and let the weakness invade her fully. She would court sleep and lose her fear to dreams.

"You'll no get there from here."

"Will I ever get there?"

He shook his head.

Tess squeezed her hands in helpless frustration. "You mean that I will marry you and never leave or be murdered for my refusal and never leave."

He said nothing immediately and Tess took that as an indication that she had the truth of it.

"But I am willing to allow you time to get used to the idea," he finally said and pushed away from the wall to approach her.

He spoke not a word as he strode toward her, but locked her gaze, his eyes the only shining thing in the shadowed corridor. One large hand flattened against the stone beside her head, the other taking her jaw to raise her face to his.

Tess closed her eyes and held her breath, not wanting to look into those blue eyes. She was quite sure they might steal her soul if she allowed it.

"I was prepared to offer you a bit of freedom within the castle," he said quietly, his voice floating over her like cold, clear water on dark, mossy stones. "Obviously, that will no happen now. We shall return to the tower."

Tess found herself nodding and opened her eyes to find him staring, his eyes moving from mouth to eyes to hair and back to her lips. She thought immediately of his kiss. Abruptly, his countenance hardened, and he released her and walked away, clearly expecting to be followed. She did so haltingly, half of her still expecting punishment for her attempt to escape.

He continued toward the dreaded tower room, but Tess thought her cell now seemed immensely free. Free from him and his eyes. He'd threatened much but had yet to truly harm her. She had only the danger of his kiss to fear.

LONG AFTER THE EVENING meal had been eaten and the trestle tables had been moved to the outside walls to allow room for those who would later make their beds inside the main hall, Conall found himself seated alone at the only remaining table. He stared pensively into his tankard of ale, ideas swarming through his mind. Ways to make Tess of Marlefield accept that which he'd desired for so long. He'd have liked nothing better than to retake Marlefield the way it had been wrested from his family. He dreamed of returning and waging war with Sir Arthur, killing him slowly, having his vengeance.

But that would risk the lives of the few remaining MacGregors and put into jeopardy not only the safety of the MacDonnells but also the trust he'd worked so hard to gain from them. He'd become their laird not because they shared his vision of revenge, but because they thought him the man to see them safely into an uncertain future.

The MacGregors, on the other hand, entirely supported any plans he'd made for Sir Arthur and Marlefield. However, they were possessed of long memories and hard hearts and likely now a bit discontent with this pale version of retribution.

There were times when Conall often felt torn between his loyalties. First and foremost, he was a MacGregor and his duty—his honor—demanded he avenge his slain father and kinsmen. Conall had never considered abandoning this responsibility and knew in his heart that if he ever hoped to be free of the horror of that night so long ago, he needed to finish this.

Battling for attention within was his commitment to the MacDonnells. They were one family now. The old MacDonnell, having no sons, had reared Conall as his own from the age of seventeen for one purpose: to be laird of Inesfree, to be father and defender, provider and protector of both clans.

Conall sipped lazily at his ale and considered these burdens—nay, not burdens, he'd never considered them so. But he was ever aware of the utter disquiet within him. It had little to do with the weight of responsibility upon him, this much he knew.

He wasn't so soft as to name the discontent as loneliness, but he recognized there was indeed an emptiness. This, he knew as truth, stemmed entirely from the massacre at Marlefield all those years ago. And curiously, while he strove mightily for revenge, Conall could never completely convince himself that the vengeance he sought, once had, would alleviate the pain or restore that missing piece of himself. So much of him would always refuse to be happy, would always deny him the simpler pleasures in life. A nagging insistence deep inside warned him never to betray his murdered kin by enjoying his own life while they had been so cruelly cheated of theirs.

"Ach, now here is a man either so deep in his cups, he is beyond the powers of the peripheral visions, or a man who chooses to ignore my august presence."

Conall turned to his captain, who sat not more than three feet away from him. His huge booted feet were propped atop the table, his back pressing into the chair, tipping the front legs off the floor. Conall guessed that John had been sitting beside him for quite a while. His captain's tankard sat nearly empty upon the table.

Conall acknowledged his captain with a tip of his head.

"Well, now," John began, holding his drink upon his belly, "I was watching you and wondering what might be keeping you so quiet and thoughtful like and then I got to thinking and decided it must be that piece o' fluff up in the tower, the one that thinks she'll survive past a score of years if she dinna accept your proposal."

Conall pursed his lips thoughtfully, debating if he truly wanted to have this conversation with John. Tonight.

"There must be a way to convince her that it is in her best interest to wed me," he finally ventured.

"Boy," John said, bringing his chair onto four legs, leaning his elbows on the tabletop, "she dinna give in at the threat of death. She dinna seem to be changing her mind while you keep her locked away."

"It has only been a few days. Maybe she needs a good month up there to change her mind." But he knew he'd not be able to give that order.

"Listen, boy. She dinna yield with a blade at her throat. What makes you think a few bugs and itchin'll make her concede?"

"I have no idea."

"Have you thought of wooing her?"

Conall turned to John, one of the few men remaining of his father's guard and the only man at Inesfree he would trust with his life. He stared at him as if he'd lost his mind.

"Woo her?"

"Woo her. Court her. Romance her. Whatever it takes."

"She is Arthur Munro's daughter."

"Aye, and a beauty at that!" John said with a pointed look. Another man might have grinned at this, his own cleverness, but Conall knew John Cardmore rarely smiled.

"She is the enemy," Conall argued.

John stared at Conall as if he should know better than to believe that this would have any bearing on the situation.

"But you already find yourself thinking on her."

Conall sighed. There were few things he had ever been able to hide from John.

"Thinking of ways to coerce her...or—"

"For whatever reasons," John interrupted with another knowing look, "you are thinking on her. It'd be hardly a man who was no taken in by beauty like that. We've nothing like that here at Inesfree. Haven't seen that kind of beauty in many a year. Your mam had it. You'd probably no recall. She was one to turn your head, was Muriel."

"Beauty has nothing to do with my plans for Tess."

"Aye, but sure it does help things along."

"Christ. You are speaking as if it is necessary for me to desire her, to care whether she has warts on her nose or no. I need to wed her, that is all."

"Wed and bed her, and dinna be forgetting it, boy."

"That is a given."

"And easier to do when the wench is as bonny as she. And then that brings me to another idea I was mulling over. You ken these women, they think so highly of their purity and whatnot. If the wooing dinna work, just take her and surely she'll be screaming at you to marry her."

Conall stared at John with a hearty frown.

John waved a hand. "Aye, no rape. More like, coercion—which brings us back to the wooing."

Shaking his head, Conall considered this. Sure, she had responded encouragingly to his kiss but that was under false circumstances, and he'd not likely evoke a similar response any time soon.

"Time," he said absently. "Time is all I need."

John shook his head, clearly sensing that he'd not made his point as neatly as he'd have hoped. "Time is what you've little of, boy. Arthur Munro will no sit back on his arse and wait for you to snatch Marlefield out from under his nose."

"He'll have no choice. He will no dare storm Inesfree, knowing I am prepared for him. He has no option, save that he wait."

The old soldier was quiet for a moment, then addressed again a subject they had discussed several times over the last few months. "You need to be declaring for Edward," John reminded him firmly. "Aye, and I dinna care if you mean it or no. Only inviting English to come insisting if you don't."

Conall snorted, his response would be the same as it had been. "Let those highborn nobles scrape and claw to save their necks, picking out lands and heiresses in England for their 'loyalty'—I'll no betray—"

"It is about no having your head separated from your shoulders, boy."

"We haven't been bothered as of yet," Conall reminded him. "Inesfree's position is out of harm's way."

John only shook his head, his craggy features settling.

Leaning back on his chair, Conall once again considered the frightened woman two floors above him. He'd thought long and hard over this revenge he planned. One did not arrive overnight at such an undertaking. Abducting Tess, marrying Tess, made the most sense. Marlefield would be his and when Sir Arthur challenged him for its ownership, as Conall knew he would, he could kill him without repercussions.

He'd thought—admittedly little—over the prospect of wedding with one who was born of a murderer. But any doubts in this regard were easily put to rest. As he'd said to John, he need only wed her and bed her—the bedding, he now knew, would prove no hardship. When complete, when his child grew in her belly, he needn't have any more to do with her. She could be ignored, be sent back to her own clan when the birthing was done. No child of a butcher would raise his own children. Tess would be sent away.

CHAPTER 5

"Lady Tess?"

Someone called her name.

"Tess? Wake up."

Sweet voice, soft hands upon her shoulder.

"Mother?" Tess lifted her head, opening her eyes, pushing herself up from the fur throw. The woman Serena knelt beside her, a gentle smile upon her pretty face.

"Good morn," said the woman. "I truly am sorry to rouse you at such an hour."

Tess considered the pre-dawn gloom that shrouded the bleak tower room, then turned her gaze back to Serena, a question in her eyes that she was too tired to put into words.

"We must move quickly, my lady," Serena cautioned, helping Tess to rise from the floor. "I've brought you what I dared from my own morning meal for we are lucky that I have always been up and about before dawn."

Tess, still groggy, perhaps even wondering if she might be dreaming, was led to that solitary table within the room and pushed down into the chair. Upon the table sat a trencher of bread and cheese and a mug of mead. Bewildered, Tess could only stare at it, the implications of what Serena was doing yet to rouse her.

"Eat quickly, Lady Tess," Serena advised. "I dare not be here longer than necessary."

Tess needed no further urging. She ate, happily and heartily. Until she thought to ask of the woman, "Why are you doing this for me?"

"Because it is wrong, for whatever reasons, to starve you so," Serena answered softly. The blue eyes watched Tess steadily and it was apparent that she was aptly named. Everything about her was serene. There was—even now as she defied her laird—a calmness about her, which Tess guessed was rarely rattled. "Make no mistake, Lady Tess," she warned. "I do this because it is right, but I'd not help you escape Conall."

Tess did not question this. Serena's loyalties were her own and not subject to Tess's examinations.

"I do apologize if my...deed yesterday brought any trouble to you." When Serena smiled charitably, Tess added, "But please understand, I will try again. If that means at your expense, I do apologize now."

"You are foolish if you think to escape Conall, my dear," said Serena with a matter-of-factness that unnerved Tess. "He is intent upon his goal. You are the tool to achieve it and he shall not be denied."

"Does this strike you as honorable? Is what he does to me acceptable because he is certain and clear on his path?"

"Do not judge Conall by this one act, Lady Tess." Seeing that Tess was about to interject, Serena went on, "And do not judge him by that which you do not know to be true."

"There is, in every rumor, a base of truth," Tess defended, having finished the sparse offering of bread and cheese. She sipped slowly of the mug of ale.

"You will soon discover what is truth."

Tess shook her head as she swallowed. "I'll not be here that long."

"Then I wish you luck in your endeavor, my lady. But know I do believe that Conall's wish of a marriage would not truly make you unhappy."

"You cannot possibly know that," Tess argued, but quickly waved a dismissive hand. "It matters not, as it will never happen."

Serena considered Tess for a long moment. Then she removed the empty tray from the table and moved toward the door. "Conall believes in this," she said at the door. "He believes that he wants you for what you can bring to him. I predict that it will take little time for him to realize that he needs you for what you can give him."

With that ambiguous prediction, Serena left Tess alone.

SHE WAS NOT GOING TO change her mind.

Conall decided to face this probability after more than a week of keeping her locked in the tower. She was stubborn and proud and not of a mind to appease him. She obviously cared little for her own life, as his threats to end it had not produced the desired end—or perhaps her loyalty to Sir Arthur was greater, Conall could not yet be sure.

Sitting atop his huge destrier, watching the practice field where a dozen or more young lads were presently tutored in the proper use of the quintain, Conall wondered how deep his supply of patience actually was. He'd not thought himself possessed of this much, that was sure. Had Tess Munro been a man he needed to break, a warrior who held information he sought, or any other person of Scotland's larger war, he'd certainly not have shown such forbearance.

She was Tess Munro, spawn of the man who had destroyed his life, and as such, should have been treated accordingly, or at the very least, as Conall would have expected of Sir Arthur had he any of Conall's kin within his grasp.

But he couldn't. He looked at Tess and saw barely beyond her beauty. He was aware of the thin veneer of fragility hovering about her, ready to crack at any moment, yet she was curiously strong in the face of his oft-seen fury. She'd witnessed his rage, had withstood his brutality, and still she refused to accede to his wishes.

This determination of hers was something to be envied, something laudable even—but not when she stood in defiance of him. This only caused him to wonder what sort of person rallied to loyalty for the likes of Sir Arthur Munro. True enough, he was her sire, a fact which might elicit the required amount of devotion, he imagined. Conall questioned only how she could muster such enthusiasm for the task of holding true to loyalties never before tested. Loyalty in word and deed were entirely two different animals, and loyalty to Sir Arthur must prove difficult under the best of conditions.

Conall shook his head, weary for answers which refused to come.

He needed more time with her. His current method was unsuccessful but there had to be a way to gain what he sought. Every person had their price, every soul its breaking point. But to break Tess. Could he do it? Could he obliterate all that he presently found so captivating about her? Aye, he thought her captivating, had been quite put under her spell the very moment he'd touched his lips to hers. And it was lessened not a whit by her present bedraggled condition, for in truth her beauty, though he perceived there was none to rival it, 'twas merely half her allure.

She was possessed of a rather quiet dignity, even in the face of harsh provocation. Conall pictured the stubborn set of her delicate chin, unaccustomed to showing such resolve, he guessed. He brought to mind her eyes, that soft liquid green that brewed to fire as he ignited her temper or tamped to pools of shimmering emerald when drenched in fear.

As often happened when he began to think on her, Conall found himself possessed of a need to seek her out. 'Twas madness, he knew that much and was never fearful of admitting at least this to himself.

What was it about her that had so completely fascinated him? Surely beauty and bravery alone could not ensnare him so fully.

All the same, he could not resist the pull toward her.

Cursing so foully even his captain raised a brow, Conall dismounted and made short work of the distance to the tower, leaving several men to stare after him in conjecture.

He took the stairs three at a time and continued to curse as he climbed, feeling foolish for such sure folly. He was supposed to be the one to subjugate her, not the other way around.

The door to the tower was open, he noticed as he neared. Frowning in alarm, he quickened his pace and then breathed in relief as he saw Serena exiting, an empty tray in her hands.

"Oh, laird," Serena cried in a whisper, trying to balance the tray and close the door at the same time. "I didn't think to see you this afternoon."

"Clearly," he said dryly, his gaze enveloping both her frightened stance and the well eaten tray. "Sharing your vittles again?"

"But, laird, 'tis not right to starve her so," Serena argued.

"I would no ken, as you've yet to allow me to try. 'Tis the second time, Serena." He had watched her steal away from Tess's chamber two days ago, the sun not yet risen. "Dinna disobey me again."

"Yes, laird," she capitulated meekly, lowering her head as she left.

Conall entered the tower room, finding Tess leaning listlessly against the wall beside the only window. From this corner of the castle, she had a view only of a small portion of the western outer bailey, the hills of Godit's Rise, and the forest beyond. Perhaps at dusk she might enjoy the sunsets, but Conall could not know this for sure. She sighed and Conall wondered if she only ignored his presence. He was content just to watch her. He saw only her profile, for she kept her eyes focused on the horizon. Her recently washed hair—another boon provided courtesy of Serena unless he missed his guess—hung in damp, curling waves of dark auburn. When it dried, it would shine with rays of amber and gold, tinged minimally with hints of red, enticing him to touch, to seek the softness each curl promised.

He watched as she inhaled deeply of the fresh afternoon air. Her brow, swept bare of hair, wrinkled as if 'twas not enough. She faced the window fully then, palms pressed flat against the cold stone on either side of the opening, leaning her head outside.

This was Tess in supposed privacy, unguarded, her face wistful, not wary. Her stance portrayed longing, not desperation.

Like everything else about her, Conall wanted in on this.

"What do you think on when you stare so pensively out that window, Tess of Marlefield?" He stepped fully into the room, coming near enough behind her to touch.

She did not startle, and she did not turn to face him. In a melancholy voice, she spoke words best saved for her dreams.

"I imagine that I can see Father or Alain charging over that hill to save me."

"They may yet try," Conall responded, his own voice clear and low. "But they would no find success."

Tess finally turned around, lifting her head to stare without trepidation at him.

"You are so very sure of your prowess in battle and that of your men?"

"Aye." He crossed his arms over his chest and might have laughed out loud at her expression then, falling a bit at his certainty. "Rescue will no come from that end, lass."

"From where then?"

"Only from yourself."

"By my marriage to you?"

"'Tis the only way to save yourself."

"A high price to pay for a life I'd not wish upon my enemy."

Conall chuckled and was aware of those green eyes watching him curiously. Her fear of him had lessened—since he'd yet to murder her as she'd originally dreaded—but now in her eyes, so very expressive, he read something else.

Tess of Marlefield was intrigued by him. Or at the very least, simply curious about the man who held her life in his hands. Conall would give some thought to press that to his advantage.

"Since you've been so kindly treated to a bath and a meal," he said pointedly and noted that she had grace enough to blush—obviously Serena had confided to her that these benefits did not come complete with the laird's approval. "I will now take you to the kitchen where you will spend your days until you change your mind."

"You think to make me a slave?"

"I can make you whatever I want, lass."

Now it was Tess's turn to proclaim the upper hand. "But never your wife."

He frowned, which seemed to enliven her momentarily. "'Tis only a matter of time. Soon you will think of Inesfree as your home."

"This will never be my home," Tess said stiffly. "Not willingly."

Conall moved closer to her, inhaling the fresh scent of Serena's lilac soap which surrounded her. He leaned in, his face a hand's span away from hers. Her eyes widened and she backed against the wall.

"Aye, lass, I beg to differ. There are many things you will claim never to do or say willingly. And I think it will take an embarrassingly little amount of time to prove you wrong."

"You cannot know that—"

"Would you kiss me, lass?" He asked, his breath on her face.

"Never!" She shook her head, visibly unnerved.

"Never *willingly*?" He taunted, a crooked grin lighting his face.

He moved yet closer, relieving her of the ability of speech. Tess shook her head.

Conall kissed her. Not as he had on that first occasion, with tenderness and ease. His mouth moved against hers with calculated fierceness and a sense of ownership, as if he'd kissed her a thousand times before. She struggled and gasped, which allowed his tongue to enter and tease her own. Huge hands encircled her, drawing her small form against the power of his. As she was so small, one arm could wrap entirely around her, leaving the other then to explore the heretofore untouched softness of her hair, delving deep through the damp curls, finding her scalp, holding her to his kiss. She continued to struggle against him, pounding at his arms, twisting her face away, an impossibility with his hand at her head. He persisted in his assault, never harshly but with a measured assuredness. He was aware of the shiver that racked her body, exactly when the fight in her ceased. He did not crow with glee for his own tremor shook him, reveling not in her response for truly there was none, but in her acceptance. At the taste of her, the very real feel of her softness in his arms, Conall groaned aloud in pleasure, then realized that her hands no longer pushed but clung to the plaid across his chest. Her manner had changed, and while not yet exploring, her lips no more thinned in unwillingness but grew pliable with interest, but not daring enough to reciprocate.

Remembering the reason for this kiss, though more reasons he did not need, Conall lifted his head and regarded her closed eyes and parted lips. He watched with keen curiosity as her eyes slowly opened and her teeth worried her bottom lip in consternation. She knew what would come next, he imagined. Though while she continued to resist meeting his eyes, indeed persisted in staring at his mouth, Conall had quite a time of it trying to recall the next part of his little lesson.

Ah, yes.

"Never willingly, sweet Tess?" He now did gloat, not of a mind to mask his wolfish grin.

"You beast!" Was all she could muster presently. And perhaps she might have struck him but Conall, still grinning like the very devil, staring at her lips to see if their proven softness was so obvious to the eye, took up her raised hand to lead her from the tower room. For the briefest span of a second, he considered her hand in his and the strange new heat that crept up his arm.

"Let us see to your duties."

CHAPTER 6

Tess followed Conall in mortified silence. He was right. It had indeed been embarrassingly easy to disprove her claims.

My God, what else might I give to him under such persuasion? she wondered with a sinking heart. She had determined that she might suffer many assaults to her pride while under his captivity. She had also determined that this she could accept, knowing her pride would be easily made whole again once she was rescued. But this assault on her mind, body, and senses—how would she ever recover from that? Even now, her anger heightened at the memory of his callous boasting, Tess could think of little else save the feel of him, what exactly he had done to her resolve and more importantly, how mere touch alone could accomplish this. His kiss had been drugging, tempting her beyond reason to seek out that which her body craved, more of his seduction.

What a horrible, dangerous man.

All thoughts of the MacGregor's nefarious deeds ceased as Tess, unaware of their destination, was led into the bright sunshine of the inner bailey. She stopped and was surprised when he allowed her hand to fall from his. Tilting her head to the sky, she breathed deeply of the fresh air she'd not encountered in over a week. Lost in her exultation, she closed her eyes and was totally unaware of the brilliant smile that lit her features.

When she opened her eyes finally, Tess found the MacGregor considering her with a pensive frown.

"Come," he said abruptly.

She didn't move, but dared to say, "I'm sure the kitchens can wait for me."

He grinned but there was no humor in it. "Aye, princess, but I've more to do than see to your fancies."

Tess opened her mouth to refute this but quickly thought better of it. Let him work her if he desired. She would then be allowed out of the tower. She was unlikely to escape if she remained locked away.

Tess chose to ignore the fact that the beast was laughing at her. She glanced around the bailey, a huge courtyard filled with milling and working serfs and servants, the tall, thick walls lined with a score of warriors.

All staring at her.

It was unconscious, but she stepped nearer to the beast as she met the eyes of several of the MacGregor people. They were of various shapes, sizes, and ages, but all confronted her curious glance with eager animosity.

I am the victim here, she wanted to shout, but dared not. Glumly, she realized that she might actually be safer in the company of the beast and followed where he led, wondering all the while at the peasants' obvious loathing of her. She did not know them and likewise they knew her not at all. Were they upset because she'd foiled their laird's plans by refusing to wed him? Tess wondered that they could not understand her rejection, for would they not have balked at being spirited away from *their* home? Carried off by monstrous fiends intent on God only knew what? Locked in a tower with barely enough food save for the scraps provided by the only person who was not of a mind to reject her outright? Knowing this, would they not then concede that she was acting not unfairly or cowardly or without reason?

Tess sighed, still trailing behind the beast.

"Come," he threw back at her as she lagged. "'Tis no the chapel stroll we're about."

"I've seen your chapel stroll," Tess answered pertly. "I've not the speed for it."

The beast then lanced her with that ferocious scowl of his, but Tess had by now determined that she was not to die by his hand, at least not for any small infraction. Hence, her daring was greater and her skin a bit thicker. But she increased her pace, if only to be farther away from the damning glowers of his people.

He led her around the side of the castle, into the large kitchen area at the rear. Tess imagined this large and bustling room could also be reached by walking straight through the main hall and she wondered why the MacGregor had not taken that more direct route. She was not allowed to ponder this for she was hastily put into an apron and curtly introduced to Cook, a robust man who was, unlike the beast and his warriors, more round than tall, with two close set eyes and many extra chins. But he did not glower at Tess and she breathed a small sigh of relief.

"Eagan," the MacGregor said to the cook, "Lady Tess is losing interest in our fair Inesfree. I think it is boredom. Let us keep her busy." Conall turned on Tess and pointed beyond her.

Tess swiveled around, aware of the enormous amount of activity in this kitchen. Marlefield had a regular staff of about ten kitchen people. There were at least twice that number here, all hard at work in a room that might fit twice into Marlefield's kitchen. Along the inner wall, which backed against the main hall, a long hearth stretched the length of the room. Tall enough for the beast himself to stand inside, it consisted of several different heating sections, including racks for spits, hooks by which to hang kettles, and long stone shelves where meat pies might be baked.

Tess felt the curious glances aimed her way. She raised her chin, intent on hiding her trepidation from these judgmental people. But there was little obvious hatred here, just curiosity, save for one man. As large and broad as the beast, he stared with downright malevolence from across the room. He was dressed not as these kitchen serfs, but as a soldier, with a dreadful looking ax dangling from his leather belt. Tess met his dark eyes, black as evil, and again found herself drawing nearer to the beast for safety.

She stepped back unconsciously, near enough that the beast's hands settled on her upper arms as she bumped into his chest.

But Tess did not startle at this close encounter for the evil black eyed man was moving toward her, his eyes locked with hers.

"'Tis Ezra," the beast said at her ear. "He'll be at your side whenever you are about your duties. I would advise you no to displease him."

Tess drew a fortifying breath as the soldier stopped before her. "Good day, Ezra."

His lips thinned but he said nothing.

Undaunted, for Tess imagined he could not kill her without his laird's say so, Tess ignored him and likewise Conall, and approached Eagan, the man in charge of the kitchen.

"What shall I do?"

She'd caught him off guard, his expression said. With small humor, she watched the fat man look from her to the beast and back again. Obviously, he'd not expected much work from her but quickly had her set up at a wooden plank counter, washing and dicing vegetables for tonight's dinner beside a young girl who could barely control her giggles as her eyes strayed every other second to the handsome MacGregor.

In short order, the beast left the kitchen with a reminder to Tess that Ezra would be watching her. Tess looked up, found the disgruntled soldier propped against the wall nearest the door which led outside, an ale in hand, and disregarded him as untroublesome, so long as she kept about her work.

For the next several days, Tess's schedule was consistent. She was escorted by the never pleasant Ezra to the kitchens every morning at dawn and remained there until sundown, with spare time only to eat her meals—which she was now allowed twice a day—and to see to personal business. Tess did not mind the kitchen duties as she had been unaccustomed to lazing about Marlefield. What this work did to her hands and her back, was another matter altogether. Standing still, about one chore, sometimes for hours, quite often Tess retired immediately after the last meal with an achy back and dry, cracked and peeling hands. However, there were advantages to be had by such work. On the third day in the kitchens, Tess absently wondered to Cook if he planned to use marjoram in the stew over which he labored. When he offered her no more than a blank stare, Tess went back to her work. But not ten minutes had gone by when Cook was at her side, asking if *she* used marjoram in her stews.

"Well, not me personally," she answered with a laugh. "I had little to do with the running of the kitchens. But I do know marjoram was always used for stews and broth. It enhances the broth as well as the flavor of the meat. Surely, Inesfree's garden grows marjoram."

Cook looked perplexed. "I'd not ken that, Lady Tess," he said, for he was one of the few people that addressed her directly and perhaps the only one, aside from Serena, to apply the 'lady'. "I'm still working off last year's dried herbs. Old Felix died this past winter—he'd a been the one to keep the gardens. Perhaps you wouldn't mind taking a look. Maybe a stray plant grows."

Tess shrugged and glanced at Ezra. Surely, she would need his permission and escort if she wished to keep her head attached to her body. Cook followed her glance, and with a chuckle, waved Ezra over, quickly explaining that Tess was needed in the garden.

Ezra gave Eagan a distasteful frown but said nothing. Only when Eagan appeared to have emerged victorious in the stare-down that ensued did Ezra move, walking away from the kitchen and through the larder to open the door that led to the inner courtyard of the castle. Tess followed, eager to embrace this change in routine. Once outside, Ezra stopped and propped himself against the exterior wall of the kitchen, next to the castle's immense pile of chopped wood and barely glanced her way.

Tess wished she had any kind of power at all; she had never wished harm on another person, but she'd sorely like to see this insolent man be given some kind of comeuppance. Annoyed, she slapped her hands on her hips and glanced around. This large inner bailey was one big square, surrounded on all sides by the castle. At the front, across from the hall, the gatehouse and garrison loomed up and over the inner gate of massive wooden doors that sat open during the day. Tess spied the smith's shop and the stables and the bakehouse, the last recognizable by its lower roof and numerous chimneys. But was she supposed to guess where the garden might be—*oh dear Lord, was that it?*

She stepped closer to what might have been at one time two separate fenced in areas with neat rows of vegetables in one half and herbs in the other. Presently, it was too overgrown to discern individual plots. The interwoven branches of the wattle fence were so damaged they might actually be irreparable. She saw no raised tufts of earth for a gardener to sit or even one drainage ditch anywhere inside either section. She had been well schooled in the importance of these features from time spent in the gardens with the novice nuns at the cloister where she'd spent her early years.

She hadn't any idea where or how to begin but crept closer to see if anything useful at all might be found or retained within. It was then she noticed that ground seemed to be missing right where the garden met the wall of the keep. Curious, she investigated by pulling at the brown vines that had latched onto the stone. She was surprised to find that the ground was not missing here; rather, the vines obscured steps that led down into a timber framed underground root cellar. Sunshine did not reach this far corner of the yard, so the interior was dark. She could make out a narrow space, maybe fifteen feet in length, not quite under the wall of the kitchen. One timber wall was lined with shelves and these were filled with dozens of small crocks and flat pans of wood, some sprouting greens, likely planted from seeds of last year's crops.

This now, was a start.

Tess ducked her head to exit the little cellar and approached Ezra, with a careful effort to appear undaunted by his perpetually glowering visage.

"I shall require some tools," she said. She thought she quite successfully captured the tone the abbess had often used when dealing with the most inferior novices.

Ezra stared at her. His mouth moved in a way that suggested he only worked at some bothersome bit of food stuck between his teeth.

"Do you speak the common tongue?" She dared to ask. Then, in a lame attempt to show a superiority she certainly didn't feel, she asked the same question in French. When he still only stared at her, she turned and began to walk away from him, resigned that if she must find the tools herself, the stables or the smithy would be good places to start.

She had only taken three or four steps when she felt her hair tugged roughly from behind. She yelped as she was nearly yanked off her feet. She turned, bent now, to find her hair still in Ezra's meaty grasp. Instinct bade her reach up to defend herself and remove her hair from his hand. "Let me go, you boorish oaf!" He smiled at her. He actually smiled, though Tess was quite alarmed to see the complete lack of humor in his dark and nasty eyes.

"Ezra!"

Tess froze, knowing she had never been so happy to hear the beast's thunderous voice. She kept her gaze locked on Ezra, her eyes narrowing, not entirely sure how or why the beast's presence emboldened her.

"Ezra!" He called again, closer now, in a voice Tess easily recognized as his barely-controlled-rage tone.

Tess straightened, feeling Ezra's hand only now loosening from the long strands. She jerked the rest of her hair free before he released all of it. She didn't turn to face Conall, whom she could feel behind her, but kept her eyes hard on the miserable mountain before her.

But then she heard the captain, John Cardmore, standing close as well, his deep voice exploding with greater fury than his laird. "I'll gut you myself! Get back to quarters!"

Ezra's eyes left her, though still his scowl remained, and he stepped around her, so close she felt his arm brush her shoulder. Tess remained absolutely unmoving.

Conall stepped in front of her, standing just where Ezra had. Tess's eyes remained fixed, settling on the plaid covering his chest as it entered her field of view. She released her breath and felt her limbs turn to pudding. She stared at her hands, one still holding the length of her hair. They trembled.

"Here now, lass, what did you do to provoke him?"

Tess immediately recognized the benefit of such an obnoxious and maddening question: it obliterated her fear, replacing it fairly quickly with irritation.

"Were you trying to escape?" He asked.

She raised her eyes to Conall, indignation straightening her yet more.

Crisply, she said, "When I do escape from that ill-mannered and ham-fisted oaf, I'll be sure to make it look quite easy." More bravado, she knew, but warranted, she allowed. "I was sent at Eagan's behest to attend *your* garden—a more disgraceful and wretched patch I'm sure I have never seen."

Conall glanced back at the offensive plot. "Do you ken anything about gardens?"

"I do. But your drudge, Ezra, wouldn't provide me tools and so I was off to procure them myself."

He seemed to consider this. "Aye, c'mon then." He began walking, his long strides forcing Tess to bounce into action to keep up with him.

"What might he have done had you not happened upon us?" She turned her eyes to him though was privy to only his profile, and thought she detected a flicker of unease cross his features, as if he, too, knew Ezra's temper to be unpredictable. "If you do actually need me alive, mayhap you'd best find another you trust more to keep me so."

TESS NOW SPENT MOST of her day outside, quite happy to repair the damage neglect had caused to the very lacking garden. The MacGregor had, after the incident with Ezra, provisioned her with several basic tools: petite spades and trowels and even a digging and cutting knife, though they be dreadfully small; several wooden buckets with long rope handles; and a larger water barrel, which had been situated between the two gardens, near to the root cellar steps. Conall had shown her to the well in the front corner of the inner courtyard, near the stables, beneath what he had informed her was the armorer's tower.

She started each morning by grabbing a bucket and heading to the well, ignoring the curious but unfriendly people who were busy with their own work. She completely ignored Ezra, who had sadly retained his position as her keeper, and who made no effort to lend any assistance at all, though it was quite a chore to lug the water-filled buckets back to the garden and even more difficult to lift and empty them into the waiting barrel. She hadn't any need of water just yet, though, as her immediate intent was only to make sense of the garden. But if she filled it up little by little now, when she did have need of water, she might have the barrel well full. She began to clear away a year's worth of weeds and found, to her surprise, several herbs and plants, struggling but surviving in the small plot. She would have liked to hack away at the intrusive larger weeds but the pathetic knife she'd been allowed required that she saw them off. Little by little, she disentangled portions of the wattle fence, stacking it neatly to the side until she was ready for it.

By the end of her first full day in the garden, she sat back on her heels, sorry for the damage this labor had caused to her borrowed gown and surveyed the results of her efforts. Truthfully, she was rather disheartened by what little progress she seemed to have made. She stood and stretched and looked around for Ezra. He was down the wall a way, talking to someone near the granary, though his eyes remained fixed as ever on her. She spent the next hour in the narrow root cellar, clearing out all the unused crocks and buckets filled with what she guessed might be compost. She moved everything outside, including all the sprouting plants and went to the kitchen to beg a broom from Eagan.

The little round cook took one look at Tess and laughed out loud. "Aye, lass, you might be wanting your kitchen job back, no?"

Tess shrugged, considering her filthy hands and skirts. "I think not." She smiled. "What's worse, these hands—" she held them up for his inspection "—or my chafed and chapped kitchen hands?"

Eagan laughed and waved one finger at her, as if struck by inspiration. He disappeared around the corner, into the linen storeroom, and reappeared only moments later with a stack of items, pressing them into those dirty hands of hers.

"Too late, lass, to save today, but tomorrow you start fresh."

Tess perused the items, finding two long aprons, two sets of light canvas gloves, and some square linens of blue. She held up the corner of one.

Eagan nodded. "Tie that hair back, lass. Get it off your face."

"Thank you, Eagan," she said, warmed by his thoughtfulness. "And have you a broom to spare? The cellar needs much attention as well."

Eagan scrambled to find this as well. Once outfitted, Tess returned to the garden.

Ezra stood in the doorway, looking as always, pleased to focus so much hatred upon her. But she disregarded him, more easily now since Conall and John Cardmore's reaction to his hands upon her yesterday assured her he would keep those paws off her from now on.

Her work continued, seemed never ending, and made the kitchen chores appear as play time now. This work was physical and grueling, and she loved every minute of it. No one spoke to her and she was fairly happy to be left alone. She enjoyed the progress she made, slow though it was, and felt that she had some purpose now, which she realized she'd never actually known before.

She saw little of the beast now, for he rarely visited the kitchens, never came near the garden, and usually was found out on the practice field. Sometimes, she would hear his voice, booming across the bailey, or through the castle at supper time. If he laughed, she never mistook that for anyone else. His laugh was unique, if rare, and more often than not upon hearing it, Tess found herself shaking her head again at the wonder of it. Such a beautiful sound. Such a wretched beast.

At night, she lie upon the fur throws, clean ones that had been kindly replaced by Serena, and thought of home. She never questioned why her father or Alain had not come for her yet. It had only been a couple weeks. Surely there was good reason to wait. Sir Arthur might be appealing to the king for assistance. Wisely, Tess stopped believing that tomorrow would be the day. That had proven much too wearying, too heartbreaking to endure.

They would come.

They *would* come.

SEVERAL DAYS LATER, she plucked vigorously at some protruding weeds, taking out today's frustration on the hapless interlopers. Oh, she didn't mind this work, truly, but she'd begun her day as was her habit by loading a bucket of water from the well to fill her barrel, only to find that the barrel, which she had filled to nearly half by slogging heavy buckets across the bailey day after day, lay on its side now. The ground all around was soaked with puddles and some of the water had poured down into the root cellar as great slides of mud. She'd set down the lone bucket and had examined the yard, looking for an obvious culprit, as it was improbable that the barrel had overturned without help. There was none, or there were plenty, as eyes watched her steadily from all directions. Ezra stood again down at the granary, his face only uglier now with the spiteful grin attached to it. She faced the barrel again and breathed deeply to strengthen her own mettle. She tried to right the barrel, but even empty of its contents, it proved impossibly heavy. She attempted to stand it up from several different directions but the weighty thing barely budged. She knew these awful people watched her, surely filled with glee at her struggles, but this only infused her with larger determination to stand the darn thing up again. She slipped in the fresh mud and fell onto her knees. She felt tears well suddenly and wondered why they hated her so. But she pressed on, latching onto one of the metal rings that circled the barrel and trying to hoist herself up as her feet were now caked with inches of thick sludge and continued to slip.

She started as a shadow fell over her, and gasped when she was yanked to her feet by a sure and strong hand. It was Conall, his touch familiar by now. Her dejection was not something she'd have wanted him to see, but there wasn't anything to be done about it. He moved her easily out of the mud, onto the dry dirt. Tess glanced down at her skirt and apron, coated with muck from the knee down.

Conall frowned and moved his eyes around, taking in the mess behind her.

"I have never in my life done something harmful to another person," Tess said, "not intentionally, not out of sheer malice or hate. I just don't understand it."

Though a response initially appeared forthcoming, he said nothing. His clenched jaw twitched, and he stepped around her to right the barrel, moving it away from the wall of the keep and onto dry ground between the two gardens. Then he went to grab her bucket, but Tess snatched up the rope before he could. Incensed at his lack of words or any offer of apology—unreasonable, she knew—she lifted the bucket and dumped it into the barrel.

"Lass—"

"Leave me alone." Anger had displaced the dejection. Tess stalked away, her knuckles white as she clenched the bucket so tightly by the rim. She filled it once again at the well and saw only the back of Conall upon her return as he strode into the hall. She held her head high—*damn them all*—and pushed herself to make six trips back and forth from well to barrel, made more difficult by the mud still clinging to her only pair of shoes.

An hour later while she cleared the last untouched corner of the garden, her yanking and pulling and cutting done with jerky motions to match her mood, she felt eyes upon her. She turned, expecting to see Ezra had closed in on her, though usually he allowed her quite a bit of distance.

It was not Ezra, but a small girl, perhaps four or five years of age. She was pretty and blonde, her eyes, with the sun behind her, as blue as the beast's.

"Hello," Tess greeted her, all anger fading at the sight of this sad looking child. Tess noticed a wilted flower in her hands. "What a pretty flower."

There was no reply. Tess came up on her knees and turned to face the girl, eye to eye though still many feet apart. "My name is Tess."

But the little girl only tilted her head as if she didn't understand the words.

"What is your name?" Tess persisted, smiling gently.

"Her name is Bethany."

Tess turned and found Serena walking toward them, coming from the hall perhaps. "Good day, Serena."

"And to you, Tess." Serena said, and stood behind the child, running a hand through the girl's golden hair. "She doesn't speak. Hasn't since the MacGregor found her on a roadside, holding the hand of her mother," Serena said and then mouthed to Tess, "Dead."

Tess frowned, her hand poised over her brow, shielding her eyes from the sun as she glanced up at Serena. "Oh, how terrible. The poor thing."

"She's rather wonderful, our Bethany, aren't you, darling?" Asked Serena, but the child continued to stare at Tess. "John Cardmore named her. She seems to like it."

"Would you like to help me?" Tess asked, her heart breaking for this wee child. There was no response.

"I've just come to fetch her for something to eat. If I didn't bring her in and sit her down, I fear she'd never eat a thing."

"Where does she live? Here in the castle?"

"Sometimes, she sleeps with me. Other times, I know not where she is for days at a time."

Tess was alarmed by this.

"Come along, Bethany," Serena prodded, taking the girl's hand in hers. Bethany resisted only long enough to offer her fragile flower to Tess, holding the bloom up in the sun, her arm stretched taut, her gaze uncertain.

Tess smiled warmly. "Thank you, Bethany. I shall keep it with me in my...room."

Bethany might have smiled but Tess couldn't be sure. Serena pulled her away and Tess was left to think about that poor child the rest of the day.

CHAPTER 7

The next day, dressed in a lighter and more serviceable kirtle of linen, and with her shoes scraped clean of as much mud as possible, Tess tended her garden. She kept an eye out for Bethany and was disappointed not to see her at all.

But she saw something almost as intriguing. A scuffle had broken out among two men in the courtyard and had quickly escalated into a full-fledged fist fight. It captured Tess's attention only momentarily but what heightened her interest was Ezra's total preoccupation with the sparring, which now had the two stout men rolling on the hard ground, over and over, swinging arms, throwing punches as they went.

Tess watched Ezra. He was completely engaged, not paying the smallest bit of heed to Tess. Quickly glancing about, Tess observed that nearly everyone in the vicinity was taken in by the spectacle. Slowly, and without great consideration, hoping the combatants would carry on, Tess crept away from the garden, toward the center of the yard, as if she only wished to witness the melee, as so many other people now did. When the crowd of people surrounding the wrestlers grew to be two and three deep, Tess ambled away casually and moved toward the stables across the yard from the garden.

She would pay dearly for this, she knew, but she had to try. With no plan, no destination in mind, and while her stomach turned at her daring, she hastened her step, concealing herself within the shadows of the stables. A furtive glance left and then right revealed its emptiness. Perhaps the stable hands and farriers were even now in that loud and cheering group of spectators. She moved quickly, ducking low as she went from stall to stall, finding most were empty. Near the end of the long row of stalls, Tess found a small palfrey mare tethered within, the gate open. She marveled at her luck.

There was no saddle, nor any time to consider one. She'd ridden bareback before—well, once, anyway. Tess slipped into the stall beside the animal, who gave only a slight nicker at her company. Crouching now out of sight, Tess considered her options. The inner gate and the larger, outer portcullis were usually open during the day, certainly while the soldiers trained outside the walls. Her heart raced inside her chest; she could feel it pounding against the hand pressed there.

"Think. Think," she insisted to herself. She knew that there were woods in which to hide herself not more than a quarter mile beyond the gate. There were few mounted riders near the gates to give chase, though the soldiers on the practice field outside the castle walls could quickly overtake her and there would be many of them—the beast included—presently atop a horse. She needed only to reach that forest at the far side of the heath in front of Inesfree. She didn't believe for one minute that she could outrace anyone, certainly not riding bareback on a little palfrey, but if she could find someplace within that forest to conceal herself, she need only to wait until the beast grew tired of his fruitless search. And when he gave up, she would ride for home.

Before she lost her nerve, Tess straightened, tipped a bucket of straw upside down, and mounted the mare.

"I can do this," she said to herself and kicked the animal into motion, thankful at least that a bridle had been left on the horse. In a few moments, she exited the stables and jerked the animal hard left toward the two gates. People still crowded around the combatants, but the noise level had shrunk, intimating the fight was over. She saw Ezra frantically spinning around, only now noticing her absence, just as she sailed through the first gate. The stunned guards atop the gatehouse watched in motionless amazement as she passed. Some-one had the foresight to shout, "Close the gate!" as Tess picked up speed. Whether too stunned, or too afraid to challenge a fast moving animal, no one barred her way. In truth, a path was cleared as Tess charged toward freedom, eyeing the now-lowering outer gate and the distance between her and it.

She would make it, she knew. It was heavy and old, rolling down-ward at a fascinatingly slow speed and in another second, Tess was safely through.

Amazed, she turned to look behind her as she cleared the outer gate. Guards atop the wall shouted, pointing, and running along the ramparts. The gate was still being lowered as Tess heard frustrated calls. "Open the gate!"

Tess would have cheered her success, but it was not won yet. Fac-ing forward again, she applied greater force to the surprisingly fast mare and soon, the edge of the woods seemed not so impossible a goal after all.

She kicked the animal again to spur her on as behind her, the portcullis reversed direction and began to rise. The alarm bells were rung, the hollow sound echoing over the heath and across the sky. Hooves thundered behind her, and Tess was sure the entire force of the MacGregors must be in pursuit. She chanced another glance over her shoulder and saw an army of soldiers emerging from the open gate to join the group coming from the practice field, led by the enor-mous figure of the beast.

A small terrified gasp escaped her. She was nearly to the forest and she had to act fast. At best, she had a quarter mile advantage. She rode as far as she dared, quite a distance within the wood, but soon the density of the forest slowed her.

Tess drew up the mare and jumped down quickly, the fear rendering her limbs useless. She fell immediately to the ground as her legs refused to support her. Gathering strength and courage she'd not known she possessed, she stood and turned the mare east, swatting her hard on the rump to send her racing away. Tess then picked up her skirts and ran as fast as she could in the opposite direction.

The stitch in her side became unbearable just as she was aware of the crashing of hooves charging into the woods, though still quite a distance behind her. She bit her lip and turned in a circle, looking for a place to hide. Ahead, she spied a rise in the terrain. Ignoring the pain in her side, she dashed toward the rise, sure it might prove a den or lair in which she could hide.

It was neither, just a lifted piece of earth that was narrow and shallow, forcing her to crouch and squeeze into it, her backside first. She pulled her skirts around her, her chest pressed almost upon her legs, her face only a foot from the ground. She managed to pull some brush and leaves about the mouth of the opening to shroud its existence.

And she waited. For them to leave or for them to find her. She listened, as still and as silent as the sun, her breath quiet little gasps for air. The sound of the pursuit, which had seemed to have been growing closer, now seemed distant and Tess thought that maybe they actually had followed the horse, which now would have them mayhap almost half a mile away.

I just need to outwait them, she thought, an actual glimmer of hope teasing her.

She was cramped in the little cave she'd pushed herself into, kneeling upon the soft underbrush. It wasn't long before her foot began to fall asleep and then a cramp began to throb in her calf. But Tess ignored this.

I just need to outlast them.

Soon, the sounds of the search party drew nearer, she thought, but could not be sure; even if she could see out from behind all the debris she'd arranged around her, she was still facing the wrong way, as the searchers would come from behind her. However, soon it became clear that the beast and his men were indeed closing in on her. The cramp in her calf worsened and were she not in hiding, she might have howled with the pain. Tess clamped a hand over her mouth to keep from crying out just as she heard his voice.

"WILLIAM! DONALD! SPREAD out!" Conall called over to the two young knights, riding side by side. "You will no find her whilst holding hands!" He gritted his teeth, having long ago lost his patience. He'd known! He'd just known as soon as he'd heard the alarm sounded that it was Tess. But he had imagined she'd hidden herself somewhere within the walls—until he and the soldiers training had witnessed her flight upon horseback into the forest.

She couldn't have gone far, he decided, his brow furrowing deeper with each step his horse took. They had overtaken the mare she'd stolen which meant that she was on foot against a mounted army. The odds of her escaping their notice—he truly didn't expect her to be running still—were near impossible.

Twenty minutes later Conall sent twelve men out in four directions to catch up with her should she in fact still be running while they meandered around the forest looking for a trace of her.

One hour later, Conall's short temper had been completely annihilated.

"That little witch," he cursed sharply, bringing Mercury's slow gait to a halt.

"The brush is too thick," his captain, John Cardmore, said for possibly the tenth time. But it was worth repeating. In certain sections of the wood, there was simply no way for man and horse to proceed. The brush, heavy thickets of intertwining and twisting undergrowth, sometimes as tall as Conall atop his steed, was thwarting their efforts. Sometimes the brush was so thick a man could not see another only ten feet away.

Conall looked up as one of the detachments he'd sent off earlier returned.

"No sign of her, laird," reported Gilbert MacDonnell, and was glad of the distance between himself and the MacGregor when a little muscle at his temple, and one again on his neck, began to tick synchronously. "We rode out north, a good few miles yet. No footprints to belong to one so small nor even a trace of that hair."

Conall lifted a brow at this, at the curious phrasing of the soldier. "That hair?" He watched Gilbert—who, on any given day, was plagued by cheeks that were always colored—shrink a bit in embarrassment as his face reddened yet more.

"Well now, laird, 'tis such—'tis all that gold in it, you ken?"

Conall only nodded. One *would* think *that hair* might make their hunt a wee bit easier, the color being so extraordinary. Conall himself had seen Tess this morning as she'd come into the bailey, escorted by Ezra for her outing into the garden. He'd stopped on his way to the practice field for just a glimpse of her. He had no intention of approaching her, but he could not completely temper the longing her beauty had wrought.

He'd thought then of the dastardly deed done to her the day before and the other several days before that—his anger at finding Ezra's hands upon her might have cost the soldier life or limb, but for John's hand on his arm. She'd been terrified then, understandably so as Ezra practiced well his menace, but that had not wrecked him so much as her tears of yesterday. She might not have even known that she'd cried then. He had noticed, it had torn through him, though in truth not nearly as much as the forlorn words she'd put to him. Later he'd taken himself to task for having any sort of emotion toward her that wasn't relevant to her position as a pawn. This was a short-lived rebuke, however; she might well be the bravest person he'd ever met in such a small package, but her heart was too unspoilt for these meanspirited offenses brought against her. For the first time, he felt a pang of remorse for his part in entangling her in his own mercenary pursuit of vengeance. She didn't belong here.

But maybe just now she'd succeeded in absconding after all. If she were successful in this attempt to be gone from him, all Conall's plans for a near bloodless return to Marlefield were for naught. It was unlikely that Tess of Marlefield would fall twice into his hands. Presently, however, Conall damned himself for worrying more over the possibility of her wandering these woods alone for even one night, let alone days or weeks, trying to escape. The forest was not friendly, and neither were the creatures within, but the cold at night and the sheer size of this vast wood was what concerned Conall the most.

With greater determination, Conall turned around and faced his men.

"Dismount!" he called and listened as his captain repeated the order three more times until the men, those at the rear of the party, too, had done so.

"Captain Cardmore, get these horses out of here," he directed as he, too, jumped to the ground. "We'll search on foot. I want every inch of this forest dissected. We'll concentrate from here backward. I dinna think she'd have gotten farther than this."

Conall abandoned the clearer path where the horses had an easy time of it and used his sword to hack his way through the dense brush. "I will strangle her when I get my hands on her," he promised, actually thinking of the harsh scolding he would subject her to when he found her.

If he found her.

Birds and small critters scurried to be out of the way, dashing for cover in hollowed logs and knobby tree holes and into underground dens. For the next few hours, until it was nearly dusk, the wood beyond Inesfree was systematically dissected. More than fifty men, never more than six to ten feet apart, about the tedious chore of inspecting every inch they trod upon, their intense gazes never forgetting to consider the wiliness and desperation of an escapee. Thus, their search included not only that which was below but also that which stretched above.

But never was there even the smallest hint of Tess of Marlefield.

Conall, near to seeing red, called off the search just as the sun began to set, bathing his soldiers and the wood in a burst of orange. He walked through the forest as the detail made its way back to Inesfree, giving instructions to John Cardmore to have the horses ready at the edge of the wood. There, the men mounted and without a backward glance, trotted off, the hunt immediately forgotten, their minds doubtless filled with images of supper and ale and their favorite wench.

His anger still not having abated, Conall sent one last glance into the trees and shook his head at the improbability of fifty men unable to find one slip of a lass.

She was here. Close by. He could feel it. Even had the logistics not been on his side—it *would* have been near impossible for her to have outrun them on foot—he just knew she was near.

She was waiting. Waiting for this. For Conall to call off the search and relinquish the forest to her.

When—not if, but *when*—he got his hands on her, he would throttle her soundly for her ignorance. For daring to brave the forest alone, in the cold and dark. For risking her safety on the minute chance that she would survive the day long journey to Marlefield—provided that she traveled in the correct direction, and did not succumb to starvation if lost, or to cutthroats if set upon, or to creatures of the wood if hungry and hunting. "Better hope 'tis only me that finds you, lass," he murmured into the encroaching darkness. His anger only grew. Not because she had dared to escape him, but because she did so in a thoughtless and dangerous manner, mindless of her own safety.

Conall hovered just outside the forest, setting himself up to outwait a seemingly fortuitous and patient Tess.

CHAPTER 8

T ess, still crouched in her concealed niche, had heard the beast's order to halt the search. She was aware of the fading sounds, the increasingly distant swish of the swords cutting deep into the forest, the waning pitch of the beast's voice as he moved farther and farther away. She was numb and cold and extremely cramped and that was all that precluded her from screeching aloud her joy at this success.

Twice, the company had moved past her. She'd felt them walk around and over her small den. Once, the tip of a sword had made a cursory sweep of the leaves she'd closed in around herself, the tip of the blade slicing across her folded knees, ripping easily through the linen of her kirtle, taking plenty of her skin along the way. Amazingly, she'd not cried out though her surprise had been great. Mayhap the firmness of bent knees, which gave not at all at the attack, was taken for hard packed earth, whereas had it been an arm or heaven forbid, her neck or face that the unknowing assailant had struck, she would have instinctively recoiled and this movement would have been felt along the line and hilt of the sword. As it was, she thought her limbs, which had been numb for hours, was all that had kept her from crying out; she'd felt only a pinch as the blade cut her.

Surely, it had been more than an hour now since she'd heard any tumult or racket raised by nearly a quarter of an army walking amid the forest. Now, she was only aware of the clamor of her beating heart, but even that had ceased to pound in her ears, settling down to a less strident pitch.

Very slowly, Tess crawled from her borrowed den, her legs from thigh to toe protesting every movement of her laborious crawl. She did not rise immediately as this would have proven impossible on numb limbs. Taking advantage of the only limbs that presently did cooperate, Tess used her arms to drag herself into a soft clearing, plopping herself onto her rump. She stretched her legs out before her and tried to work the kinks from her muscles, slightly unnerved by the complete and utter darkness of the forest, now more than an hour past sundown. If there was moonlight, it would be of little use filtered so sparingly through the trees. Concentrating on her weakened state, she spent the next few minutes massaging her legs, aware of the sticky wetness at her knees, no doubt her own blood, though presently she was still too numb to feel much pain. After a while, she finally rose and immediately collapsed back onto the leaf strewn earth. A few more minutes had passed, and she tried again, this time with greater success, loping over to the nearest tree, against which she leaned heavily for support.

The slice across both her knees cut exactly across the middle and therefore, now that feeling had returned to her limbs, each step was excruciating as the open skin stretched and pulled and tore yet more to accommodate her movements.

But Tess was determined and soon was limping awkwardly but at a clever pace from tree to tree.

She'd covered no more than fifty feet when she first heard the noise, not unlike things she might have heard earlier while the search was underway, being of a metallic nature, not borne of any creature of the forest.

As quickly as her legs would allow, she ducked behind a tree, peeking about to find the source of the noise. But she was able to see only darkness even as the sound drew nearer, even as she identified it as the jangle of a harness there was no movement to discern its exact whereabouts. Tess lurched forward, pushing away from her crutch, the tree, into an ungainly sprint, feeling as if her knees were sliced anew with each step she took. But pain was easily ignored when one's fear was greater. Branches and leaves smacked her in the face as she ran. Twice, she fell, tripped by protruding and gnarled roots and quickly picked herself up, knowing she cost herself any advantage every time she glanced behind to gauge the distance between she and her still unseen pursuer.

Soon the pounding of hooves became all too near, sounding as if any second she might be trampled as she ran. She was sure she felt the eerie hot breath of the beast on her neck and cried now as she continued to run and then suddenly the harness jangled no more, the galloping hooves ceased. Above the roar of blood pounding in her ears, above the heaving of her own breath and the clumsy trod of her own foot, she heard the heavy stamp of two feet hitting the ground and then the purposeful thud of those feet in pursuit, gaining on her, surrounding her.

She screeched as a weighty paw thumped onto her shoulder and turned her around with such force she crashed into the solid wall of a chest.

"Damn you, Tess!" she heard the beast's voice then, void of the level of anger she would have expected of him. Tess looked up but could barely discern his features through blurry eyes in this darkness.

Desperately, she turned her head to one side and bit deeply into the paw that detained her.

"Arrgh!" He raged and pulled his hand away as the other simultaneously took up one of her free hands in his. And then came the anger she'd anticipated. "Try that again and I'll turn you over my knee!" he promised in a hiss, shaking her imprisoned hand to enunciate.

"Let me go!"

He ignored her demand. "Where the hell were you off to?" He demanded sharply.

"Away from you!" She spat in his face.

"Marlefield is that way!" He shouted, pointing over his shoulder, his roar echoing throughout the forest.

"I know that!" She lied. She must have gotten a bit turned around in her fear. "I was trying to lose you."

"That, you will no do." His tone was not taunting, but still wrathful.

"I will. I will if it takes me forever."

Then there was quiet, save for their very heavy breathing, blown into each other's faces as they glared at one another in the gloom.

"Dammit, lass! What were you thinking? If I'd no waited you out, you'd have wandered this forest for days—that is, if you survived your first night."

"I would have survived. I would have made it." But this last was given weakly, as a cry of insufferable despondency burst forth. And then, in a voice hopeful of emerging strong, but weary nonetheless, "I would have made it." She was as weak now as she could never remember being, wracked by pain and the ever nagging hopelessness.

"Come on then," Conall ground out as she unconsciously leaned into him, surely about to collapse. Effortlessly, he scooped her into his arms and brought her swiftly to his steed, who was well trained enough to hold still while Conall mounted with Tess in his arms and rode slowly back to Inesfree.

ONCE RETURNED, CONALL dismounted and stalked into the castle. People about stared with fascination at their laird, holding in his arms the hostage they'd thought never to see again. He ignored them, his quick pace and stiff arms alerting only Tess to his heightened emotions. He took the stairs two at a time, and turned down the corridor of the second floor, not pursuing the steps to the tower. Soon, he'd carried her down the hall where lie the two rooms she'd previously hoped would have provided her with a means of escape. Conall kicked open the second door to the private solar and set Tess down upon a huge, firm mattress against the far wall of the room.

It was then that he saw the blood.

"Son of a bitch!" he cursed and bent to lift her skirts, uncaring that she balked at such an offense. "What have you done?" His face, so hardened with his anger, contorted now with disbelief. "Jesus, Tess!"

"Must you curse with every utterance?" She asked wearily from the bed. "'Twas your man that did this." She yawned then, and Conall wondered if she were in some state of shock for the single straight gash upon each knee was deep enough to be extremely painful though she'd not complained once of its effect.

He cursed again, this time under his breath and left her to step to the doorway and shout for Serena and Mary, her maid. When he returned to her side, her eyes were closed and he decided that perhaps it was for the best if she slept now, though he noticed she shivered. No doubt, her wounds would require stitching though it appeared that presently there was no continued bleeding to cause alarm.

His anger, a constant state this day, had yet to evaporate, even now with Tess's recapture. He straightened again and put his hands to his hips, considering her. From head to toe, she was filthy. In her hair, dried leaves or crumbled bits of them clung to several snarled locks. Upon her cheeks, once so smooth and unmarred, scrapes of dirt and surface scratches blemished the fairness of her skin, streaked by trails of tears. Her clothes were torn and muddied, and then there was the obvious sight of the slash across the lower section of her kirtle, blood dried upon her skirts and her now bare legs. Her hands were all but completely brown with dirt and debris, her short tapered fingernails now ragged and crusted with God only knew what forest foulness.

This is what she would endure to be rid of him, he surmised, and wondered to what lengths she truly might reach to be free. He ground his teeth and closed his eyes. He ran a hand through his own untamed hair and wondered how much blame he must accept for her actions. She wanted only to escape.

She began to tremble almost forcefully then.

Gruffly, he whipped open the trunk at the foot of his bed and withdrew an extra pile of furs before gentling his actions to place them snugly about her while her eyes remained closed.

The door was pushed open and Serena rushed in, her expression a sigh as she realized Tess's presence upon the bed. But then, noticing Tess's pallor beneath the grime and the harsh expression etched upon Conall's face, she cried out, her hand reaching for and squeezing Conall's arm. "Oh...is she...?"

"She sleeps," Conall informed her. "Her legs are badly grazed. Perhaps the hag should be summoned to stitch them," he suggested absently, his tone curt, not having removed his eyes from his hostage.

"Would take too long to find her. Mayhap Duncan...he is, after all, your surgeon."

"And a hack with a needle," Conall said with a shake of his head. "The hag has neater stitches."

Mary, Serena's head bobbing maid, flounced into the room just then, a shrill shriek emerging as she, too, noticed Tess. Serena, as so often was the case, immediately calmed the young maid, with a few succinct sentences.

"Mary, settle yourself. Lady Tess will be fine. Send Gowan, at his laird's behest, to find old Metylda. Her skill is needed. Fetch hot water and linen and the salve from my chamber. Go."

The little maid, clearly put at ease by her mistress's own calm, continued moving her head up and down so quickly Conall won-

dered that it sometimes did not bounce right off. Serena turned her
to face the door and the girl left to do Serena's bidding. Then Conall,
sensing that Serena had the situation well in hand, left without a
word, closing the door with an unintentional loud thud behind him.

"HE IS VERY ANGRY," Tess observed groggily to Serena, though
her teeth chattered.

"He was greatly worried, no doubt," Serena guessed.

"Worried that he might lose Marlefield, if at all," Tess said and
tried to open her eyes, which she eventually did. She found Serena
tilting her head, considering her in an odd fashion. "Do not be cross
with me, Serena. You must understand that I have to try."

"I understand, Lady Tess. But he never will," Serena answered
softly.

"I don't care what he does."

"Tess, have you any other injuries aside from your legs?" Serena
asked then.

Tess shook her head against the softness of the mattress beneath
her. "Save for the knowledge of my failure, there is no pain."

Mary returned a few minutes later with an ewer of steaming wa-
ter, several strips of linen draped over her forearm, and a vial of what
Tess guessed must be the salve. Tess observed Serena as she accepted
these items and moved the furs aside and began to clean her wounds.
She studied her quiet dignity, her gentle efficiency, that soft beauty.
"Why did you never marry the beast?"

Serena's head popped up. "Conall? Wed Conall?" And she
laughed.

"You are very beautiful. Surely he pursued you."

"My father took Conall in many years ago and raised him as his
own. Conall is...he is like a brother to me. Just as loved and equally
annoying at times."

"I did not know that you were a MacGregor," Tess admitted. "I thought that you and the beast were...you hold such a high place in the household that I thought...." she did not finish, unwilling to insult dear Serena, though she had just done that.

Serena was shaking her head. "I am a MacDonnell. Conall was named chief by my own father before he died."

"I wish you had married him," said Tess. She winced then as Serena began to apply greater pressure to fully remove the debris from Tess's open cuts.

"You think you would not be here then?" Serena shook her head again, her eyes on her work once more. "I think, Lady Tess, that you are Conall were meant to be."

"But not like this."

"Exactly like this."

"I hate him," Tess said after a while, drowsily, slipping away.

"You want to, but you cannot," Serena guessed.

IT MIGHT HAVE BEEN several minutes or several hours later when Tess woke again. She could not be sure for she'd slept fitfully, having no strong idea of time passed. The room—to whom it belonged, she did not know—was gloomy, almost dark save for the orange glow of a small hearth fire which projected dancing shadows against the cold stone walls.

Something had woken her. Glancing around, she spied a tiny figure near the window to the left of the bed.

The old hag. That must have been what had roused her from her pleasant dreams. Dreams in which she'd been successful in her escape, in which she was home, in England, and with her mother.

A small noise, a cackle really, reminded Tess again of the old woman's presence. She still hovered in the corner, her back to the rest of the room, but Tess was aware of the sound of a pestle scraping against mortar. Tess had noticed her previously, during the time she'd had chores in the kitchens. She knew that this woman, Metylda, who was as hunched as most were erect, and who seemed to have lived far beyond the years God had intended of her, lived outside the castle walls, somewhere deep in the forest. According to Moira, the kitchen maid who had sometimes shared duties with Tess, Metylda had not had a clan of her own since a summer more than sixty years ago when she'd lost a child and her husband had blamed her and shunned her and ordered her gone. Meg had whispered to Tess that Metylda was a witch who could speak to the dead.

"'Tis true," Meg had insisted. "When my own ma lay dying, we summoned the hag, and she came and carried on an entire conversation with a person at the far side of the sick bed." The young maid had paused for dramatic effect. "But there was only me and da with her and we were standing next to the hag."

With this knowledge, which Tess chose to accept as possibly half true, Tess wondered at the stability of the old woman's mind. Aside from this enlightenment from the usually quiet Meg, Tess knew only that the hag served as a sort of medicine woman to the clan, coming inside the curtained walls of Inesfree every few days to treat or heal various afflictions throughout the castle. She sometimes spent time in the kitchens though had never seemed to take much notice of Tess.

The door opened and Serena again entered the chamber, her smile, as much about Serena, never less than genuine. She perched beside Tess on the bed. As Tess trusted Serena, who appeared completely at ease with the other woman's presence, Tess lost some of the anxiety which had begun to plague her about allowing the hag to perform the necessary deed. Tess was sleepy but still cognizant of the pain in her knees, which was beginning to seem enormous, causing Tess to wonder how she had managed to walk at all earlier.

"Tess?" Serena called to her, taking her hand between both of hers. "Metylda is ready now to stitch your cuts."

"It will hurt," Tess predicted with a grimace.

"Aye, it will hurt," called the old woman, sounding almost cheerful as she turned and approached the bed. She loomed over Tess, her head suddenly seeming too large for her frail body. Her eyes, which Tess noted with horror were two distinct colors, one green, one blue, trained steadily upon her. Her hand, cold and dry and gnarled, covered Tess's forehead. She held Tess's gaze, narrowing her blue eye while Tess fought the urge to shrink further into the mattress.

As quickly as it had come, the hand upon her brow disappeared, and the old woman straightened as far as she was able, nodding approval, smiling to reveal a surprisingly full and pretty set of teeth.

"You're strong," she declared and thumped one crooked finger against her own temple. "In here. And pain, you ken, is quickly forgotten."

Tess imagined those were her words of comfort, preparation for what was to come. She tried very hard not to think of the needle, which would have to be large enough to puncture solid skin, poking through, back and forth, first one knee, and then the other.

"I think I might be sick," she whimpered.

"You'll do no such thing," the hag announced and dragged a chair from near the window to the side of the bed.

And while Tess contemplated how very agile and robust the tiny woman seemed to be, the door opened again, and Tess watched the beast himself enter and come to stand beside the bed also.

She might have groaned aloud her discomfort at his presence but could not be sure. Their eyes met and Tess knew immediately that he was still particularly angry at her for such an ill-conceived attempt to flee. To flee at all. But she was able to continue to meet his dark stare, and rather frightened enough just now that she sent him a rather beseeching look. Whether she realized it or not, she considered him the safest and surest thing in her life right now.

Then everything happened very quickly. Serena moved down upon the mattress, firmly grabbing hold of Tess's lower legs while the beast surprised her by lifting the upper half of her body off the mattress and positioning himself behind her, straddling her from behind. She was then lowered onto him, her back pressed against his chest as his arms circled her, trapping her own arms between her thighs and his, which stretched out beside her.

"Dear Lord, will it hurt that much?" She wondered.

Conall answered at her ear. "No so much as you seem to think, lass. But 'tis the body's natural inclination to flinch when stuck with a needle, and you need to remain verra still."

She whimpered. She couldn't help herself. She knew herself to be a coward, with barely any tolerance for pain.

"Close your eyes," Conall whispered, his breath fanning the tangled hair at her temple. Tess obeyed instantly. She did not need to see the needle piercing her flesh.

She felt the first prick of the needle and knew that Conall was definitely correct. Her entire body spasmed. Her back lifted while her hands dug into the hard flesh of Conall's thighs at each side of her. She knew Serena strained under the force of her bucking legs. She felt Conall's arms tighten around her, holding her snugly to his body.

"Listen to me, lass," Conall said urgently. "You must remain still. Listen to my voice. Concentrate on the sound of my voice. Right here behind you." He continued to talk, and Tess was slightly amazed that she was able to lose a small bit of her dread. His voice did that to her. It was soothing, purposefully low and warm against her skin. The words themselves were unimportant—he spoke of the last time he'd been stitched, thought he might have been stitched at least a dozen or more times throughout his life—but the movement of his chest as it contracted with his speech, the timbre of his tone soft against her ear, the feel of his body, so solid and secure behind her, lulled Tess. Soon, concentrating upon Conall, she was able to relieve herself of her preoccupation with the needle and the pain. After a while, she imagined that his voice had inherited that same quality she'd encountered before, that husky, sated yet somehow still hungry tone that he'd used when he'd uttered his very first words to her, "Now you are kissed" all those days ago at Marlefield.

CHAPTER 9

Perhaps it took the hag all of twenty or so minutes to complete her task. When she was done and had laved Tess's knees with some pungent concoction, she ordered Serena to wrap Tess's legs in linen. Serena did so, quite efficiently, while Metylda gathered up her implements and accessories in a small, leathery bag.

Tess's entire body was drained of tension, though still draped over Conall, who seemed inclined to remain as he was. She felt her shoulders drop a bit with the removal of the expectation of pain. Her fingers loosened their biting hold on Conall's thighs though he had yet to remove his own arms from around Tess.

"Dinna bend your knees, lass. No until I return to remove the threads," advised the hag, again at Tess's side.

"Thank you, Metylda," Tess said, curious as to the picture she and Conall made and the hag's possible reaction to it. But there was none. The old woman departed just as Serena raised herself from the bed, having completely bandaged Tess's knees.

"I'll check on you tomorrow, Lady Tess," she said. She bid a quiet good evening to Conall and she, too, left.

Tess stiffened again. She was alone with Conall.

"Promise me, lass. You'll no try to escape again," he demanded of her.

"I will not make that promise." Had her arms been free, she might have crossed them over her chest to accent her firm resolve in this.

"You may no be so lucky next time," he predicted, his breath once again at her temple. "Next time, you may no survive."

"But I would rather die free than live forever here."

"Your courage is wasted in this endeavor. I will no let you go." Silence then, a stalemate, until he said, his tone fairly gentle, "Lass, it's dangerous for you out there."

A bitter laugh escaped her. "Says the man who threatened my life at knifepoint."

"Aye, and well you ken I'll no be killing you."

"Then why not release me?" She almost threw her hands up in frustration.

She felt something rumble against her back. "I keep thinking you'll change your mind."

"Is this funny to you? You have stolen me from my home and my family and everything I know and love—and for what? I won't marry you. And you can just shrug it off as if my mind is merely fickle, and bound to be changed? Is a person's life so meaningless to you?" He did not answer, but he extricated himself from his position behind her, settling her back upon the pillows. "Take me back to the tower," she said stiffly. "Take me back."

"Nae, lass," he said gruffly. "The mattress will be kinder than the timber tonight."

"I do not want to stay here."

"But you have no choice."

Her answering sigh was audible, in part due to her exhaustion, in part due to the sense that she would never have her way when up against the beast.

TESS SLEPT SOUNDLY in that borrowed chamber, Conall's own, she had horrifically learned the next morning when she'd casually asked of Serena whom she had put out of bed. This explained the nagging sense that she had not spent the night alone.

The MacGregor had stayed with her. Likely to guard his prisoner, Tess guessed, and wondered if it were not possible that he might have worried for her. Had she perceived about him, aside from his anger, an emotion she'd not been able to name at the time. Was it possible then, that he brooded about her safety?

Quickly enough, before other incredible ideas took flight, Tess laid these dubious imaginings away. Conall thought only of Marlefield. Any feeling he might portray was motivated by his desire for Marlefield. Never for his prisoner. Never for Tess.

Three days later, Tess had seen Conall not at all during the day but, as was proven by disturbances within the chamber she noted each morning, knew he spent his nights here. Surely, though, not in the massive bed with her. She liked to think this was something that, even while sleeping, could not escape her notice. Possibly, the herbal mix that Metylda had left behind to help with the pain, and which Serena insisted she take twice a day, might have something to do with her sound sleeping of late.

Daily, Serena changed the linens which bound her knees. Tess was awed by the grotesque damage done to her by the sword but was assured by Metylda, who visited two mornings after Tess's misadventure, that all would heal well, with nary a scar.

It was on her forth night in the beast's chamber that Tess was disturbed from her slumber. Thus far, she had managed, despite the obvious company she was keeping, to sleep uninterrupted. Tess thought a shift in the mattress might have been what disturbed her. She opened her eyes to find Conall hovering over the bed, then straightening with something in his arms.

"What is it?" She asked.

Conall stilled. "Go back to sleep, lass."

"What have you there?" Tess sat up.

"Bethany," he answered. "She steals in every night to lie beside you. "

Tess was stunned. "Then why do you take her away?"

"She might cause damage to your legs." He sounded disgruntled.

"No, she won't. You mustn't."

"She'll go to Serena as she has these last few nights."

"No, bring her to me," Tess insisted. She was heartened that the woeful child had sought her out and then angered that Conall would so uncharitably remove her. "Leave her here," she again insisted as Conall remained unmoving with indecisiveness. Finally, with a disagreeable sigh, he replaced the sleeping child at Tess's side. Tess turned, not without pain, and propped herself up on her elbow to stare at the child, who had curled toward Tess.

Such a beautiful child. So very lonely. Tess stroked the girl's soft blonde hair, then quite happily laid her head upon her arm and soon had drifted back to sleep, with Bethany tucked into her side.

In the morning, Tess woke to the feel of her hand being held between two small ones and opened her eyes to find Bethany regarding her shyly.

"Good morn, Bethany," Tess said with a smile.

The child, as expected, did not reply. Just sat there, holding Tess's hand.

The door to the chamber opened and a man entered. It was the MacGregor's captain, Tess saw, John Cardmore.

"There you are, lass," he called to Bethany, whom Tess noted only shifted her head at the huge man. "Pardon and all, Lady Tess," John Cardmore said. "Serena's been looking for this mite. 'Tis time for her meal. I dinna hope you'd mind her creeping in here at night."

"Not at all, Captain," Tess said.

"She seems quite taken with you. Dinna take to many. I'd thought it'd harm no one to let her up."

"I welcome her company." Then to Bethany, "But the captain has come to take you to Serena, Bethany. You should go now and break your fast."

Bethany continued to stare silently at Tess.

"Promise me that you'll come again." Tess nodded and hoped the child would do the same, to show she understood. She did not but released Tess's hand and scooted off the bed. Tess watched her leave, allowing the captain to take her small hand in his.

For quite a while, Tess thought of little else save Bethany, actually craving the beast's presence that she might question him about the girl. But, keeping with his habit of avoiding her during the day, he did not show himself. Serena arrived later in the morning with a trencher of bread and cheese, followed shortly by the ever-gloomy Dorcas, who once again was charged with giving Tess a bath. The mean-spirited woman made no effort to keep her thoughts to herself, letting Tess know that her injuries were the least she deserved for the trouble she had caused the MacGregor. In spite of this, the woman was careful not to dampen or disturb the bandages about Tess's knees. For her part, Tess was happy for the bath, despite having to bear Dorcas' criticisms.

She refused any more of the drug Metylda and Serena continued to insist she needed and then was able to remain awake that night, awaiting the arrival of Bethany. She was not disappointed. Shortly after sundown, the door creaked open and Bethany's small head appeared, peeking into the room. She was not alone. Tess was quite astonished to see that the MacGregor's captain, John Cardmore, was actually the force behind the opening of the solid door.

Upon noticing that Tess was clearly not asleep, indeed, was sitting up in bed, John cocked his head to one side and said, rather sheepishly for one so large, "Ach, now I've been found out."

"You have been helping Bethany to steal into this room?" Tess asked. "Come darling," she added sweetly for Bethany's benefit, patting the space beside her. The little girl wasted no time but dropped the captain's hand and climbed up beside Tess. Tess gave her a quick hug and happily watched the child settle herself upon the bed. Tess pulled the coverlets about the small body and raised her eyes to the captain, awaiting his explanation.

"Here now, lass, 'tis only that I've a wee soft spot for the lass, having no kin of her own. She wants to be with you." He shrugged his broad shoulders. "If you'd no deny her, then neither can I."

"I thank you for allowing her to be with me." Tess placed her hand atop the child's head, marveling at the softness of her baby fine hair.

"It makes the lass happy."

"It makes me happy."

John Cardmore only nodded. Clearly, his motives concerned only Bethany. Nevertheless, Tess was truly grateful for his assistance. Captain Cardmore nodded again before moving his eyes to the child, all but sleeping already, and, satisfied that Bethany was well received, he left, closing the door quietly behind him.

Only moments later, Tess heard voices outside the chamber, raised not quite to shouts, but heightened enough that Tess recognized that of the beast arguing with his captain, though the words themselves Tess could not discern. The voices died away after a few curt exchanges. Footsteps receded down the passageway just as the door to the chamber opened again.

The beast had come. He'd clearly been advised that she was not yet asleep for he seemed not at all surprised to find her awake and watching him.

"Do not reproach your captain for bringing Bethany to me. I want her here."

"She should no be here." His tone was abrupt. He tossed his sword and belt carelessly onto the chair in the corner of the room and knelt at the hearth to stoke the fire.

"Why would you want to deny this child anything?" Tess bravely continued.

Still down upon one knee, Conall turned his head toward her. Fire played upon the contours of his face, hugging the planes, blurring the shallows. His eyes, that ever-striking blue, were rendered dark and fiery. "For her own good. She needs rules."

"She is too young to understand all that has happened."

"She has lived at Inesfree for nigh on two years," Conall protested as he rose and stretched his arms above his head.

Tess momentarily lost track of her thoughts. Conall may well be the enemy, and true enough had proven himself the very devil at times, but he was a rather remarkable presence. Not handsome as a young girl dreamed a lover to be, nor merely agreeable to look upon as a hopeful woman wished for in her mate, but there was an appeal about him, nonetheless. His body, for one, defied all that seemed logical. Too big, too muscular. Too perfect. Hard, tight skin was pulled even more taut across the bulging mass that was his chest as he stretched. His arms lifted higher in their search for ease, defining the leanness of his waist. He was big and male and powerful, and he was not at all unpleasant to look upon. Tess stared unabashedly as he reined in the stretch, rolling those unbelievably broad shoulders as perhaps he often did to relieve the day's stresses. His head fell back, his eyes closed briefly.

Truly, it could not have been designed any better. That such a brawny and powerful body was crowned by a face of perfectly rugged character. Hard, yet noble. Wizened, yet still youthful. Beautiful, Tess guessed, if one appreciated such a craggy, earthy figure. The longer she stared at him, at that face that was both handsome and not, the more Tess was sure that his appeal did merit greater consideration. Up until now, he had simply been the man who held her prisoner. Someone to be feared and wary of as he held her future, should there be one, in his hands. He was, very simply, the beast.

The beast pulled up his head. His eyes opened and lit on Tess, who immediately closed hers. She'd not want to be caught staring—gaping, as it were—and too, they had been discussing something. She was about to reply to something he'd said.... Oh, yes, that was it. She opened her eyes. He was watching her with a steely gaze.

"But she has suffered a great trauma and has no real family of her own."

"She has the MacGregors and the MacDonnells," Conall retorted evenly, though his frown was heavy.

A thought occurred to Tess. She tilted her head and asked, "Or is it just me? You don't want her to become attached to me, do you?"

The lines across his forehead deepened. But he did not respond, only shook his head and stalked to the window.

"I'd wager you made no such fuss over her attachment to Serena or John Cardmore," Tess ventured. Then, with a bit of resentment, said, "Perhaps your Munro prisoner is not what might deem a suitable companion to the child?"

MacGregor turned on her, pointing a finger to underscore his words. "Serena and John will be in her life forever!" He hissed.

"Oh," Tess said, quite stupefied. She lowered her head and bit her lip. A frown came with the dawning of understanding. After a moment, sharp green eyes lifted and connected with his. "You speak of a marriage, but you've no intention of living one. You've plans to be shot of me should I ever concede to such a course. Or, mayhap I am being too generous. Perhaps my original suspicions will prove true."

Hands on his hips, obviously short on patience, MacGregor asked, "And what do you suppose my plans to be?"

"What I originally knew to be true. You plan to murder me. If ever I did marry you, I might wager that I'd not live to see the day after."

Conall rolled his eyes and threw up his arms. "And what would be the benefit of that?" He shouted now, making no attempt to keep his voice low for the sake of the sleeping child.

"The obvious reason would be to have Marlefield, with the marriage, but the bride of your choice, with my death."

Conall advanced quickly on her, leaning over her, fisted hands on the mattress, his face inches from hers. "Think, Tess," he advised in a dangerous whisper. "Think about this for just a moment. Do you no think if that were my intention, I could easily manufacture evidence of a marriage? A certificate? Witnesses? I would need you no at all, and you would be dead already."

Tess swallowed the lump in her throat caused by his proximity and his words.

Conall shoved himself up off the bed.

"You understand that I can trust no one, least of all you," Tess argued. "And certainly not your motives, nor intentions."

"I want to marry you—"

"For nefarious purposes," she finished, her own ire risen. "Greed is not a justification for a wedding."

"And pray tell, what is?" He kicked his sword and belt off the chair and plopped down into it, his long legs stretched out before him. "Dinna speak to me of love and need as reasons. They are for weaklings and dreamers."

"As any unmarried man would claim," she contended. "When I choose a mate—"

"It will be me."

Tess only shook her head. How many times did one have to refute this? She sighed and started again, "When I marry, it will have more to do with the love you ridicule, and respect, and admiration—"

"Such as you felt for your previous betrothed?" Conall lifted a brow, his elbow on the arm of the chair.

Tess's chin rose. "Alain wanted to marry me because—"

"Because your father arranged it. Should you happen to have your way, should you manage to escape me, any future marriage—other than to me—will be for the same reason: because your sire demands it."

"That is only partly true. Alain and I had profound respect for one another."

"I was there, Tess," he reminded her, leaning forward, his voice ugly. "I saw the entire encounter between you and the esteemed Alain. I saw his love of self, his bare tolerance of you, and even your silent but futile attempts to find something in him to appreciate."

There was little to refute there, Tess reluctantly determined. The man saw entirely too much through those dark eyes. Instead, Tess concentrated on her hands, worrying the blankets in her lap. When she looked up, the MacGregor was on his feet again, doffing his mail and tunic.

She did not stare outright at his naked back and arms and chest. But she did steal glances from her purposefully averted eyes. It was not as if she'd never seen a man's bare upper body before. Still, she had never, she knew this to be absolutely true, seen anything like Conall MacGregor. All that had been hinted at earlier, when he'd stretched in such a lazy feline way, was heightened now minus his tunic. In this room, by the soft flashing light from the hearth, his skin was bronzed, every muscle and hollow shaped and caressed by the flicker of firelight.

Powerful. Somewhere, in the back of her mind, that was the word she'd always thought of in conjunction with the beast. From that very first encounter, she'd realized his powerful presence, had been terrified by it. It was still true; the perception was still correct. His body, the size, the shape, the very fitness of it, proclaimed loudly his power. At this very moment, however, Tess feared not the might but her response to the very visible and admittedly, very appealing power of the man—not the beast.

"The other reason I'd deny you Bethany's company, lass," he went on, having no idea of the tumult she wrestled with, "is because she sleeps in my bed."

"But I've been in your bed for five nights. Sleep tonight wherever it is you've been sleeping since then." He faced her again and Tess was confronted with the solid wall of his chest, barely dusted with black hair tapering down to a vee where his breeches still held onto trim hips. Suddenly, as she had never believed before, Tess imagined his eyes might actually be the safer, less disturbing point on which to focus.

Conall stared at her, a slow grin spreading across his face. "I have slept beside you, lass."

"Y-you have not." But she had suspected....

"I have." Just a statement, no smugness.

"I...I would have known," this, with doubt. "I thought you slept on the floor—"

"And give up my bed for you, lass? " He climbed in beside her, putting Tess between himself and Bethany, his size forcing her to move nearer to Bethany. "You sleep verra soundly, lass. Your hair is quite bothersome as it seems to be everywhere. But aside from that, no at all unpleasant."

He laid back while Tess continued to sit up, her back ramrod straight now with indignation. Her eyes darted around the room, seeking an alternative. With her still tender knees, she could not very well leap out of bed to sleep elsewhere, even if he would allow it. She could cry all she wanted for his exit, but it would do her little good, she guessed.

But to lie next to him.... So very close. Had Bethany not been here, she would have at least been afforded more space for retreat.

"Will you sleep sitting up?" He asked from behind her, a grin quite evident in his voice.

She made no response for he knew very well she could not. Indeed, he knew exactly what troubled her at the moment and no doubt enjoyed her discomfort. This sure knowledge, of course, raised Tess's hackles. No doubt, he found joy in her predicament, which perversely made her want to show him that it affected her not at all. As casually as was possible while her stomach roiled, Tess pressed herself back upon the pillows and knew immediately, without a doubt, that the bed had shrunk.

CHAPTER 10

S he did sleep soundly.

Many hours later, very close to dawn, Conall was awake, turned to face Tess, propped up on his elbow. He had learned these last few nights that there would be little sleep for him so long as Tess lie in his bed. He should have found another bed. But he would not leave her.

There was something worth noting about how he felt having her here—or rather, knowing she was here, safe, and with him. He could not dispel the image of exactly how she had stared up at him when the hag was just about to start stitching her legs. He was the laird of all people MacGregor and MacDonnell and had been for several years, but he would swear that no one had ever looked at him like that, with need. She'd been fearful and she had looked to him to calm and comfort her. He was not at all immune to how powerful and satisfied that had made him feel.

But now, how could he possibly sleep knowing that she was so close? Within arm's reach. When every breath taken brought the scent of her to him.

Her hair, as he'd told her earlier, was everywhere. It was splayed about her head much as a crown, long enough unbound that some of it was tucked under his hip, other strands curled around her own arms. Conall lifted a lock, brought the tress to his nose, rubbing it back and forth while he watched her. Her closed eyes formed half-moons across her face, the shadow of her lashes striking out against her cheeks, long and thick.

Bethany's head was tucked into the pillow on the other side of Tess, their faces close. Their skin was very similar, Tess's being of a rather porcelain quality, much as the child's. Releasing the lock of hair, Conall ran the pad of his forefinger over Tess's cheek. So soft, he mused, moving his finger down along her jaw. It was quite a natural progression for him to trace the outline of her mouth. The extreme softness and alluring fullness of her lips intrigued him, seduced him. She turned her head, only fractionally, perhaps in response to his touch. Her lips were mere inches from his and it took barely any movement to claim them. Softly, for he wished only a taste. He did not want to waken her. But just a taste of Tess was not nearly enough. She sighed beneath him and he deepened the kiss, sliding an arm underneath her back.

She woke almost immediately, her initial reaction confusion, stiffening in his arms, until she heard his voice against her lips. "Just one taste, Tess." And he covered her mouth completely, hoping to swallow any dispute. There was none. Whether this was due to her sleep-shrouded mind or her liking of the kiss, Conall did not know. She relaxed against him. He forced her mouth open with his own by means of gentle persuasion, aware that her hand now touched his bare shoulder. His tongue sought hers, played against it. Conall shifted on the bed, bringing his head fully over hers, stretching a hand out upon her stomach, where it made a slow journey upward until it settled on her breast. She stilled but did not protest. Conall cupped his hand entirely over her breast, wishing for much less clothing, turning the budding peak between thumb and forefinger. She whimpered, a sigh of pleasure really, and Conall was nearly undone.

On the other side of Tess, stretched out along the wall, Bethany squirmed in her sleep.

With a sigh of his own, one of resigned disappointment, he placed his forehead against Tess's brow.

"Now I am doubly sorry for the child's presence but you, I imagine, are feeling well protected," he said. "Go to sleep, Tess."

ARTHUR MUNRO ROSE NAKED from the bed and thoughtfully poured himself a goblet of wine from a tray left earlier. He cared not that the whore in the bed no doubt cringed at his bare form, which had over the years, expanded while it drooped. He cared not for any of her thoughts; she was merely a body to use. He offered her no drink, but in fact bade her leave. "You may return to that husband of yours," he said coldly, knowing as well as she that her spouse, a Munro soldier, had a very keen idea of where she spent her evenings.

She'd thought to raise her own position at Marlefield by giving Arthur what she, in her ignorance, believed to be the foundation of all his desires—gratification, domination. Arthur Munro knew of her scheme, had read well her ambitions in such hopeful, transparent eyes, but gave little heed to her plans. He would use her well and good, so long as she suited his present desire. When he tired of her, she would be dismissed, replaced. She was of no consequence.

Accustomed to his changeable moods, the woman, Meyra, slunk from the bed and dressed herself, neither quickly nor quite slowly.

"Perhaps tomorrow—?" she hinted, leaving the question hanging between them, as she neared the door.

"If I want you," Arthur said from the window, "I will send for you." He heard the hollow soft thud of the door closing and drank deeply of his wine. An excellent cellar, had MacGregor, from which Arthur still benefitted.

This brought to mind his daughter, still bound by the younger MacGregor. That the boy had survived at all had been something of a shock to Arthur when he'd learned of it several years ago. And that the boy had landed on his feet—not only finding a home with the old fool, MacDonnell, but actually benefitting from his association with the man, to become his heir, now chief of the MacDonnells.

Arthur's lip curled. He'd never, not once in his life, been handed anything so fine as a ready-made kingdom. He had to work ceaselessly for all that was his. And now, it seemed, his work had yet to be finished. Marlefield only remained his for the time being until Arthur removed this threat that could take it away from him permanently.

He sipped again, drawn into his own thoughts, recalling a time when he'd been impressed with the daring of the 'little MacDonnell' as MacGregor had been known while he raided the border English, before his fame had grown enough to have his true name known far and wide. That was when Arthur had learned the truth, which he'd feared for many years.

A survivor.

The name bandied about, the legend that grew, the man Arthur himself might have admired for his daring, was none other than Douglas MacGregor's spawn, fighting beside men like Wallace and Andrew Moray.

Arthur had seen him from afar, at Falkirk not so long ago, before he'd turned his own men away from the carnage that was to be. It had occurred to him, that just as he'd discredited the father, so, too, could fall the son. It had been relatively easy to convince those Scotsmen worthy of the purpose that Douglas MacGregor had been a traitor to them all. That it was Douglas MacGregor and not himself who had supported secretly Edward I and England; that he'd regularly recruited, financed and dispatched men and arms and gold to England. That Scotland indeed was better for his death.

None had questioned Sir Arthur. Some might have congratulated him, ferreting out such disloyalty, ridding the world of such a scourge upon humanity as a traitor. Happily, they had agreed that Marlefield was certainly best suited in Arthur's hands— though it had been proposed and agreed upon that it should not remain a Munro estate as Arthur was well compensated by his own holdings and castles in both England and Scotland. It was then that the contract had been first drawn up, ceding Marlefield to his first son-in-law upon Tess's marriage. This had—until now—never presented itself as a problem. Marlefield would always be his, as he knew that Tess would only marry whom he deemed acceptable.

Arthur chuckled briefly to himself now. Perhaps, it was best termed as *whom he deemed most malleable.* Alain Sinclair was perfect. A second son of immoral character, he had few prospects, which was precisely why marriage to Tess so appealed to him. He had no interest in either running an estate or ruling a clan. He cared only for his entertainments, which he happily found in Edinburgh. This, too, pleased Arthur. Marlefield would, in essence, remain his forever.

Tossing back the remainder of his wine, Arthur placed the goblet on the tray and sought his bed. Stretched out, arms folded beneath his head, he stared blindly at the ceiling and thought of Tess and the MacGregor.

He'd not been able to dishonor or discredit the younger Mac-Gregor so easily as he'd hoped. Apparently, the boy's honor was strung like chain mail around his person. A planted seed here or there, as he'd craftily done many years ago against his father, had not injured the boy, as he was championed in many areas by many people. But Arthur was not a man given to casual efforts. He would succeed, 'twas only a matter of time.

Tess, on the other hand....

Likely, the twit had already been forced to wed and had been well bedded for her trouble. But there was a hope that the stubbornness he'd tried to break in his daughter, had served him well now in her captivity. Arthur knew her not well at all, having had little interest in her very existence until she had proved useful—but he knew this: Tess Munro was set to stubbornness as only her mother had been. And her mother, God rest her wretched and wavering soul, was as willful a person as were the great warriors of their time. With this recollection, it was easy to believe that Tess had refused and somehow evaded marriage to the MacGregor.

Arthur knew well enough of young MacGregor's honor—he'd tried long enough to vanquish it—to believe that MacGregor would not kill Tess over her refusal. This afforded Arthur a lean bough of hope on which to cling. If he could not regain Tess, but if she had managed thus far to elude marriage, there was still time to save Marlefield.

He found it nearly distasteful to contemplate the murder of his own daughter—but necessary to his desires. It was unfortunate that Tess remained his only legitimate child and heir, but it wasn't to be helped. He'd not planted a fruitful seed in almost a decade, despite the advent and subsequent departure of a second wife and then a third. It was therefore unlikely that now, at the age of two score and nearly ten, he'd sow so fertile a field—even if he had a mind to take another to wife.

"You know what needs to be done," he spoke to himself, scratching his head. He rose quickly and dressed himself.

Though he knew it to be nearing midnight, he quit his chamber and found his way to the steward's room. There, he found the sharp-eyed little man busy counting coins into a leather satchel. "Tis as you said, a thousand pounds to Edward. His man awaits."

Arthur nodded. "Quickly, then, for we've other business to direct."

The steward nodded, his raw, bony fingers quickening their pace. When all was counted, the satchel was closed by a drawn cord and set into a small wooden chest, packed tight with linens.

"See to it," Arthur said impatiently when the steward had looked to him for further instruction. The little man hefted the chest with great difficulty onto his shoulder and left the room, returning in only a few minutes, empty-handed.

"Where is Sinclair?" Arthur asked.

"Within the castle, my lord," the steward answered. "Abed, likely, at this hour. Nothing here to hold his interest." Sly and sunken eyes glittered at his quip.

"Mm," Arthur murmured, agreeing. "Fetch him. I've a job which perhaps only he can perform."

"Could it not, my lord, wait 'til morn?" The factor dared to ask.

Arthur cursed. "Like as not, it could, man! But I've a mind to discuss it now. Fetch him!"

"Yes, my lord."

Arthur watched with hard eyes as the aging man scurried away, much as a rat, Arthur thought absently.

Another thousand pounds would slight his coffers not at all. He laughed at his own mad cleverness, wondering if instead he should offer Sinclair thirty pieces of silver to get the job done.

TESS AWOKE THE NEXT morning, as she often did since coming to Conall's chamber, alone. Initially, she gave this little thought until an inkling, just a shadow of something began to form in her head. Conall had slept beside her last night. But there was something else.... A dream. She had dreamed of kissing Conall. He had risen over her and claimed her lips and touched her body and dear Lord, she had relished it. She had shown him secret longings by answering his kiss with little restraint. The dream had been short-lived, but its memory was etched upon her, indeed, still caused a fire to sweep throughout her.

Tess shook her head, chiding herself in the wake of such traitorous thoughts, be they only dreams. She was not so wanton as to crave such carnality.

Was she? He was the enemy, for the love of all that was holy! He was to be loathed and reviled and... and not desired. Tess mentally shook herself.

When Serena came, Tess asked after Bethany and asked if she might return to the tower today. Her knees were all but healed. They pained her not a great deal. She would even return to her garden chores to show she was entirely healthy to be gone from the beast.

"Bethany is in the kitchen," Serena answered first and then shook her head sadly. "I am sorry, Tess, but Conall says you are to remain here... indefinitely."

"For what purpose? That I may not escape again?" seethed Tess.

Serena did not answer, only assisted Tess with her morning ablutions and settled her at the handsome table in Conall's bedchamber where Tess angrily shoved food around the trencher but pushed little into her mouth. Serena tidied the bed and opened the tall doors which led out onto the battlements. "'Tis a lovely day, Tess," she observed, and Tess tilted her head in Serena's direction, though she saw nothing of the blue sky or bright green of spring.

After a while, Serena left, offering to bring Bethany up to keep her company later in the afternoon. Tess nodded at this, losing a bit of her anger, which truly had no place in Serena's presence.

She stood and walked stiffly to the opened door leading outside. Curiously, she stepped out onto the battlements, the long and narrow balcony that stretched along this wall of the keep, entirely surrounding the castle's inner bailey. It was a beautiful day indeed, but the air, as always, was chilled and Tess re-entered the chamber to search through the trunk at the foot of the bed—Conall's trunk, containing Conall's belongings. She gave no thought of trespass, finding several tunics and trews and hose. At the bottom of the trunk she spied one of the MacGregor's plaids and pulled this item out to consider its worth. Too long, by far, but if wrapped properly, it would provide ample warmth. With no care for proper pleats, Tess swung the plaid around her shoulders and again took herself out into the fresh air, pulling the tall doors closed behind her. She had never been afraid of heights and so leaned over the stone wall.

Below, there was little activity. Tess saw only a pair of young boys, playfully sparring with their wooden swords until a passing woman swatted one boy upside the head and tugged him by the ear away from the other, who had himself quite a fit trying to control his laughter over his friend's trouble. Tess smiled despite herself and looked farther. In a far corner, there was laundry being done, a huge boiling pot the centerpiece for this labor and several household serfs attending. Tess found Dorcas among the women washers and her smile faded. This explained the tired woman's rough hands. Further down the wall, away from the center of activity, Tess saw two older boys, pages perhaps throwing something against the wall. She straightened and walked down along the balcony until she stood directly over them and leaned again over the embrasure between the rising teeth of the merlon.

They were dicing, she determined, spying the crudely made cubes of animal knuckle bones. Tess watched as the smaller of the two, a blond-haired lad, dropped coins into the other boy's hand. The other, perhaps a year older with darker hair and a lanky frame, then tossed the dice, crying jubilantly when he took more coins from the blond youth.

Tess watched for quite a while, finding herself rooting for the smaller boy as the other was too peacock-like in his strut. She could not see so well as to read what dice came up at each roll but could easily discern the winner and loser by the boys' reactions.

She spied something that drew her attention away from the boys dicing below. Further across the yard, at the rear wall of the castle, she noticed a gate not much taller than herself. Tess straightened and wondered how often it was used. She wondered if it were difficult to open, maybe rusty with age and unemployment.

"Oh, my."

CHAPTER 11

At that moment, Conall was thinking on Tess. He'd done little else since rising this morn, having much to consider. He'd awakened to the feel of Tess beside him, recalling instantly their kiss during the night. What manner of man was he, he wondered, that he was able to resist her charms? Resist? No, he'd not been strong enough to do that. But he had somehow managed to stop what he had started, despite the swelling belief that so much of what he wanted might be found in her arms. Forbearance such as this was often the memory a man called upon when faced with future hardships. He had withstood—with great steadfastness, he decided—the lure of Tess in his arms. He could, no doubt, slay dragons. He could do anything.

That brought a rare smile to his face. He shook his head at such fancy. Doubtless, Tess recalled nothing of their embrace last night. She'd been imbued with sleep, troubled not at all by their intimacy. It was altogether possible that she imagined she'd dreamed the entire episode, if she were indeed affected by any shred of memory at all.

Serena had suggested that he might consider explaining to Tess his dictate that she was to remain within his chamber from now on. Serena had informed him that when told of this decision, Tess had appeared ready to do battle. With this in mind, Conall approached his chamber, giving Gilbert MacDonnell, charged with guarding the door when Ezra was otherwise occupied, leave to seek his ease for a while.

Conall entered, his eyes going directly to the bed, where of late he was accustomed to finding Tess, narrowing dangerously at the empty space upon the mattress.

"Tess?" he called, his tone instantly suspicious. He spun around, taking in every corner of the room in one quick, swiveling glance. "Tess!" Louder now as she did not appear before him. He cursed when it was obvious that again she had managed to escape him.

Gilbert, apparently not having gone too far, barged into the solar, sword drawn.

"Put that damned thing away, boy!" Conall growled. "Did she pass you?"

"Nay, laird." Gilbert's face was blank, his eyes darting nervously around the room.

His lip curled up in displeasure, Conall noticed that his trunk had been opened. Someone had rifled through his belongings. Frowning heavily enough to move the hapless Gilbert several feet out of his reach, Conall stalked toward the balcony and swung open the doors. He looked left and then right and immediately he breathed again, spying Tess at the far corner of the battlements, leaning over the embrasure.

He straightened and bumped into Gilbert, who had followed him and peered around his shoulder.

"What the—?" Conall spat. "Go. Leave."

"Aye, laird," gulped Gilbert and he left.

She hadn't escaped. She hadn't tried.

But his anger was still heightened, if only because of his reaction to her supposed disappearance. He had feared... and not the loss of Marlefield.

Quietly, Conall approached Tess. Hung over the wall as she was, her upper body and face between the alternating merlons, she was not aware of his presence. As he neared, Conall frowned at what he heard. She was talking to herself, quite animated. He heard her small hands clapping nearly soundlessly. Intrigued, Conall peeked over the wall, still a few feet away from her, and saw what held her interest.

Two boys—who would be severely reprimanded later—diced at the wall at this far corner of the bailey. Tess cheered or groaned, obviously championing one of the two.

Conall came up behind her, and still she did not turn. When he finally noticed what was different about her, he liked at once the sight, the very idea of Tess wrapped in his plaid. It was several lengths too large for her, and likely outweighed her even, but it suited her and absurdly thrilled him.

Tess stilled and Conall thought she realized his presence. But she only stared ahead and not down, no longer watching the gaming lads now. He placed one hand on each merlon on either side of her just as she straightened and whispered, "Oh, my."

Then a voice boomed—Conall would know John Cardmore's voice anywhere—hollering at the boys to see to their duties. Tess jumped as did the derelicts below her, coming up hard against Conall's chest.

Startled, she pivoted quickly, so instantly frightened in fact, she seemed near relieved to find Conall. She placed a hand against his chest—he was that close—and smiled in relief.

"You startled me."

Conall grinned, glancing down between them at her hand. Tess yanked it away with a look of horror about her that suggested she'd not known she'd placed it there.

Tess shook her head. "You scared me, that is all."

Thoughtfully, Conall took a bit of his plaid into each of his hands, rearranging the folds over her shoulders. "You're wearing my plaid," he observed, hardly able to contain a crowing grin.

"To keep away the chill."

"But I like the way you wear it, lass," he said, his hands still upon her. "I like the look of you bearing the essence of me." He was enjoying the goading, enjoyed tremendously the near rolling of her eyes.

"Make of it what you will, MacGregor," she said with a shrug. "If cow dung would keep me warm and was readily available in this length, I would wear it."

Conall laughed. She hated to so much as give an inch, she was that stubborn.

"Aye, Tess, you do entertain me." He watched her eyes, never comfortable when he was this close, flicker again and again to his lips. When he said no more but only waited, she finally raised her eyes to his. And still he said nothing, waiting.

"Don't kiss me," she breathed after a long while.

"Then stop staring at my mouth," he warned and was quite delighted when she did not. Well, she tried, but as soon as he'd said the words, her gaze had guiltily switched to his mouth, only for the briefest of seconds before she looked again to his eyes, her cheeks pinkening.

Conall lifted a brow, as if to say that she had been warned and lowered his head, his hands tightening on his plaid. She whimpered, he heard that, barely audible but he was attuned to the smallest reaction from her and quickly silenced her mewing with his lips. Reminiscent of last night, as softly, as experimentally as he'd pursued her then, he touched her now. Still as stone she was beneath him now, frightened, he was sure. And Conall knew well the fear. Relinquishing the power you thought you held, giving it up to this. Just touch. But he cared not—he would later, but not now. Just for now, Tess.

He slanted his head, accustomed now to the size of her, exactly the angle her height required of him. It was not uncomfortable, despite the differences in their size. He pulled her closer by way of the plaid, where still his fingers held. But they itched. To touch more, to feel more. Start with this, he told himself, tasting Tess with his tongue. She tried to shake her head. He would not let her escape this. But when he tasted a saltiness upon her, he groaned and pulled away.

Why did she cry?

"Please don't do this to me," she begged, burying her head in his chest, not to find comfort there, not because she wanted to be there, but to hide her face from his.

Conall stared over her head, releasing the plaid, putting his hands on her upper arms, solidly but not with the intent to soothe or console.

It was sinful, what she did to him. He no longer felt the need, the urge as the aggressor, to scare or seduce his victim into compliance. He wanted her response to be spontaneous and impulsive, as his need of her appeared to be. He wanted her to need him, need *this*. He consoled himself only with the sure knowledge that she truly hadn't any idea of the power she held in her tiny hands.

"Let's go," he said, bringing her head up. Before she could ask—indeed, having no clue why he should still entertain such plans—he told her, "I have business to attend in the village. Since you seem to be quite taken with places outside these walls, I thought you might wish to accompany me."

After an initial expression of great guilt, she offered a cautious yet wondrous smile, which served as some consolation since he was not still kissing her.

THEY LEFT THE GATES of Inesfree behind them and were confronted with an intimidating expanse of green. Tess sat eagerly before Conall atop his great steed, relishing the feel of the breeze upon her face, which was strong enough to hike her skirts up to her knees. It had been a long time since Tess had ridden like this. At Marlefield, Sir Arthur did not approve of her ability to ride, a knowledge her mother had insisted upon, which had seen little use as her father rarely allowed her the opportunity. But never had she been capable of handling one of these huge destriers; presently she liked the feel of the solid animal beneath her. With his size, one did lose a bit in speed, but this was easily countered by appreciation for his sheer power. The mare she'd appropriated almost a week ago was not nearly so large as Conall's beast and that terrifying ride, she scarcely recalled.

He inquired of her knees, and her injury, and if this riding was perhaps causing more harm to her.

It was not, actually. "And I wouldn't care if it did. I want to ride."

Conall had taken a path to the west, onto a well-beaten trail, which was extremely narrow in sections. They skirted round a small loch and soon came into the village, not unlike any other village of a great castle, being a cluster of thatched cottages with small pens attached to many. They stopped before the largest of these homes, nearly twice the size of any other.

A woman stepped from the dim interior, her hand across her forehead to shield her eyes from the sun, a child of no more than one straddled on her hip. "Chief MacGregor," she called. "Good day to you."

"And you, mistress. Is Evan about?"

"Gone to field, I fear. He'd not known you were to come or like as not, he'd be waiting. Please, come inside," she offered, her eyes curiously on Tess.

"Thank you, no," Conall declined. "I'll find Evan, for I've matters to discuss with him." He turned the horse, steering him between two smaller cottages across the way and up a slight incline which leveled off to reveal a field of chestnut brown dirt, as far as the eye could see. He'd tightened his arm around Tess as they climbed, and her hand clung to his at her midsection. "Might the riding be too rough for your knees?' He asked yet again.

"Not at all," she told him, and raised a thin brow at this consideration from him.

Conall stopped for a moment, his eyes scanning the horizon until he spotted several groups of men and boys, at the farthest corner of the field. He directed the horse across the freshly turned earth, great black and brown clumps of soft mud, until they reached the laboring men. Several turned and greeted their laird, tipping their hats or raising a tool in salute. Conall reined in beside a man of middling years, whose eyes were a kindly brown, as pretty as Tess had ever encountered.

Leaving Tess in the saddle, Conall dismounted and greeted the man. They stood a bit away from Tess and as there was little need for raised voices upon this vast but quiet field, Tess was left to hear only snippets of their conversation. This man was Evan, she knew, extremely small and wiry, coming only to the height of Conall's shoulder but of a great intellect, his eyes told, and feared not of physical labor it seemed, the sweat and flush about him telling all he'd been active this day.

Conall spoke to the man for almost ten minutes, in which time Tess was left to handle the prancing steed. Amazingly, an entire five or more minutes had gone by, while Tess stared at the MacGregor's back and listened to the hypnotic timbre of his voice, before she realized that beneath her sat an opportunity for escape.

Immediately, she glanced around with a guilty expression, as if she feared someone might have actually read her thoughts and determined her debate.

Escape.

She contemplated kicking the animal into motion. Just go, ride away. She looked up, beyond the beast, across the field to the rolling hills that might lead to freedom. Something paused inside her. She would never know what stayed her hands from flicking the reins.

Conall turned and squinted up at her. Their eyes met, hers a pained expression as she tried to keep her thoughts hidden. But Conall's expression undid her. He gazed at her with something akin to pride, the smallest quirk of his lips beginning a slow satisfied smile, as if he simply enjoyed that she was near. His eyes, that heated glow warming her, showed a growing gladness.

Tess understood at once. She had not fled, and Conall was pleased.

She had pleased Conall.

Conall turned around again, giving his full attention to Evan.

Her stomach somersaulted. She had found favor with Conall and this, in turn, pleased her greatly. His simple, content smile had sent something warm and sunny to course within her and Tess had neither the will nor the desire to make it go away.

The horse began to prance in agitation of waiting, or perhaps in response to Tess's heightened emotions. He was a huge beast and without Conall, Tess was considerably dismayed at having to settle the animal herself. He snorted and pawed the earth, dancing now in growing impatience.

Conall turned again, noticing Tess's increasing efforts to calm his horse. Still conversing with Evan, he made his way back to Tess, while Evan followed, as if they only strolled while they talked. He took the reins from Tess's hands, his eyes on the animal, telling Evan that he expected supplies to be brought within the next few days and perhaps repairs might begin in a week. His horse stilled instantly with Conall at his side. And then, as if they were friends or lovers of long-standing, Conall placed one hand, which held the reins, upon Tess's thigh, the other upon the big horse's flank, calming both. But he listened still to Evan, who stood on the opposite side of the horse, telling Conall that things were proceeding as planned.

"Fine, Evan," Conall said and climbed up behind Tess, an arm sliding around her waist to draw her near. It seemed involuntary really, almost a natural reaction—she had to hang on to *something*—to place her hand upon the back of his again. "I'll see you in two days' time at Inesfree with the complete list," Conall said.

"Yes, laird," said the small man. "Good day to you."

Effortlessly, Conall turned the horse around, now controlled under his master, carrying the pair back toward the village.

"Evan is somewhat of a steward," Conall explained as they rode away. "A liaison, if you will, between the villagers and me. He makes all the arrangements for repairs to the cottages, which need to be finished before the May Day feast."

"That is only a month away," Tess commented.

"To expedite the necessary repairs, we set aside one day, and everyone comes together, from the village and Inesfree. The men work, the women feed us and chatter, everything finished in one day."

"Very productive," Tess decided.

"The work gets done and we celebrate our good deeds at the May Day festival."

Tess had heard talk of this festival during her time in the kitchens, and more recently from Serena. Indeed, the very air around the keep seemed to vibrate and crackle with the excitement of the forthcoming event. She might have assumed it was as similar as any castle's May Day feast, but she had been happily corrected, informed that no castle's spring festival compared to Inesfree's.

Conall and Tess passed again through the village and soon it began to fade behind them. At the loch which they had earlier skirted, Conall stopped and dismounted.

"Let us walk," he said and pulled Tess to the ground, and she found herself not unhappy to remain away from the keep yet longer. They walked sided by side, along the small rocks that braced the loch, the horse ambling along behind them as Conall held the reins in his hands.

CHAPTER 12

"Why did you no bolt whilst I spoke to Evan?"

She'd known he would ask. She had no answer, other than to say, "I feared that I might fail again." That wasn't entirely true, she admitted to herself.

"Then stop trying, lass," he suggested simply.

She smiled without humor. "Would you?"

Conall nodded, not in answer to her question, but in recognition that it was a fairly put query. "Nae, Tess. Like as no, I would escape—or die trying."

"Then you must accept my need to do this also," she insisted.

"To return to what?" asked Conall as he bent to select a flat stone, which he skipped expertly across the water. "What, or who, at Marlefield do you miss the most?"

"My freedom," she answered without pause. "If I had nothing to return to, I would yearn still for freedom."

"And were you free there, Tess?" He turned his head to consider her, but Tess stared straight ahead, her hands clasped before her.

"Freer than here."

"But no completely," he guessed.

Tess shrugged. "Are any of us, at any time, completely free?" she wondered.

"Every person, I suspect—those no burdened by captivity—creates his own chains. Responsibility, loyalty, expectations—all deterrents to true freedom."

"Is that how you feel? Does being laird restrict you?"

"No at all. I am respected and needed. Inesfree is no a burden. It is an honor."

Tess sighed. "While I am quite without purpose—aside from your plans for me. At Marlefield, I have no responsibility at all, nothing to do save that what I wish," she said and bit her lip, as if wondering for the first time why this was so.

"You are the daughter of a laird. Surely, you ran the household, cared for the serfs."

Tess shook her head. "I've only lived at Marlefield this past year. The system of management within the keep was already in place."

"Where were you before then?"

Tess did not look at Conall, but she heard the frown in his voice.

"At Craignairn Abbey, near Haltwhistle. My mother and I lived there for as long as I can remember. She'd miscarried so many times my father sought a divorce as he needed legitimate sons."

"He was granted the divorce."

"Yes, after several years of lobbying for it. He remarried twice. Both died in childbirth, having produced no living heir." Tess sought to change the subject, never comfortable talking about herself. "So why have you not married?"

"No reason to," he answered simply.

"Could you possibly expand upon that vague reply?" She liked the feeling that had come over her, not of attention to Conall, though this was always in her, but of her ease with him now. Without the pressure of seduction and being outside the keep, which seemed to detach them from their assigned roles of captor and captive, Tess felt quite comfortable walking and talking with him, even bold enough to pursue this new topic.

Conall chuckled. "Aye, I can. I've found none I could live without and none with something I needed. Until you, that is," he clarified with a wry smile in his voice.

"None you could live without?" Tess turned her head to frown at him. "But you don't believe in love," she challenged, ignoring the last part of his reply, which she knew referred only to Marlefield.

"I speak no of love, but of need."

"Is there a difference?"

"Mighty."

"Please explain," Tess laughed, "as someone who does not believe in love, how you can compare it to anything."

"I ken love. I have loved," Conall said firmly. "I just dinna think it needs to be an all-consuming thing, that makes you become someone you are no, trying to please a person you can only hope is worthy of it."

"Did you not have love from your mother? Or your father? Surely, a parent is worthy of our love."

He threw a glance at her, a brown arched. "Is your sire worthy of your love, lass?"

Tess considered this. Not her response, but the way he asked the question, as if he knew her father was difficult, as if he knew there was no love.

"I was asking of your parents."

Conall nodded, an acceptance of her unwillingness to answer his query. "My mother died when I was very small. I barely remember her, only snippets and aye, a sense of love." He shrugged. "Perhaps I dinna actually remember, perhaps I only ken what John tells me about her. My da loved me, I ken."

"My mother loved me. 'Tis the only love I have known, I suppose. You were right about Alain—my betrothed—he didn't seem very interested in..."

She felt him staring at her. She'd said too much. Tess stared at her hands and made a show of swiping nearly undetectable wrinkles from her kirtle.

"Interested in what, lass?"

Tess lifted her shoulders, waving a hand, searching for expression. When she said nothing, Conall spoke. She could feel his eyes on her.

"In loving you?"

She stopped walking and gave this some thought, not the question but her reply. "He wasn't interested in *me*, actually. Seems odd, that you wouldn't want to know someone you were about to marry." She pointed into the woods. "Look." There a handsome doe stared warily back at her. "Oh, she's beautiful." She moved toward it, happy to put this conversation behind her. Leaving the rocky shore of the loch for the short grass of the incline, Tess lifted her kirtle and hiked upward. She struggled a bit, as the angle of the incline was steeper than she had suspected, using her hands upon the earth to assist her efforts. Here, she felt the effects of the recent trauma to her knees. But then Conall was beside her, taking up her hand, seeming not to struggle at all, still holding the horse's reins, guiding her effortlessly toward the ridge.

She reached the top to find the deer had fled. She might have continued along the short grassy path but Conall stopped, releasing her arm. He turned and stared at the view offered by the ridge. Tess turned, too. She gasped at the sight before her.

Atop this rise, one could surely see forever. Hills and mountains and valleys were covered in new spring grass and sharp gray rock, some peaks shrouded by mists, the view endless. Below was the loch and to the left, the village. Conall directed her gaze to the right, where rose Inesfree, its very majestic presence proclaiming all the land in sight its own.

"'Tis Godit's Rise," he said. "The first MacDonnell to come was said to have stood at this spot and proclaimed, *'God, it's—'* but was left speechless by his awe. Thus, it has ever been known as Godit's Rise."

"A clever tale," said Tess with a suspicious crinkle in her brow.

"And truth." Conall surprised her by collapsing onto his back on the ground, now releasing the reins to allow the animal to graze. "I've a mind to rest a while."

Tess searched about in consternation, glancing at Conall, his legs stretched out, one foot crossed over the other, eyes closed, arms under his head. What was she to do now?

"Tess, have you no need for repose?" He asked, without opening his eyes.

"I am plagued by repose of late and well you know it."

"But suffer your laird's need of it."

"'Tis not my laird you are," she said quietly but dropped carefully to the soft grass. She made a show of arranging her skirts about her legs. She'd thought she'd allowed for enough space between herself and Conall, a safe distance. But at her remark, Conall opened his eyes and rolled to his side, coming up onto his elbow, which now placed him within reach of her.

"Aye, I am no," he said, without rancor. Just thoughtfully. And then, "Lass, you said your mother loved you, but you didn't sound very convinced of it. Was she no a kind person?"

Tess was quick to correct. "My mum was the sweetest, most gentle person. She just didn't... she couldn't really love me."

Conall frowned. "All mothers love, tis...just nature," he challenged.

"It wasn't in her nature, I suppose. Oh, she was lovely, mistake me not," Tess was quick to defend. After a moment, while her eyes stared straight out over Inesfree, she offered, "Truly, my mum was the finest person I had ever known—so fragile and beautiful I often found myself just staring at her in awe—but she had demons, I am afraid. Her mind would wander. No, more than that, it would plague her and harass her and so often she would...." Tess shrugged, her words trailing off. "She wasn't well, and not entirely capable of love at all times."

And, rather as an afterthought, "This would have killed her though, my being...gone."

"And your sire?"

Tess thought for a moment. "I barely know him. While they were married, he spent much time in Scotland and we remained in England. Any memory I have of that time, before we were moved into the abbey, is fuzzy. I remember being hopeful, looking forward to his rare visits, but then I recall—" she shook her head and stared away from him, "I was disappointing to him, I always felt."

She seemed to shake herself within, but did not look at him, only gazed upon the hills and mists. But soon enough as he continued to regard her, her cheeks reddened in response. "Do not stare at me," she reprimanded, her voice a hurried whisper.

Conall said lazily, "Endure this, lass, for the alternative would scare you even more."

"I am not afraid of you." It hadn't sounded very convincing. She turned to glare at him. "I am not," she said again, this time with more bravado than truth, staring into those blue eyes, trying very hard to convince herself. He tilted his head, looking at her still, his eyes telling her she should not make statements that she knew he could so easily discredit.

But he did nothing, save to lie back down and fold his arms under his head.

"May I ask you a question?"

"You just did."

"What? Oh," and she grinned at this bit of foolery, and saw just the barest quirking of his lips. Tess played along. "May I ask you another question?"

"You did it again."

Now Tess laughed out loud, but caught herself, clapping her hand over her mouth. She shouldn't be enjoying the company of this man. Not at all. But her eyes danced.

"I am about to ask you a question," she said, pleased with her own cleverness.

"Hmm." He smiled fully now thought his eyes remained closed.

"Why Marlefield? Why me?" She asked, sorry to see the smile disappear from his handsome face.

Conall opened his eyes, but didn't move otherwise, just watched the clouds rolling by, seeming to consider his words.

But he didn't answer, or didn't answer soon enough, so that Tess now regretted even more dispelling his lighter mood and asked, "Did I confuse you? That was two questions, actually. Would you like them asked one at a time? I can space them out...."

She saw his chest move a bit and he threw a glance at her, his lips quirked again. And she felt better.

"'Tis war time, lass," was his very vague reply. He kept his gaze upon her. "I am sorry you are the pawn for you seem like a decent enough person—though entirely too stubborn for my purposes."

Tess shrugged. She would not apologize for her behavior while she remained his captive. Of course, while she wouldn't actually express regret for having foiled his plans, she was sorry for the circumstance between the two of them. She looked at him, at all that maleness, those riveting eyes, those very able hands, capable of keeping a person—even a pawn—very safe. She thought of his kisses and realized it was indeed a shame, this circumstance.

"'Tis only war, and no personal—no you and I anyway."

Her nod was slow, though she wasn't exactly sure what he meant. It seemed decidedly personal—or did she only wish that? "But...why am I still here?" She didn't think she needed to add, *while I still refuse to wed you.*

"You'll wed me yet, lass, mark my words."

That was an infuriating condition, his apparent ability to read her very thoughts. Tess thought it wise to change the subject.

"Do you fight for Robert Bruce?"

"I fight for Scotland," he answered, so simply, so matter-of-factly, she knew it to be an integral part of the man.

"For Bruce and Scotland, you mean to say."

"Always, only, for Scotland, occasionally beside the Bruce."

"And pillaging and raping and murder are necessary deeds to ensure Scotland's freedom?"

He opened his eyes and Tess knew in that moment that she'd gone too far by repeating sheer supposition, rumors of which she'd yet to be shown any evidence. Gone was the light blue of ease in his eyes, replaced by frowning depths of deep blue, colder, she imagined, than any loch in winter.

"Have I raped you, Tess?"

"No," this, a mere squeak.

"Have I stormed Marlefield?"

"No."

"If I raped you, Tess, would that make it easier to sustain a hatred you believe you should feel? A hatred that diminishes by degrees with each passing day?"

With mounting regret for having opened her mouth in this arena, she stared at the hands in her lap. At this last theory examined, she lifted her eyes to his, sure the rapid color rising to her cheeks answered his question.

She *should* hate him. She had—at one time. But he'd proceeded to prove himself not the monster she'd anticipated, nor quite the one she'd dreaded. Tess considered herself not at all prepared to deal with this Conall MacGregor.

MacGregor the Murderer she could well take on. Fear and hatred could, as he'd guessed, sustain a person. She could confront a beast and stay true to the Munros with relative ease. But she knew not what to do with his kindness, found herself at a loss when confronted with something so simple as a smile from the man. Truly, Tess was lost.

"I have to hate you, that is all. It is my duty," was all she said.

Conall stared at her for a long moment. When he spoke, his tone was relaxed, no sense of smugness detected. "You want to," he said. "To hate me, that is. I think therein lies your greatest struggle."

CHAPTER 13

Tess hadn't lied when she'd told Conall that she wasn't afraid of him. And while she wasn't so naive as to believe that she knew him well—sometimes not at all, it seemed—she'd been his captive for many weeks now, and he had yet to fulfill any promise of harm to her. She felt quite safe in her belief that he wasn't bent on her destruction, even as she continued to thwart his well-laid plans. Curiously, though Conall and Tess had spoken of marriage, he had not again demanded that she wed him. She wasn't sure what steadied his head or hand in this regard.

What she was afraid of, however, was her very own self. Or—more succinctly—her rather ungovernable response to that man. He was correct; she didn't hate him and perhaps she never had. Any loathing, real or hoped for, to which she'd tried to cling, was, as he'd said, waning day by day.

And this was a great and shameful quandary.

Maybe in another time—another life perhaps—she'd want to know more about him, would want to be kissed by him, and experience the full promise those kisses teased at. But now, she had no business keeping any emotion for him save the ever-fading hate. And she just couldn't do it.

She needed to get away from him before it truly was too late. He may not be quite the beast she'd once thought, but she was still and would always remain nothing more than a pawn.

He'd left her alone these past many days, to both her pleasure and, sadly, her chagrin. She'd returned to her kitchen and garden duties and had given up trying to have herself removed from his bedchamber. But even in this, Tess had adopted a careless insolence; her exhaustion at night meant she wasn't even bothered to wakefulness by his coming and going in the chamber. But then, she hadn't seen Bethany in the last few days and nights, either. This, too, fueled her ill-spirits of late.

The only speck of relief—it wasn't great enough to be construed as joy—was that the evil-eyed Ezra seemed to finally have been discharged of his duties. She hadn't seen him since her return to her chores, and though no mention was ever made to her, he had not been replaced, either. She didn't dare question it, since she'd never been comfortable in his presence anyway and was thankful that she needn't suffer him any longer.

And so it was, that on this day, more than a week after her scrambled dash away from Inesfree, that Tess sat once again in the herb garden. Rains had threatened all morn. The sky churned up gray and dour clouds, whisking them across a sunless sky. Serena had been kind enough to loan her yet more pieces of apparel; today it was a hooded gray cloak. There wasn't much to be done in the garden, but she was still happy to remain out of doors as long as possible, despite the depressing weather.

Soon enough, the rains did come, and Tess hitched up the basket of plucked herbs onto her hip and started back toward the kitchens. She thought she spied Bethany. Across the inner bailey, a child with blonde hair, just about Bethany's size, darted through the light shower and the outer gate, out of Tess's sight. Curious, she followed, her hood pulled low against the rain, hoping to catch up with Bethany before she disappeared. Tess walked briskly but never came upon the child again, even though she'd walked almost halfway around the square outer bailey. She was surprised to find herself near the postern gate and the back door to the larder and kitchens.

She stared at that gate, the one she'd discovered while watching those boys dicing many days ago. There was none about to stop her or question her. She walked further, and with only one last glance to be sure there were no witnesses, she lifted the latch.

It did not budge. Tess frowned and squinted at the handle. It should just lift out of the brace, but it did not. True, it was old and rusted, but it should at least have budged. She tried again, and used two hands now, but to no avail.

Tess turned around, scanning the yard again, her mouth pinching a bit in confusion. With a frustrated shrug, and now chilled by the continued rain, Tess began walking back from whence she'd come. The outer gate and bridge were almost out of sight when she heard the call to raise the gate. Wondering if Conall might be among the coming party, she waited only long enough to see that it was, instead, old Metylda entering on her rickety cart, pulled by an impossibly aged nag. The old woman obviously felt the same as Tess did about the rains, her head likewise covered in a dark and heavy cloak. She turned her cart left, toward Tess, aiming for the back of the outer yard, where she usually stood her rig, closer to the kitchen. Metylda barely lifted her head and did not see or greet Tess as the cart rolled past Tess. The old healer might request to see Tess's knees again, to discern for sure that her ministrations had been helpful, so Tess was bound to meet up with her inside.

Tess returned to the inner courtyard, intent on getting out of the rain, but looked back, just in time to see Metylda stepping slowly from the seat of the cart, her movements judicious. She reached under a heavy woolen blanket, which covered much of the bed of the wagon, and withdrew her little leather satchel, which contained her medicinal herbs. On solid ground now, and with her head still lowered, Metylda walked rather spryly into the kitchens.

Tess's eyes remained fixed on the covered bed of the wagon. A person might lie under that blanket and never be noticed.

THE RAINS BROUGHT CONALL and his men back to Inesfree earlier than expected. They had not been training today, but had, over the past many days, been shadowing and disrupting reivers along the border. The borderlands between England and Scotland had borne the brunt of the battles waged between the two warring nations. Sadly, their little towns had been mostly wiped out, castles burned, people killed and forgotten, and farms obliterated by the English's love of burning everything in their wake. The people of the borders, understandably, were distraught over what little care had been shown them. Many of them had begun to turn the tables by plundering lands and homes and keeps on both sides of the border, while refusing allegiance to either Scotland or England. Of late, several of these loosely related groups had been hitting close to home, pillaging the small towns of Ainfield Plain and Swalwell, and these only a quarter day's ride from Inesfree.

Yesterday Conall had received a missive from the Kincaid, its chief advising of increased activity of these reivers. Conall and Gregor Kincaid had plans to meet up at the end of next month to ride to Wallace's side, and both thought it imperative now that they settled the reivers' increasing brutality before they departed their own homes.

Today's outing, with about fifty of his men, had succeeded only in showing him where the reivers *had* been, as they'd come upon the burnt out village of Langley Moor. Likely, the assault had taken place the day before, as the remains of the crofter's huts, burned down to heaps of ash and bodies, barely smoked yet. If there had been survivors, they were gone as well, not even lingering about to bury the dead.

No clues had been left to identify the perpetrators, and though the area had been scoured and the next closest villages visited throughout the morning, they knew no more than when the sun had risen.

Death disturbed Conall. Senseless death and ruin infuriated him. They would head out tomorrow and try to discover which band of border reivers might be responsible. His best plan might be to charge into the reivers' lands and start knocking heads to get the answers he needed.

Conall nodded up at the soldiers atop the gate as he passed underneath. He was weary and wished only for a hot bath and tall ale.

And Tess.

That thought had not come completely unbidden. He'd been thinking on her while riding back to Inesfree. When did he not, really? He didn't understand the reasoning, didn't question the logic or lack thereof behind it, only knew that he'd missed her this past week. It was foolish, he knew. But the day had been miserable, and thoughts of Tess had calmed him. Not even carnal thoughts of kissing or touching and all the things he wanted to do to her, but just...her.

It was time to force the marriage, he knew. He needed to wed Tess to regain Marlefield. He wanted to marry to bring Tess to him. She was not immune to his touch or his kiss, of that he was certain, ofttimes thinking it befuddled and thrilled her as much as it did him. If they were married, she would yield. Marriage would remove an obstacle, allow her to keep a bit of her pride, he guessed. It would make her his.

His head would never allow him to say these things out loud, certainly not to any MacDonnell or MacGregor, but he knew he wanted Tess as his own, and he needed her to want it as well.

Conall left his mount with one of the grooms who'd come running through the rain as the soldiers approached. The boy took the reins from Conall and John and two more soldiers, leading all four horses back to the stables. On down the returning line, grooms continued recovering horses. Drained warriors, silent with the weight of the day's trials still upon them, were glad to be within sight of the keep.

The men stepped inside, welcomed by a strong fire in the main hall, and the warmth it provided. Several soldiers took up seats upon the benches that would in a few hours be home to their supper. Serving wenches scrambled at their arrival, scampering off to the kitchens to fetch ale. Conall allowed the men their ease; they'd witnessed atrocities today and were certainly permitted any attempt to drown them out.

He had other plans and took the stairs two at a time at the end of the hall. Inside his chamber, there was no Tess. It dawned on him that at this time of day, she would still be about her kitchen chores, and Conall retraced his steps.

Inside the kitchens, there was no Tess. Conall approached Eagan, not oblivious to the stillness that always overtook the kitchen upon his appearance.

"Where is Tess?" He asked the round little man.

Eagan looked around, as if he hadn't given her any thought for a while. "She was here," he said lamely. And then, with a worried look at his chief, "But that was quite a while ago. She went to gather herbs and..." his voice trailed off as dread contorted the cook's usually composed expression.

Conall's nostril's flared. He spun on his heel and headed outdoors. The rains continued to fall. Only a few people moved about, only those with someplace to be, heads covered and lowered against the rain.

There was no Tess.

She couldn't have, he thought.

She wouldn't have dared.

He turned around in the yard, his boots eating up mud from the ground. Rain splashed on his bare head and face. He swiped his hand angrily from forehead to chin, swiping water away. His curse then would have raised the brow of the devil himself.

"Sound the alarm!"

TESS THOUGHT HERSELF extremely lucky this day. If she had planned an escape, it would have involved all of these perfect opportunities. Metylda's coming to the castle; covering the bed of her wagon because of the rain; the old hag making another stop after Inesfree, to a small village further north, where Tess stealthily clambered from her hidden spot within the healer's wagon. 'Twas only the rain that annoyed her, but this even had only to do with the chill, and that she would most definitely survive.

From the village at which Tess had fled from the hag's wagon, she'd headed south, into the woods. At least she thought it was south. She was only slightly unnerved to have no idea where she was. Evening would come very soon, and the darkness that would come with it frayed her nerves just a bit more, but Tess trudged on. The only strategy she'd managed to form in all her time since leaving Inesfree was that she needed help to get back to Marlefield. To that end, she'd thought to enlist aid within one of the many villages that dotted the Scottish countryside. She hadn't dared seek help in the village where she'd exited Metylda's wagon, on the off chance that the beast actually figured out how she'd managed to flee him this time. If he suspected or somehow figured out how she'd quit the walls of Inesfree, he would trace Metylda's steps, which would bring him to that first village at which the hag had stopped.

The rain needled her cold flesh and her knees had long ago begun to protest so much ungainly walking through the forest. It was fortunate then that she spied a lone thatched cottage, across a flat expanse of tall grass with a dark forest of trees behind it.

Cautiously, Tess approached the house, which showed no signs of occupation. Not a single light shone on this dreary day and not a thread of smoke rose from the chimney. But shelter, however undesirable, was welcome and Tess neared the door just as it swung open from within.

She jumped back, startled.

"Who comes?" Demanded a man, who Tess decided immediately had seen more years than even Metylda. He was tall and thin and slightly bent, his eyes milky and sightless and settled just above her head. His garb was untidy, the original color of his ragged tunic lost to time, his breeches stained and tattered. One shoulder of the tunic hung off an impossibly thin shoulder, while his sparse hair clumped in wispy patches around his head.

"I am Tess," she offered hesitantly and watched his head move very slowly so that he appeared to stare almost directly at her. "I have become lost in the wood. May I take shelter inside?"

The old man straightened to this full height, perhaps the height of the MacGregor even, and announced, "Such a bonny voice. It's raining, you ken."

"Yes, I do know that," she said with a small laugh.

"Then come in now, won't you? We're no idiots to keep you out in the rain." Holding onto the door, he shuffled his feet backward and Tess entered the cottage.

It was dark within, at which Tess frowned, until she realized that a blind person would have no need of candles. The cottage was only one room, and filthy at that. Cobwebs hung all around, not only in the corners and the thick rafters. The floor, pounded earth, was puddled in some areas. The few pieces of furniture were ancient and gave the impression of frailty.

"Do you live here alone?" She asked.

"All my life," he answered, still hovering by the door. "Go by the name Angus Kilkenny. Have a boy—Fynn, he is—comes 'round on Tuesdays, brings me game. Sit down. Sit down, lass."

Tess did not precisely trust the constancy of that lone chair, but she was weary and so sit she did.

"I have water from the stream, here in a jug...somewhere," he said, moving away from the door and searching with his hands atop the table until his fingers settled around a tankard. He turned and Tess found herself rising already, lest he be forced to find his way to her.

"This is very kind of you, sir." And she drank deeply. The water was surprisingly clear and refreshing.

"Angus is all," he said. "No 'sir' hereabouts," and he chuckled, a raspy little laugh that made Tess smile. "I've bread, too, though it be moldy by now, no doubt."

"Thank you, Angus, but I am not so hungry," she lied. She glanced around his 'kitchen' which was no more than a shelf built into the wall, that held a tin bucket and a few wooden trenchers. There appeared to be no foodstuffs at all. Tess wondered how he survived, but then considered his very lean frame.

Tess glanced at the still-open door and measured the darkening day. "Angus, would you mind if I made a fire?"

The old man's bushy brows rose over suddenly brightened opaque eyes. "Ach, now, that'd be grand. Only ever have fires on Tuesdays when Fynn comes. Too dangerous, ofttimes," he explained vaguely.

Tess rose and perused the items near the hearth, which was heavily filled with ashes. She employed a thinner, flat piece of wood from a pitiful supply on the floor to move the ashes to one side. She arranged what little else was available to her, wishing she'd paid more attention to the boys who'd always kept the fire burning in any place she'd ever lived. Perhaps there was enough, she guessed, of kindling, logs, and dry pine needles.

"An' now you can be telling auld Angus how it is you've lost your way," said the old man from behind her.

"Oh, well," answered Tess, not wanting to lie to him, but certainly not about to reveal to him the whole truth. "I'd been detained down at Inesfree for a while," she hedged. Upon the spare and rough mantel, she found both flint and steel, and even the remnants of a char cloth. "Today, it was imperative that I start back home." There. Not quite a lie. "The rain seems to have turned me around a bit."

Tess struck the steel down across the sharp edge of the flint many times before she found success, which she then pushed immediately into the char cloth. She set down the fire implements and picked up the char cloth, lowering herself and the cloth to the kindling inside the hearth.

"Inesfree, you say? I once brought my wares down there. Sometimes leathers, sometimes fabric, if I could get 'em. Back when the MacDonnell was alive. Long ago."

Her tiny fire popped and sizzled, growing quickly. Tess stood and surveyed her handiwork, then stretched her hands out to warm them.

"That's nice, lass," Angus said. He'd taken up a seat on the bench at the table.

"Come closer Angus," Tess said. "It's so nice and warm." She touched his arm and he rose without opposition, allowing Tess to lead him to the chair, nearer the hearth. He patted her hand, before she'd released him.

"Do you know the current laird, the MacGregor?" Tess asked of him, keeping her voice neutral.

"I haven't been down that way in years, since before Fynn was birthed," he said with an aimless shrug of his narrow shoulders. "Might smoke me some pipe, now you've made so nice a fire," he hinted.

Tess glanced around, found his pipe atop the mantel, set apart from the flint and steel. A soft flax pouch sat next to it—what he smoked, Tess could only imagine. She pressed both into his hands. "You fill. I'll light it." She left him to insert the pipe into the pouch, with such familiarity he needn't have sight, while she selected another thin piece of wood and lit the end of it. She returned to Angus, just as he finished pressing the filling down tightly within the pipe. "Here," she said, and he placed the pipe between his lips. Tess joined the small flame to the filling and Angus drew deeply upon it until it was well lighted.

"Aw, but aren't you an angel," he said, settling back into his chair, the pipe now hung between his lips.

Before she sat, she stood at the door, surveying the wide clearing that was Angus's front yard. Dusk had definitely settled. "It has stopped raining," she told Angus. "Mayhap, I should try again to find...my way."

"Getting toward dark now, lass," Angus noted, his teeth still clamped 'round the pipe. "You'll sleep here. Might be Fynn'll come tomorrow. He'll be able to see you where you need to be."

"Has he a horse?" Tess inquired, intrigued by the possibility. She closed the door and finally removed her cloak, setting it upon one end of the bench while she sat at the other end. The cottage was cozy now, aglow with soft light and warm air.

"Of sorts."

"Angus, do you mind me asking why you stay here?" Tess dared. "I mean, all by yourself."

He shrugged again, a comfortable enough motion, Tess thought he must do it often. "Nowhere to go. My boy is gone too much to have his own hearth. Trades up and down, he does." He began to talk of what Tess assumed had been life before he lost his sight, telling her of his youth, much of it spent fighting wars for Alexander III, upon the Isle of Sky. There was a way about him, his eagerness to talk, which suggested to Tess that he'd seen no company other than his own son for many a year. Tess was happy to listen, comfortable upon the bench, warmed by the fire and Angus's melodic speech, though she felt her eyes drooping after a while.

"You take the bed, lass." Angus offered, after he'd been quiet for a few minutes.

"Angus, I'll not put you out of your bed. I can—"

"Nonsense, lass. 'Tis often that I do catch me winks here." He waved her off with a frail hand.

"You have no idea what this kindness means to me, Angus."

She hadn't any intention of sleeping too long. Tomorrow was not Tuesday, she knew, so it was unlikely Angus's son actually would come and she dared not stay longer than necessary. It was her plan that she should push on very early in the morning, to be further still away from Inesfree.

She didn't need much persuasion to climb into the stiff bed, harder than she imagined, though surely more comfortable than the cold wet ground outside.

CHAPTER 14

S he woke next to the feel of a hand, huge and warm, clamped over her mouth. She tried to bolt upright but was unable—the long fingers of another hand were pressed around her throat. Eyes wide with fright revealed near complete darkness. The fire had died, and Tess knew not what had become of Angus. Squirming and clawing at the hands gained her naught but an increase of pressure. After a futile moment, Tess stilled, though her own fingers remained tensed over the mammoth, detaining paws.

"Give me one good reason no to kill you here and now, Tess."

Had her mouth been disengaged, she might have actually sighed her relief upon realizing the voice as Conall's. But quickly enough, her fright did multiply. His words and his tone had been chilling. Here was an anger she'd yet to experience from him; seething, quiet, controlled. It frightened Tess as nothing before had.

After a last shove against her mouth, to emphasize the breadth of his rage she was sure, he pulled away, then removed the other hand from around her neck.

Tess coughed and fought for breath while he hauled her abruptly to her feet from his bed. She glanced quickly about but did not see Angus.

"Move," Conall commanded and pushed her to the door.

"Where is Angus? What have you done with Angus?"

He didn't answer. He continued to shove her, out the door, and into the utter dark of night. Tess thought she detected at least a dozen soldiers waiting there. But no Angus.

She pushed back against Conall, holding her ground. "Where is Angus?"

"There are penalties, Tess," he clipped cryptically. Roughly, he threw her up onto Mercury's back. "People who abet runaways are punished." He climbed up behind her though he did not wrap his arm around her middle as he usually did.

"Oh, Lord in Heaven!" she cried. She was forced to hold onto the pommel as the group galloped away. "He is blind! He did not know I was escaping—please tell me you haven't killed him," she begged to be assured, her own fright at Conall's mighty wrath forgotten as her distress over Angus's fate increased. "Please—"

"Your accomplices will always be punished."

Tess let out a sharp cry, her shoulders sagging as the implication set in. Oh, God, he had killed that kindly old man.

TESS'S HATRED FOR HER captivity grew tenfold over the next few days. Angus's death lay heavily over her. It was entirely the Mac-Gregor's fault that the poor man was dead, but Tess found that it was *her* heart that ached with guilt. And with this weighing mightily upon her, she feared she would never escape Inesfree and Conall Mac-Gregor.

Never again to see Marlefield, or even so much as a friendly face.

After her return from this most recent escape attempt, she'd been summarily thrown into the tower again by Conall. He'd said not one word to her during that long ride. She'd yet to see Bethany. And Serena—always kind, always gentle—had shown herself once, sans food, only to inquire in a bristly tone if Tess had need of Metylda for any reason.

So now, three days after that fateful misadventure, Tess was no further ahead. Indeed, she was suffused with a sense that she was, again, nearer to the status at which she had begun at Inesfree: a hostage with neither rights nor kindness. Without mercy. Without food.

Soon, she imagined, she'd be without her mind, for one did not suffer these ups and downs without some defection of wit.

She was cold and damp and hungry and no doubt this contributed to her lack of hope and confidence. And, too, her failed attempts were disheartening to a ruinous degree.

Upon the furs once again, Tess rolled onto her back, flinging an arm over her head. She stared at the ceiling but found little there to hold her attention. She'd already counted the timbers and the stones within this wretched room. She'd not like to find herself counting raindrops next, though like as not it would prove productive, as the rains had yet to abate.

As a child, she had always prayed for rain. Her mother, of a charitable yet variable character, hated the rain. She would retreat to the inner sanctum of their rooms within the abbey, finding comfort in herself. Her changeable nature had, at these times, unnerved Tess, but the songs she'd sung, to keep herself calm during the storms, had soothed Tess and haunted her still. There had been a quality about her mother's voice—peaceful, lulling, hypnotic—as her soft little chants carried through their apartments, filling Tess with tranquility. To this day, Tess ached to hear her mother's voice in song.

CONALL HAD THREE TIMES approached the tower, and three times had retreated without entering. She needed to know he played no game. She must understand—be reminded—that his desire to once again possess Marlefield played a foremost role in every action, hers or his. Every word, every deed, every thought should be undertaken with only one objective in mind. She must never guess anything other than this to be true.

He would never admit—not to her nor anyone else—that the larger issue here, and the greater part of his fury was a result of the ache he'd felt when he realized she actually wanted to leave him. Repeatedly, he'd shaken this off, feeding the anger instead, over any possibility that this was only about his feelings being hurt. He needed to be able to look into her eyes and remain hard and unyielding and fearsome. His dealings with her prior to her most recent flight had been motivated more by softness than anything else. That was done now. He'd allowed her some freedom, had thought she'd accepted her position here, at Inesfree and in his life, had thought indeed she'd accepted him, and her fate. Their fate.

And so, for the fourth time, he climbed the stairs, resolved now to contend with Tess. As he reached the landing of the second floor, just as he placed his foot upon the first step of the stairway that would lead him to the tower, he became aware of a humming sound. It was melancholy at its brightest, its fluid tone a soft, somber cry. He stilled for a moment, seized by a heightening anger, and then charged up the steps and barged into the tower.

But he found, as he entered, only Tess, upon her back, one leg settled atop the opposite knee, rocking to the hum of her song.

"Get up."

She tilted her head upon the fur, looking at him upside down. He noted immediately that she was in a terrible state. Unkempt, uncaring, she regarded him.

"Ah, the Lord does come now," she said tartly though made no move to rise as he'd commanded. Indeed, her knee still moved in time to her song of a moment ago.

"You do try me, Tess," he snarled. She ignored him, fueling his already frayed temper. She had in her hands, which rested on her stomach, a small torn piece of fabric, perhaps from her dark overskirt. She threaded it between her slim fingers, one end unraveled into dozens of loose strands. "Get up, I said." She moved not at all, save for her hands, fiddling with the fabric. Conall was at her side in an instant. He shoved his booted foot into her hip. "Move. Now."

"I think not."

"Goddamn it! Think you I'd no kill you now because I haven't yet?" Still, her hands toyed with the piece, ignoring him. There was an urge then to shove his foot at her with greater might. To provoke her into...something. She began to hum again, as if he did not stand above her engulfed in a towering rage that had much to do with her near successful escape—her very perseverance in this course—and more to do with this ungovernable desire for her, even now. Abruptly, he took her wrist in his, pulling up his arm, forcing her to come to her feet or chance being dragged. She rose, dropping that damn scrap of cloth, her eyes only momentarily wary. She knew her trouble was deep but was willing to accept her supposed doom for the very chance to rattle and vex him.

Set upon his own course, and with no great desire to accommodate her shorter steps, Conall led her down several flights of stairs and out into the yard. Several persons halted their business to stare, though in this everlasting drizzle, there were few about. He knew Tess eyed him critically. He could feel the burn of her glance upon his back as he pulled her along. He waved away the guard at the inner gatehouse and marched through the outer bailey. Nearer to the portcullis, he gave a call for it to be lifted, his stride unbroken as he ducked under the slow rising gate, forcing Tess to do the same. He continued to drag Tess, through the tall grass, cutting through a sparse copse of short trees until they reached the stream which sometimes afforded Inesfree its fresh, clear water if the well were dry.

There, Conall stopped, though his arm continued to move, bringing Tess around to his front. Without hesitation, he lifted her into his arms, holding her slight form to his chest and waded into the stream. She made not a sound; no protests came forth. And when he directly dropped her into the icy water, she was silent still.

She went under immediately but surfaced quickly enough. As the depth here was slight, she just sat there, covered up to her breasts, her knees bent above the water. She might have inquired of his purpose, she might have shivered in the cold, she might have railed at him for this abuse. But she did none of these. Her eyes met his, watchful, curious perhaps, but without the fear she should have been feeling.

This lazy vigilance prompted Conall to ignite some other emotion. "Take off your clothes."

She frowned at him, more confused than leery.

"I'll no have you filthy when I take you."

And here was the fear he'd courted. Those pretty eyes, now highlighted by spiked lashes, widened. Her bottom lip trembled. She began to scoot away from him. Conall lunged for her, catching the front of her soaked kirtle as she fled, yanking her up so that she fell upon him, forcing them both down into the water. She kicked and screamed as he circled her waist with one arm and hauled her out of the water, suspended at his hip. With as much care as the limited amount he'd shown her today, he dropped her onto the bank of the stream. She cried out and Conall forced her onto her back and rent her wet kirtle in a single stroke. He stared for a moment at her shape, outlined by what remained of her sodden chemise, a savage fire burning within his eyes. Her nipples were all but completely visible to him, hardened circles of rouge beneath the transparent material.

Easily, he gathered her striking hands, pinning them above her head as he came fully atop her. He pressed his lips to hers, holding her mouth despite her squirming. She sobbed and he pressed on, refusing to be dissuaded, despite the ache it brought.

TESS WENT LIMP BENEATH him.

She cried still, but not for what he was doing to her.

I am not afraid. He will not hurt me. He will not. She cried because he thought he needed to do this. He needed to bark, but he would not bite, she knew. She just knew this was true.

He stopped, just dropped his head into her neck and her hair and stayed very still, save for his heavy breathing. Her eyes remained closed as rain continued to pelt them.

Long seconds later, Conall shifted just as Tess put her hands on his shoulders. When his face was above hers again, when the rain was blocked, she opened her eyes, saw the struggle in his. Placing one hand on either side of his face, she asked, her words slow and laced with sorrow, "Is it anger? Or is this really you?"

His nostrils flared and some noise came from his chest, but he did not answer.

"Riders a comin'!" Came a call, through the hard rain, from the castle wall.

Conall pushed off the ground and rose to his feet.

Tess let her shoulders relax, and felt the tension leave her body.

He stood over her, sluicing rain from his face with his hands, as large and fearsome as he had ever been. He stared down at her for a moment, their eyes locking. She did not shrink away, though surely her relief had become a physical thing for him to perceive, and watched his eyes darken. There was still a fierceness about him as he reached out a hand to her.

"Get up," he said, pulling her to her feet. He was abrupt and curt, once again stomping swiftly along the path, through the rain, ignoring her as her bare feet slipped and sputtered in the wet grass and mud. Her clothes, what remained, hung in shredded rags, her hair no doubt as filthy and bedraggled as the rest of her, and still, she suspected, there was the light of panic in her eyes. But Conall paid no heed. The gate was lifted at his call and lowered as they cleared it. Tess was pushed onto the ground at the foot of the wall with the admonition, "If you move, you will never leave the tower again," which Conall had to shout to be heard above the now pounding rain, before he stalked away, up to the battlements to view the arriving party. He returned momentarily, to find Tess huddling yet in the hard rain, against the wall. "I'd have recognized him anywhere," he said, his mood still dark. "Your betrothed arrives, Tess. Shall we greet him?" he raised a brow at her.

She had thought the timing to be perfect. The riders might have saved her from his furor but now knew she had been mistaken. The coming of Alain now, while she looked as she did, was beneficial only to Conall. She would be disgraced. Alain would take one look at her, and that which he had perhaps only wondered at, he would now believe to be true.

"Open the gate!" Conall called, his deep voice carrying over the torrent of rain. "Come, Tess. Greet your betrothed."

It would have been easy to have disobeyed him then, but Tess feared she would, in this hunkered down position, appear even more broken than she actually was. She stood and clutched the shreds of her gown together and walked stiffly to his side. Let Alain see her. She would hold herself proud. She had betrayed no one.

Alain's party rode slowly through the open gate, Sir Arthur's banner flying high above the standard bearer, though against the rain, it did flounder. Tess was able to pick out Alain immediately. Despite the helm that shielded all the oncoming faces, Alain's person was obvious. Even amidst such inclemency, his attire seemed undisturbed, not shot with mud, nor drooping with saturation. The group halted and Alain raised his helm.

In different circumstances, Tess might have snorted with laughter at the comical expression upon her betrothed's face. He was shocked, to say the least, at her appearance. And true, standing straight and bold when dressed only in one's chemise and torn asunder kirtle, and soaked through at that—which no doubt showed Alain and any who thought to stare a great many parts of Tess—was scandalous and deserving of censure. But what struck Tess was only that Alain appeared not so much distressed at what horrors she obviously faced at the MacGregor's hands, but that she had been reduced to this unsightly and offensive state.

"Take her inside," Conall said, quietly, and one of his men hurried to do so.

Only then did Tess allow herself to yield her brave stance, giving Alain a pleading look that surely bespoke of her fear and hope for salvation.

She was grabbed none too gently, the show of brute force must be carried through, and hauled away into the castle. Quietly, she went, abandoning all her hopes to Alain.

She was taken to the tower room again, left alone behind a locked door in her ruined garments, her body once more chilled to the very core. She prayed fervently that whatever Alain was about, he would prove successful

Tess sank to her knees, wondering truly if she would ever be warm again, and considered Conall's earlier behavior. Some dam within him had broken today. Though Tess on occasion believed him to be the very devil, she would have never imagined that he'd have behaved as he had. Her dismay was also born of sadness, she realized. She honestly examined her emotions in regard to this: despite everything—their status as enemies, his kidnapping of her, his initial harshness toward her, her own attempts to escape him—she'd truly and naively thought that there existed between them some inexplicable connection and certainly a desire for things that had nothing at all to do with captor and captive.

Exhausted and cold, Tess collapsed on the fur throws. Absently, she wiped mud from her arms and from her face, pulling her wet hair up above her, away from her skin.

She would forever hate the rain.

CHAPTER 15

"Parading Tess before me in such ungodly condition has answered the first of my few questions," Alain Sinclair said when he and Conall were alone, seated at the lord's table in the hall. Alain had been offered wine and food, which he had declined. He slapped his gloves onto the table, showing an anger which Conall believed might actually be real. "I take it she has been used, well and good."

"She is a hostage," was all Conall said.

"Then you had no plans to wed her?" The younger man looked affronted.

"Wed a Munro? For what purpose?" Asked Conall.

Alain only shook his head. "What are your terms for release?"

"There will be no release," said Conall, lifting his tankard to his mouth. He drank deeply, then swiped the back of his hand across his lips, happy to let this fop think him a barbarian.

"No release? Then why did you take her?"

"To harass Munro."

"You have stolen a man's daughter only with intentions to harass him?"

"The first of many harassments, to be sure."

Alain frowned at this. "That is between you and Sir Arthur. I should tell you, however, that this first harassment, has done little in the way of nettling the man. Sir Arthur cares not much for his daughter. I come here of my own accord. Her father thought Tess not worthy of saving."

It was quite a feat for Conall to contain his ire over this. "You mean he thought it impossible to rescue her."

Alain shook his fair head. "Not at all. I impart that it was considered that a plan should be created to have her killed—for reasons which I am not at liberty to discuss."

"Munro instigated these plans?" His tone was quiet, controlled.

"He would have, save that circumstances changed and he—well, there was no longer a need."

Conall mulled this over. After a thoughtful moment, he asked, "And why is it that you have come, if no at Munro's behest?"

"I was betrothed to Tess—"

"Was?" Conall lifted a brow.

"The betrothal was forfeited when Tess was abducted."

"By you?" He was quite aware of the muscle ticking within his jaw.

"By Munro. As I have said, circumstances changed."

Conall leaned forward, elbows upon the table, hands around his tankard. He stared not at Alain, but straight ahead, his gaze fixed upon nothing. "I know of the clause which cedes Marlefield to her mate upon her marriage."

"Then why haven't you—?" Alain began.

Conall cut him off. "Are you saying, with your cryptic and garbled speech, that Munro has somehow managed to have that dictate nullified?"

"Yes. As soon as Tess was taken, he sped directly to the council. He convinced the council that Tess had taken it into her head to marry an Englishman. The council has no idea she is here and immediately agreed that it was of utmost importance that a Scots castle not possibly fall into English hands due to the fickle mind of a lass."

Conall nodded. After another long moment, he asked again, "So why is it you have come, Sinclair?"

Alain offered a harsh, self-deprecating chuckle. "Even I, and I fancied her not at all, could not have lived with myself if I'd done nothing to try and help her."

"Munro knows that you have come?"

"No."

"If she were to be returned, would he kill her?"

Alain shrugged his shoulders. "No reason to—or he'd have set his original plan into motion."

Conall leaned back to study the man. Alain Sinclair's eyes were without guile. Truly, he had no reason to lie. As he had said himself, he had no desire for Tess, and as effeminate and toady as he was, Conall had a pretty good idea where Sinclair's interests did lie. It was possible that good conscience alone had brought him to Inesfree, that and perhaps a virulent dislike of Munro, as his voice, when he'd been forced to say the man's name, had emerged as a snarl.

But then, Conall couldn't exactly be sure. Were his answers just *too* perfect?

Conall stood. "You may take shelter at Inesfree tonight until you depart in the morning." And he left the dais, walking away.

"Do I not at least get to see Tess? Will you not even consider releasing her to me? I am willing to—"Alain sputtered, clearly unprepared for this hasty departure, faced with his own fruitlessness.

"No." Conall called back without breaking his stride.

"Dammit, MacGregor! You cannot keep her thus, abusing her as you do..."

But Conall heard no more as he rounded the corner and advanced upon the stairs to his chamber. He'd learned much tonight, most of which was disturbing to his cause. There would be no bloodless return to Marlefield. Munro had anticipated his motive and had rallied, and prevailed. Conall had never anticipated that a supposed traitor would have been able to even convince a council that the sky was blue, let alone to void a contract parcel.

He ran into Serena in the passageway outside his chamber. It was obvious, as she leaned against the wall beside his door, that she waited for him.

"Conall, tell me. Who is that man? Are you letting Tess go?"

Conall reached for the door handle. "That man is her betrothed and no, Tess will no be released." His other hand kneaded the back of his neck.

"What happened today, Conall?" Serena asked, apparently desperate for some reassurance that he wasn't as dishonorable as he'd almost proved himself to be. "What did you do to Tess?"

"Nothing she didn't deserve," he snapped, but at Serena's cry of horror—over Tess's supposed abuse or his fall into indefensible wickedness, Conall could not guess—he added harshly, "I did no rape her, Serena. She is still as pure as the fucking driven snow."

Serena straightened with indignation. "Oh, Conall—"

He waved her off, with an order for a bath and a meal. He paused, then added as he pushed open his chamber door, "And have a bath sent up to Tess. She'll need food as well. And wine." He watched Serena nod though she moved not at all. But Conall ignored her, entering his room, closing the door behind him.

Inside, he leaned heavily against the door, tipping his head back upon the thick wood. He closed his eyes, his thoughts mayhem. Nothing—not one goddamn thing—was proceeding as planned.

Marlefield was falling through the slight grasp he'd had upon it. Tess—good God, he'd done nothing right where she was concerned. He'd not started out as he meant to continue. His plan from the start had been to instill fear as a way of coercion. But he'd found himself, time and again, looking into those perfect green eyes and losing all his aptitude to effect terror. After her initial refusal to wed, and though he assured himself he would never reduce himself so much as to actually woo the child of his enemy, all his subsequent actions had amounted to just that. He would defend it as strategy, but understood it was more about want and need. In short, his desire for Tess had begun to override that of his desire for Marlefield.

And just when he'd found anger enough to re-establish the fearfulness in her, he was slapped in the face with information that made him ache for her.

No one would save her. None save the ineffectual Alain would even try. Her own parent, bound by blood, had plans to murder her lest she cost him something that had never been his anyway. She should never know this. Never find out how quickly and easily she had been cleaved from Sir Arthur's life, and doubtless that of every Munro.

While she waited in vain, perhaps prayed daily for deliverance, she was, and had been from the moment of her abduction, dead to any she imagined might support her.

Conall was the only person to whom she might have proved useful.

And now, he too, no longer had any need of her.

SERENA SOFTENED TOWARD Tess after a fashion, though Tess stalwartly refused to apologize for escaping, as she deemed it her duty. After what Conall had almost done to her, she felt she owed no apology to anyone. As it was, Serena had come to the tower room several times more, offering a bath and nourishment and even clean furs, but Tess ignored her, likening her to Conall, and his cruel intentions. After a few days of this, only Dorcas, and sometimes even lesser persons, delivered her food. The witch, when she came, only thumped the tray heavily upon the table, saying not a word, as if any attention to Tess was beneath her. Tess didn't care. She didn't even bother to ask after Alain. Whatever his mission here, he'd not been successful, or she'd not still be locked away in the tower.

Whenever she thought of Angus, she cried. She would never tell Conall—if she ever saw him again—but she would never again risk someone else's life to save her own. The death of Angus might be the one thing that broke her, she decided. She didn't know how to make that better. There was no way to undo what had been done, and there was no way to forget about it, either. It gnawed day and night at Tess.

She considered actually marrying Conall, but to what end now? He'd done—nearly—his worst. If she hadn't capitulated when threatened with her own death, what might marriage gain her now but a possible release from the tower?

Tess's muddled thoughts were interrupted by the door opening. She was crouched in the far corner, in the shadows of the tower room. Usually, she heard footsteps before the door opened.

The shadows hid her face, she knew, and thus her surprise, at finding it was Conall himself who entered. She felt herself pressing further into the corner. She wrapped her arms around her drawn up knees.

He said nothing but walked over to the lone window, from which Tess no longer looked out. After a few minutes of silence, he turned and leaned his hip against the stone beneath the window. He crossed his arms over his chest and considered her.

Tess didn't move. She didn't need to; he couldn't see her face. She didn't even need to avert her gaze. His eyes were dark still, but they were not the eyes she remembered, being neither struck with anger nor brightened by purpose, and certainly not lightened with the intent of kissing her. They were tired, she decided, weary. Indeed, his entire body and posture screamed this as well.

"I will apologize for my behavior," he finally said, his voice deep and low.

Tess could only stare at him. When it became apparent that he would say no more, she wondered if she was expected to reply? To...

what? Forgive him? She felt, above the unease churning in her belly, a formidable anger rising.

She started to speak, but having not done so in many days, had to clear her throat when no sound immediately came forth, and begin again. "Do you speak to the murder of Angus? Or your treatment of me?"

He wasn't baited, indeed seemed unperturbed by her brashness. "At the water's edge."

"Oh, that." She struggled for indifference but feared she hadn't quite hit the right note exactly.

His eyes darkened. He pushed away from the wall and strode to her, stopping when only inches separated his feet from hers. His hands were fisted, though they only hung at his sides.

"I—I have never in my life behaved like that. I wouldn't have—" he stopped. He shifted his weight. "I am sorry, Tess."

"Your apology, I fear, is likely for your benefit, rather than my own." She strove to maintain an even tone in the face of his growing annoyance. "My mother used to say an apology is a fine means to have the last word."

He regarded her a moment more. She detected a resignation about his tired features, which caused Tess only a momentary pang.

Let him stew, she thought. *Let him taste guilt*. He deserved it.

Conall turned and went to the door, which remained half open. He pulled the heavy timber wide and stepped out onto the landing at the top of the stairs. He stood there for several minutes, while Tess chewed her lip.

Someone came. She detected the soft and light brush of feet slowly moving up the stairs. Still tucked in the far corner, Tess leaned to her left, to peer around the door. Conall's huge form blocked her view. Two shapes, one tall and one short, advanced toward the tower room.

Tess slowly stood at the same time Conall moved again, backing into the room, as if he led someone.

When Conall fully stepped aside, Tess clapped both hands over her mouth in dazed joy.

Walking into the tower room were both Bethany and Angus. Tears surfaced and fell instantly. Tess watched beautiful little Bethany, holding Angus's hand, lead the blind man into the room. Bethany's eyes moved from the floor and their steps to Angus's face, watchful and so very dear.

Tess rushed across the room, falling to her knees in front of Bethany. The child didn't smile, but her brightened eyes told Tess that she was happy. She squeezed Bethany into a teary and joyful embrace. She kissed her face and her hair and pressed her again into a hug. "Oh, I am so happy to see you, darling." She pulled back and looked into the little girl's eyes, smiling like an idiot, while the child silently contemplated Tess. She didn't care. She kissed Bethany again. And then she stood and faced Angus, placing her hand on his weathered cheek. The old man smiled, covering Tess's hand with his.

"Angus," was all she could think to say, her joy in sobs undoing her.

"Aye, lass." The old man smiled. The scent of good tobacco hovered about him. He wore clean and tidy breeches, hose and tunic. New shoes of soft leather covered his feet and his formerly long stringy hair had been trimmed short and neat.

Tess hugged him. Angus stiffened in surprise at this, though he patted her back with his free hand. She continued to cry, unable to stop.

"Promise me, Tess," Conall said from behind her. "No more."

She closed her eyes and bit her lip. From his tone, she understood that his 'apology' was now complete—and with purpose—and she owed him something now, her vow to never again attempt to flee Inesfree.

Tess released Angus and turned to Conall. While he appeared as he ever did, large and foreboding, it was also apparent that he was holding his breath. She grasped at once that this gesture served another purpose: returning Bethany and Angus to her was the greater part of his apology.

She nodded shakily, smiling and crying still. It was an easy promise to give. "No more. I promise." She gave no thought at all to the fact that she had just pledged her life away.

She felt Bethany take her hand, the other still holding Angus's, and Tess knew she would pledge him anything at all right now.

His eyes, that mesmerizing blue she was sure would never *not* affect her, relaxed ever so slightly as he gave a quick nod, though his jaw remained clenched.

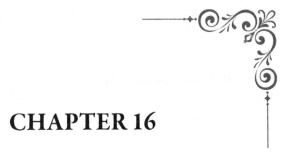

CHAPTER 16

"**D**o you have any idea what you're about with the lass?" John Cardmore asked Conall, in his frank and aggressive way, but showing a frown that suggested he, himself, was sore confused by the whole situation.

Conall offered a scathing chuckle. "I have no idea, John." He sighed loudly. "She twists me in knots. She will no bend—tis I who bends, it seems—and on any given day, I want to throttle her and send her away and..." His hands had moved while he spoke, punctuating his words and thoughts. He just wanted to take her in his arms and make her feel whatever it was he fought against any time he was near her. He wanted to be gentle, make her forget every pain he'd caused her at the water's edge. "She torments me." He raised his eyes to his captain and friend, found the old man staring at him with a growing comical look about him. Conall frowned, "What?"

"God's teeth, boy! Are you daft?" Now John, too, scowled heavily. "Dinna you ken when you're in love?"

Conall's jaw fell. "In love with Tess?"

Inside his grizzled old face, John Cardmore's eyes rolled with exasperation. He threw up his hands in frustration. "Jesu, if I dinna spell everything out for you, you'd ever be without a clue. Moping whilst she's gone. Eyes dogging her whilst she's here. Bringing her boons to make her smile. Conall, me boy, you got it bad."

"I am no in love with Tess," Conall argued, his words slow and thoughtful.

"If the bird quacks, it's likely a duck, boy," said John sagely.

And the old man, who'd barely smiled over the past fifteen years, guffawed noisily, his teeth flashing, slapping his knee at his own clever wit. And to himself, when Conall had abruptly left the table and the otherwise empty main hall, "Ach, now John, how we do like that boy." And he chuckled some more.

"WELL, NOW," SAID ANGUS, sitting comfortably in a sturdy chair in front of the huge hearth in the main hall, "I dinna rightly miss it, was lonely most the time." The hounds had taken to the old man, and at least one or two were forever at his feet, and at his side when he moved. "The laird is kind enough to give this old man a better home, and a full belly every day. He says he's gotten word to Fynn about me change of circumstances."

Angus's happy smile, uninterrupted even as he pushed the pipe between his teeth, was one of Tess's favorite things these days. "That is good news, indeed," Tess said. "Won't you come outside with me, Angus? I've had a comfortable chair set within the herb garden. The sun shines. You could keep company with me while I work."

The old man's bushy brows rose over his cloudy eyes. "Well, don't mind if I do." He uncrossed his legs, left his pipe in his mouth and stood. "Where did the bairn get to?"

"Who can say with that child," was all Tess could offer as she took Angus's arm and walked him out of the hall. "She'll be 'round at some point, I imagine." But it was strange, as Bethany had quite taken to Angus and was often by his side, watching him with a such a keen interest, trying, Tess assumed, to understand his blindness. She was very protective and watchful of Angus. Tess liked that. She knew Angus did, too.

Tess steered Angus out of doors.

"Ah, warm today," he commented, lifting his face just a bit toward the sun. The leathery surface of his skin told Tess he had often spent time outdoors.

"Wonderfully so," she agreed and brought him across the yard to her little plot, sitting him in the chair she herself had commandeered from the hall only this morning. "There."

Tess set to work then, while Angus sat contentedly beside her, listening to all the goings-on within the yard. And when the sound of the gate rattling upward reached her ears, she gave it no thought at all.

Hardly any words had been spoken between Conall and Tess since he'd revealed Angus and Bethany to her in the tower room over a week ago. Without discussion, the door to the tower room had been unlocked and she'd resumed her tending of the garden, though she'd been sadly informed by Eagan that he no longer needed her in the kitchen. No longer required by Conall, she'd thought, but didn't argue. She was happy to fill up her day with Angus and when tolerated, with Bethany. And she truly hadn't thought of escape since.

Three nights ago, Tess had returned to the tower to find that the entire chamber had been swept clean and a fire burned cheerfully from the rarely used hearth. In addition, a striking carved headboard and bed had been fitted into the room. It was covered in a delicate embroidered blanket of fine and soft cream wool. Underneath, the furs were heavy and thick over a canvas-covered mattress filled with straw and feathers. Tess had never seen a bed so beautiful. Across the room, nearer to the hearth, sat another bed, this one much smaller, with a similarly embroidered blanket and clean furs. Tess did not know whether Bethany was pleased or not by their new circumstance, but she had every night since slept in the tower with Tess.

The morning after her reunion with Angus and Bethany, Tess had sought out Serena. She'd found her easily, overseeing the half dozen laundresses making soap in the large closet off the kitchen. The lower half of the faces of all the women, Serena's included, were covered with the veils of the wimples they wore today, pinned up over their mouths and noses, offering protection against the caustic lye. Tess met Serena's pretty brown eyes as she stirred the hardwood ashes and water inside the metal bucket, suspended over a low flame.

Serena gave a brief nod and tapped one of the elderly laundresses to take over stirring the pot, removing that woman's narrow eyes from Tess, then moved toward to the door where Tess waited. Together, the two women stepped out into the corridor.

Tess caught Serena's strong hands in her own. She met her brown and wary eyes straight on. "I don't want to be forever begging forgiveness from you," she began earnestly. "So, I propose that I never again treat you so poorly, when you have been nothing but kind and wonderful to me." When Serena said nothing, Tess pressed on. "I am sorry, Serena. It was wrong, my behavior toward you. I am deeply shamed."

The other woman squeezed Tess's hand in return, her shining eyes seeming to hint at a smile beneath the veil. "Oh, Tess. You do try me!" But she hugged Tess, who teared instantly at such generosity from her.

"Oh, thank you, my friend," Tess cried into her shoulder. "I could not have borne it if you hated me."

Serena pulled back sharply, her hands on Tess's arms, her gaze fierce. "Never could I hate you, Tess. You have a difficult circumstance, I do know. You are allowed... your missteps. But please, no more," she requested with a nervous laugh.

Tess grinned ruefully. "I won't. I promised him." At Serena's quizzical look, Tess explained, "For Angus, and for Bethany, I've promised I won't ever again try to flee."

This pleased Serena greatly, Tess could see.

"You are a better friend than I deserve, Serena. Truly."

TESS HAD ONCE AGAIN filled the basket beside her with several varieties of herbs. Deciding it must now be nearing noon, Tess knew Eagan would need the marjoram and rosemary for the dozens of pheasants that he would prepare for tonight's dinner.

Tess rose and stretched but reined this in as she spied Bethany flying by. Bethany and a boy about her age ran around the bailey, ducking between the unmoving cart and wagon. They sped around two soldiers near the smithy and past two seated knights, both wounded, idling their time by whittling.

"Bethany is playing with a fellow her own age," Tess said, for Angus's benefit, as he sat nearby. She'd just yesterday told him of the brief and incomplete history of Bethany, and how she hadn't spoken since the MacGregor had found her. "They're darting all around. She looks happy."

Angus smiled. "As she should, aye, lass?"

"Oh, indeed," Tess agreed, hands on her hips while she continued to watch the pair, a soft smile enhancing her features. Eventually, they ran out of sight.

"Has she blonde hair?" Angus asked, pipe in hand, slanting his head.

"Yes, and bright blue eyes." Tess picked up her basket and reached for his hand. "I've finished up for today." They began to walk back into the keep, as Tess continued, "She doesn't smile, not outright. But I can see it in her eyes. They lighten. It's a wondrous thing to see."

"Bairns should always smile," Angus observed, shuffling alongside her.

"I think it will come," Tess continued. "Her hair, by the way, is thick for one so young." Tess laughed a bit. "Though it never did meet a comb it enjoyed." Angus chortled at this and she went on, painting a picture for him, "She is too thin, I sometimes think, but seems overall very healthy. She has a child's pure skin, with only ever a slight flush about her cheeks, though no freckles at all. She is darling now, but she will be a great beauty one day."

They entered the keep, leaving the sun out in the yard.

"Like you, lass," Angus guessed.

Tess gave a small smile and bumped her shoulder lightly into his. "I'm passable, I'd say."

"More so, I'd guess, or the laird would no be so keen on you," came this bold statement.

This stopped Tess, which caused Angus to halt as well. "He is no such thing."

Angus leaned toward her and lowered his voice conspiratorially, "They all stare at you, I ken, but his is ... brooding. I can feel it." He drew out the word 'feel'.

All teasing aside, Tess thought to inform him, "Angus, you now know my circumstance here. *They* all hate me. I am the outsider, and half-English at that. Never mistake it for something it is not."

"He dinna hate you and well you ken it. And they do stare, lass. They dinna want to, but they canna help themselves."

Tess made a face and started walking again, bringing Angus along with her.

"You are a fanciful old man, my friend," she told him, trying to put an end to the conversation.

"He's here now," Angus said. "He's watching you. Can you no feel it?"

Unnerved, Tess lifted her eyes and scanned the hall.

"Am I right?"

"Yes," she answered unconsciously, her eyes on Conall, who was indeed at the end of the hall, at the family table atop the dais, his eyes most definitely on Tess. Gooseflesh rose on her arm, but she didn't know whether to attribute this to Conall's heated stare or Angus's unseen knowledge of this. She met Conall's eyes and moved not at all.

"You need only to smile, lass. That's all."

Tess did smile, nervously, mayhap more as a reaction to Angus's foolish statements and this silly mischief. But Conall smiled back at her. Surrounded by his bailiff, his clerk, his steward, and several of his soldiers, apparently about the castle's business, he paused and smiled back at her, just lifted his lips ever so slightly, as if he, too, were surprised by this turn of events. The men gathered around him then turned to see who had earned this rare boon from their laird. Tess blanched a bit, as these faces showed not any façade of agreeableness to match their chief's. Her cheeks heated to such a noticeable degree that she felt Angus's comforting hand cover hers.

Now unsettled, Tess scurried along, forcing Angus to accelerate his normally unhurried pace. Scrupulously avoiding letting her eyes stray again to the far side of the hall, she settled Angus in his chair by the hearth, and made a quick exit out the main door, heading to the kitchens the long way around to avoid having to pass close to the table, and Conall.

SHE COULDN'T VERY WELL avoid him completely, Tess determined the next day, still nervous about any possible encounter with Conall. She'd been allowed more freedom and didn't want that spoilt just because she couldn't seem to be within eyesight of him without losing her breath. "I just have to learn to deal with it," she resolved, skipping down the stone steps, wondering what exactly *it* was, deciding that any further investigation into *it* was foolhardy.

She had desired to be out of doors again today, but the sound of rain dancing off the stone of the keep had changed her plans. She sought out Serena instead, hoping she might be of assistance for an idea Tess had chewed upon late last night.

As she reached the landing, Tess turned the corner to reach the lower stairs and promptly collided with Conall's chest. His hands reached out to steady her, and Tess wasn't wholly certain how she successfully tamped down an exclamation of surprise.

She should have been frightened to be in such close proximity to him—after what had happened the last time they'd been this near, the last time they'd touched—but she was only aware of the distracting sensation of his touch, warm and familiar. For a moment, they only stared. His gaze appeared neither unfriendly nor unkind.

"Sorry," he mumbled, and his cheek twitched. He dropped his hands from her arms.

She shook her head to ward off his unnecessary apology but could produce no words to strengthen this. Voices belonging to those busy in the hall below drifted up to them, the only sound around them for a long moment.

"I'm headed off to—"

"I was looking for—"

They'd spoken at the same time, words rushing out to fill the uneasy air between them. Short bursts of edgy laughter escaped them both, emerging as strong puffs, as if they'd been holding their breaths. Tess breathed in the scent of him and swallowed hard.

"I'll be taking a party to the border," he said, and Tess considered that he'd never before informed her of his plans for any day from the time since she'd first come. She had no idea what that meant, *taking a party to the border*—though the heavy leather breastplate covering his chest had not gone unnoticed—but she acknowledged the delight she felt that he'd shared it with her.

"I'm off to find Serena. I thought she might help me with a project," she told him, to which he raised a brow. "I wonder if I might be allowed some fabrics and sewing notions." When his expression didn't change, she rushed on, "I had often made my own clothes at the abbey. Here, I am stealing all of Serena's," she said with a nervous laugh, "which hardly seems fair. I could—"

Thick brows lowered briefly over his dark blue eyes. "We have clothiers in the village," he said, "they depend upon the income."

Tess bit her lip and pled her case. "I would not infringe upon their trade. Angus and I, now, we are only extra persons. It would not reduce their income." He seemed to consider this. "I haven't anything, really, to occupy myself," Tess continued, "now that I ...am not needed in the kitchens."

Oh, and here she had been faring so well, putting words and sentences together before him without sounding like a halfwit. But here he was, ruining all that, just because he'd lowered his eyes, and was now staring at her lips.

Her breathing changed, came rather in short little bursts while his eyes lingered on her lips. He raised his gaze to hers, and this she recognized—that light in those beautiful eyes, heated and rapt. She leaned toward him, the movement so small as to almost be indiscernible. Or maybe not, as he moved nearer as well. Now Tess's eyes were drawn to his mouth, saw his lips part and already, she anticipated the feel of his kiss. Her stomach knotted, not unpleasantly.

Conall lifted his hand, about to touch her, she blissfully realized, when footsteps sounded on the steps behind him, quickly coming closer. Before Conall and Tess had completely moved apart, John Cardmore appeared on the landing.

The older man's huge paw sat upon the hilt of his sword, as it usually did while he moved, to keep the weapon from swinging so wildly. He stopped abruptly just off the top step, realizing their presence. His countenance registered only mild surprise, but Tess was quick to note that his mouth, within the close-cropped beard, quirked a bit. He sketched an abbreviated bow to Tess and turned to Conall. "Thought you'd gone for a lie-down or such," he harassed his laird. "The lads be waiting on you."

Conall nodded tightly, which should have sent John Cardmore back down the stairs, but he remained and tucked both his hands into the leather and steel belt circling his waist, over his tunic and light armor. His head swiveled between Conall and Tess, raising brows at both of them. When Conall made a noise, that might have been an annoyed growl, and swung his eyes back to Tess, the old soldier winked at her quickly before she returned her own gaze to Conall.

"You may have the fabrics," he said gruffly, and waved a hand to include other things, "and whatnot."

"Thank you," she said softly and watched him turn to leave, followed immediately by his captain.

She only thought she understood John Cardmore's laughter as it drifted up the stairs to her.

CHAPTER 17

"Tess," Serena called her attention from across the table. Tess raised her eyes, swiveling her neck a bit as she did. She truly did enjoy sewing and the creation of new things, but it made her neck weary, to be ever bent over the fabric and threads.

"I hope you don't mind sharing a room with me come the end of the week," Serena continued. They were perched upon stools in the main hall, which was actually no place for this chore, but the light here was so much more suitable to the task than any other chambers of the keep. "With the May Day festival, Inesfree will be host to several noble families," Serena explained, "though certainly less than we might have seen in times of peace. However, we are of a certain expecting the Brodies, the Cockburns, and the Dunbars. Your tower room would be perfect for the Brodies, as they have several children."

"Of course," Tess conceded without hesitancy. "Truly, 'tis not mine to withhold. But recall, I do bring Bethany with me." She held up the piece she'd been working on, pleased with the second of the sleeves she had made. This joined the first, set aside on the table, and she reached for the rest of the cut fabric to work on the body of the léine she was making for Angus.

"It will be fun. We can snuggle under the furs and stay up late, talking about people we do not like," Serena said with a twinkle in her merry eyes.

"Why, Serena MacDonnell!" Tess teased a chastisement, ruining the effect by making a face and telling her friend, "I'll bring my list of names."

"You will come out for the feast, won't you?" Serena asked.

Tess had no idea. True, she had more freedom now since she'd given her promise, but ultimately, "That would be up to your laird."

They worked until mid-afternoon, with Angus close by, perched as usual upon the chair near the hearth which was roundly considered his own. For a while, Bethany was found at his feet, using one of the hounds as a pillow, while Angus entertained her with muted tales of the Battle of Largs. Only once had Tess been forced to call out a caution to the kindly old man. Though his voice had been soft, nearly sing-song, Tess had chanced to hear, "...and then, when the blood of the heathen marauders' dripped from every Gael sword, and their heads were cleaved—"

"Angus!"

He had been leaning forward, swept up in the tale or his own memories, but sat back again at Tess's chiding. "Ach now, sorry, lass", he said, tilting his head a bit as he carried on with the telling while Bethany sat enchanted underfoot.

When the morning rains had all but evaporated, and their needlework had been put away, Tess and Serena and Angus and Bethany headed outside the walls of Inesfree to inspect the orchards. Likely, Tess was the only one who gave any thought to her actually stepping foot outside the walls, certainly while Conall was not in attendance. In her mind, she reasoned it was permissible; she had pledged to stay, and she hadn't any plans to flee.

The spring grasses were tall with the help of the rains of late, but they stayed mostly on the worn path from the castle. Tess inquired if it was safe to be outside the walls, but Serena had turned her back around to face the huge walls of Inesfree. Serena pointed specifically to the soldiers visible on top of the front wall, watching them.

"They've their crossbows ready, should any dare to accost us," Serena further explained, then pointed lower, toward the ground, not fifty feet behind them on the path, where two more MacDonnell soldiers trailed behind, crossbows in hand.

They reached the orchards, larger than Tess would have expected, but in need of their annual spring clean-up of weeding, pruning, and bird-scaring. Bethany pulled her hand away from Serena's and darted off, chasing spring buds and several busy squirrels. They would not labor today but needed to take an inventory of work needed.

"I smell almonds. Only see those when Fynn brings them in from Spain or Italy." Angus noted. He breathed long of the scent emanating from the blooms of the trees nearest him.

"That's the cherry tree flower," Serena declared and predicted, "There'll be great cherries this summer."

Angus squeezed Tess's arm, which she'd held along the path. "Park me by that cherry tree, lass. I'll catch me winks in the open today." Tess obliged, settling Angus against the trunk of the nearest fruit tree. She watched him lean his head against the purplish brown bark and close his eyes.

Serena and Tess meandered among the trees, discussing the work required for a productive orchard.

"I don't know much about orchards, Serena," Tess admitted.

"I used to be in love with the gardener's son," Serena confided, threading her arm through Tess's. "I'd spend many a summer day right here in these orchards."

"Where is he now? The gardener's son?" Tess wondered.

The dark-haired woman smiled sadly. "He was killed at Falkirk. His da only passed this last winter. Inesfree has been, you may have noticed, without a gardener since then."

Tess had indeed noticed. "Serena, that is a terrible loss for you. I am so sorry." Just then, Bethany darted past them, her blonde hair flying out behind her, her arms splayed wide as if she were a bird. The women smiled at her.

"We were children, it seems now," Serena replied wistfully. "It was so long ago. So many are gone from Inesfree—I don't think we've half the souls we did ten years ago." An air of melancholy hung about her tone. "I hope I live to see the end of this war."

A charging of horses brought, first, the pair of soldiers quickly to the side of Tess and Serena, and next, a double-lined column of riders into view, headed toward Inesfree. Tess gathered up Bethany; Angus was undisturbed by the clamor. Tess and Serena, and the soldiers, too, breathed easier when they noticed it was Inesfree's own returning, with Conall at the lead. Their relief was quickly obliterated, however, when they noticed, as the army drew nearer, the grim countenances of the party, and then, sadly, several bodies draped face down over their mounts.

Tess cast her eyes to Conall and gasped when she saw his fierce countenance. Her hand covered her mouth, her heart breaking for the anguish she found in him.

SUPPER THAT EVENING was both miserable and voluble. Conall sat gloomily at the head table, his hand toying with the ale-filled goblet before him. He listened with half an ear to the talk around him, while knowing that John sat close, lost in his own reverie.

"Is no like they could've known we'd come," Gilbert MacDonnell said near the middle of the room. Gilbert ignored the peasant—Ena, Conall thought her name might be—at his side, who hoped only for a scrap of his attention. "And when, tell me, did reivers start fighting like they was soldiers?"

A chorus of agreement drenched the air.

Donald MacDonnell called out from the next table, "Spineless, is what they are. They ain't no soldiers! Parading and raiding, all upon them that canna defend themselves. And none to answer for it."

"They'll be answering yet more on the morrow!" Claimed another. More cheers.

And on it went, until finally it settled, and their own dead were considered.

More solemn now, toasts were made and joined for the men who had died.

Conall looked up to find John now standing before him. His captain drained his goblet and pounded the cup onto the table in front of Conall. He gave Conall a surprisingly clearheaded glare, infused with promise. "We'll head out at first light and I'll no be caring if they know we're coming for them. We'll chase 'em to hell and further, if it be needed."

Conall nodded grimly and John stepped away, making his way between the still crowded tables and benches to quit the hall completely.

Little by little, as the midnight hour came upon them, the room cleared.

Conall left the hall later than usual, having drunk too much ale. He took the stairs to his chamber rather prudently, unwilling to be found passed out at the bottom come the morn. At the landing, he paused, his gaze lifting to search the passageway to the next higher floor. There was no inner debate, just action as he continued up the next set of stairs, rather than turning toward his own bed. With a guiding hand upon the wall, he reached the top floor and stood before the door to the tower.

It was late, he knew, and she would be long asleep by now. Carefully, he turned the knob and entered. He closed the door behind him and stood silently for many minutes, surveying the entire chamber in the dim light of the deadening fire. A soft orange glow bathed the entire room, brighter near the fire itself. He liked this room now and was satisfied with the installation of the beds and those fripperies. There were also, he noted, several other recent additions—a second chamber pot, tucked under Bethany's tiny bed, where she slept with arms and legs splayed in more than a few directions; three dying flowers, protruding from a dull silver cup, perched on the table against one wall; a crudely made trunk, of some light colored wood, piled high with dark and light fabrics, at the foot of the larger bed. He only eyed these items briefly, his gaze searching for the occupant of the bed. Conall pushed away from the door and stepped noiselessly to the side of the bed.

Tess lie on her stomach, her arms wrapped tight around the feather pillow, her face turned away from him. He leaned over her, wanting to see her.

Some ember in that dying fire popped loudly. Conall straightened as Tess startled and turned over, settling her head upon the pillow that only seconds ago she had been embracing. Her eyes slowly adjusted and found him. She seemed to wake further, though appeared not frightened by his presence, only met his gaze drowsily.

He just stared at her, having no particular idea what it was he sought from her. Maybe only a few seconds had passed before she moved, away from the center of the bed, turning back the furs and bedsheet. An invitation.

With methodical movements, he removed his breastplate and sword and belt, then sat on the side of the bed, on the wood frame, and pulled off his leather boots. Without rising, he turned to find her eyes, saw only the soft, liquid green though he could assign no emotion to them. Wearily, he stretched out beside her, not bothering to pretend he hadn't a need of her. She remained on her back, so that he only skimmed one arm and hand across her to drag her nearer, burying his head in her hair and her shoulder. The length of his body was pressed along hers. She allowed this. He was not of a mind to wonder why, but felt her hand in his hair, holding his head to her.

Presently, this was all he needed.

BACK ON THE TRAIL THE next morning, Conall and his army returned to the borderlands. Yesterday, he'd underestimated the reivers and had brought only a quarter of his army with him. He'd not make that mistake again, feeling once more the wrenching guilt for the loss of life. This time, more than two hundred men rode behind him.

It would be another hour before they reached the lands of the Carruthers and Selbys and Musgraves. While yesterday had been disappointing, it had not been completely unproductive, for they'd learned from people and villages nearby that these clans were the most active and reprehensible reivers. The Scottish Carruthers were responsible for the massacre at Langley Moor. After yesterday, the Carruthers would be reiving no more. That left the English Selbys and Musgraves to deal with today.

Conall clicked his tongue and spurred Mercury up the steep incline of Dalkeith Beinn, the steepest and tallest hill they'd ascend today. From here, they were offered a fair view of all the land south of Bonnyrigg, mostly forested and rocky, with only a few flat heaths and dampened moors. And while the windswept and striking landscape appeared inhospitable, Conall knew that a greater unwelcome waited beyond the tree line.

As they moved slowly across the ridge of Dalkeith Beinn, he thought again of Tess. He'd risen before the sun and permitted himself only a moment to gaze upon her before departing. He had held her, or she him, throughout the short night, neither ever sufficiently wakeful to have pursued more. He'd been left only with impressions of warmth and welcome and wonder, all reasons enough to return to her.

Down the hill, fully into the borderlands now, Conall kicked his steed into a ground-chewing gallop. His army followed suit, with John Cardmore crowing brashly within the throng, well aware what presently hurried the young laird along.

The MacGregors and MacDonnells had barely gained a mile from the bottom of Dalkeith Beinn when there rose before them an oncoming army, easily twice the size of Conall's troops. They came from lower ground, that one moment the horizon was clean and clear and in the next, as if salmon springing from the crisp water of Loch Earn, an army swelled before them, dust billowing out behind them as a gray and perfect backdrop.

Conall raised his fisted hand to rein in his troops, his scowl fierce, until he saw the banner in the forefront of the oncoming horde: scratches of blue, gray, and green, highlighting the profile of a stag's head.

Lowering his hand now, Conall actually sped up, a grin lighting his face.

The two armies met amidst the mountain heath and willow scrub somewhere between Bonnyrigg and Lasswade, their chiefs not reining in until they were side by side.

"I'd have known that woodpecker from even a mile away," said the leader of the joining army. He stretched out his hand, clasping his forearm to Conall's, as they hadn't done in over a year.

Conall shook his head at Gregor Kincaid's oft-used quip, giving an admiring glance at the eagle adorning the MacGregor banner. "I'd rather that," he returned, tossing his head toward Kincaid's flag, "than the rendering of a kitten your niece gave you last Michaelmas."

Gregor Kincaid made a face and lifted his shoulders, granting only small appreciation for Conall's humor. Gregor and Conall were of an age, having fostered together as young lads at the castle of the mighty and still-revered Sir Hugh Rose. Of a similar height, and both endowed of legendary prowess in battle, the likeness between the pair ended there. Gregor, though impressive, was leaner where Conall was brawny; both his hair and eyes were a medium brown; Gregor was possessed of a cheerful temperament compared to Conall's more serious nature.

Conall nodded at Gregor's bloody claymore and took in the Kincaid army's sweaty horses and men, steeped in the stench of death.

Gregor grinned. "About your work, I'd be guessing. Came across some nasty English and they were in me way." He shrugged, his humors fine, as if he hadn't a choice in the matter.

"They wouldna have been Selbys or Musgraves, would they?" Conall asked.

"They might have been both," Gregor told him, and explained how his army had run up against some border reivers, and while they'd had an easy time routing them, the English had been joined by another militia. Gregor grinned like a cocky devil, "Would've been rude no to give them some as well."

Conall barked out a laugh. "Near Duns and Greenlaw?"

Gregor nodded. "The same."

"And where are you headed now?"

Gregor offered up another smile. "You'd probably no ken it, some wee spot dubbed Inesfree," he teased. "The lads want to swing 'round a Maypole."

Conall grinned, shaking his head at his friend's incredible timing and smug wit.

CHAPTER 18

For the first time, Tess joined Serena atop the wall, awaiting the return of the laird and his army. It was early evening, the air was cool, and Serena was wrapped up in the gray and brown plaid of the MacDonnell while Tess stood at her side, pulling the borrowed gray cloak more snugly around her.

Tess had no idea that Conall's army was so large. She watched many hundreds of mounted men come into view over the hills, exactly opposite the setting sun. At this distance, she could not find Conall.

"Kincaids!" Someone called out from further down the wall, and a cheer went up with the castle yard.

"Kincaid and Conall are great friends," Serena explained for Tess's benefit. "His forces are much larger in number. Conall will be happy to have him here."

Tess nodded and watched as the armies drew nearer. Many broke off before reaching the castle, and as the lines thinned, Tess could now distinguish two different banners, and the two men leading the pack to Inesfree. She spared only a glance at the Kincaid chief, but found herself looking anxiously upon Conall. She determined by the tilt of his head, even before he was close enough to confirm, that he was staring back at her. He was unharmed, she determined, breathing easier, but when he was close enough for her to feel the heat of his gaze, those silly butterflies commenced whirling about in her stomach.

Serena took her hand just as the flags passed under the barbican. "Come." And she pulled Tess across the gate tower and down the steep steps to join the parties below.

Tess felt a bit awkward, maybe even a bit misplaced, but she followed along, urged as she was by Serena's tugging. They were met in the yard by Conall and a man who was of his same height, but whose demeanor soon gave the impression of being day to Conall's night.

"Gregor!" Serena happily called out and kissed him upon both cheeks.

Tess met Conall's eye, returned his nod of greeting, and offered a small half-smile for his safe return. She hugged her great cloak more tightly around her, keeping hold of Conall's gaze, as his appeared in no hurry to leave hers—until the man named Gregor stepped immediately and purposefully before Tess, putting Conall behind him.

"I am Gregor Kincaid," he announced, his eyes dancing. "I dinna right care who you are, lass, but you should ken I aim to be completely at your mercy."

Serena giggled and swatted his shoulder from beside Tess.

He pretended an affront. He took Tess's hand in his, ignoring her scandalized expression. "Or your disposal? Your beck and call?" He placed his other hand over hers, despite Tess curling her fingers uncomfortably within his.

"Oh, Gregor, do leave off," Serena chided, all in good humor.

Tess hadn't a clue what to make of this man.

Conall stepped around him, his dark frown giving the impression that he did not share Serena's affinity for the man's playfulness. Almost glowering at his friend, Conall disengaged Tess's hand and kept it held by his own.

"Lady Tess Munro," Conall said, "I am sorry to introduce you to Gregor Kincaid, chief of all Stonehaven."

Gregor's playful expression shifted subtly. "Munro, you say?"

Tess kept his gaze but felt her expression harden just a bit; her chin raised, supposing he was taking her measure.

But he only smiled again. "A glorious pleasure, indeed, Lady Tess."

After a moment, Gregor Kincaid turned back to Serena, took up her hand now, and began walking toward the keep. Tess heard him say, "Munro, he says. Here's a story, aye?"

Tess looked up at Conall, whose expression advised her to disregard Gregor Kinkaid, though she saw no true displeasure in his eyes. Still holding her hand in his, they followed in the wake of Gregor and Serena.

Tess had never dined within the hall, and as they entered the keep, she saw that many people were already seated at the long trestle tables. Nervously, she watched Gregor and Serena make their way toward the family's table at the front of the room. Unconsciously, she slowed, tugging lightly at her hand. Conall, a step in front of her, turned at her resistance. He realized what had given her pause and gave a brief nod, a gesture of assurance meant to communicate that all would be well. Her palms turned instantly damp and her stomach churned but she followed anyway, keeping her gaze on his broad back to avoid eye contact with any who might take exception to her presence.

"Perhaps I should return to the tower," she suggested, but this faintly given idea was lost in the din of the crowded hall. Before she knew it, she was next to Conall at the main table, and he was holding out a chair for her.

Tess sat and looked around. To her left, at the center, sat Conall, who was pulled immediately into conversation with the priest, Father Ioan, seated on the other side of the laird. If the little round man was surprised to see her in the hall, he did not say, but rather lowered his head and his voice so quickly to Conall that she thought he must be imparting urgent and secretive news. Next to him sat Leslie Mac-

Donnell, the castle's steward, whom Tess knew not at all, save for the pinched lip stares he sometimes offered when she did happen upon him. His value to his laird was evident by his position at the head table.

Serena sensed Tess's unease, and reached below the table to squeeze her hand where it had sat nervously upon her knee. Her friend offered an encouraging smile. Fortified by this, Tess considered the jovial mood of the occupants of the room.

'Twas not so crowded as the hall might be were there a true banquet, but it was near to full. The low fire in the hearth was barely required, all these bodies adding warmth. A light haze of the smoke that ever lingered about the keep hung above the tables, reaching to the timber of the ceiling. Brown and gray—of the tables, the rush-filled floor, the peasants' garments, the very air—were the predominant colors in the room, brightened only rarely by more cheerful shades: a bouquet of spring blooms lying atop a table, a brightly dressed rag doll held tightly in the arms of a child.

The haunting sounds of a Celtic harp drifted across the hall, and as Tess looked around for the minstrel, she reveled in the wistful atmosphere created by the lovely music.

Trenchers of food came first to the chief's table, which prompted all those still milling about to find their seats. One by one, kitchen girls and pages delivered the meal, fresh from the kitchen, to each of the tables—hot lamb custarde and braised greens and peas, and tasty parsnip pie with raisins.

"You had success today at the border?" Tess asked of Conall, while they supped.

He was either surprised by the question or perhaps more by her attempt at conversation. He set down his eating knife and took a long swallow of his ale, then rested his forearms on either side of his trencher, as if he were unaccustomed to eating and talking at the same time.

"My efforts were no so much thwarted, as redundant," he answered, casting a glance above her head to acknowledge Gregor Kincaid, seated on the other side of Serena.

When the women turned their eyes to Gregor, he only shrugged, spearing beans onto his own knife. "Only that we happened there first," he said and shoved the vegetables into his mouth, hunkering down over his food.

Conall shrugged as well. "Saved us the hassle. The reivers will be silent, at least for a time."

"But there is still another war," Serena reminded them, "and as pleased as I am to see you, Gregor, I think your stopover begs an inquiry."

"We will ride for Elcho Park after May day," Conall explained. "William Wallace himself has taken up a position there, disturbing the English and defectors in the area. We'll give him some assist." These words were softly spoken, meant only for ears very near to him.

Tess swiveled her head to Conall when he'd revealed these plans. His dark eyes rested upon her, anticipating her reaction.

What would become of her? Did he wonder that as well? Did he trust her to remain, only because she'd given an oath that she would?

Would she remain, if given true opportunity to flee? Or, would she choose to keep on at Inesfree? She must be honest with herself about her current circumstances: truth be known, she was not unhappy and had purpose in caring for Bethany and Angus, enjoyed a deep camaraderie with Serena, and took pride in her responsibilities, tending the herb garden, sewing and needlepoint. She'd had no purpose in her father's home. And, too...there was Conall.

She could not ignore, first, the near-constant, if unwelcome, appeal of the man, nor, secondly, the temptation—dare she think it, the potential?—of her own response to him. Certainly not after these last few days.

"I would wish you God's grace, and a safe return," she said, opting for the most generic reply. He continued to hold her gaze, his own thoughtful.

Tess spent some of the evening with Bethany and Angus, just sitting with them near the hearth, giving Angus details of the goings-on in the hall, while Bethany dozed in her lap. The hall had a carefree ambiance tonight. It was possible that this was the usual mood of the supper hall and Tess wouldn't know this, having never before taken part. The harp had been united with another instrument and the music turned from subdued to jaunty, prompting several occupants to begin to dance.

"There is a woman," Tess was telling Angus, her voice low, "and God love her, she has as many years as my own father, pushing herself—I cannot think of another way to describe it—upon a youth with her dance. His face is beyond red. The chorus you hear is his mates, urging him on, though he seems most resistant." It might have been quite humorous, save for the boy's palpable mortification. "She's lifting her skirts—oh my," Tess kept telling, though her eyes widened at exactly how much the old woman exposed to the boy.

Angus chuckled beside her. "He canna run?"

"They won't let him," Tess explained, watching as the older men around him, soldiers and peasants alike, circled the woman and the boy, refusing to allow the youth's escape.

"Best thing can happen is the music stops," Angus guessed, and when it did at that very moment, he and Tess shared even greater laughter at the perfect timing. After a moment, Angus asked, "And where is the laird now?"

She didn't have to scan the room to know, had kept half an eye on him since taking leave of the table. He'd remained and was now surrounded by his retinue of soldiers and advisors. "He plots with his war council and the Kincaid," she informed Angus. She looked left and right, then whispered to Angus, "They will join William Wallace himself in a sennight or so."

Angus nodded. "As he should. Freedom will no happen by the will of one man alone."

She tried to take interest in other things and people around the room but found her eyes returning to Conall. He stood larger and taller than any man around that table, save for Gregor, and even he was not so broad as Conall. His size had at one time intimidated her, but that was long ago. She thought boldly of him pressed against her, holding her tenderly, an impossible thing to imagine if you'd not experienced it firsthand.

She mused to Angus, "Seems to me, if you were upon a battlefield and you witnessed the coming of Conall MacGregor as your enemy, surely you would turn and run. I know I would."

Angus tilted his head and lifted his brow. "You haven't as yet."

She continued to watch Conall as he rose from the table and dismissed the men around him. Tess wondered if he might be equally as attuned to her, for though she'd not once found his eyes upon her while she'd sat with Angus, he seemed to know exactly where she was, and his gaze settled on her without having to search around.

She watched him walk toward her, wondering if she would ever get used to the great appeal of Conall MacGregor, that sure stride, the wide shoulders, those piercing eyes. Tess's heart skipped a bit, then quickened as he neared. Realization dawned finally that whatever it was that kissing led to—she had only been educated in the basics—it was inevitable between her and Conall. And this thought did not displease her. It might well have something to do with her desire for more of his kisses, or mayhap it was the way he stared at her now as he neared, all that smoldering intensity churning her belly and breast, teasing her into acceptance. Tess felt a flush warm her cheeks.

He reached her and Angus near the large fire against the courtyard-side wall, his eyes scanning over the three of them sitting there.

"Aye, laird," Angus said, bringing Conall and Tess's eyes to him, both amazed at the man's uncanny ability to know when someone came near, and who that someone was.

"Angus," Conall greeted. "I'll carry the lass up for you," Conall offered and reached to carefully pull the sleeping Bethany from the old man's arms.

Tess said good night to Angus and kissed his cheek and followed Conall out of the hall.

UP IN THE TOWER, CONALL settled the child onto her small bed. Bethany roused a bit, so that Tess sat on one side of the bed and fussed over her for a few minutes. Conall thought that might be something he could never do; likely, he and that small bed frame, in pieces, would crash to the floor. He strained to hear Tess's gentle murmurings at Bethany's ear but could not.

He busied himself with the small fire in the hearth, removing the belt that held his sword to keep in out of the way as he went down on one knee. He poked at the logs, making sure they were in a position to keep a low fire burning at least for the next hour. When he stood and turned again after several minutes, Tess was standing as well, her eyes on him.

Conall sent a glance to the small bed and found Bethany's eyes closed again, with no lines marring the perfect skin of her forehead. He reached for the belt and sword he'd discarded only moments before. He hadn't any reason to stay.

And yet, he had no desire to leave.

Tess spoke, drawing his eyes again to her, though her gaze focused only on his sword and the hand that held it. "There might well be danger if you go to Wallace's side. All of England—indeed, some of Scotland—seek his capture, or demand his surrender."

Conall nodded. "Aye. Wallace has only Scotland's interests at heart, but he'd be the first to tell you, he does much of his thinking with the blade of his sword."

"But you are not like him," Tess guessed, tilting her head at him, finally meeting his eyes, "in that regard."

"You dinna ken that," he told her. "You haven't seen me in battle."

In response she gave a little laugh, which raised Conall's brow. Her eyes even danced a bit now. "Angus has informed me that I have," she confided. "He sees much for an old man without sight. He is quite sure that we—you and I—battle daily."

Now Conall smiled. His eyes swept over her, considering her skin, turned creamy and gold by the light of the fire, and her eyes, shy but not wary.

"You've no heart for battle, lass." And yet, he'd never met a person, man or woman, young or old, who had stood their ground as fiercely against his ire and rages and menaces as Tess Munro rather regrettably and regularly had.

"I do not."

"Do you even now plan your escape, knowing I'll be away?'

Her eyes darkened. Softly, she insisted, "I promised I would not."

"Then we can be done with battling?"

"I would like nothing more," she said, and he did realize a bit of relief washing over him until she added, "Yet I am a prisoner here, if only now by my own vow."

"You dinna have to be."

Her eyes jumped back to his. If any previous statement Tess Munro had uttered had ever shocked him, nothing, he was sure, would ever compare to her next words.

"I am considering that." And she held his gaze still, her green eyes even more remarkable with her newfound fearlessness.

If he kissed her now....

His teeth gnashed together, warring with indecision, which he rarely had cause to do. He would leave in one week. If he kissed her now, while she actually appeared as if she might welcome it, everything was changed. Everything. If he should not return, if he should fall beside Wallace, what would become of Tess? His chest tightened, a new fear sitting heavily there. He needed to plan for the possibility of his death. There was, aside from Inesfree and its people, now Tess to consider as well.

He stepped toward her, stopped only a hand's breadth away. Her eyes lifted as he neared and stood so much taller. Conall set his palm against her cheek, and felt her hand settle upon his chest, her touch whisper soft. His hand slid around her neck and pulled her closer still and she nestled her head against his chest. He bent and pressed a long, slow kiss to the top of her head. He breathed deeply of her scent, infused with the heat that consumed him whenever they touched.

Conall turned and left the room.

He would return from Wallace's side. He *would*.

CHAPTER 19

As Tess knew well by now, Inesfree's master twice annually hosted a large bazaar: in winter at Michaelmas; and in late spring on May Day. The people of Inesfree and the surrounding area, and occasionally some from as far away as Edinburgh and Glasgow came to the four day celebration. They filled the two baileys with their food and song and wares to sell and brought entire families, pitching animal skin tents in the grass and heath where they might sleep off their indulgences outside the walls. Any given day during the May day feast, one might count as many as a thousand heads. Inesfree's steward would record in his ledger a tally of six hundred cattle, three hundred chickens, one thousand pheasants, and hundreds of smaller game assembled and slaughtered for the banquets held round the clock. It took the half a year between the celebrations to prepare for the next, for there were kegs to fill, tables to construct or upkeep, arrangements to be made for the nobles attending, salt to store, ice to procure and keep, and a host of other necessities which called for Leslie MacDonnell, the castle's steward, to oversee every detail, major and not.

All week long, people had arrived, slowly at first, a trickle here and there of a family or small group of travelers. By late last evening, the bailey had been filled near to overflowing. From the window in Serena's chamber, which she now shared with Tess and Bethany, Tess had watched the goings-on, intrigued by such gaiety and revelry. With a song ever in the air, people danced and frolicked, exchanged money for goods, and the large outer bailey was transformed into the largest of several marketplaces. She watched wistfully but not with enough longing to want to join in.

On the morning of the first day, Tess once again offered her services to Eagan to aid with the never-ending cooking schedule. It was like nothing she had ever witnessed before. The kitchen now teemed with scores of people, the air within oppressive. She was crowded between people working at the chopping counter she'd at one time had mostly to herself. After only a few hours on the first day, she gratefully accepted a long square of plain linen from another girl, Moira, tying the kerchief around her head as the others had, centering the flat fold along her forehead and knotting it under the hair at her neck. It offered only slight and short-lived relief, taking the hair off her face.

This overwhelming crowd and frantic pace prevented Tess from noticing Conall's arrival. So often, a room seemed to still at his entrance, but there was so much to be done, that barely a soul had their head turned away from their chores. Indeed, while the room bustled, there was little noise, save for the clanging of pots and the sound of knives slapping down onto wood, or sometimes Eagan's harried voice giving instructions.

She did not realize Conall's presence until she turned at the touch of his hand on her elbow. His bright blue eyes showed no lack of good humor. Her smile, though weary, was reflexive but her hand went immediately, nervously to the kerchief in her hair.

"Come with me, lass," he said, the hand at her elbow sliding down to her hand.

Tess faltered, desire and duty sparring inside. She cast anxious eyes to those around her, saw their sidelong glances, some upon her hand held in his, and understood it might not be well received if she abandoned her position. She shook her head, "I cannot. There is much to do—"

"Aye, and there are plenty to do it," he countered, tugging at her hand.

Tess was torn. She sent her gaze to Moira, the girl who had shared the kerchief with her. That girl moved her face and eyes in such a way as to express that she did not relish being put into the position of giving Tess leave, or denying her.

"You can return in a wee bit," Conall cajoled, as Tess had never heard him do before.

Tess set her small knife upon the table and followed Conall. He led her out the nearest door, past Eagan, who only stopped his own work long enough to consider the pair and then Tess's empty spot among the workers.

Conall propelled her into the bright sunlight, despite Tess's unease. Outside, he tucked her hand into the crook of his arm as they pushed their way through the throng of people. Smells of dead animals and well-tanned leathers and too many bodies flooded her nose. The local peasants were given the preference of setting up their stalls and tents within the walls, though these spaces were few, and Tess was delighted to see such handsome and varied wares from Inesfree's own.

A woman hawked woven baskets and an old man sold grotesque necklaces made of both human and animal teeth. A lad shouted that he had "the finest fabrics this side of Edinburgh". Tess grinned at the fraudulent advertising as the fabrics looked like any other gray and brown wool she might see in any village from here to London. Another lad in brightly colored garments strolled by, juggling flaming torches. Tess drew closer to Conall, squeezing his arm, sure that his size was all that kept them from being jostled about by so many moving bodies.

Conall glanced down at her, his eyes so light and trouble-free at this moment, Tess felt an immediate pleasure.

"This is magnificent." She smiled up at him.

He nodded, alight with pride, then quickly pulled her out of the way of a man walking upon long wooden legs, standing twice as tall as Conall. Tess stared, aghast and amused, and they laughed together.

Tess sensed that people stared as she and Conall walked about. Their eyes were hard yet, unwilling to like her. There was no question in their eyes about who she was. Obviously all knew of the Munro prisoner. Were she to make eye contact with any, she would know immediately if they be Inesfree's own or not, depending upon their returned gaze, be it friendly or not.

They rounded the entire outer bailey and Conall steered her outside the castle walls, where stood dozens more booths and stalls and still so many people, crushed near to the castle itself. Beyond the mob and the grounds of the festival itself, tent after tent stretched almost to the tree line. There was only marginally more space out here and Tess held tightly onto Conall's arm. He spent some time talking to the tinkers and tradesmen and vendors, as well the chief was expected to do. He purchased sweet rolls and ale for her, which she happily accepted; once he picked up a gaily colored scarf and held it up to her cheek, considering, then laughed as she frowned, thinking the piece too garish for her tastes. Tess began to wonder if he paraded her around intentionally, trying to foster some measure of acceptance among his people. Would her presence be tolerated for having found such favor with the chief of the MacGregors and Mac-Donnells? Tess immediately dismissed the idea. In all probability, the people would only assume their laird played now with his toy, his leman.

They had been about the fair for several hours when they came upon Gregor Kincaid, who carried a cup in his hand, and appeared to have sipped often. He was surrounded by Kincaid and MacGregor and MacDonnell soldiers alike, a boisterous bunch who pounced upon Conall and drew him into rambunctious conversation. He was asked to settle a debate about the strongest of the men, which he tried to shake off with a few glib remarks. They carelessly ignored Tess and her hand slipped away from his arm.

"Do you enjoy the fair, Lady Tess?" Gregor asked, having sidled next to her.

She pasted on a pretty smile, somewhat uncomfortable outside the safety of Conall's reach. "It's rather remarkable," she told him.

Gregor paused, watching a pretty peasant girl saunter by, her own eyes returning Gregor's admiring stare, her wide lips tilting upward until she turned her head away. Gregor seemed to catch himself, responding to the amused lift of Tess's brow with an exaggerated shrug and a devilish gleam in his eye.

"You dinna fit in here, lass," Gregor said, seeming suddenly sober.

Tess lowered her eyes. Even Gregor had seen it, the rather universal dislike of her.

"I promised not to leave," was all she could think to say, as he appeared to wait a response.

"A promise made under duress," he said, the hand and cup swaying with his words, "is no really a promise at all, is it?"

Tess lifted her gaze and stared at Conall's friend, trying to read his brown eyes. She said lightly, "I wasn't aware there were degrees of promises, or that the keeping of them could be optional."

Gregor barked out a laugh, spilling a bit of his ale. "Aye, Conall has excuses too—why you're still here though you'd no wed him yet, why he needs to watch your every bluidy move, why he suddenly has no taste for war."

"I did not—"

He made a show of waving his hands, spilling more ale, staving off her argument. Curiously, Tess was not frightened.

"Lass," he said and stopped moving, pinning her with his sharp eyes, "you may no belong here, but it is where you are. He will no let you go, and I'm wondering if you truly want to be let go." He surprised her by wrapping one big arm around her shoulders, giving her a rough squeeze and laughing yet more. "'Tis verra good, lass. Verra good."

And then he was gone, entering the circle of the soldiers surrounding Conall, calling out loudly, spiritedly, "I'll take on any man here!" He thumped his chest. "C'mon you feckers! Who'll take me?" A great and encouraging cheer went up and they closed around him, the pack growing.

Tess caught sight of Conall deep in the midst of these rowdy men as his gaze turned toward her. She pointed toward the rest of the market they'd yet to see, letting him know where she'd be. He nodded, his head risen slightly above those around him. She understood there were expectations for him, as laird, to participate, to judge, to partake, and was not bothered by this at all.

Carefully making her way alone through the congestion, Tess approached the line of vendors. She strolled amiably about, perusing the handcrafts. She stopped to envy some beautifully detailed embroidery upon crisp white scarves. The scarves themselves, though fresh, were indistinct, but the sewn designs, some tone-on-tone, some subtle pastels, were outstanding.

"These are remarkable," she commented absently, giving no thought to the fact that once having spoken, her words—despite their kind intent—invited the people to speak to her.

"And not for sale to the likes of you." The merchant, a stout woman with short, beefy hands, glowered at Tess.

Inwardly cringing but outwardly hoping to remain unperturbed, Tess lifted her hands in resignation. Obviously, this merchant was one of Inesfree's own. "I've no coin to make purchases, mistress. I only admire your work."

"Move on, jezebel," the woman snarled. "Me work is no concern to you."

"I am sorry to have troubled you," Tess murmured and stepped away, strolling with greater trepidation to a hastily erected stall several booths away from the unwelcoming woman, to find that vendor pointedly turning his back on her.

She continued to walk on, leery of making eye contact with any person now. Glancing around, it seemed she was beginning to draw a crowd. Forced to admit she would indeed find greater welcome at Conall's side, she turned and began to walk his way, looking about for the sight of his dark head. She had strayed farther than she had intended and could not even see that large group of soldiers, or even the main gate of the castle.

She was roughly bumped from behind, stumbling with the force of the shove. Her heartbeat quickened as people rapidly began to close in on her, knocking and elbowing and bumping. Her kerchief was torn from her head. She was too small to see above the people pressing suddenly and madly around her and was now completely unsure of even which direction she faced.

Unexpectedly, a gap cleared, and Tess breathed easier, considering that panic had almost set in. She moved on, but her eyes continued to swivel, as she tried to get her bearings. Something sharp and unyielding smacked down upon her head. She cried out, and her vision blurred. She reached a hand up to where she'd been struck and felt the wet stickiness of blood at the back in her hair. With her other hand, she reached toward the ground, as her legs buckled. She struggled to remain upright, watching people walk past her, all now with eyes focused with great malevolence upon her, it seemed. True horror crept into her chest.

Conall would come for her, she thought, hanging on to that surety.

A rock, not too large, but thrown with sufficient force, struck the back of her leg. When she instantly turned around, shocked, another struck her arm, followed immediately by several more striking her face, chest, and the hands she held up to defend herself. The stones kept coming, some thrown with such malice as to make her cry out, others seeming only a rude nuisance. They ripped open skin and gouged red welts into her arms and legs and head, one heaved with such intent and power that when it connected with the side of her head, she stumbled again, the scene before her blurry and gray.

Of course, she had heard of stonings. She imagined them to be a singular ambush accomplished by a riotous mob, shouting and cursing, branding the victim with an alleged crime, wishing them loudly to hell or worse. But this was frighteningly surreal. No circle of evil formed around her. No calls for death could be heard.

Tess sank to the ground as the stones and rocks continued to pelt her, eerily aware of their attempts to inflict pain without being noticed. They continued to walk about, as if strolling without destination through the festival. There was about these people a grumbling undertone of determined evil, a rumble here or there as a stone-thrower passed close by her, but there was no volume to their voices.

Her mind began to dim from the pain of the persisting assault. She watched with battered and fearful eyes as they milled about. For a moment she imagined that she recognized Ezra among the crowd. He would help her surely—if only to avoid displeasing his laird. But there was no help forthcoming. She pressed her cheek against the hard earth, felt the dirt cling to a gouge near her ear and tried with great steadfastness to concentrate upon that small pain. Tiny granules of earth clung to the blood and imbedded themselves into her open skin, burning, stinging. A foot met with her back and another with her stomach.

Inhaling as deeply as her suffocating fear would allow, Tess smelled the ground beneath her, turning her senses away from the pain and upon the scent of the earth, the unkind fragrance of a well-traveled path. The serfs' drab garments slid past her, all browns and similar shades, lacking even the smallest hint of brightness. Unimaginative, earthen, like their spirits, and she wondered that no one had ever thought to introduce color into their lives. They dressed as matter-of-factly as they murdered, without design and with a conscious effort to go unnoticed.

I will die here among this quiet throng, she thought.

Casting her tear-filled eyes about, Tess saw a familiar face.

Alain was here. He had come for her.

No, it couldn't be Alain. In a subtle gesture, this man held his cowl close to his face in an attempt to conceal himself. Certainly, this man resembled Alain so closely they could be brothers, but Alain would never have wanted to be seen, live or not, in such dreadful, coarse garments. Her blurred eyes had deceived her. It was not Alain at all.

And still, Conall did not come.

Tess closed her eyes, aware that her body, curled into itself, occasionally jerked and tightened with each rock or foot that found its mark.

Finally, when her tenuous hold on consciousness began to fade, she heard her name being called. Suddenly, large hands lifted her up, away from the bloodied dirt. She might have thought it angels come to carry her home, save these hands were strong and blessedly familiar.

"Tess!"

She murmured something unintelligible, as speech was nearly beyond her, her body not her own just now. She tried to focus on Conall's face. What she saw, what she would never remember later, was the fierce ache in his eyes, that of unmitigated fear.

Before she might have stowed away the wonder she fleetingly experienced at this, she was lifted into the air, against the strength of his chest. She cried—for who would not have?—and felt nothing more as Conall's long, sure strides conveyed them quickly inside the keep.

CHAPTER 20

Sometime later, Conall stormed out of the keep, roaring as if consumed by the fires of hell, charging through the still crowded inner bailey, overturning tables and booths as he went, venting this unrivaled fury. A man stepped unknowingly into his path and received an unrestrained fist in his face, while Conall's countenance remained a display of torture. He quickly exhausted his immediate need for the release of rage. Breathing raggedly, he stumbled to right himself from his last wild barrage of destruction, slowing the swinging of his arms to an eventual halt. He was aware of the fright that surrounded him as people backed away nervously. None would meet his eye. In the gray-orange light of only a few bonfires at dusk, he considered those he knew, those who now slunk away with fear—not guilt, he knew, never that—and those who dared to meet his stare unblinkingly and taunt him. *She deserved it.*

"Do you think she wants to be here?" He called out, his voice cracking on the shout. "To see your hatred and live with your scorn?" Wiping the back of his hand across his mouth, he waited for more breath to loudly proclaim, "She has tried repeatedly to escape me! I hold her *against her will!* I tried to force her to wed me that I might regain Marlefield!" Still drawing air into lungs that sputtered against it, he slowly turned about to take in all around him. "I threatened her at knife-point and still she refused to wed me. She vowed to kill herself before wedding with me. She had a family and a man to love and I stole her away. You'd no do the same if you were she? You'd no hate me and every one of us? You'd no watch the hills for your father or your lover come to save you?"

These were not questions put out which required answers, but merely an attempt to make them understand. His voice said as much, the anger easy to define but his desperation more palpable. An odd quiet descended with his silence. Only the shuffling of feet, the crackling of fire broke the stillness.

Fearing what these unprecedented emotions might do to him in the middle of the market, he walked through the separating crowd, only to turn again to consider the faces that watched him so warily. "You shame me. I'd never have thought it of Inesfree." Clamping his teeth, he ran a hand over his dark eyes and stubbled jaw. "The next person to threaten or harm her or disrespect her in any way will answer to me. And may God help you then."

He finally stalked away, into the night, struggling to grasp the myriad emotions that gripped him. He *was* shamed by their hatred. He was furious at their actions. How dare they harm Tess in the middle of his own castle!

Far away from the open gates of Inesfree, Conall slumped against the cold, unyielding trunk of a giant elm. His head found a place to hang in his hands, his elbows supported by knees that surely would have buckled had he remained standing.

She was going to die.

He had to face this fact. All those bruises, the lacerations, the blood. She was so tiny, so very small.

Ah, God.

He didn't want to see her. He couldn't be with her now. He wanted it to be quick, before he returned. Her breathing had been so shallow. Her eyes had not opened. He'd brought her to his room, had placed her upon the wide bed, had bid Mary fetch the old hag and Serena and whomever else she imagined might save her. But he'd seen enough of death and its likeness to know she'd not survive this.

All because he'd brought her here. Because he'd wanted Marlefield. Because he'd believed it rightfully his. Because he'd never accepted her refusals. He'd refused to believe that she wouldn't eventually give in to his persuasions or succumb to his wishes simply to avoid her fear.

In his tortured mind, he pictured her bright eyes, watching him with great curiosity when she thought him inattentive, and lately with a softness he'd never known he craved. He pictured her hair, that indefinable hue that had fascinated more than he, and imagined he could at this very moment feel the softness of it. He saw her hands, so small when engulfed by his....

Now covered in blood.

"Ah, damn. Damn!" He stood abruptly, his face red and perspiring, and made short work of the distance between himself and Tess.

He found her not as he'd left her almost an hour ago. Lying upon his great feathered mattress, her torn and bloodied gown having been discarded, her body bathed, she was clad loosely in a fresh cotton gown which covered her from neck to toe.

Without a word, with the barest of gesture from his still grim countenance, Conall dismissed the quietly crying women from the room. The crone and Mary filed past him, sniffling as they left. Serena stood before him to tell him on a sob that Tess was as comfortable as they could make her, and she departed, closing the door with a soft click behind her.

He drew a chair close to the bed and took up a position at her side. There was little of Tess to recognize though her face had borne the least of the assault. He'd never seen her so still, eyes closed, the left one swollen grotesquely. She looked very peaceful. Always with him, she'd been stubborn, her chin set or squared; or melancholy, her features joyless. Of late, on rare occasions, she'd shown signs of a revival of spirits, something he'd hoped might become more pronounced and regular.

Never this, though. Never this paleness nor this quiet.

"I did this, Tess," he whispered harshly, "and I canna fix it. I can punish them. I can slay each and every one...but I canna help you." He took up her hand, tracing a pattern about her palm, marveling at the blue veins, so slim and transparent, visible on the back of her hand. The other hand he wouldn't touch. It was swollen to nearly twice its size, purple and so very incriminating.

SERENA ENTERED CONALL's room several hours later to find him sitting still in the large chair beside the bed. He did not sleep.

"Conall, I shall sit with Tess," she offered and tried to guide him from the chair.

"Leave us."

"Conall—"

"Leave us!"

Conall waited until Serena had gone before taking up Tess's hand again in his.

He would not leave her. Not now. Inexplicably, he now wanted to be with her in the end. Should she wake, he would be near. She would know he was here.

He would tell her—what? That he was sorry? No, he still believed he'd have done anything to have Marlefield. But then, he'd never considered this. Having known Tess, he faced the weakening conclusion that he would not have chosen to sacrifice her life to have Marlefield back.

I have murdered her, he thought grimly. *As if I, myself, had assaulted her, I have murdered her.*

The minutes turned in to hours. Conall alternately stayed at her side, holding her hand, or looked out the window, onto the scene below, where life continued while Tess barely fought for hers.

This angered him.

"You are no even trying," he hissed, once again at her side. "You're a coward, Tess Munro. You'll let your fear win. I believed your will greater."

She did not respond, of course. Frowning, breathing heavily through his nose, he laid his head upon her hand.

The door opened after another long hour. It was near to dawn now. Conall had dozed. He raised his head as the crone entered, the perpetual bag of herbs and whatnot swinging from a cord at her waist. He looked at Tess.

She slept still. She hadn't moved at all.

Metylda stood at the opposite side of the bed. She imparted nothing immediately, just stared at Tess while Conall waited.

"She will live, you must ken," the hag finally said, though her eyes did not move to Conall.

"She is too small...for this," he said impatiently and waved a hand to indicate Tess's appearance, which spoke loudly of her condition.

"But she is no meant to die for you," Metylda murmured in her cracked voice, so reminiscent of the crags of Scotland, aged and wise. She untied the bag from her hip and placed it at the bedside table. "When she wakes, stir a pinch of this into wine. For the pain."

He had no reason to believe the crone knew of what she spoke, other than that she sounded so damn convinced of it herself. And, too, the fact that it gave Conall hope made him eager to cling to it as truth.

He watched Tess with great hope over the next hours. At times, she breathed easier, it seemed. Her pulse was strong now, stronger than even an hour ago.

Shortly after dawn, Gregor Kincaid crept into the room. He moved to stand opposite Conall, drew in a sharp breath at Tess's appearance, and breathed, "Jesu." He was neither so heartless to not be moved by the very wretched visage of his friend, nor so obtuse as to not notice that Conall did not take his eyes off her.

"I am to blame," he admitted to Conall. "I left her. I caused the ruckus—"

Conall shook his head and turned to Gregor, all that boldness and sureness—of which Gregor had always been so envious—gone now.

"I want them hanged."

"Aye." Gregor had expected as much. 'Twas only right.

"I dinna care if they threw one stone or ten, or if they only watched and did nothing, I want them named and found and I want them hanged. John'll ken what to do." And he returned his gaze to Tess.

After a few more minutes, Gregor squeezed Conall's shoulder and left the room.

By the time four more hours had passed, Conall was completely sure he was not just being hopeful. Tess's breathing was indeed smoother. The bruising, about those few parts of her body that he could see, those not covered with her night rail or bed sheets, had begun to turn ugly shades of red and blue and purple.

An hour later when Tess began to moan in her sleep, Conall was convinced she would survive this. He called for Serena to procure some broth. She would need to eat. And her hair would need to be washed again for the gash upon her scalp had bled through the night, causing tendrils to clump together in sticky strands. Perhaps the women should bathe her entire body again, rid her of as much of the crime against her as they could.

While Conall left Tess only momentarily to fetch Serena and the others to attend her, she roused. For just a moment, a small speck of clarity, brought above the pain, Tess woke and called his name.

There was no response to her plea. She called again... and began to wonder if she only imagined that she spoke.

"Conall?" He did not come to her. Tess closed her eyes again and allowed sleep to claim her once more. A lone tear slid from the corner of her eye, eased into the hair at her temple and mixed with the blood.

"I DEMAND THAT YOU WAKE," Conall told Tess eight hours later. He'd stayed with her throughout the day, but other than an occasional escaped moan or cry, she'd not fully roused, and Conall was now angry. She'd shown more mettle in her dealings with him. He knew she was made, on the inside, of sturdy stuff. She wouldn't have refused him his wish of wedding this long if she weren't.

So why in the hell wouldn't she wake?

"This will no win you favors, Tess," he warned with little tolerance. "Keep at it and I'll no allow you your garden, nor your precious Bethany." Growing weary, Conall once more slumped into the chair at her side. "I'll throw Angus out," he said, his voice cracking. "You'll never see him again, I swear." He took up her hand, as he'd done a dozen times or more, and linked their fingers. He liked the look of their hands twined together. His was big and dark, and though he'd never much given thought to the appearance of his own hand, to see it now, together with Tess's pale and fragile one, it seemed...validated.

Her hand squeezed his.

Conall's eyes flew to hers and found her watching him, her lids half open, the expression within as haunted as any he'd ever witnessed.

"Tess?"

"I kept looking for you," she murmured. She tugged feebly at her hand.

Every bit of guilt and remorse and self-reproach he'd willingly let torture him over the past day and a half was nothing compared to what her words had just done to him.

Conall loosened his fingers and watched hers slide away, aware that with this gesture, something fled from him. He stared at her fingers and knew a vague, inexpressible fear. His own face suddenly blank, he inquired about the extent of her pain, truly sorry that she remembered any of what had transpired.

"Everything—it all hurts," she finally said, her voice scratchy.

"I'll fetch Metylda," he said, standing so abruptly that the chair on which he'd perched flipped over behind him.

She shook her head against the pillow. A tear slid away from her discolored eye.

"Please... don't leave me." She tried to move, or shift, and sobbed pitifully, almost silently.

Conall was at a complete loss. He couldn't leave her. He didn't want to touch her, certain that it would bring or arouse pain. He was afraid to even hold her while she cried. A hard pain surged through his chest and tightened his throat.

"Just tell me what to do," was all he could think to offer.

The door opened, and Conall turned helpless eyes to see who came. Both Metylda and Serena entered, and Conall knew a profound relief.

Upon noticing Tess's wakefulness, both women hurried to the bedside.

Serena sat right down near Tess's hip. She didn't hug her friend, possibly afraid to bring her pain as Conall had been, but softly rubbed her arm and moved the hair out of Tess's face while she continued to cry. Conall's brows rose as the hag, too, settled herself upon the bed, opposite Serena. It was the hag who spoke first. Conall had never heard such tender speech from the old woman.

"Here now, lassie, you get it all out, go on now. Just cry it out." Her gnarled fingers hovered close but did not touch Tess. "'Tis an awful thing what they done, no way 'round it. You cry for now."

And she did. Great, racking sobs overtook her, until her body shook, and her breath was lost. Serena and Metylda cooed and comforted her, and just let her cry.

Conall's throat was on fire, his teeth gritted so tightly that pain shot down his jaw and neck. But he remained. She'd asked him not to leave her.

After what seemed an interminable amount of time, Tess's tears were exhausted. Her cries fell silent and her breathing slowed. Metylda stood and fetched the pouch she'd left with Conall earlier, then stepped around him and out the door. Serena remained with Tess, now motionless again. Serena whispered something to Tess, who shook her head briefly in response.

When the old woman returned, she held a cup of wine. She stirred in several pinches of whatever herbs were contained in her pouch and swirled the cup in her hand.

It took the efforts of both Serena and Metylda to help Tess rise enough to drink from the cup, and she moaned twice during the process. Conall wanted to help, but feared his hands were too big and clumsy and would only hurt her more. He stood with his arms folded over his chest, feeling helpless still, his muscles screaming against the tension in him.

The women remained for another quarter hour, and Conall thought their presence certainly was of comfort to Tess. She slept again, with the aid of whatever that hag had given her in the wine.

CHAPTER 21

Conall rarely left his chamber, or Tess's side. Whenever she woke, she was immediately given another draught of Metylda's herbs and slept soon after. By necessity, he'd met several times with John and Gregor and even Leslie MacDonnell, taking these meetings sometimes just outside the door. When the women bathed and changed Tess, Conall took that opportunity to see to his own quick bath and a change of clothes. He'd advised Serena that Bethany was absolutely forbidden to see Tess right now, but that Angus most certainly was welcome.

Alone with Tess, a full three and a half days since he'd borne her bloody and bruised to his chamber, Conall sat again in the chair at her bedside while she slept. He rubbed a hand over his forehead and scratched through his hair. A full wide yawn overtook him just as someone rapped at the door.

It opened to reveal John and Gregor. Conall stood to meet them, watching two pairs of eyes look beyond him to the bed. They were now nearly accustomed to exactly how battered her tiny frame and face appeared. Yesterday, John had been staggered by the sight, his lip curling with such distaste and anger, he'd been forced to take an abrupt leave, though he hadn't been within the chamber for more than a minute.

"We have six now," John said, one hand on his hip, the other covering the top of his sword. "More to come."

"Aye, they'll start talking once they ken they're bound to hang," Gregor added. "One we have is a woman."

Conall looked sharply at him. "And she will hang, too."

"Aye," they all agreed.

"The grounds are cleared," Gregor said, folding his arms across his chest. "Your steward and bailiff saw to that, everyone gone now."

Conall nodded.

Gregor continued, "I sent a rider to Elcho Park to tell Wallace we'd be delayed some. Should have word back on his direction in a day, maybe more."

Tess made a sound from the bed and all three men turned their attention to her. Conall approached while John and Gregor hung back.

He reached automatically for the herbs and wine.

"No more," Tess objected.

Conall stopped and turned to her. "'Tis meant to get you to the other side of the pain." She was trying to sit up, and because neither Serena nor the old healer were present, Conall was compelled to assist her. He gentled his touch as much as he knew how and shifted her upward with hands under her arms. She clung to his forearms, her face a mask of pain, though she made not a sound. Today, the bruises on her face showed much less swelling, though her left eye was still half closed from the injury around it.

John stepped forward and turned the pillow up on its short side, against the wooden headboard, just as Conall settled her backward.

"Shall I call for Serena?" Conall asked.

Tess shook her head and let her eyelids fall closed for just a second. When she opened them, her gaze swept over John and Gregor. "Did I interrupt?" She asked.

All three were quick to insist she had not.

"Aw, now, lass," John said kindly, "it ain't right what they done, so here we are, about to make 'em pay."

Her eyes found Conall, a question within.

He nodded. "Some of the persons who attacked you have been apprehended."

"And?"

"They will hang," Conall answered simply, firmly.

"Am I to be freed?" She spoke slowly, as if it would cause pain if she did not, but the question raised brows.

"Tess—" He did not, of course, remind her of her vow to stay. Again, guilt suffused him.

"Will you release me?" She persisted, her words measured and implacable.

Conall said nothing.

As fierce as he'd ever seen her, she met his hard gaze and uttered evenly, "If I'm to stay, and you do this, their hate will grow tenfold."

He breathed a spasm of relief, realizing that leaving was not her desire.

Silence hung in the chamber.

"The lass is right," Gregor finally said.

Conall turned and leveled Gregor with a mighty scowl. His friend at least had the grace to not appear happy about her suggestion or his own entertainment of it.

Through gritted teeth, Conall insisted, "They need to be punished."

"You cannot kill them," she protested.

"But lass," John Cardmore butted in, "dead men dinna throw stones. And who else would dare, if a hanging awaits them?"

Tess sighed, dark circles under her eyes that had little to do with her injuries. "But it will only intensify the hate, if they're hanged because of me."

"What do you suggest?" Gregor asked, unconcerned with the steam seeming to rise off Conall.

Her shoulders lifted and fell. "I-I don't know. Could I meet them? Could I talk to them?"

Conall resorted to shouting as Gregor and Tess discussed this not only as if he weren't present, but also as if he were not already fuming. "Absolutely no!" He struck the air with his fist. "I don't want them even breathing the same air as her!"

Gregor stayed him by raising a hand to make him stop. "Why no? Let them see what they've done," he suggested while Conall's seething increased with each word.

"Are you daft—"

"Let them meet her, talk to her," Gregor persisted.

Nearer to the bed, John began to nod, his expression thoughtful. "The devil you ken and all that. Let the lass decide after she meets 'em if they deserve to die."

Conall's eyes were wide and alarmed, upon Gregor and then John.

Tess spoke up, turning Conall's attention to her. "But make it public," she added, which caused Conall to appear to have fits. "If they choose to be belligerent, if they are merely evil by nature, everyone will see this, and see that they were given a chance. And if they persist with...with their hate, then you...should punish them. But what if they're sorry, or were just caught up, or—"

Conall had had enough. He roared, with great disgust, "Of course they're sorry now! They're about to hang!"

"Maybe no public, lass," said a voice from the open doorway.

All three men within the room turned to find Angus standing there, one thin hand just touching the door jamb.

Tess smiled.

"Least no too public," Angus continued, "you're no up for that." He took one more step into the room and John approached him, lending his arm to bring him to Tess. He deposited the older man at her bedside, in the chair Conall had used.

A lone tear slid down Tess's cheek, though she smiled to see her friend. She bent forward and touched her forehead to his. They whispered, though none too quietly, as the three men heard the exchange.

"I am happy that you cannot see me like this, Angus," she confided.

"Bruises fade, lass. And you're still the bonniest one in the room, like as no."

Tess smiled, but even a short laugh was beyond her.

"I only worry, lass—what if they're awful? What if they keep with the hate, even after they ken you? You've a soft heart, and that's the bruising I'm worried about."

Tess considered this, a small frown gathering before she answered. "I think the worst of them now...or I believe the worst. Might it help if they proved me wrong?"

"Aye, it might. Maybe just in the hall, then. Informal-like, surrounded by those who do love you. You could hear their side, and they yours."

"But what if I'm wrong, Angus?"

The old man searched for and found her hand, holding it firmly. "Then you have to let 'em hang, lass." He turned his head, just a bit, knowing Conall stood behind him. "But do it quickly, laird, whilst the evidence of their crime remains. Let 'em see what they done."

IT WAS HAPPENING AGAIN. Oh, God. She wasn't strong enough for this.

The stones came, flying at her as if heaved from catapults, never missing their mark, large and gouging deeply. She fell and covered her face, her fingers clawing into a ground that was not so much rough earth as one solid but smooth hardness. She cried and screamed, and Alain was there again, as she'd believed him to be before. This time, he endeavored not to hide himself but enjoyed the

melee. He watched eagerly, laughing loudest, his undiluted glee setting others to cackle devilishly as well. Ugly sounds, their laughter.
Mean and hard, echoing ceaselessly in her ears.

"Tess! Tess!"

Conall. Angry again.

"Tess! Wake up!" He shook her shoulders.

Tess moaned and opened her eyes, dispelling the nightmare with
a final whimper.

Conall was here. In his chamber. She was safe, after all.

He sat on the edge of the wide straw mattress, his hands having
released her shoulders, but close still, on either side of her. He was
dressed only in his tunic and breeches.

"You were dreaming of it," he guessed, and there was no need to
define the 'it'.

Tess shuddered and offered a jerky nod, her eyes darting around
the firelit room. It had been so real, surely the assailants lurked within, watching, waiting.

"'Tis only you and I," he said, having glimpsed her horror. "Tess?"

She breathed heavily but said nothing, just slumped further
down into the mattress, closing her eyes.

Tess opened her eyes again when she felt Conall rise and step
away from the bed. She didn't feel so much achy and bruised as
she did restless, filled with a need to be gone from this bed. She
hadn't any idea of the time, save that it was night, the window only
blackness. She sat up, which proved less painful than she'd expected,
and settled the bed sheet and furs around her waist. "I'd like to see
Bethany tomorrow."

Conall turned to face her again, considering all of her, looking
pointedly at her bruising, gauging her healing. They had decided,
within her first wakeful hours, that Bethany should absolutely not
see her body in this state. But Tess, too, now scrutinized the visible
scars, noting the discoloration was faded now to yellow and light

green, and the salves that Metylda had provided had effectively reduced any open skin wounds to mere scratches this many days away from the incident. "I can cover my arms," she suggested, but that left her face, which Tess frankly had no desire to see. Yet, she didn't want to scare the poor child. For the hundredth time, she touched her fingers to her swollen eye. She looked to Conall for his opinion.

He returned to the bed and sat down beside her. Tess lowered her hand, watching his face as he gently touched her chin, turning her face to the light of the fire. "'Tis no so bad today."

This close, she noticed something she hadn't since first waking. She was very accustomed to his eyes and the many manifestations of their intensity. But now, while he sat so near, she noticed the distinct lack of fire, the absence of purpose, and no evidence of residual anger. He seemed almost detached.

"Something is troubling you," she guessed.

A tiny spark lit his eyes, but perhaps this was only surprise she'd recognized his mind was occupied elsewhere.

He drew a long breath. "Lass...I dinna ken how to say I'm sorry to you."

She certainly hadn't expected that. When she answered, she only spoke what came to her mind. "True, this wouldn't have happened to me if you hadn't stolen me. 'Tis just fact." His eyes found hers, looking pained by this truth. "Yet, I do not believe you are a person who promotes hate and evil. I-I want to blame you," she said, sorry for his growing discomfort, "but only because that would be easy, to try to understand the hatred of one person rather than hundreds." Tess sighed, wearied by that thought. "But the truth is—and I don't think you can deny this to me—that you do care about me and wouldn't wish harm upon me." These were possibly the boldest words she'd ever spoken.

Conall's entire expression seemed to soften, though he said nothing.

Before he might have spoken, either to confirm or deny her supposition, Tess said, "But I don't want to be killed. And I think you need to make me a promise—that if, after I speak to these people, they remain fixed in their hatred, that you will release me from my vow. I will never be safe here if they cannot be made to understand their hatred is misplaced."

Conall removed his eyes from her, turning his head to stare away from her. After a moment, he nodded.

This should have brought her immense joy, the thing for which she'd wished so long was within her grasp. And yet, she only felt saddened by the very idea of not being at Inesfree, with Conall.

"I canna put off leaving," he said, causing her more distress.

Leaving? Dear Lord, she'd nearly forgotten. Since he'd mentioned that he would join the great warrior of Scotland, William Wallace, battles had been waged inside her own head, torn between so many desires, not least of which was for Conall's safety. On the heels of this, she prayed often for peace—everywhere—but mostly, she tussled with her allegiance. Being half-English and having lived for many years a sedate and delicate life within the cloister, she'd never known another person aside from her own father who was Scottish. In England, the people of Scotland had been painted with a rather broad brush stroke—they were heathens undeserving of sympathy and would all be better off once Edward I finally had his way with them.

Yet, she was also half-Scottish. And her allegiance, which she suspected greatly favored Scotland, had more to do with the people inside this castle and was not at all related to the Scottish blood given from Arthur Munro—and this, in spite of how long she'd lived in fear here, in spite of even this most recent offence committed by Inesfree's own.

"You should put it off no more," she told him. Tess tilted her head and wondered, "Might you have gone sooner to Wallace's side had you not taken me?"

Conall shook his head. "No. I'd spent the winter with him, until Edward chased us about. When the nobles swore to Edward in February, it seemed a good time to regroup."

"You weren't required to swear allegiance to Edward and England?

"Aye, I am. But I'm no verra political and I've a smaller house, and for the most part have stolen beneath the notice of the English. But it's time to claim our freedom."

She looked down as his hand moved, reaching from where it had rested just next to her thigh. He picked up her hand, the one that had suffered much battering at the May Day feast, his fingers gentle upon her palm as his thumb traced the fine veins upon the back of it. She was well familiar with the escalation of her own heartbeat at the warmth of his touch.

"Why do you put off the leaving, then?" She asked, to the top of his head while he continued to stare at their hands.

His wrist flicked slowly to bring her eyes to where lie his. As ever, his hand was larger and more sun-darkened, the veins that marked paths being raised and corded. In contrast, hers was tiny and pale, giving no intimation of strength when coming up so short compared to his.

"For this," he said.

Her eyes jerked away from their hands, but he'd not yet lifted his own gaze. When he finally did, she witnessed again that warmth and desire whose absence she'd noted earlier.

He kissed her only briefly, softly, just breezing his mouth across hers, eliciting a sigh before her lips were abandoned. Tess struggled mightily to rein in her disappointment. She'd closed her eyes, expecting—needing—his kiss and when she opened them, it was to see him stand from the bed and stretch. She did not trouble herself to remove her gaze from him. She was hard put to contain her own sorrow for his leave-taking. But perhaps, on this night, she would like to lie beside him, just to feel him near, to know because he was so close, she was safe. Nightmares would recede into that place where Conall was not. She would close her eyes, feel safe, and pretend there was naught else between them; no history, no battle, no fear. True, it was wrong and sinful, too. But he'd just agreed to let her go, if she couldn't somehow manage to prevent him from hanging the persons who'd attacked her, if she failed to make them or help them abandon their hatred.

She must, though. She just must.

"CONALL?" SHE CALLED to him softly.

He froze, the long slender rod he'd used to adjust the logs within the hearth suspended in mid-air, his eyes held captive by his thoughts of her and the swaying of the flames. Tess had never called him by his Christian name before this moment. Her tone was neither coy nor frightened, but soft, hesitant, testing the sound upon her tongue. Slowly, he straightened and turned. She sat as he'd left her. In the dim interior of the chamber, from the small distance across the room, he leveled his gaze upon her and waited. He watched her eyes dancing around him, nervous.

He wondered what other long-denied truths or unwilling promises she might force from him now.

When finally her eyes met his, she asked, "Will you...lie here tonight?"

If ever there had been put to him a loaded question, surely this was it. He approached the bed, towering over her as he reached the side. She didn't shrink away but met his gaze, not boldly but with a certain resolve.

"Would you have me sleep here, Tess?" He had plans to do so but would let her think the choice was hers. He hadn't sought his own bed, despite Tess having taken up residence within, since the attack, so afraid of causing her more harm, physical and otherwise. But here she was, appearing not so much frightened as sad.

She nodded, and it was obvious she disliked admitting even this. But any ire her stubbornness might have bred was diminished when she said, "I would...I would want to lie next to you."

Had there been sufficient light, he was sure he'd have spied a flush creeping up the creamy expanse of her neck. His own heart raced. He had to know.

"Why? Why now?"

She closed her eyes, perhaps to gather courage. But he wouldn't coddle her in this regard. She hadn't done so for him.

"I don't want to be afraid."

That was enough, he decided, and entirely sufficient. He nodded thoughtfully.

In his mind, he dove into the bed beside her and took her into his arms with particular urgency. In reality, he guessed this was not what she sought. And, too, in the back of his mind remained his thoughts of riding away from Inesfree and leaving Tess behind.

Without great care, he doffed his tunic, and tossed it onto the trunk at the foot of the bed, thinking to spare her the removal of his breeches and braies. He watched her shimmy her bottom and herself further toward the wall and climbed in beside her and lay on his back. He raised his arms, placing one under his head, offering the other to her, holding it above them until she understood and shyly moved toward him. She placed her hand upon his bare chest and lowered her head into the crook of his shoulder. Conall lowered his arm around her. He stared at the open timber of the ceiling, pretended she didn't smell so fresh, or that her hair didn't feel so damn soft against his naked skin, and that her kisses weren't known to be so affecting. But this was an ineffective ploy. Her entire body was pressed against him, her breasts teasing his ribs, her thighs rubbing against his own.

The devil himself had not imagined torture such as this, he thought. Conall might have found a rare amusement in the situation had it been anyone but he who suffered.

He didn't sleep for a long time. He'd just promised her he would release her if she couldn't by some means transform Inesfree's dangerous and unreasonable loathing of her. And he only had a few hours to figure out a way to make her stay when she failed to do so.

IN A TINY COTTAGE IN the village, far outside the curtained walls of Inesfree, another man stared pensively at the ceiling above him. 'Twas not a cottage, truly, he'd decided earlier. Nothing more than four walls, barely that, and a roof that surely leaked during the rains. A hut. A hovel, he'd have called it. But it offered slightly more warmth than the cold Scots night and, too, there was the added warmth of the whore beside him.

Whore, there was a term. He laughed inside. Whore, in this girl's life, would have been a tribute. She was the widow of a mason who had died rather suspiciously—he liked that bit—with hair that would give straw a good name and a disposition that goats might envy. She'd proved unimaginative upon the mattress despite the coin he'd enticed her with.

Yet, his options had been spare. These villagers, with such gray and dreary lives, and their severe distrust of travelers or any person who thought to encroach upon their squalid line of shacks, had tested Alain almost to the point of violence.

But encroach he had. He had his thousand pounds to earn yet.

He might have earned it already, without even raising a finger if these same dull people had done the job for him. He remained now only to learn if Tess had survived the brutal attack. He'd been just as shocked as Tess had been when that first stone had struck. As the stoning had continued and Tess had fallen, his interest had risen. He had no experience with murder and had truly dreaded the task to which he'd been set, had wondered if he could actually do it. Could he snuff out a life? Would he opt for a painless end to spare his own squeamish nature? Or might he find grim pleasure in a violent scene? He might never know. The choice had been stolen from him, and not without a breath of relief.

At this very moment, Tess might be dead.

She had seen him.

In bed, one hand idly scratching at his chest, he considered the consequences of being seen by his quarry. Lost in his own horrified glee that day, he had stared quite unabashed—had surprised even himself—as she lie upon the ground, blood covering so many parts of her slim body. When her eyes had found him, it had taken only fear of discovery to avert his fascinated gaze from her tortured body.

And then that brute MacGregor had swept into the beautifully quiet scene and had removed her from all that evil. But had he been in time?

They had not married yet, Alain had learned firsthand from that mammoth of a man weeks ago, and had it confirmed by the sullen villagers. Yet, there was something indelible between his one-time betrothed and the MacGregor. Alain had seen it. Had witnessed that Scotsman's eyes when he'd found her. He might have been facing his own death, his eyes had shown such fear—surely a telling moment. Alain knew immediately the MacGregor's alarm had little to do with any possible loss of Marlefield. What Alain had seen in Mac-Gregor's eyes and actions when he'd come upon Tess's battered body told Alain that everything—every single word—uttered from Mac-Gregor himself at their lone meeting had been a lie.

It was not in the plans that she be returned to her father, but Alain now believed that his chances of actually earning the thousand pounds already paid to him were virtually nil. Alain had witnessed that feral gleam in the MacGregor's eye and that meant he'd never be able to spirit her away from him—even if he had help from Tess herself. It was unlikely she would ever again be allowed to be in so vulnerable a position as she had been in the market.

He'd thought to question again in the morning the recalcitrant villagers. He must know that Tess was indeed dead—he truly could not conceive that she had survived such heathenism. Confirmation of her death was the only reason he'd remained in this dreary and inhospitable place. Were she dead, the coin was his and he could move on. If she was not, he was sure that his own continued existence—he imagined Glasgow was fine at this time of year—was likely only guaranteed if he returned the coin to Arthur Munro. He wanted nothing to do with either her madman of a father or her even more dangerous lover.

CHAPTER 22

"I still dinna ken why I'm taking advice from an old blind man," Conall whispered harshly to Gregor the next day, when the 'trial' was about to begin.

Gregor leaned into Tess, who sat between the two chiefs. He grinned and shrugged. "Because he was the smartest man in the room?"

Conall threw him a dark look, which perfectly advised Gregor of his exhausted tolerance. He gripped the thick wooden arms of the chair.

This did not go unnoticed by Tess. "I should be the nervous one," she said and gave him a soft, imploring look, hoping he knew she needed him to be strong for her.

They sat together, all of them—Tess in the middle with Conall and Serena to her left, and Gregor and Angus to her right—upon the dais at the laird's table. John stood in front of them, feet braced apart and hands on his sword. The hall was otherwise empty while they waited.

Tess self-consciously touched her fingers to the skin around her eye, deciding that it might actually feel less tender, as if the swelling had decreased yet more.

Her hand was pulled away by Conall. He settled it on the arm of her chair and covered it with his. It was meant to be comforting, to tell her not to fret, but her stomach was so unsettled as to be almost painful and she feared at any moment she might just start crying. They needed to see all the damage done to her, she knew, but was certainly ill-at-ease about her appearance, despite Serena's best efforts with her hair and gown.

"Neither too formal, nor too fashionable," Serena had insisted, regarding how to wear her hair. "We don't want to intimidate them. We want them to see you as someone just like them." With that in mind, she'd only brushed out Tess's long hair and tied it with a single ribbon at her nape, leaving the length draped over her left shoulder. Tess wore a plain blue kirtle, which laced up from the waist to the modest neckline.

And she waited. It had not been easy to leave the safety and solace of Conall's chamber. Conall had insisted he would carry her down to the hall, but Tess's need to at least *appear* strong was powerful and she'd walked down the stairs with careful steps, aware of Conall's glowers and grimaces while she continued to refuse his help.

She'd practiced, again and again in her mind, words she might say to these people. Staring now at the twelve waiting stools lined before the main table, she still couldn't fathom that people could truly be so evil to wish death upon a person they did not know, and who had presented no threat to them. Wishing was one thing, but to go a step further and carry out such a deed was an extremely frightening thing to consider. What kind of person did that? She hoped that murder hadn't actually been their intent. Maybe they'd only wanted to scare her, or simply remind her that she was unwelcome. Maybe it had just gone too far....

The doors opened. Tess breathed deeply and watched as Inesfree's bailiff led the shackled offenders inside the hall. He used a long iron rod to prod them forward. To a man, each of the accused's eyes, went immediately to the table and the occupants. But across the distance from one end of the hall to the other, Tess could perceive no emotion in their eyes.

Though she held herself very still, Tess's lips trembled to find, among the accused, a boy of not more than twelve or so, and a woman, thin and unkempt, weeping openly. When they came to the stools, the bailiff gruffly told them to sit and they did so as one. Now, not one would meet Tess's gaze.

That was fine. It gave her opportunity to consider them. She recognized only a few, and only by sight. Aside from the boy and the woman, they seemed just average peasants, hardened by the very circumstances of their daily lives, but cowed now by this particular situation. Tess couldn't be sure this had anything to do with her, and their part in her attack. Their current meekness could be a result of their belief that they were bound to die.

Next, several dozen soldiers entered the hall, taking positions along the wall on either side. They lined up—with near equal distance from one to the next—and stood at attention. Conall had told Tess the rest of his army would be, during this assembly, directly outside the keep. As the open doors had brought a stridency of noise from outside, Tess believed the entire village must now be surrounding the keep.

After the soldiers, the families of the accused, mostly wives and mothers and sisters, filed into the hall, keening and crying as they entered. "Mercy," was called and sobbed many times until John Cardmore brusquely called for silence.

When all had settled, and the room was near to full, Conall stated to those who sat in the chairs, "You are charged with attempting to murder. It had been decided you would hang without so much as this benefit, for your treachery against the house of Inesfree, and against one under the protection of the house of Inesfree." He paused—dramatically, Tess thought—before pronouncing, "'Tis only at Lady Tess's insistence that you be allowed to plead your case. She has no wish to see you hang."

"Mercy" and "praise the lady," were exclaimed now until John Cardmore once more shouted for quiet. "And if you make one more noise, you'll be tossed out!"

Conall turned to Tess and inclined his head, squeezing her hand, which had remained covering hers.

Her heart thudded in her chest. Her palms were damp upon the arms of the chair.

She swallowed visibly and faced the accused. "Would you look at me, please?"

They did. Slowly, reluctantly, and with obvious uneasiness, one by one, they raised their eyes to her. The accused woman whimpered loudly now, confronted with the evidence of her crime, written upon the still-bruised eye and the discoloration of Tess's cheek and neck and hands. John Cardmore did not instruct her to shush. The young boy only appeared sorrowful and afraid. The others, all men, some as young as twenty and some as old as fifty, looked at her with varying degrees of fear and regret. Only one, who sat at the end, stared at her with tight lips, seeming to withhold a snarl.

Tess asked, "Do any of you claim to be innocent?"

No one answered.

Tess nodded, considering her words.

"Have I personally done anything to you, or the people of Inesfree, to have warranted your treatment of me?" When there was again, no answer, she persisted in an even tone, "Anything at all?"

She looked from one pair of eyes to the next. She saw no defiance, no current loathing. "You, sir," she addressed the man at the end, whose eyes yet held a bit of an edge. "Have I wronged you somehow? That you should want me dead?"

He wanted to say something, she could see. His body jerked a bit, the cords in his neck stood out, while he clenched his jaw to keep himself silent. His eyes strayed to Conall, but he said nothing.

Tess continued, "It is no secret, I was stolen from my home. I was brought into an enemy keep and nearly," she cast a glance sideways at Conall, surprising all by showing a quirk in her lips, "forced to marry. Against my will. Yet, I did not take it out on you, nor even your laird. I did, however, try often to escape, much to your laird's chagrin, and when he re-captured me this last time, he made me promise not to try again. And I did. I've kept my promise, and I intend to keep that promise always." She stopped and cleared her throat. "I don't need you to like me. I don't even need you to pretend that you like me. But can you promise me that you'll neither wish me harm nor cause it? I know...I know I wouldn't harm any of you." She watched as their expressions altered gradually, until most were watching her now with some combination of confusion and hope. "If you can promise—and intend to keep the promise—then you shall not...you shall walk out of here today, free."

No one answered. And one by one, they dropped their eyes to their chests. Her shoulders, stiff from holding such an anxious posture, slumped now, this hard blow of failure twisting her already fretful gut. She'd so wanted to believe they really weren't hateful people. "Only a vow to not repeat your actions, that is all," she urged. "I don't think you really meant to do me such harm."

The boy looked about him, at those who sat at his left and right, his eyes anxious and frightened again. Another quiet sob overtook him when he realized none would speak, and he was, presumably, too frightened to speak first, or for himself.

"Please say something to save yourselves," she begged, so unwilling to see people die because of her. Some looked up at her again, startled. Tears now slipped from her eyes and she nervously brushed them away. She leaned forward. "I couldn't bear it if you were to die." She felt Conall's and Gregor's and Serena's eyes on her and knew they would be disappointed with her pitiful pleading.

Near complete silence filled the hall, save for Tess's quiet crying. Many seconds passed while her crying was the only noise. Finally, Conall stood, about to proclaim their sentence, since none had chosen to accept Tess's offer.

"I'm sorry, miss," the accused woman whimpered. "I dinna mean—I never meant—"

"I promise," called the man sitting next to the woman. Tess moved her eyes to him and saw a lone tear travel down his dirt-stained cheek.

"I won't ever hurt you again, lass," said the oldest man in the group, his voice steady and firm, his eyes thankful.

Tess's cries turned to joy as one by one, they promised or apologized. She clapped a hand over her mouth to prevent embarrassing herself further with outright blubbering.

The young boy wept openly, staring unabashedly at her. "I'm sorry, miss!" he wailed. "I promise not to ever do it again, not to anybody."

"Oh, thank you," Tess said through her tears. "Thank you."

Conall sat back down. Tess could almost feel tension washing away from him.

Finally, all of the defendants had made some statement either in apology, or as a promise given, which satisfied Tess immensely, save for the man at the end, though his eyes now watched her with much less animosity. He said nothing.

Tess regarded him, silently pleading with him to say something. Anything.

Finally, he lowered his head to his chest and wept. He mumbled something, but the words were lost in his sobbing. When he raised his eyes again, Tess saw only fear, and his eyes were on Conall.

"It was me," he said through a sob. Shaking the dark hair off his forehead, he admitted. "I started it—I bashed the rock into her head." All this was confessed through his weeping, while snot dripped from his nose and spittle followed the words out of his mouth.

Conall pushed his chair back and stood abruptly, his lip curling, about to charge. Tess grabbed at his fisted hand. "No," she cried.

Gregor had risen as well. Tess lifted her other hand to stop Gregor.

One of John's hands wrapped around the hilt of his sword, prepared to draw it from the scabbard.

"No," Tess insisted loudly. "Enough."

The man had gotten control of himself and, with an air of resignation as if he expected still to die, went on, "I am sorry, lass, but hang me anyway. I've brought shame—to myself and my family. I thought he hated you. I thought you hated us."

Still clenching Conall's fist and Gregor's arm, while they remained standing on either side of her, and while Conall's breath snorted out of his nose rather than through his clamped lips, Tess kept her eyes on the man and asked, "But how could I hate you when I don't even know you?"

He had no words, just shook and lowered his head, crying again.

"But will you promise me that it will never happen again—not to me, not to anyone?"

"Tess, no," Conall growled.

Their gazes met and she could see that his temper and his forbearance were stretched beyond thin.

"No," he repeated, with more emphasis. "This bastard was responsible—"

"This *man*," Tess interrupted, aware that every person in the room held their breath, straining to hear her soft words to their laird, "has apologized and is sorry. He has admitted he was wrong. He did not need to make the claim that he did; he could have very easily just spat out a promise to be free." When he seemed not swayed at all, she pressed on, "Please. He doesn't need to die, not if he's truly sorry."

Calls for mercy came again, first one then a second, until dozens of strident and begging voices could be heard.

"Now, goddamn it all, knock it off!" John's voice thundered above, but the cries kept coming.

Tess kept her eyes on Conall, who met her beseeching gaze with his own displeased glare. After what felt like an eternity, he tore his gaze from her, holding up his hands for silence.

Tess dropped her hands to her lap.

When the room quieted again, Conall addressed the man. "This morn, I wanted you hanged. Now, I want to kill you with my bare hands. and I'd want it to be painful, and slow," this last, delivered with a sneer. The man nodded, accepting his due. Conall continued, "She just begged for your sorry life. If you don't do something worthwhile with it, I will kill you. And if you ever even look sideways at her, I'll kill you."

The hall erupted in noise again, as cheers and cries of gladness resounded. Tess stood from her chair and walked behind Conall while he continued to glare at the man. Her steps were halting, with the pain she still felt. Another hush fell upon the hall, as every eye in the room watched her slow and painful progress from behind the table, down the step, which caused her a visible grimace, and toward the shackled group.

From her peripheral, she sensed the movements of Conall and John. She stopped and turned, just in time to see Gregor put one hand on the table and vault over it to be within only feet of her now. "I'm fine," was all she said and approached those who had attacked her, well aware of how close those three did stand behind her.

The bailiff struck his iron rod into the chair of the one nearest him, and the man bounded to his feet. The others followed suit, standing from their stools, their eyes on Tess. She stopped before the first man and took in his grateful gaze. He mumbled, "I promise," again and Tess hugged him and thanked him and asked his name.

"William," he answered but otherwise seemed to be at a loss for words.

Tess moved on to the next, the woman. She repeated the embrace and expressed her gratitude and asked her name as well. "'Tis Marta, and God bless you, Lady Tess."

As she approached the next, he announced, "I am Gilbert, milady, and I am ever indebted to you." He closed his eyes, his jaw quivering when she hugged him.

The boy was next and stood at just the same height as Tess. She placed her palm against his cheek, considering how young he was. "My name is Miles, Lady Tess." His fear was gone, and that was good, Tess thought. She embraced him warmly.

She continued to each person, standing shackled before a stool, until finally she stood before the last man, the one who'd declared to have started the entire attack. Conall and Gregor drew closer. The man wouldn't meet her eye.

"What is your name?" She asked, cognizant of his efforts to gather composure.

"Ranulph," he said, his voice weak.

Tess hugged him warmly, with true sentiment, while he lowered his head to tuck it on her shoulder. When she disengaged herself, she asked in a low voice that only he could hear, "Ranulph, will you promise to never harm another person unless you're defending yourself or your family or an innocent?"

"Aye, I do. I promise," he whispered back, and finally raised his eyes to her.

They weren't unkind eyes, she knew immediately. They were warm and intelligent, and Tess smiled at him. No longer whispering, she asked, "And what is your occupation, Ranulph?"

"I-I am a tanner, milady."

"Do you enjoy that?"

"Aye, verra much."

"Would you be averse to helping my friend, Angus?" She turned and indicated the old man, who'd never moved from his seat at the table, but whose sightless gaze hovered somewhere near Tess, his smile fond. "At one time, Angus was a master tanner," she said, not sure if that were actually true, the 'master' part anyway, "I think he'd be quite pleased to have some leather work to occupy his hands."

Ranulph's face was not the only one to show surprise, though this was immediately overtaken by a want to please. Eagerly, he nodded. "Oh, aye, milady, I could at that. I've more work than I can handle, and my boys are too young yet to train."

"Wonderful. Perhaps come up to the castle Monday next and let's get started."

She continued to smile but turned her eyes to Conall, while Ranulph continued to stare at her, his mouth hanging open, his awe apparent.

Her legs were near ready to buckle, and her head throbbed almost unbearably. She'd only taken one step before Conall was at her side as if he'd sensed her growing weakness, his arm sliding around her, one hand taking the one she'd reached out to him. She'd pushed herself too far, she knew, but, oh, it had been worth it.

Conall led her from the hall, while the bailiff busied himself unshackling each of the relieved attackers. They had barely turned the corner to gain the stairs when Tess collapsed. Conall reacted quickly, catching her as she nearly fell, taking her up into his arms and bearing her up the steps and into his chamber.

CHAPTER 23

He watched her sleep.

Conall had yet to know a coherent thought from the moment he'd carried her out of that hall, or to fully comprehend all that she had accomplished today. His mind was a jumble of exactly how brave she had been, how they had gawked at her with such wonder, how she had so easily and effectively turned their belligerence and fear to appreciation and thankfulness.

He shouldn't be surprised, he knew, reflecting on how she'd handled him since coming to Inesfree. Coming? No. He'd stolen her, had snatched her from her home and had brought her to this place that reviled her, and he'd had every intention of making her life miserable. But she had turned all the tables, so that he was begging for just one smile from her, or maybe one more kiss, and forcing oaths from her that she would never leave him. Not Inesfree. Just him.

And now she would stay. She wouldn't leave him.

He couldn't remember the last time he'd even thought of Marlefield, or his pursuit of that vengeance.

Good God, what had she done to him?

And what was to become of them now?

The door opened and Angus entered, the old man now accustomed to finding his own way about the keep. "She sleeps?" he guessed, and shuffled further inside, until Conall met him to lead him to the chair he'd vacated.

"Aye, she sleeps," he told him. He stood behind Angus, his hands on the back of the chair. "Like as no, she'll sleep until morn."

The old man's head moved up and down. "Aye, and dinna she earn it," Angus stated, his pride evident.

"How did you know her meeting with them would no fail?"

Angus didn't respond immediately, but when he did, his tone was thoughtful, reflective. "I dinna have eyes to see, laird, but you and I both ken her heart is pure. She's soft, and maybe too much so, but they only had to meet her. I knew she'd turn 'em around." Angus crossed one leg over the other, showing one knobby knee. "She turned you, though you likely fought it."

"Wasn't the plan," Conall said, and Angus chuckled softly.

"Plans made can sure enough be improved. Off with you now, get about your lairdin'. I'll sit with the lass for a while."

"DO YOU THINK THAT'D have worked if she were ugly?" John asked.

Gregor spit out his ale and howled with laughter. "Aye, and here she is with her eye all blown up and her cheek still three shades of green and purple, and they're all bending at her feet, ready to swear fealty."

"Aye, she was a feckin' queen today," John said, still filled with incredulity over what had transpired earlier, what she had done. But then he cackled, "I thought Ranulph might piss himself!" He plunked one ankle down over the other, his feet on the table in the main hall.

"The lass'll be washing snot from her hair for a week," added Gregor.

They chortled more, but settled down after a moment, each thoughtful again, considering the whole of the day.

Sobering for a moment, Gregor said, "I canna believe she pulled it off. I have never seen anything like it."

John nodded, his brows rising. "'Tis the same what she did with the boy," he said, referring to Conall. "Just took him longer to bend the knee, so to speak."

Gregor acknowledged this with a wry grin. "I'd have done the same." When John gave him a hard glare, he waved it off. "No like that, old man. She's all his—as if she'd notice any other. As if he'd let her." He chuckled again. "But damn, between the two of them and all their making eyes at each other, I'm no sure who has it worse."

John's eyes creased a bit at this, but he said, stroking his beard, "I've never seen him like this." And after a moment, "I'd call 'em blessed, but for that Munro is her father."

"Aye."

THE NEXT MORNING, TESS left Conall's chamber, and vowed she'd returned to her own tower room that night. For now, she wanted to see Bethany. She moved through the main hall and saw only a few people milling about, and walked to the kitchen, not finding Serena or Angus or Bethany anywhere. She approached Eagan, who saw her coming and offered her a jowly grin.

"Aw, now, lass," he said when she reached him, "'tis good indeed to see you about."

Tess rubbed his arm affectionately and returned his friendly smile. "I was looking for Serena or Bethany or Angus." She noticed the porridge, which still hung from the kettle at the hearth. She grabbed up a wooden bowl and helped herself with the ladle that remained within the pot. She sat at the lone stool at the counter upon which Eagan worked and broke her fast with the spoon Eagan handed her. "Mm, solid food," she marveled. "Or nearly solid." She grinned at Eagan.

"Good morning, Lady Tess."

Tess turned from her morning meal to see two of the kitchen girls, including Moira, the one that had previously loaned Tess a kerchief, entering the kitchens and bobbing their heads at her. They had rarely spoken directly to her before. They smiled at her now.

"And to you," she called back to them, her words slow. They went about their work, their arms laden with breads from the bakehouse.

Tess turned her eyes back to Eagan and felt a tightness just there, behind her eyes and nose. The cook inclined his head and grinned at her, and kept about his work, rolling out an impossibly large mound of dough for what Tess assumed would be the crust for some meat pie.

"I believe Lady Serena took off for the village," Eagan informed her, "about finding the mistress Elena who dyes the wools she spins. But I haven't seen Angus this morn. Now, the child, well she scampered through the kitchen much earlier, but she heard the laird's voice and went about finding him, I guess."

While she ate, she chatted a few more minutes with Eagan, neither one making any mention of her ordeal, for which Tess was thankful.

"I'll spend some time in the garden today," she informed him and inquired, "what can I bring you?"

His hands, soft and rounded upon a long and thin rolling pin, paused, "I have still the rosemary from last week that you'd brought, but I could do with some winter savory and more thyme, I would think."

Soon after, Tess had searched throughout the castle and inner bailey but found none of the three she wanted to see. Deciding to attend the garden as promised, she headed that way. She stepped outside just as the smithy was passing by, his beefy hands filled with dozens of worn iron horseshoes, about to be re-forged, no doubt. He lifted his gaze and tipped his head, "Morn to ye, milady." Tess's smile was reflexive but oh, so happy. She greeted him as well, tucking her hands upon her hips, taking in the bustling activity of the yard. She needn't avoid eyes today.

When she turned to her garden, she finally saw Angus, walking beside Gregor Kincaid, only a few feet away. Tess noted both Gregor's slower pace, surely to keep to Angus's speed, and the basket he swung from one hand.

"Good morning, Angus," she called, "and to you as well, my lord."

Gregor spoke first, though Angus's thick brows rose with pleasure. "Just Gregor, lass. Nothing lordly about me, aye?"

"Morn to you, lass," Angus said.

They stopped in front of her. Tess noticed the basket contained about half dozen small perch. She made a face at Gregor, at this sparse offering.

He laughed, "Ach, now, lass, 'twas just for fun. We'll leave the providing fish for the whole castle to those who ken what they're about, aye, Angus?"

"Right so, lad. Aye, but it was nice, to wrestle once again with the wee morsels."

Tess considered this. With Gregor's help to situate him upon the banks of the loch, Angus wouldn't have needed sight to sit and hold a line or pull it in when engaged. She gave a sidelong glance to Gregor, wondering if he, like Conall, was often mistaken as harsh and intimidating merely because of his size and bearing, when in truth they were kind people, who cared about others.

"Will you join me in the garden for a while?" She asked Angus.

"In a bit, lass, if you're still about it. The lad had me torn from me bed before the sun did shine," he said, looking not at all displeased about this circumstance. "Might have need of a wee lie-down just now."

Tess smiled at this and bid them good day, turning once again to her garden.

The ground was damp, but not muddy, and Tess could see little that required much labor, despite her inattention over the past days. She turned toward the cellar, tilting her head inquisitively as she noticed a nail affixed to the rim of the barrel—which had not been there previously—and saw that her water bucket hung by its rope handle from that nail. Closing in on the barrel, about to reach for the bucket, Tess saw that the barrel was filled near to the brim with water. It hadn't rained heavily enough to fill the entire barrel, she knew, pressing her fingers to her smiling lips.

She collected the thyme and savory, as requested by Eagan, but only set her gatherings outside the perimeter as she'd forgotten to bring along her own basket. She knelt carefully upon the moist earth and began to grab at the few weeds, thinking to save herself more work a few days from now. She wasn't about this too long before she heard Conall's voice. She didn't need to turn her head, as he approached on his horse before her. Tess was pleasantly surprised to see Bethany upon the saddle before him, looking even tinier in such proximity to Conall, and atop the great destrier.

Tess's breath caught, in amazed but happy response to the smile that Bethany wore, as the big horse trotted them nearer to Tess. She had rarely, if ever, been witness to any expressions save that of inscrutability or outright sadness from Bethany and was captivated by the transformation of the little girl's face, never recalling a sight more joyful.

Conall caught sight of Tess and reined in very near to her. He dismounted quickly and swung the still smiling Bethany down from the saddle. Tess imagined a normal child would have cried out with glee as Conall gave her an exaggerated swing in the air before setting her onto the ground. But Bethany, despite her beaming, made not a sound. Happily, though, she rushed immediately to Tess when

Conall had released her. She flung her arms around Tess's neck and squeezed tightly. Tess was astonished, her arms instantly returning the altogether unexpected embrace. Over the child's head, Tess's eyes, now watery with joy, asked a question of Conall. He only shrugged, though his smile was equally wonderful, Tess decided.

She didn't want to let go. Ever. But Bethany loosened her hold and stared at Tess as if she had not just done the most miraculous thing. Bethany, meeting Tess's eyes while she was still on her knees, traced her tiny fingers over the bruise around Tess's eye.

"'Tis nothing, sweet," Tess brushed it off. She was about to make some excuse for it, but Bethany surprised her yet further by opening her mouth as if to speak. Tess's eyes widened, waiting, her breath caught. But no words emerged, though the child's expression fell, becoming sad, forcing Tess to realize the child was not deaf, only mute. Just because she didn't speak, didn't mean she couldn't hear. Finally, Tess acknowledged only, "It is done, Bethany. I am well." After a moment, seemingly mollified by this, the child moved off to a flowering plant and bent her head to sniff at the blooms. Tess sat straight again, still gape-jawed, and watched in wonder, until she felt Conall nearing her. She looked up to see his hand outstretched and placed her own in his before she gave it any thought, allowing him to gently pull her to her feet.

"Thank you," she said and mechanically dusted off her skirts. But her eyes turned quickly back to Bethany.

"I found her in the stables this morn," Conall told Tess. "She's been with me all day, out training."

Tess swung her eyes back to him. "Oh, Conall, is that a good idea? To have her seeing such violence, even if it's only training?"

"Aye, 'tis fine," Conall explained. "Today was mostly instruction from John and then simple archery practice. I've brought her back now so we can get in to some heavier training this afternoon before we leave."

Tess nodded, appreciative of his consideration of the child, and pointedly resolved not to consider his imminent departure.

Just then, a small wasp entered the garden, swooping very near to Bethany's head and dancing in the air around her. The child's blue eyes turned owlish in fear and she dashed away from the plants, rushing to Tess, who scooped her up in her arms. "It's fine, darling," Tess soothed. "He's gone, that silly old wasp." Bethany picked up her head from Tess's shoulder to glance around. "He wouldn't hurt you, darling. You're too sweet. Wasps only like the bitter, sour tasting people. Laird MacGregor has been stung many times," Tess said tartly, with a saucy glance back at Conall as she took Bethany with her, inside the keep.

CONALL STOOD FOR A long moment, watching Tess walk away, her step a bit halting yet, as she carried Bethany into the keep. A strange feeling had come over him, something unidentifiable, something he wasn't sure he could ever remember experiencing before. He didn't name it immediately, but he explored it in his mind, reliving the last few minutes since he'd approached Tess in the garden.

He shook his head and looked around the bailey, wondering if anyone could sense that something had happened to him, that something was different. The feeling was so foreign he felt the need to scrutinize it carefully. He'd been pleased himself today when Bethany had, without words, expressed an interest in accompanying him. He'd tried to temper the encouragement he'd felt as she'd stayed so near him around all his soldiers. It wasn't fear of the large and brutish men that had kept her close, but just a want to be with him. He'd let her hold the large bow and told her one day he would teach her to use it, when she was taller than the piece. If this pleased her, she did not show it, but had seemed interested in the weapon and the training of his men. Then he'd thought to return her to the keep but had noticed Tess in the garden first. So many emotions had played across his mind upon first spying her glorious hair, shining so brightly in the bailey. There was no Ezra, hadn't been in some time, and yet there she sat, alone, unguarded, seeming to be content with her garden, in his keep. And when she became aware of him and Bethany, her surprise had quickly turned to open delight to see Bethany for the first time in days, and amazingly, he'd watched her joy increase tenfold when Bethany had rushed into her arms. Why had that affected him so, to see that teary pleasure overtake her? Was his own joy determined by hers? And just as he'd struggled with those questions, she'd spoken to him, addressing him only as Conall, as she had only recently begun to do, as if they were familiar. And friendly.

And then—then!—she'd teased him! As if they were not enemies, as if they had known each other forever. True, it had been for Bethany's entertainment, or benefit, but she'd smiled at him—saucily, to be sure—but the effect of it was almost...playful?

"You plan on mooning' much longer, or will we get to work this day?"

Conall turned to find John Cardmore atop his own steed, eyeing his chief with what Conall recognized as humored self-satisfaction, and this, too, seemed not to bother Conall at all. He had much to contemplate still, but his captain was right: he couldn't just hang about like a simpleton all day thinking on Tess's smile.

He mounted up, ignoring John Cardmore, and turned the horse around to follow the older man back to the training field. His own thoughtful smile stayed firmly in place for more than half the ride.

TESS ENTERED HER OWN chamber late that evening, an inner smile still with her. She couldn't remember a happier day, not for a very, very long time. Bethany had stayed with Tess long after they'd taken leave of Conall. She didn't think Eagan had minded that she had returned to the kitchens and told him she'd help with some of the day's work. The cook had agreeably tasked Tess with the beans and broth, and she taught Bethany how to snap off the ends of the pods, tossing the trimmed pieces into a large kettle in which they would boil for the meal. Tess had found a tall stool for the child to stand on. It kept her at waist height at the counter upon which Tess had previously worked. They returned to the garden to fetch the bounty she'd picked earlier, and also gathered mint and parsley, adding that to the kettle, with the beef stock Eagan had provided. While normally Tess might have stirred the large pot whilst it cooked, she removed it from the hot flames so Bethany could use the tall wooden ladle to mix the soup well. Bethany, of course, never said a word, but Tess was quite sure that the little girl's usually mysterious and haunted expression had been replaced today with pure pleasure.

Neither Conall nor any of his close advisors were present for the evening meal, so Tess chose to join Angus at the lower table, nearest the hearth. She sat Bethany beside him and watched her stand on the bench seat, to be of a height with Angus, and hover close to him, touching his shoulder while he supped. Angus patted her hand with one of his, while the other attended his meal. Eventually Tess sat the child down and encouraged her to eat as well.

Serena entered the hall, returned from the village, her cloak and gloves and basket still upon her. She quickly noticed the threesome at the table and approached with a beautiful smile, pulling off her gloves as she came. She kissed Tess's cheek and laid her basket and gloves upon the table. "I am so happy to see you about, Tess."

She sat down and greeted Angus and Bethany, who scrunched up her face at Serena, which caused both women to laugh.

Serena summoned one of the serving girls and soon had her own meal in front of her. The four of them sat for quite a while, amiably supping together and sharing their day, Tess telling them of all that she and Bethany had done together in the afternoon. While Serena spoke of her very busy day in the village, Tess listened happily and couldn't help but notice a warmth that surrounded her. For the first time in her life, she felt as if she had a family.

It was well past dusk now, but Tess wasn't thinking of sleep, her mind still reliving the events of the day. She was waiting for Conall, wondering if he might seek her out, debating if she dared approach his chamber. She wanted to discuss all that had happened and ask for more details about his time with Bethany, ask him what he thought it all meant, if he thought it might continue.

She thought to ready herself for bed but put that off until she saw Conall. She spent a bit of time unplaiting her hair and combing through the length of it with her fingers, for lack of a brush. She had not quite finished this when the door opened, and Conall entered.

Tess jumped up immediately, flinging her hair over her shoulder, meeting him as he closed the heavy door behind him.

Though she could barely contain her eagerness, Conall actually spoke first.

"Why are you no downstairs, lass?"

"Downstairs?" She titled her head, her brow crinkling. "Oh," and she waved a hand, "it was time I returned here." And giving that no more thought, she charged on, her smile bright, "Conall, just wait until I tell you about my day!" She grabbed his forearm in her excitement to have his ear. "Bethany spent the entire afternoon with me. I taught her how to make the beans and broth. And she stirred the pot—her little hands could barely move the spoon around the big kettle." Tess gave a little laugh. "Oh, but I think she loved it! And then," she continued, "she helped me chop up all the mint and—"

Conall kissed her—suddenly, simply—took her face in his hands and kissed her. It was rather sloppy and took Tess completely by surprise, but she didn't resist. *Oh, my, where has this come from?* raced through her mind, but was quickly expelled by the feel of him, the taste of him. It was needful and urgent, his mouth devouring her as he had not in so long.

Tess answered in kind, swept up instantly, her hands still on his forearms, now gripping tightly, opening her mouth to him. She felt, before she heard, the low growl that emerged from somewhere deep in his chest. Conall skimmed those hands down her neck, and across her shoulders, sliding them around her back, forcing her to move her own arms and hands, unconsciously sliding them higher to wrap around his neck, curling her fingers into his hair.

She tasted wine on his tongue as it moved around hers. Still not quite sure about the proper form, or the rules for kissing, she could only follow his lead. She did what he did, pulled him closer, kissed him back, and found herself wanting more.

And then he stopped. He pulled back, breathing forcefully into her face, and put her at arm's length. Tess looked into his eyes, but couldn't read anything, wasn't sure what she thought she saw—control? Lack of? Hunger? His jaw clenched. He dropped his arms and walked around her. Tess stayed as she was, confused, facing the door, wondering what she might have done wrong.

She shook her head. "No," she said firmly.

From behind her, after a moment, "No?"

"No," she repeated and turned to face him, but he'd sat near the fire, his hands splayed out on his thighs, his eyes on the small flames. "No, you can't do that. You can't ruin this day for me," she told him, the words, the thoughts tumbling out, unformed.

He'd raised his eyes to her, giving a rather irreverent laugh.

"It was such a beautiful day. I was so happy. And you're trying to ruin it—"

"That's why I stopped—"

"But I don't want you to stop," this, vehemently, and, as attested by her expression, surprisingly.

Conall closed his eyes for a moment. "Tess, if I hadn't stopped—if I touch you again, I will no be able to stop, and you'll accuse me of using today's happiness to...."

He didn't finish. Tess considered this. She'd braved plenty already, and now caught herself before she said something remarkably stupid, giving him leave to—

But... "Weren't you happy today?" Her voice was small.

Conall lifted his extraordinary blue eyes to her. She returned his stare and begged for the truth with her eyes.

CHAPTER 24

"*Weren't you happy today?*" she'd asked.

Conall was amazed and fairly flooded with a need to touch her.

"Aye." He rose and returned to her, absently tossing his sword and belt onto the end of the bed, while he held her eyes. His intent couldn't be more clear, yet she only breathed in and out, deeply and slowly, otherwise still. His last two steps to her were rather hurried, and while the thorny reminder that he shouldn't be doing exactly this only days before he might well ride to his death ruefully coursed through his mind, Conall could not restrain himself from pulling her hungrily into his arms.

She lifted her face, fully expecting his kiss, which captivated him. He placed his mouth over her soft lips, felt another quick intake of breath from her, and wrapped his arms completely around her so that the entire front of her was pressed provocatively against him. He loved the way she kissed, neither too sloppy nor too noisy, and certainly enjoyed the urgency he felt in her, matching his kiss, seeking more. He felt her lift her hands and twine them into his hair while her tongue, as he'd taught her, turned around his own. There was so much more he wanted to show her.

Conall shifted them while they kissed and walked her backwards until the bed was directly behind her. He lowered her, reaching one hand down while holding her with the other, and brought them both upon the mattress. He held himself up on one arm so she wouldn't

bear all his weight. He left her lips and trailed kisses down her neck
and to her ear. She smelled of lavender, her skin warm under the at-
tentions of his mouth. One hand fussed with the corded belt at her
waist, leaving it strewn about the bed when it was untied. His hand
skimmed over the soft wool of her gown, defining her stomach and
ribs and her breasts with his touch. A small sigh escaped her, and he
brought his lips back to hers. He took her mouth with greater need,
cupping his hand fully over her breast, pressing himself against her.
But it wasn't enough.

His hand left her breast and began to bunch up both her kirtle
and her surcote until many folds were in his hand at her waist. He
raised the entire length of the fabrics over her head, carelessly tossing
them aside when all her hair was free, leaving her adorned now only
in her sleeveless chemise. Impressions of blush-tinted skin and wonderfully rounded breasts and an intoxicating curve of hip teased him
before he joined their lips again, his hand finding her bare arms, the
skin here just as heated and soft as parts he'd already touched and
tasted. He touched her breasts again, torture he thought, so close
to naked. Her nipple was already peaked, which made him pause to
use his thumb and forefinger to provoke it to stay risen for him. She
whimpered at this and Conall answered with a groan, knowing immense power and incredible weakness at the same time.

He was hard, had been since almost the moment he'd touched
her, but when her small hands moved away from his hair and neck,
over his shoulders, and down his arms, he shuddered at what those
caresses did to him. When she grabbed for his tunic, as he had hers
just seconds before, and began to lift it upward, he grew even harder.

He abandoned her lips only so long as it took to remove his shirt.
He hadn't intended to be rough with her but found himself tugging
almost desperately at her chemise, trying to free her breasts, so that
the thing just tore under his insistence. He didn't care, and she didn't
seem to either, so he came on top of her, pressing their naked skin to-

gether, and felt a furious heat inside him burn much hotter when his
hard chest met with her heavily rounded breasts.

"God, lass," he breathed, nearly undone. He suckled her lower lip
and moved to kiss her cheek. He tasted a saltiness and drew back,
breathing heavy, looking intently upon her. Her eyes had been shut
tight but opened now as he stilled.

"Why do you cry?"

She shook her head, another tear escaped and slid down into the
hair at her ear. "I don't know." Her eyes closed again, and her head
moved faintly, side to side. "Because I don't want you to stop."

"You and I are enemies no more, Tess," he said, his voice low and
husky.

"No, we are not. I guess these are happy tears."

He was still, but only until her small hands pulled him back to
her. He gave her another scorching kiss, sliding his hand over her
belly, around her hip, and across her bottom, pulling her against his
erection, rubbing himself on her. Her tongue stopped playing with
his, just for a second, while she gasped, and then she set her hips in
motion against him and kissed him again with a need that was equal
to his own.

Soon, he pushed her again onto her back and his mouth replaced
his fingers at her breast, arcing his tongue across the bud, then moving on to the next, drawing her nipple fully into his mouth, using
his teeth and his tongue so that soon she began to writhe under
him. He pushed her chemise down more, away from her hips, down
her thighs. He lifted his head and sat back on his knees, pulling the
garment down over her feet. Her skin pinkened under his gaze. He
touched the fingers of his left hand to her ankle and traced a pattern
up her leg, over shin and knee and thigh, his eyes hungrily following.
Whisper soft, he skimmed those fingers over the triangle between
her legs and up across the flat of her stomach, back to her breasts,

just gliding across, aware that gooseflesh followed in the wake of his touch.

He lifted his head and met her darkened eyes, noted her shortness of breath, and whispered huskily, "You are perfection," before he took her lips again. He worked the laces of his breeches, the only remaining barrier, fumbling a bit in his eagerness, and then more so when the ties refused to adhere to his wishes. Finally, they were pushed down and off his legs and he laid at her side, touching so many parts of her.

"Oh," was all she said, other words escaping her presently. And then, "Oh," given now lower, deeper, as his fingers moved beyond the curls between her legs to stroke her. Her legs fell open to him, and his fingers moved further, to the very center of her. Tess writhed against his hand, her eyes closed to what he hoped was the same blissful torment he now felt. She whimpered softly and arched her back as Conall slid one finger inside her, his own growl deep and satisfying at finding her so deliciously wet for him. His finger moved in and out of her, which opened her eyes, showing him both her innocence and her hunger. His mouth reached for and took her nipple again and he felt her reacting shudder against him.

He could make her come right now, he figured, but knew that more than anything, he wanted her to come with him deep inside her, to tighten and throb around him. He shifted, sliding his finger out of her, and positioned himself between her open legs. Her hands found his shoulders, his lips found hers, his erection pressed against her heat.

He lifted himself only fractionally; he needed to go slow, needed her to stop moving against him like that. "It will hurt, lass," he said, so much regret in his voice as he pressed the tip of his cock just to where she was open and wet for him.

"You won't hurt me," she said, her voice husky and seductive, nearly finishing him. She tilted her hips against him. He shifted forward, embedding himself. And he knew he had to force it but couldn't bear the thought of the pain it would bring. But he did it anyway, thrusting within deeply and quickly. She cried out and he told her he was sorry, and he forced himself to not move though it nearly killed him. And then Tess began moving her hips against him and he groaned, a deep rumble surfacing before he moved with her.

He thrust deep, being fully surrounded by her wet folds and then withdrew, over and over again, faster and faster. Tess tilted her head back upon the pillow, arching her back. And he knew exactly when she came for the way she brought her eyes to his, her mouth open and panting, her gaze telling him she hadn't any idea it would feel like this. Conall felt his own orgasm crashing over him with such force, he felt near broken for it and could scarce move in and out now nor catch breath enough to even moan aloud.

Still and silent, though yet connected, they lay entwined like that for several minutes until finally, Conall could lift his head. He braced his forearms on either side of her, felt her small hands slip around, under his arms and across his back. He touched his lips to hers, just a drained and weakened kiss, all he could manage at the moment.

He lifted his eyes to her, found hers bright and not unhappy upon him. They were heavy lidded and filled with wonder. She lifted her head off the bed and kissed him back while her hands clung to him.

The last thing he wanted to do now was leave her body, though he feared his arms could hold him no more. He slipped out of her and rolled to her side, taking her with him.

"Mm," she purred and placed her head on his chest. Conall slid his arm under her, drawing her nearer. He felt her hand and her long thin fingers gliding experimentally over his chest.

Conall stared at the ceiling, slicing through the emotions overwhelming him just now.

TESS FELT HIS HEARTBEAT against her ear, nestled into his chest. She liked the feel of their skin touching like this. She liked everything. Everything they'd just done, everything she'd just felt.

She thought they might have dozed for a while. When she heard him speak, and felt the words come from his chest, she felt as if they'd woken her.

"Truth, lass, I'd no wanted to do this before I left," Conall told her, his hand rubbing lightly along her arm while her hair tickled his nose.

She didn't lift her head, just considered his words. "But you did *want* to do this?"

"Aye, but only from the day I first met you."

A lazy but happy smile touched her lips. "Why not before you leave?"

A long silence. She felt his deep breath under her cheek.

"Might be, I dinna return."

"You must, though." She didn't even want to think about that possibility.

"Aye, but it dinna work like that, lass."

She felt tears gather but staunchly refuse to let them fall. So, she changed the subject, "Is it always like that?"

"Jesu, I hope so," Conall said with a laugh. "'Tis different each time, no just quicker or slower, or this way or that, but," he paused, maybe to search for words, "the intensity, the precise way it feels... it's hard to explain."

She turned her face on his chest, caught his eye. She wanted him to kiss her again. She wanted him to want this, too. "I feel like now that I know, I'm always going to... want this with you."

Conall lowered his eyes to catch her gaze. His was very intense. He shifted, turning a bit onto his side, bringing their faces close. "The same thing I've wanted with you for so long—this—" he kissed her lips, "I will want again." He kissed her again, sliding his tongue over hers. "I will want it soon, and then tomorrow. And after that," he said into her mouth and kissed her yet more. He turned her onto her back again, his hand finding her breast. "And long after that."

TESS AND SERENA, ANGUS and Bethany, and scores of others stood in the yard, under the light fog and mist of the cool morning, ready to bid farewell to the majority of the MacGregor, MacDonnell and Kincaid armies. The sky, the air, the yard, everything was gray. Tess held Bethany's hand as the child stood beside her in her little gray hooded cloak. Beside her, Angus and Serena wore matching stoic faces, staring straight ahead, while the armies gathered just outside the gate, awaiting their lairds.

She'd so wanted *not* to cry. But that was going to be hard to do. He wasn't even standing before her yet and she felt her lip quivering.

And then they came from the keep, Conall and John and Gregor and a half dozen more men, their expressions grim, their strides purposeful. They were a sight to behold, these magnificent soldiers, dressed in full battle gear—chain mail, breastplates, tabards, and gauntlets—no sign of fear, motivated by grit and valor and justice.

Tess met Conall's dark gaze immediately, noted the furrowed brow and drawn mouth, and felt her heart flip. He came to her first, removing one glove to place his palm on her cheek. His eyes were fierce, but she saw a promise in them. She tried to be brave, tried to smile and nod for him. Fingers reached around her neck, drew her near. He pressed his lips to her forehead. And she cried now, her hands clinging to the leather of his breastplate. She closed her eyes, committing this to memory, the feel of him holding her. Too soon, he released her.

Around them, others said their goodbyes as well. Serena hugged Gregor tightly and Angus shook his hand. "You come back, lad," Angus insisted, to which the usually easy-going Gregor nodded curtly, his expression solemn. "Aye, Angus."

Then John stood before Serena, giving her a fatherly embrace while Gregor stepped before Tess. "I'll get him back to you, lass."

She couldn't speak but thanked him with her eyes and hugged him tightly. When he released her, she managed to say, "And you and John, too. I'll not be happy with anything less." He nodded.

Conall took up Angus's hand, shaking it firmly. "Be well, Angus."

"Aye, laird," Angus said with a slow nod, and offered the lone moment of levity. "I'd say I'd keep my eye on the lass for you, but then...."

Conall and several others chuckled, and Conall squeezed the old man's thin shoulder.

Then John stood in front of Tess. "You take care of the bairn now, aye lass?"

"You know I will," Tess promised him. "I plan to have her welcoming you home with her own words, John."

The robust old man's eyes watered as he enveloped Tess in a great bear hug.

The longest goodbyes were from John and Conall to Bethany. They each went onto their haunches to be at eye level with her, speaking in low voices, assuring her they'd see her soon, and that she was to mind Serena and Tess. John vowed to teach her to ride upon his return. Bethany stared at them, clearly not understanding the gravity of their leaving, but she returned their hugs and watched them curiously as they stood, her finger in her mouth.

Conall came one more time to Tess, kissing her fiercely upon her lips, not caring who witnessed this, or what they might think. She felt his arms slide around her and pull her close and tight.

"You'll be here when I return?" He wanted to know

She nodded without hesitation. "I promise."

And then he was gone, following John and Gregor and the others to climb swiftly upon their steeds and trot out of the yard, not one of them turning their heads, not even for one last glance.

It was several minutes before any in the yard moved. But the mist had turned to a light rain and soon the riders were only specks in the distance. Tess scooped up Bethany in her arms and Serena slid her hand into the crook of Angus's elbow and they made their way back into the keep.

THEY QUICKLY GREW ACCUSTOMED to having fewer people about the castle. The evening meal might only see a dozen people on any given day. And while it made for so much less work, there hung about the keep an air of sadness. Serena and Tess did their best to soldier on. They scheduled much time together, and with Angus and Bethany too, sewing and spinning and even subjecting the keep to a thorough cleaning. As summer was almost fully upon them, they were thankful to be able to spend so much time out of doors, in the orchards or the village or down near the loch, where Angus sat contentedly fishing, while the ladies lounged nearby with small needlework. And always, though Tess thought it was needed less and less, two MacGregor soldiers were never farther away than a dozen feet or so, at Conall's insistence, she was sure.

Ranulph had kept his word and had appeared at the keep only a few days after Conall and the armies had left. He was nervous, Tess could see, when she encountered him in the hall. She tried to put him at ease.

"Good day, Ranulph," she greeted him kindly. "I will fetch Angus for you." She'd noted that he carried with him tall baskets of uncut leathers and tools for the work. "He likes to sit in the yard on sunny days," she said, while the man had still not spoken. "Do you mind working out of doors?"

He shook his head.

"Have you eaten yet?"

He nodded.

Nonplussed, and not knowing how else to put him at ease, Tess went in search of Angus. She found him coming up from the storeroom at the back of the kitchens, led by Inesfree's steward, Leslie MacDonnell.

"Angus, Ranulph is here," she told him and waited at the end of the corridor.

"Aye, lass," he answered, using his hand as a guide along the stone of the wall.

"He appears to be still unnerved," Tess told him. "Mayhap you can set his mind at ease?"

"Aye, lass," said Angus and continued to walk by her, heading toward the hall.

Tess turned to Leslie. She never spoken a word to this man, but curiosity bade her ask, "Angus was in the storeroom?"

Tess hid her surprise as Leslie MacDonnell all but smiled in response. "He was. Curious about our store for the coming winter."

"But it's barely summer."

Leslie nodded and they moved further down the hall, toward the kitchen. "A verra smart man, that Angus," Leslie commended. "He made some good points, which the laird and I had discussed before his departure. We've a goodly supply now, but if a siege were to be laid upon the castle, we would be in dire need, and quickly."

"A siege?"

Leslie waved off Tess's alarm. "Unlikely at best, lass."

Tess thought on this but knew nothing of supporting a castle with food and necessities for any length of time. It had not ever been a concern that she'd been made aware of, whether in the cloister in England or at Marlefield. "Should we do something to increase our preparation?"

Leslie shrugged. "We can request more grain from the farmers, but until the harvest comes in, there's not much to be done. I'll make a note to inquire of the livestock births this year around the village. Monies might be paid to those willing to sell anything above and beyond what they can use or afford to feed themselves."

Tess nodded and thanked him for his time and went in search of Serena. They were working on two tapestries for the main hall. Serena had actually been working on them for almost a year and was glad for Tess's offer of help. When finished, each would stand more than twice the height of Conall but offer so much throughout the winter toward keeping the warmth within the hall and the drafts without. Tess had suggested that they make smaller ones for the chambers, and Serena happily agreed.

CHAPTER 25

A week later, Serena and Tess sat once again in the hall, the growing tapestry spread across the two rollers of the loom. Last winter, the machine had been disassembled as there had been none to help Serena. At Tess's insistence, the loom once again took up a generous portion of the hall, which saw little use these days. Daily, Serena taught Tess the intricacies of weaving a large tapestry.

Bethany was under the table closest to Tess, having found again a hound as a pillow. Bog child and dog enjoyed a morning nap.

"How long, actually, do you think they might be gone?" Tess asked. She'd asked this also of Leslie MacDonnell and Angus and even of Eagan, who'd given her only a blank look and a noncommittal shrug.

"Conall was gone for almost six months last year," Serena said, keeping her pretty green eyes upon her work, as she carefully wove the weft over one of the initial vertical threads and under the next. Occasionally, she would pause to beat down the emerging web to ensure that the load bearing threads, or warps, were completely covered by the weft threads.

"Were you afraid then?" Tess asked, taking the drawstring from Serena as it reached the middle of the loom, she now weaving as Serena had instructed, first over then under, bringing it ever closer to her side.

Serena splayed her hands upon the finished parts while Tess worked her side. "My father had so often been gone to fight, that it affected me to lesser degrees with each subsequent departure."

"My mother and I lived with nuns for nigh on seven years," Tess confided. "I've never known this, someone going off to war, with no assurances of their return."

Serena offered a sympathetic smile, but Tess didn't see, her eyes steady upon the weaving. "Sadly, 'tis just normal life here. Why did you live in a cloister?"

Tess shrugged. "My mother could bear no more children, so my father set her aside. He was granted a divorce eventually."

Serena's thin brown brows lowered. "How unchivalrous."

"When I think back on it, I believe it was for the best. What little I know of my father, having only lived with him this past year, I don't think I'd have liked to have grown up in his presence."

"He is a hard man?" Serena guessed.

"Very," Tess answered. "I enjoyed the cloister very much. It was peaceful, and because my mother was a lady we had our own suite of rooms and were not expressly governed by the rules to which the nuns were subject." Tess smirked, "Which was fine by me, as they were forced to rise at all hours of the night and morning to pray." She turned at the edge, and began weaving, over and under, aiming the drawstring back toward Serena.

"And your mother died?"

Tess nodded. "She was ever a sickly person, both physically and otherwise," this, rather matter-of-factly, though it still hurt to think about the loss of her dear, sweet mama. "When did you lose your mother?" She asked Serena.

Serena stared off, over Tess's head, pondering. "I was about eight or nine, I guess. She died in childbirth. My new brother died a few days after. I remember, at the time, being more upset about the loss of my brother. Not that I didn't mourn my mother, of course, but I had been so excited to have a sibling."

"Your father never remarried," Tess guessed.

"None would have him," Serena said with a small chuckle, then covered her mouth at her own impertinence. She explained, "My father was the kindest man, he truly was. But he wasn't at all...he was...well, he was ugly."

"Serena!" Tess's eyes widened, so surprised by this admission.

Serena shrugged while she laughed. "'Tis true! His face was just so...I don't know, he was just not attractive."

"Oh, my."

"He really was wonderful, and I loved him dearly but faith, he was a sight." Serena clapped her hands over her mouth, shaking her head. "I can't believe I just said that. How awful am I?"

Tess, of course, did not reproach her, or otherwise add to her embarrassment, but enjoyed a good giggle over Serena's honesty.

Their laughter was interrupted by a MacGregor soldier entering the hall, escorting a stranger toward the two women. The guards who were never far from Tess rose from the table they'd been sitting at and came to her side just as the stranger neared.

Serena and Tess raised their gazes to watch the men approach. The stranger was at least twice the age of Tess herself, she guessed, and stood rather straight and tall, and sported a lean figure. His hair was the color of sand, and his eyes a pleasing and soft brown. He was dressed only slightly finer than the peasants, his wool and linen garments simple, but clean and not at all threadbare.

"The Ladies Serena MacDonnell and Tess Munro," the soldier said, by way of introduction. Tess tilted her head, having found something very familiar about the man, though she did not believe she had ever met him before.

He smiled handsomely, his eyes settling appreciatively upon Serena. "I'd have come sooner if I'd known the ladies of Inesfree were so comely." He cast a glance at Tess but only briefly before returning his gaze to Serena.

The soldiers remained, hands on their sword hilts, eyes fixed on the man.

Tess watched, her eyes darting from Serena to the man and back again, sighting the prettiest blush staining Serena's cheeks. They seemed happy only to ogle one another. With a fine grin over this lengthy but silent exchange, Tess cleared her throat and asked, "And who might you be?"

Serena caught herself and averted her eyes, running a hand over her thick mane of dark hair.

"Aye, I'm called Fynn," he said, addressing Serena, "and I'd be searching for me da."

"Angus!" Tess cried happily. She jumped up from her stool, leaving the drawstring upon the finished part of the tapestry. "I'll fetch him straightaway. He'll be so happy to see you!" And she dashed out of the hall, her guards in tow, still smiling inside at this man's coming, and at the eyes he and Serena were making at each other. She discovered Angus sitting with several other elderly men around the smithy's open barn, his pipe clenched between his teeth, listening to whatever stories the smith shared to hold keep these old men amused.

"Angus," she called. "Fynn has come!"

His head turned at her voice, his brows lifting. A complete happiness enlivened his features. He made to stand just as Tess reached him, offering her arm. She guided him as he shuffled along, with greater speed than she'd ever seen, into the hall.

Upon returning, Tess put her gaze immediately upon the pair she'd left behind, seeing still a blush about Serena's pretty cheeks while Fynn stood before her, arms crossed over his chest, a grin accompanying whatever words he was giving her now. But he turned soon, following Serena' eyes as she noticed Tess and Angus.

"There he is!" Fynn called and it was evident, from the expressions on both men's faces, that theirs was a very sturdy and favorable relationship.

Tess delivered Angus to his son, who gave his father a rather sweet and gentle hug. "I've missed you, da."

Angus's sightless eyes had never shone so bright. "Aye, been too long, Fynn."

Tess supplied a stool, onto which Fynn settled his father. He rested his hand on Angus's shoulder and proclaimed, "You keep good company, da."

Angus nodded, his grin wide. "Aye, the lasses. Good they are to this old man, and aren't I blessed?"

"When I received the message," Fynn said, "I shook my head, wondering what to make of it, and however did they finally get you out of that old shack. 'Course, now I see 'twas no hardship, coming here."

Angus chuckled, holding his pipe upon his knee, which sat upon the other.

"Have you traveled far?" Tess thought to ask. "Should we send to the kitchen—"

Tess noted that Serena made a face, suggesting that she chastised herself for presently forgetting her duty as lady of the castle. Tess sent her a reassuring glance while Fynn politely refused, said he had to settle his horses and cart, but that he wouldn't mind being received for supper.

"Of course," Serena said, finding her voice again.

Fynn excused himself, taking a happy Angus with him to keep him company and catch up on each other. The soldier followed the pair out of the castle.

When the three men had cleared the doorway completely, Tess turned wide eyes upon Serena.

"What?" Asked her friend, her fresh blush challenging her pretense of innocence.

Tess burst out laughing. Serena soon joined, her hand finding and settling on her chest, as if to slow her heartbeat.

FYNN WAS CONTENT TO enjoy the hospitality of Inesfree for several days. Being a man of trade, he offered precious salt for Inesfree's cellars and several bottles of wine, which Leslie MacDonnell gratefully accepted, knowing that wine had to be imported, usually from France, and could be quite costly. Serena was effusive in her appreciation—her pink cheeks having become a fixture as long as Fynn was around—and even more so when he produced several large bolts of beautiful silks, in gorgeous shades of soft blue and saffron yellow and one, the softest shade of pink Tess was sure she had ever seen.

As lovely as they were, as adoringly as both Serena and Tess gaped at the silks, both women were quick to refuse such a precious and lavish gift. Fynn was very serious when he insisted, "'Tis more I owe you! Giving me father hearth and home, and me not having to fret on him. Now you'll be accepting all this, or I'll be taking the old dog away with me."

Tess and Serena quieted instantly, fearful that he might carry out his threat.

"Ach, now, I only goad you," Fynn had said, with a robust chuckle which brought great relief to the ladies.

He'd made himself quite comfortable during his stay, which seemed to please everyone. Tess even saw him in some discussion with Leslie about what Inesfree had need of, which he might supply upon his return. He was ever of a good nature, which surprised Tess not at all, as his father was the most affable and even-tempered person. He joined their family at supper each evening, though they still eschewed the larger table upon the dais in favor of the cozier trestle table lined up with the others on the floor. Fynn entertained them with stories of his travels and it was apparent that he had the perfect, pleasing personality for his chosen profession as a trader. "Could've talked Christ off the cross, his mam would say," Angus told them, his smile proud.

But he departed too soon, they all agreed, though Tess confided in Angus that she believed he'd be seeing his son quite regularly. "Not that I think you'd missed it, Angus, but your son was definitely quite taken with dear Serena."

"Aye," Angus acknowledged, nodding approvingly, "he always had an eye for the brunettes."

Tess punched her hands onto her hips. "Angus, how do you know that Serena has brown hair?"

"Aw, now, lass, can you no hear it in her voice?"

No, she most certainly could not. But this amused Tess and she had to ask, "So what color is my hair?"

"Now there's a riddle, to be sure." He was filling his pipe, dashing it against the palm of his hand. "You sound blonde, I ofttimes think. But every once in a while, I canna deny I hear red."

Tess laughed at the fanciful man, pulling a long tress in front of her. He wasn't exactly wrong, she decided.

SOME DAYS, TESS MANAGED to get through almost the whole morning without thinking of Conall. Some days.

While she'd known, before his departure, that she would fret over his safety, she hadn't actually given thought to exactly how much she might yearn for him.

But as the weeks went on, she agonized over things she couldn't remember Exact conversations evaded her and sometimes entire scenes were too foggy to be of any use. Tess ached to recall every minute detail about him and cried for that which she did remember as it was maddening in its deficiency, leaving her only to crave more.

She begged for dreams. Safe in her chamber at night, she made deals with God to deliver Conall unto her in her dreams, to give her new memories, to help recall the old. If she closed her eyes, she might see Conall coming to her. Atop his steed, his eyes—oh, God, would she ever be able to clearly recall such a blue? —fixed on her. He might smile at her. He would speak, his voice would wash over her, just as it had in reality. She could hear the sound of his voice, could almost invoke the feeling it roused in her, even now.

He might touch her in these dreams and Tess would yearn for a body she could press herself against. She'd close her eyes and pretend that just for a moment Conall was there. Conall was real. His arms were around her.

She missed him.

She was, then, grateful for exactly how busy she was during the day. She and Serena had committed themselves to much more work, mostly in an effort to keep their minds busy, which meant they rarely sat idle while the sun was up. The tapestry was nearly half complete when a month had passed since the army's departure. They joked that they might see grandchildren aiding them with this very project, it was so large. They also knew that their attention to the tapestry was certainly distracted by Fynn's gifted silks.

They'd decided they'd treat themselves to one gown apiece, and one for Bethany, with Serena choosing the yellow fabric and Tess the pink. Bethany's gown would be fashioned from the blue silk. This would still leave much of the fabrics for more designs, should they choose.

"But we must agree," Serena challenged, "that we are not permitted to work on our gowns unless we've given a fair amount of time to the tapestry."

Tess agreed, as the gowns would be a frivolous extravagance, and they would need to earn them. She had Bethany near, trying to get the child to hold still long enough to perceive some measurements. Bethany was intrigued by the blue silk, her little hands smoothing over the fabric, but impatient with Tess's turning her this way and that.

"You might just find one of her other little gowns," Serena suggested, smiling at Bethany's efforts to be away, "and surmise a pattern and size from that."

Tess sighed and agreed. She kissed Bethany's pretty blonde head and playfully swatted her bum, to send her on her way.

Bethany laughed and skipped away.

Tess's mouth fell open. Serena's eyes lifted from the pattern she was cutting.

Bethany laughed.

They gaped at Bethany, and then at each other.

"What's that I hear?" Angus called from beside the hearth, across the room.

With her hand to her chest, almost in disbelief, Tess answered, "That's Bethany. Laughing." She cried almost and looked again to Serena, whose expression still displayed her own shock.

"Oh, my," Serena breathed.

Angus uncrossed his legs and turned to face the women, his face hopeful, waiting.

But Bethany made not another sound and didn't seem to have any idea what she had just done. She plopped down beside her favorite hound and lifted his ear, turning her head to peer inside.

They hovered over Bethany and kept her close the rest of the day, waiting for another sound to come. But it did not.

"It's all right," Tess insisted while they supped later that evening, after Bethany had finished eating and stolen away from the table. "It's a start, right?"

"I still can't believe it," Serena said. "Did we imagine it?"

"We most certainly did not," confirmed Tess. "But what can we do? How can we help her to get the sounds out?"

Serena had no answer, sadly shaking her head, but Angus suggested, "Maybe that's how," he said thoughtfully. "Sounds, no words."

"What do you mean?" Serena asked.

"Well, I'm no rightly sure, lass," he admitted, "but I'll be giving it some thought tonight."

The next morning, Tess entered the hall to find Angus sitting once again by the hearth with Bethany at his feet. She sat with her legs crossed under her, one hand upon the hound—Jakke, Tess thought his name—while she stared with a scrunched up face at Angus.

"Oo, oo," Angus was saying, slowly and carefully. "Aa, aa."

Serena came to stand beside Tess, still quite a distance from the pair, watching Angus raise his brows and point to Bethany, indicating she should make those sounds now. But while Bethany's mouth opened, nothing emerged, and her expression hinted only at confusion rather than interest.

"Oo, oo," Angus persisted.

Tess grabbed Serena's hand and marched them over to Angus and Bethany, an idea moving her. She sat on the floor next to Bethany, upon the rushes, and pulled Serena down beside her. "Oo," she joined in.

Serena likewise did the same, understanding what Tess might be thinking. "Oo."

"Oo," Angus said again, his tone encouraging.

Bethany looked from one to the next, her little face letting them know that she understood they expected something from her. Her mouth opened again and all three held their breath while her lips appeared to move, almost as if she were trying to let the sound come out but didn't quite yet know how to make that happen.

Angus leaned further forward from his chair, reaching for Bethany's hand. He found the one in her lap and brought it up to his throat, placing her little fingers against his Adam's apple. "Oo," he said again several times, putting enough space between each sound that she could feel them separately and comprehend that it came from his throat.

Curiously, Bethany pulled her hand away and placed it against Tess's throat.

"Oo," Tess obliged.

Bethany smiled and moved to Serena, repeating her silent request with her small fingers now at Serena's neck. Serena moved her fingers, so they were centered. "Oo."

Serena took Bethany's hand and placed her fingers against her own neck and gave an encouraging nod.

A sound emerged, though it sounded nothing like "oo." But they didn't care, Bethany's eyes widened, and Agnus and Tess and Serena cried out with joy. So enamored of her own accomplishment, and the cheering that came with it, Bethany clapped her hands together excitedly and then put them back on her throat. "Ahhh."

Angus leant back and slapped his knee, his smile wide. Tess hugged Bethany to her, though the little girl kept her fingers at her own neck, "Ahhh."

Serena erupted in laughter, her eyes welling.

Just then Fynn walked into the hall and brought all eyes to him when he asked, "What's this about?"

Many sets of happy eyes turned upon him. Bethany squirmed out of Tess's arms and hurried over to him. If he were surprised, he didn't show it, only raised one brow and knelt down to her. Immediately, she placed her fingers against his throat.

"Say 'oo,'" Serena instructed, still smiling.

He gave a quizzical look but did comply, which sent Bethany racing around him, clapping her hands again, her own smile most joyous.

Poor Fynn hadn't a clue what was so exciting about this until his father said, "Bethany, show Fynn here what you can do."

Bethany stopped moving, and staring at nothing in particular, pressed her fingers against her neck and said, "Ahh."

Fynn eyes lit up. He clapped his hands and made a big fuss over this, which delighted Bethany yet more. He came to the ladies and helped them to their feet, first Serena and then Tess.

"How did this happen?"

No one had an exact answer, and no one seemed to care, though Serena said, "Angus did this." They regarded each other with shining eyes, reveling in the joy of the moment. Angus gave a hearty chuckle over Bethany's continued antics, skipping around calling out, "Ahh," with her fingers pressed to her throat. Soon, she stopped and sank to her knees before Jakke, who lifted his head off his paws. Bethany looked under his chin and squished her fingers into his fur.

"He canna make the sounds, lass," Fynn told her cheerfully, "no like you."

UNDER THE CANOPY OF an ancient yew tree, the MacGregor sat next to the Kincaid. Gregor leaned against the thin and scaly bark, eyes closed, though the occasional lifting or furrowing of his brow indicated he was acutely tuned into their surroundings. Jamie MacKenna sat across from Conall, his large hands clenching and releasing, seeking physical or emotional release, Conall could not say. MacKenna's elbows were draped across his knees, his head turned to the left, where stood William Wallace.

"Bruce himself was sent off by Edward to find you, to bring you in," Jamie said. "That was only few months ago." His voice was, as ever, low and rumbling, more a reverberation from his chest than words from his throat.

William Wallace squatted down on his haunches near to Jamie. He stared from one man to the next, his thumbnail digging at some bit of rabbit stuck in his teeth. His broad shoulders lifted only slightly, acknowledging this might well be true. "That was then," he said after a while. Larger by far than any man present, with lengthy flanks and massive arms, he spit the offending piece of food from his mouth, his deep set blue eyes following the trajectory and path of the bit. "He'll come around again. I ken he's got his reasons, keeping his head, keeping his lands, biding his time." He scratched his fingers through his close cropped reddish-brown beard. "You ken as well, he's no pawn of Longshanks."

"Aye," said Gregor, though his eyes remained closed. "And let Edward relax now, believing all the nobles who signed with him are true to their letters."

"They stand with Edward when his grip upon Scotland is strong; they stand against him when the tides do turn," said Jamie, with some disgust.

"But if not Bruce, then who?" Conall wondered. "Edward will find someone to betray you. A peace was offered and you dinna accept. He'll no stop until you're dead."

"Three hundred marks, Edward has promised, to the man that makes you headless." This from Gregor, his grin impudent.

"Aye," said Wallace, with a deep and bitter laugh, "but you ken the offer of peace was no related to the bribe—he'll no give me three hundred marks for my own head. Aye, they'll come. Stirling castle gone now, too, so that only we remain. But freedom should no die with me, nor any of you."

"You've got hundreds with you now," said Conall. "Back to where you started in '96. And so, we begin again. Build the armies, win the battles, loosen his grip, and the tides *will* turn."

Wallace tilted his big head toward Conall, his smile thoughtful. "Sufficiently simple, aye?"

Gregor opened his eyes, staring up at the evergreen boughs above. "Let us go, then, to make trouble down near Yrenside. The constable at Dundee is one of Edward's own, and I ken he's no making life easy for his wards."

Wallace nodded. They'd talked this strategy earlier this morn. His ragtag army of peasants and farmers and freemen, emboldened by the strength and numbers of the MacGregor, Kincaid, and MacKenna armies, was eager for a fight. They'd last ambled near Stirling, just after it was finally taken by Edward but had turned away from the sheer number of English still holding the castle, with nary an opportunity to let blood.

Conall watched Wallace stand and stretch and walk away from the yew tree. The larger-than-life man that Conall had met almost eight years ago was no more. The fight lived still within him, but the bite was gone. The spring treaty between Edward and the Scottish nobles—and more notably, the Bruce's signing of the shameful agreement—coupled with his largely ineffective trip abroad to curry favor and friends in other courts, had cut deep into Wallace's spirit. In his mind, no reason existed to betray Scotland as he believed that living without freedom wasn't living at all. Yet, curiously, he was distinctly sympathetic to those who were not sturdy enough to withstand the burden to concede, almost as if he understood that men like him, stalwart and unfaltering and true, existed only rarely.

This put Conall in mind of Tess. She shared Wallace's truism about living free, and hadn't he suffered because of it, he thought with grim humor. He'd been gone now a month but had yet to find a day that he did not think of her—damn, he'd yet to pass an hour without thinking on her, despite the company he kept and the stakes at hand. He feared losing all recollection of her smile. He feared meeting his death—as he never had before—and being then de-prived of the chance to make things right with her, for her.

Conall laid back against the mossy rocks that surrounded the giant yew, closing his eyes, bringing to mind her face. But the image scattered quick enough when Gregor spoke beside him.

"You've got the best circumstance."

Conall opened his eyes and shifted his head toward his friend.

"You close your eyes, you've got something worth seeing," Gregor said, only the smallest evidence of envy in his tone.

Conall grinned and shut his eyes again. Yes, he did.

CHAPTER 26

July and August flitted by, a routine settling over the inhabitants of the castle. The women worked studiously upon the tapestry still, the fields and orchards grew and bloomed and yielded, and Bethany began to use actual words. True, they weren't always easy to understand, sometimes frustrated both speaker and listener, but there was enough progress that the child could make her wants and needs known—and on occasion, her displeasure.

With the harvests came much work—not least of which the reaping itself, though Tess and Serena had little to do with this labor. They did, however, receive the laird's share and were made busy drying and pickling and salting large stores for the winter months. This put Leslie in a fair mood for several weeks, watching his inventories grow.

Fynn was a regular visitor and Tess was pleased to witness a romance blossom between him and Serena, the pair often finding occasion to disappear outside the castle walls, causing Tess to feel both envy and gladness for her friend.

Angus and Ranulph spent many hours together. Ranulph could be found within the castle several times a week. Though Angus's age constrained him somewhat when it came to quantity, he took considerable pride in the quality of his work, as did Ranulph.

Presently, laid out upon one of the tables in the hall were dozens of finished leather bridles. The bits were supplied by Ranulph, and Angus worked the leather to accommodate these in many assorted sizes, that they might fit destriers or work horses or palfreys. Tess had been amazed to watch his seasoned and worn hands use the tools so proficiently, make perfect measurements, and rarely have missteps. Regionally, there was only small need for the bridles, as so few people aside from soldiers owned horses. But Fynn had taken crates of these south and east and had buyers offering considerable coin for the fine craftsmanship, which lined the pockets of all three men. Aside from the bridles, Angus also helped with the sporrans and footwear and gauntlets that Ranulph had already been producing. The peddling of these—once the needs of the locals were met—fell now to Fynn as well.

While Tess and Serena sat nearby, their hands busy with mending, Leslie joined Angus at the table. He'd offered his assistance to the record keeping of the leatherwork business, as Ranulph and Angus were not literate, and Fynn not good enough with figures to see to the task. Leslie kept one log book, recording all expenses, production, inventory, and profit, eschewing any monetary boon for the aid he gave.

"A superior product once again, Angus," Leslie praised. "No sure how it is you have time for anything else." He began to tally the number of bridles just as Ranulph entered the keep.

Ranulph bid good day to all present and added several baskets and crates of leather goods to the table for Leslie to record. Fynn was expected any day and they were eager to send him off with his largest supply yet. Ranulph inspected Angus's work with sincere enthusiasm. "Aye, I've much to learn yet."

"Ranulph," Tess called, "can we send some fish home with you tonight? We've too much for the next few days, and I'd not like to see it wasted."

"Aye, that's very kind of you, milady," Ranulph said, having weeks ago learned to speak around her. "Bridie'd be thankful, as the mutton and pottage do grow old," he continued, speaking of his young wife.

"I haven't seen Bridie in so long," Serena lamented. "I understand she's busy, what with the help she gives you in the tannery, and then caring for the boys, and surely so much else, but tell her I'd love to see her."

"I'd like to meet her," Tess said, much to Ranulph's delight. "Oh, we should visit her, Serena. 'Would be ever so much easier than to have her take time out of her day to traipse up here to the castle."

"Wonderful!" Serena agreed. "Would that be alright, Ranulph? Might we visit one afternoon next week?"

"Aye, if you'd not mind," Ranulph answered, seeming quite pleased by the request. "I ken she'd like to see you again, milady, and to meet you as well, Lady Tess."

FYNN RETURNED AS EXPECTED, the next day, late in the afternoon. As he often did, he spent his first hours with Angus and Ranulph and Leslie, preferring that business was taken care of first so that it could be set aside. He spent most of his time traveling outside of Inesfree, often to larger towns and ports where trade was done. Fynn regularly brought news to Inesfree of the goings-on outside of the castle and village. Though they always hoped for word of Conall and Gregor and their armies, they knew this was unlikely, or at best, the news would not be specific to their loved ones. But he'd told them of King Edward's siege of Stirling Castle, to the south.

"With twelve siege engines, they come!" Fynn said, his astonishment clear. "But Stirling held out."

"But I thought there was a truce," said Serena.

"Aye," responded Fynn, "and so Stirling Castle was the last major stronghold, still refusing. Edward's engineers built a siege machine, right there at Stirling and when they surrendered after many months, Edward would no allow it. He wanted to try his new machine first, and then he accepted their surrender."

"So that's it?" Tess asked. "Now all of Scotland has conceded?"

"Ach, no, miss," Fynn insisted. "It's all just words. There are indeed many traitorous Scots but for most of them, it's just biding time, until the tides turn again. That's what your men and Wallace are about."

This appeased all those gathered round only minimally.

An hour later, as Tess readied herself for bed, Bethany already sleeping upon her cot, there was a knock at the door.

Tess called for entry and Serena poked her head around the door. Tess had no idea why Serena should visit her at this hour but sensed pretty quickly that it had something to do with Fynn, as her eyes—indeed, her entire face—shone brightly.

Tess didn't have long to wait, as Serena closed the door and pronounced immediately, "He wants to marry me!"

Tess's excitement promptly matched her friend's. "Oh, Serena!" The girls embraced and Tess recalled that Bethany slept so near, and whispered, "Did he...officially ask you?"

Serena shook her head, though her joy was not diminished. "He will have to ask Conall, of course."

"Have you—?" Tess began.

"Kissed him?" Serena guessed and nodded with girlish excitement, her hand covering her heart.

Tess actually referred to other things, though she supposed the vague air of innocence that still surrounded Serena answered these questions.

"Fynn says he hates trading now, because it takes him away from me."

Tess felt the warmth of such a sentiment and was truly happy for Serena.

After a little more conversation, Serena took her leave, anxious to find her own bed, or perhaps Fynn himself, Tess wondered.

Tess sighed and stared absently out the window of her tower. It was now the third of September. She watched idly, appreciating the colors of the setting sun, shooting arcs of purple and orange and red across the sky, up over the tree line. She had the length of her hair pulled over her shoulder, braiding the mass of it against her breast. She sighed, thinking Conall had been gone now almost four months. She wondered often what he might be doing. Staring at that same sunset? Routing the enemy? Saving lives? Thinking of her? Without any proof, she somehow knew he was safe yet.

She clung to this.

TESS AND SERENA WALKED into the village several days later, each with a basket hanging over one arm. Tess's borrowed cloak and Serena's soft plaid were closed tight against the stiff wind and cooler air. They were followed, as always, by two MacGregor soldiers, walking behind at a respectful distance.

Serena was speaking of Fynn, of course, and Tess silently delighted in Serena's newest habit of beginning so many sentences with, "Fynn says....".

"Will Fynn give up his trading when you marry? Tess asked.

"We haven't actually discussed it, but I do hope so."

"I do, too—for your sake. It is dreadful when someone you love is gone so long," Tess said, thinking of her own longing, wishing Serena did not have to suffer this.

Tess paused and glanced back at Serena who had stopped walking and stared at Tess with a smile that had begun slow but widened quickly. Tess stared back, waiting for an explanation for Serena's strange behavior.

"You are in love with Conall! I knew it!" Serena cried. She moved closer and grabbed Tess's hands, shaking them excitedly. "Will you marry him now?"

Tess didn't necessarily try to do an about-face, but she reviewed her own words. She let out an almost inaudible gasp, realizing what she'd just said and to whom she referred. But....

A rather ironic chuckle bubbled up. "He hasn't asked in a while."

"Oh, but he will!" Serena predicted, squeezing Tess's hands.

"Because he still craves Marlefield."

Serena shook her head. "Conall will always crave Marlefield—as would you if your home were stolen—though I daresay—"

"What?" Tess shook off Serena's hands to hold her own up, palms facing her friend, almost defensively. "What did...why did you say that?"

Serena breathed heavily and briefly shut her eyes. When they'd opened again, there were lighted with resignation.

"Because it's true!" Serena replied with rare impatience, which startled Tess. "He should have told you," she said. "Your mother should have told you—though maybe she'd hadn't any idea of her own husband's machinations. You and Conall were to be betrothed." She held up her hand when Tess opened her mouth. "'Tis true. It was so many years ago, Conall was younger than you now. Marlefield wasn't an ancient home, but it belonged to the MacGregors, for several generations at least." Her words tumbled out quicker as she continued, "The MacGregors have long sought Scottish independence, and Conall's sire had refused to sign the Ragman Rolls—they'd never vow fealty to any but a Scot. Your father pretended a desire for an alliance, but in truth, 'twas a ploy to curry favor with the English king and gain himself another castle and land." She shook her head and waved her hand, her irritation clear. "Conall should have told you. 'Twas no trivial scheme, his taking of you—your father had murdered all but handfuls of his clan, including his own sire, before his eyes. 'Twas only John that saved him."

Tess hadn't any clue what to do with this information. She barely blinked, still gaping at Serena, trying to process this monumental cache of truth. While it explained much—not least of all her father's agitated loathing of Conall, and Conall's powerful wish to claim Marlefield—it raised many questions as well. All these words spun 'round in her head. True, she'd known her father was a hard man, but she'd never—not once—thought him capable of such treachery.

"My father—murdered Conall's family." Her horror choked her.

Serena gripped her arms firmly, drawing Tess back. "And it hasn't anything to do with you, Tess. Your father's sins are his own just as Conall's actions and reactions are his."

Each breath in and out of her chest felt as if it were composed of heated and barbed steel. "My God, how can Conall even stand to—"

Serena shook her. "Because it has nothing to do with you! You didn't commit any crime. You had no idea of any of the treachery—neither your sire's nor Conall's!"

"But how can he not hate me as well?"

"Why? Because of kinship? That's ridiculous. Tess, would you hate Conall if you'd learned that his father had killed yours?"

"No," she answered quite easily, but thought to add, "though I would not allow myself to love him."

Serena gave a short laugh. "I believe he did try."

Tess found no humor in this.

Serena pressed, "Tess, you are not your father and Conall knows this."

"I know that," Tess finally said. "My father—it has never been about me. But I'd thought Conall..."

"Yes. He does," Serena said, finishing Tess's thought. "Whatever it began as, you know—you know!—that is dead. It hasn't been about Marlefield for a long time."

This had teased her for a while. She often rejected it, favoring stubbornness over hope. Serena's ferocity just now insisted she finally acknowledge that it wasn't about Marlefield. Conall's eyes danced before her, the blue so clear. She recalled his kiss, gentle and stirring and needful. And his temper, after the incident at May Day, all that ferocity wasn't about Marlefield, she knew, only her.

"I love him." She saw nothing just now but his face. Tess covered her mouth with her fingers. But she could not take it back. "It's not anything I'd imagined." Her words were slow and slight and musing, "It clutches my chest and waters my eyes and takes all my breaths."

Serena smiled wondrously and hugged Tess to her.

They continued on to the village, though Tess had nearly lost interest in the purpose of their visit. She wanted only to return to the castle, to her tower room, and confront all this information and dissect it and tear it apart. She tried to relive conversations and moments with Conall, applying all this newfound knowledge, but was at a loss to create any different circumstance than the present: that she was in love with him, but still hadn't any notion if he might return the sentiment.

They passed by large wheat fields now shorn to the ground and the tithe barn, larger than most of the homesteads, before reaching the crofter's cottages, which were clustered around several crossing roads. Each tenant's space was large enough for their own dwelling, a farmstead, and a garden. The village shared a communal pastureland, which sat on a rise at the north end of town.

Serena led Tess past the first few cottages and turned up the grassless walk of the next, slighter larger than the others, with whitewashed stone under the fresh thatch of the roof. She rapped smartly upon the wooden door and stepped back to wait. The two soldiers remained at the road, their backs to the cottage.

The door opened and filled with a young woman, whose bright and friendly green eyes passed nervously over Serena and Tess. Tess thought her very pretty indeed, with stunning red hair and a most disarming smile to accompany those pretty eyes. She stood taller than Serena, with lanky arms and a long neck.

"Milady," she greeted, "tis fine indeed to see you again."

"And you, Bridie," Serena returned, "and this is Lady Tess Munro."

Bridie turned her gaze to Tess. "I ken well who you are, milady, and I canna say I've ever been more pleased to meet anyone."

Tess believed her, so transparent and constant was her gaze. "The pleasure is mine, truly. Your husband and Lady Serena speak often and fondly of you."

"Aye, but where are my manners? Come in. Come in."

They stepped inside and Tess was surprised to find the interior of the cottage so pretty and cheerful. Either Ranulph or Bridie herself had whitewashed the walls inside as well, brightening the sizeable main room which served as their eating, living and sleeping area. The room was very long, with a wide bed and small trunk at one end, the wall nearest hung with many garments in assorted sizes. In the center of the room sat the hearth, under a purposeful hole in the roof, and at this end near the door was the family's dining table, just large enough for four, with squat benches on either side of it. Kitchen utensils hung from pegs on the wall near the table and in the corner, stacked neatly, sat many buckets and pots and crocks.

Bridie waved her hand toward the table. "Please sit."

They did, setting their baskets upon the table.

"We've brought you some black bun," Serena said, pulling the linen away from the pastry covered fruit cake.

"And honey." Tess revealed several small crocks in her basket.

Bridie expressed her joy over these items and thanked the ladies effusively.

"'Tis very kind, indeed," said Bridie, "but then I ken you would be." Bridie offered to carve some of the black bun, but Serena insisted it was for her and Ranulph and her boys.

"Aye, they're gone with old man Creagh, putting the cows to pasture."

"How old are your boys, Bridie?" Tess asked.

"Five and seven now, but they're growing up fast these past few weeks with their da gone so much." She was quick to add, "Aye, but milady, dinna think we're no grateful for... well, everything."

"Not at all." Serena quickly put her at ease. "But, Bridie, Tess and I have been discussing something, and it has to do with all this extra work for Ranulph. And we have an idea."

THIRTY MINUTES LATER, they left Bridie's home, feeling quite pleased to have the matter settled. The MacGregor soldiers moved off the walkway to let them pass and fell into step behind them.

"Oh, she's quite lovely," Tess said of Bridie.

"Isn't she though?" Serena agreed.

They talked and walked, and Tess made mention that she was sorry that she'd not asked Bridie if she were any good with a needle.

At the question in Serena's eyes, Tess explained, "I cannot, after all, wait until Bethany grows old enough to help us with that bloody tapestry."

Serena laughed at this. "We should have started with the smaller ones."

Coming just upon the ledge of Godit's Rise, which showed the castle below, they saw immediately that the entire area in front of the gate was filled with hundreds of mounted men. Soldiers. It took not one more second to find the blue and gray banner and distinguish the eagle centered upon it.

Conall.

CHAPTER 27

Conall nearly bounded off Mercury before the animal had stopped fully. The boys from the stables would come to collect the steeds, but he paused to hastily untie several items from the worn leather saddle bag.

His shoulder was thumped, and he turned to find John giving him one of those fish-eating smirks he so loved to bestow, knowing very well what had Conall behaving so anxiously.

John said nothing, just tipped his big head and pointed beyond Conall, to the west toward the path from the rise.

Conall turned and saw several persons coming from the direction of the village, moving swiftly. He recognized instantly two Mac-Gregor soldiers and in the next instant identified the forms of Tess and Serena, though their heavy outerwear concealed much.

She was far away, across the field, coming just from the bottom of Godit's Rise. He was sure at first that his eyes deceived him. But no, it was Tess—bright hair, beloved face and all. Ah, that face, which had haunted him for months, became clearer as she neared. While all those around him still moved forward and through the gate, Conall's hand fell away from his saddle bag. He stared for only a moment before, besieged with great purpose, he began to walk toward her.

He was home. And Tess was here.

He marched across the field, leaving the castle and army behind, his starved gaze only for her. She picked up her skirts and began to run toward him, the hood of her cloak falling away from her hair. Conall lengthened his own stride.

Upon the great open field of Inesfree, against a backdrop of a dark gray sky, amid the tall grass of the late summer, they met neatly in the middle, neither stopping, but crashing into one another. His arms engulfed her, his lips crushed against hers, devouring her. Her arms hugged him close, clawing into his back. In the swift breeze, her hair fluttered outward, her skirts flapped against their twined legs while the wind billowed his tunic much like a sail, save for where her arms pressed against him.

When he pulled back, she cried out. But his hands cupped her face, his eyes darting from one feature to the next. "Dinna cry, lass," he said, a laugh, entirely jubilant, in his voice.

"Oh, Conall," she cried, but it was stirred with a nervous laugh. She hugged him tight again, laying her head against his chest. "Oh, I have dreamed of this."

Above her, Conall closed his eyes and held her tight. If he only dreamed now, it was too steeped in rightness to take for granted. He was holding Tess. He needed to absorb this, feel her, burrow deep inside and never surface.

Inhaling of her clean, fresh scent, Conall knew the fears that had plagued him for so many months—that he might return to Inesfree to find Tess gone—were unfounded. "You stayed," he said, breathed into her upturned face. "Why?"

Because I love you. Those were the words he wanted to hear. Until this very moment, despite the haunted dreams and the ache he'd known for just one more moment with Tess, he'd not realized he'd craved those words.

Until now.

"I promised."

She continued to press her head into is chest. She couldn't see his interrupted joy at what had been a rather remarkable homecoming.

Stiffening, he lowered his hands. That damn promise. For Bethany. For Angus. It had nothing to do with him, save that he'd used it to keep her here. Because he couldn't bear the thought of Tess not being here, not being with him.

He could not deny the disillusionment he felt. He'd just survived months and months of brutal and bloody fighting—some of the worst he'd ever seen—and had watched William Wallace, that great hero of this long war of independence, grow more and more desperate and weary. He'd begun to feel as if Scotland might now be actually further away than ever from complete freedom, and through all this rarely a day, sometimes not even an hour, had passed that he hadn't thought of Tess, and his desire to be with her.

"Conall?" She lifted her head, now sensing his sudden detachment.

"I'm to meet with John and Leslie," he said evasively. Dismissively.

Her hands slipped away from his shirtfront and all that animation faded from her features.

"Just like that?"

"Just like that." He kept his gaze hard.

The stricken look on her face nearly softened him, made him beg. The light fading from those most remarkable green eyes almost undid him. But then she clamped her lips and turned away from him.

He sighed, the long breath releasing all that pent up hopefulness and the discontent that came with the reality of their reunion.

Oh, I have dreamed of this, she had said.

That was something.

Her retreating figure drew his attention.

She held her shoulders straight and her head high, arms swinging at her sides as she marched away. The tall grass reached near to her thighs, but she stalked through it as if it swept only her ankles. She would leave him, just like that. Conall frowned. No argument? Just walk away? His frown creased into a full-fledged scowl. "Son of a bitch." He cursed his own stupidity. Hands fisted at his sides. And he ran her down, reaching her quickly, the swaying grass certainly no hindrance to him. She turned, at the sound of his pursuit, just as he reached out and grabbed her arm.

Fresh tears shimmered in her eyes, darkening the orbs to emerald. She fought to stave off a trembling of her lips.

"Tess," he said, decidedly uncomfortable with the words forming in his head. "I had hoped you might have thought of me, maybe...missed me." And he waited. Endlessly it seemed, while she regarded him, fighting still the threat of tears.

Her expression registered only the briefest hint of surprise, but then softened, her face tilting, her eyes lightening.

"I would have thought that my ungainly gallop across the field to meet you might have said as much." She said, her tone even, clinging yet to her own hurt, he guessed.

Conall nodded, holding her gaze, and his hand moved down from her upper arm, waiting until she turned her hand into his. She did so, slowly. How he loved the feel of her hand, so very soft and small, engulfed in his. Always, this had been good.

"I've been away for too long," he said, by way of excuses for his untenable behavior. "I forget how to...be 'round you." He was staring at their linked hands.

She stepped closer and put her free hand on his cheek, bringing his gaze to hers.

"Not like that." A slow smile emerged.

He laughed and swung her up in his arms, relieved by her forgiveness. God, she felt so damn good here. Her arms, wrapping around his neck, brought with them a peacefulness he'd not experienced in so long.

They walked hand in hand toward the castle. The large open space in front of the gate was stilled filled with most of Conall's army.

Those with family inside had probably already found their loved ones, might even now still be in their arms.

"Gregor?" She asked.

"He'd left more than a month ago," Conall told her. "Was talk of some English bringing trouble down near the border. We'll meet again. But I see you're near bursting with news to share."

Conall grinned. She was nearly bouncing beside him.

She nodded excitedly. "I'd almost forgotten—no, I hadn't forgotten, 'tis too huge to have forgotten, but then you kissed me and...well, where is John?"

Conall glanced around at the faces as they walked through all the horses and men and finally gained the outer, then inner bailey. "There." He pointed to the captain, holding up the rear foot of one of the large destriers, inspecting the shoe.

"John!" Tess called out as they neared. The big man turned, and upon seeing Tess, set the hoof down gently. He stood straight and faced Tess, barely in time to catch her embrace. The old man's eyes close while he hugged her back. Conall knew that feeling, that warmth, that irrefutable sense of peace John felt just now.

Tess released him, her eagerness tangible. "I know you have much to share," she said. "Supper is probably a fine time to fill us in, but—oh, my—so much has happened. You must come with me!"

It would have been impossible to resist her enthusiasm, which they had no desire to do, and they followed Tess into the keep.

Only a handful of soldiers had reached the hall as of yet. Conall's eye scanned the room, satisfied that it appeared almost exactly as he'd left it. Even Angus seemed not to have moved, perched as he was by the hearth, though perhaps he sported a newer tunic, courtesy of Tess, Conall guessed. Tess walked immediately to Angus, then bent down, her back to him and John near the door. When she straightened and turned, he saw that she held Bethany in her arms. The transformation of the child shocked Conall. She seemed years older, her hair pulled back into neat braids, these tied up atop her head. She was dressed in a miniature version of Tess's burgundy gown, complete with matching metal belt and the same embroidery about the collar. And her face—she was smiling and appeared so carefree. Conall was stunned at this change.

She spotted Conall and John and her eyes widened, her joy evident.

"Cone!" She cried out, her arms reaching for him.

Conall's jaw dropped. He looked at Tess, whose own delight was a beautiful thing. Conall and John exchanged glances, wearing similar dumbfounded expressions.

He moved swiftly and claimed Bethany from Tess.

"Cone!" She said again.

Conall nodded, barely able to contain his emotions. He did not bother to hide these feelings, just buried his head against her and squeezed her tight, letting this new joy wash over him.

Bethany squirmed though—she had more to say. Conall lifted his head and turned them to face John, who only now moved, walking slowly at them.

"And who is that?" Tess forced Bethany's attention to the captain.

Bethany scrunched up her face, making silly eyes at the older man as he so often did to her. "John," she said finally.

Conall had never seen his captain cry. Not ever. Not when he'd lost his wife, nor any of his three sons. Not when Conall's father had been murdered. Never once during the last few months when they'd seen more death and brutality than ever before.

But he cried now, unabashedly. Tears fell from his eyes and a strangled noise came from deep inside. Conall handed Bethany off to him and watched Bethany throw her arms around the big bear's neck.

Tess stood with her hands covering her mouth. In joy and awe and wonder. Her own eyes were wet. Even Angus, his head tilted and listening, displayed a supreme satisfaction.

"Angus, my friend," Conall knelt down to the blind man and touched his knee.

"Aye, now, laird, 'tis good to have you home." His voice was gentle.

Tess was crowding John and Bethany. "Bethany, what do we say when someone comes home after being gone a long time?"

Bethany looked at Tess, frowning while she tried to remember. Her little hands twisted over each other.

Tess nodded.

"Love you."

Tess laughed. "Yes, that, too."

And that was enough.

"That's the highlight, of course," Tess said. She slid her hand into the crook of Conall's arm as they watched John and Bethany. "But oh, there's so much more."

Conall didn't quite have words to define what he felt, but whatever it was, it warmed him and soothed him and heartened him, and he knew he couldn't ever remember a time when he had felt like this.

Leslie MacDonnell stepped into the hall and came straight to Conall. "Laird, 'tis happy we are to welcome you home."

Conall shook his hand, appreciating these thoughts.

"Leslie," Tess said, "we should make arrangements for the garderobe to be available to Conall and his officers. Let's have Henry and Donald and Richard keep the tubs filled and warm and fresh. And maybe offer some of Fynn's wine?"

Leslie raised his brow at this request. "Wine in the garderobe, Lady Tess?"

Tess nodded. "Why not? They deserve it. Let them relax without any care. Doesn't it sound lovely?" She'd glanced at Conall.

Leslie laughed. "Sounds like we'll have a bunch of drunken naked men right soon, lass."

Tess giggled as well, and said with mock severity, "Make sure they don't drown."

Conall watched this exchange silently, a bit befuddled. *So much more*, indeed, he thought, recalling Tess's words from only a moment ago. He hadn't any idea that Leslie had even known Tess's name, and certainly had never witnessed his very staid steward ever laughing. Laughing, for Chrissakes!

And, Fynn? And, wine?

Leslie had disappeared, about Tess's bidding no doubt. Tess stared up at him with a pretty smile as if even this very significant change still had nothing to do with the surprises she had in store for him.

Serena entered the hall, still with her plaid draped around her, holding the hand of a tall man with steady eyes, who showed not the slightest hesitation coming to stand before Conall. Serena's bubbly smile and merry eyes enlightened Conall a bit to her attachment.

Serena embraced Conall, delighting in his safe return and introduced the man as Fynn, Angus's son. The picture was becoming clearer.

Conall shook his hand, allowing some approval that the man demurred not at all.

Conall threw a glance at Tess, who shrugged offhandedly though he could well read the pleasure in her eyes.

"A great pleasure, MacGregor," Fynn said. "And a great debt I owe you for your care of me da."

Conall only titled his head.

But Tess didn't allow him the opportunity to make the man prove his worth.

"It's too short notice to properly feast tonight," Tess said, "but we will sup as usual and I'll talk to Eagan about how long he'll need to prepare for a proper welcome home repast."

Conall didn't need a feast, though knew they were customary for an army returning after so long a time away. What he needed, after that bath she'd tempted him with, was her.

He reached for her hand, pulled her away from whatever she was just about to say to Serena and turned them both around so that his back blocked her from view of everyone present.

"Lass, I'm headed off to that respite you promised in the garderobe—I feel I haven't been clean since I left." He pinned her with his gaze, making sure there was little question about what he was thinking. In a low and husky voice, he added, "And I suggest you find my chamber in the meantime. I will no be long, and you should be naked." Pretty words, maybe the actual end of the evening, might have served him better, he knew, but having seen her and kissed her and touched her, he hadn't that kind of patience just now.

And she didn't seem to mind, maybe felt a little thrill herself. Her eyes had widened, but he was well aware of the breathy little rush of air that escaped her. She nodded, barely, tightly, and her lips parted. Conall squeezed her hand and headed toward his bath.

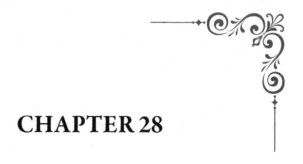

CHAPTER 28

T ess was an agitated mess.
　　Be naked?

While his words had exhilarated her, had indeed stirred those dormant butterflies, it was his eyes, that incredible blue of his gaze promising such delight, that had set her in such a dither.

She stood now in his chamber, as requested, debating how, exactly, to be naked. She'd actually stood for many minutes, chewing her lip, trying to decide how to proceed. Just drop her gown and kirtle to the ground, and stand awkwardly, waiting? She glanced around. Sit in that lone chair? She wished that capricious maid from Marlefield was here to ask; she'd seemed to have an extensive knowledge of these matters. Butterflies indeed! Tess placed her hand over her belly, as if that might thwart the excitement that danced there.

Forcing herself to do *something*, she removed the metal belt, fashioned of many rings linked together, and laid it on that chair. She kicked off her soft shoes and pulled her braid in front of her and began unraveling it. She was thinking just now that in a very short time, Conall's naked body would be pressed against her. She closed her eyes, recalling exactly how that had felt, his chest pressed to hers. A warmth was felt inside at this remembrance, starting near her chest but lowering to settle between her legs. She breathed deeply and let herself enjoy how that teased her.

When her hair was completely loosened, she pushed it all back over her shoulder and unlaced the bodice of her gown and pulled it up over her head, adding that to the chair as well. She sat, still in her long sleeved chemise, upon that trunk, and lifted one leg to untie her garter and roll down her thin hose. She raised the other leg and did the same. The door opened just as she pushed the fabric down over her ankle. She lifted her gaze, her hands still.

Conall stood there, dressed only in a fresh tunic, his plaid seeming to have been wrapped rather hastily. He held his sword and belt in his hand and wore no shoes. His gaze, upon her now bare leg, was hungry.

She couldn't be sure if what crawled around her belly just then was nerves or excitement. She swallowed and applied her gaze again to her task, removing the hose and laying both upon the chair with her gown and belt. She turned, standing straight, her hands on the strings of her chemise, and watched Conall close the door and drop the brace before propping his sword against it.

He faced her, standing only a few feet from her, his hands on his plaid, unwinding it as Tess unlaced her chemise. Conall dropped the plaid around him and lifted his tunic over his head.

Tess let her eyes wander over him, completely naked now. Her mouth opened as her breathing changed, taking in his perfect form, those impossibly wide shoulders and his magnificently sculpted chest, his flat abdomen and trim hips on top of his well-muscled thighs. She was shy yet to stare overlong at his arousal, but even her passing glance, showing his want of her, created a heat and wetness between her own legs.

He was discolored in several spots and she knew she'd have questions later about the origins of those black-and-blues but just now, as he waited, she pulled loose her chemise and let it fall to her feet with a confidence she didn't exactly feel.

They stood now, not close enough to touch, but completely bare. She watched his jaw tighten as his eyes raked her. She felt a blush heat every part of her body that his eyes caressed. Tess took one tentative step toward him, their gazes locked now, and he closed the distance with his own sure step. He lifted one had to stretch it out upon her hip, just rested it there, his eyes following, feeling her. Tess's nipples hardened. His other hand found her other hip, and his fingers sunk into her flesh, not forcefully, just enough to pull her near. First his erection touched low on her belly then her breasts met his skin, just grazing under his own nipples. Tess gasped or moaned, she didn't know which, and his mouth found hers just as all space between them vanished. No simple kiss, this, as they came together open-mouthed, tongues finding each other as his hands melted from her hips, sliding around to her buttocks, his fingers grasping the underside, pulling her up against him. Tess's arms gripped his shoulders as he actually lifted her off the ground, never breaking the near-bruising kiss. His hands had moved under her thighs, bringing her legs around him as he walked them toward the bed. Tess felt liquid heat surface as the very center of her was so open and exposed against his stomach, but only briefly before he lowered both of them onto the furs that still covered the mattress. He broke the kiss to take one nipple into his mouth, her hands now in his hair, encouraging him. She shifted her hips, seeking movement against him, a glad cry forming, knowing her would soon be inside her.

"I cannot wait," she moaned, shimmying against him.

"I've been dreaming of this for months, lass," he groaned, moving to the other breast, giving the same generous attention with his tongue and teeth. "I'm no about to finish yet."

"You can go slow later," she told him, making no effort to mask her need, her hands reaching for his cock. He shifted and rose from her breasts and her fingers found him, wrapped around him and moved up and down as he'd taught her, while his lips claimed hers again. A lone drop of liquid came from the head and they both moaned, with Tess now directing him between her legs. God, she ached.

She touched the tip of him just to the core of her and felt herself contract right there where she opened to him. She pulled her hand away to fit herself against him. The tip of him was pushing into her and need so brutal built inside her she whimpered. Conall groaned into her mouth then lifted himself, his hands on the bed to leverage himself deeper until he was fully inside her. He lowered his head briefly, almost to his chest and stopped moving so that only Tess moved, slowly, just feeling him inside her. Then with greater purpose, she tilted her hips so that he was deep and then not, and deep again until he joined her actions and they moved rhythmically together. Her fingers dug into his broad shoulders as their growing need demanded they move faster and faster.

Every sense of hers was fixated on the exact feel of him thrusting inside and sliding out. Yearning soared, twirling deep within until she was frantic underneath him, searching for that promised release, aching to have it burst upon her. It did finally, and she cried with soul-throbbing pleasure, as all that slaked decadence flowed about and within and over her.

Conall exploded right after she did, calling her name while he continued to thrust into her, until finally his movements slowed as his head nestled into her shoulder. She inhaled the scent of him, musk and horse and man, closing her eyes while her breathing slowed, finally.

Conall lifted his head, his own breathing nearly returned to normal, his skin glowing with a bare sheen of perspiration.

"I'd live again those last many months to come home to this," he said and kissed her forehead and her cheek and her lips.

"Might have been better if you'd just stayed and we were doing this all the time."

A drained laugh rushed from him. "Aye. Or that."

Conall rolled to her side and gathered her close, so that her back was pressed against his front. They were quiet then, just breathing and thinking and feeling.

After a while, as her eyes began to droop, she asked him about all those bruises covering so much of his beautiful body.

"'Tis just war, lass." He sounded equally groggy.

"But is it done now?"

"No until we're free."

A minute later, "I should go down to the kitchens, give Eagan a hand."

"Aye," he murmured.

And they slept.

WHEN SHE WOKE, TESS was scandalized that she had slept, naked in his arms in the middle of the day when there was so much to be done. She scrambled quickly from his thick and warm arms, thus rousing him. Conall rolled onto his back and stretched his arms upward then tucked them beneath his head to watch her hurriedly dress.

She knew he watched, which maybe contributed to the length of time it took her to find the proper end of her hose to begin with. *Should've donned the chemise first*, she thought, finally having one length of hose situated over her foot. She stood sideways and rolled the hose up to just over her knee and tied the garter round it, then repeated this action with the other hose.

"Tess," he called when she finished the second one. She turned and looked at him, standing completely naked save for those garters and hose. She was glad for the length of her hair, which concealed much. She waited. When he said nothing, just lay his gaze upon every inch of her body, causing heat to rise, Tess placed her hands on her naked hips and tried to appear stern and not aroused again. In truth, between his heated regard and the sight of him lying there, so magnificent upon the furs, she was sore pressed to contain a shiver.

"Don't let that thing stand up now," she warned, her voice lacking any sort of reprimand. "I've work to do."

This elicited a grand bark of laughter from Conall, who climbed from the bed and came to stand before her.

She lifted her hand between them. "I'm serious."

"Aye, lass, as am I."

But he only kissed her lightly and turned to open the trunk at the foot of his bed. Tess warred with her disappointment, staring at his broad back and those wonderfully shifting muscles as he bent to retrieve items from within the trunk.

"Keep gawking, lass...." He said without turning, a beautiful threat in his tone.

Tess shook herself and pivoted to find her chemise, hearing yet more laughter from him. The pleasure of their love-making had certainly faded by now, but the warmth and joy at their ease with each other gratified her nearly as much.

CONALL RETURNED TO the hall, having waited until Tess had been gone for several minutes. Not for one second did he believe any adult downstairs hadn't a clue what they'd been doing for the past few hours but it had helped to relieve her apprehension and so he had played along.

He'd come into the hall to find that bastard, Ranulph, sitting with Angus, a bit of leather goods about them, their hands busy braiding strips into long belts. His lip curled unconsciously, though he recalled Tess's invitation to the man to come to Inesfree. Aside from his abilities upon the battlefield, there were other uses for Conall's immense size. He strode directly and assertively to where they sat, delighting in the troubled look upon Ranulph's face as he neared.

Tess emerged from the kitchen just in time to ruin his attempt at intimidation, calling out cheerfully—purposefully, Conall was sure— "Aren't they wonderful, laird? I bet even London itself hasn't a tanner with as much skill as these two."

Conall noticed Angus's silent amusement at the whole scene while he let his eyes rest intimidatingly upon Ranulph, even as Tess came to stand beside him.

With great innocence, she asked, "You remember Ranulph, do you not?"

"Aye, I do." He let his voice continue to menace.

Ranulph stood slowly. Angus's hand stopped braiding, just sat holding the strips while he listened.

"Laird, I would express my appreciation for all—"

Tess waved a hand, her smile still tenaciously and exasperatingly bright. Conall could just feel it, though he'd yet to remove his gaze from the man.

"He knows well of your gratitude, Ranulph. He's happy to have you here, what with the extra income you've brought to Inesfree, and the care you've shown Angus, and too, for being such a great friend to me. He is elated, I assure you."

He didn't look it.

Angus's shoulders were shaking, and he'd lowered his head to his narrow chest.

Conall would have words for him later, as well, but for now, he just turned and walked away.

SUPPER WAS A LIVELY affair. It began first with Conall giving a full account of what the army had endured and achieved while gone to Wallace's side. He stood at the center of the family table, with Tess and Angus and John seated at his right, and Serena and Fynn and Leslie at his left, and spoke with carefully chosen words.

"The war is no finished, and freedom is no yet ours. But I tell you, as I stand here, if no for the bravery and steadfastness of our own William Wallace, we'd be now completely under the yoke of Longshanks." Cheers were called out and Conall paused to acknowledge these. "His continued resistance to the English is a reminder that Scotland belongs only to us, and that we must defend her unto the death." He lowered his voice and said solemnly, "To this end, we lost some of our own and we owe them a debt, and gratitude for our lives, that likely we'll no ever be able to repay. Forty-six men gone these last months, and not one, I swear, will have died in vain. Freedom will be ours." More shouts and calls for freedom. Conall raised his cup, "To the MacGregors and MacDonnells felled at Tobermory! and Kirkcudbright! and Linlithgow!" This time, the answering cheer was thunderous as cups were raised throughout the hall.

"And we canna forget," Conall continued, and waited for quiet again, "their families belong to us now, as they ever have. 'Tis our honored duty to provide protection and succor and aid."

"Aye, aye" was hollered and repeated from table to table.

Conall sat, and peasants poured from the corridor, arms laden with trays and trenchers of herring and pike and salmon, as if they'd waited around the corner for their laird to finish speaking. These were followed by puddings of egg and cheese, and baked apples with honey. The harp was strummed from the far end of the hall and conversation grew spirited once again.

Conall sat, looking around at those gathered in the hall. Aye, it was good to be home. His eyes fell upon Ranulph, as he sat with some laughing red-head and two boys that surely must be his own sons.

Perhaps Tess caught his eyes resting upon her 'friend', perhaps she noted his tightening jaw. She placed her small hand over his as it sat on the table.

"I don't want him here."

She completely ignored his dark tone which would have at one time sent her scurrying. "I'm very sorry to say that not only is that impossible, but it's about to get worse."

"I dinna even want to ask what that means."

But this didn't stop her from explaining. "Now that Ranulph and Angus have so much business, we thought it best if he and his family moved up here to the castle. Bridie and the boys have been left too much on their own, more so now that Ranulph has started traveling with Fynn. Bridie can help in the kitchens or the laundry—according to Ranulph there isn't anything she cannot do. Serena promises her fruit tarts are mouthwatering. And, Leslie has agreed to begin instructions for reading and writing for Bethany and Bridie's boys. But don't worry, it doesn't take away from his own duties as I've been helping Leslie in the storerooms."

There was so much information in these statements, Conall felt as if he'd been gone not only months but years. As laird, and as one with a keen interest in his own castle, he asked, "Does their croft sit empty?"

"No. They're to let it out to another family."

"Why dinna Serena help Leslie in the storerooms?" Not that he took any issue with Tess working there, but Serena was essentially the lady of the manor.

"She's too busy trying to learn how to keep the records for Ranulph and Angus, which Leslie has been teaching her. And, too, she has been visiting market towns lately, trying to find a better source for the hides. The business has expanded so much, Ranulph's supply has been wiped out and his present supplier of hides cannot keep up. Leslie says that Inesfree is making much more coin from Ranulph's tithe with this growing business, as compared to what he'd produced and sold on his own."

"It's no too much for Angus? He is verra old."

"He is much happier working, this I know. He wants to contribute; this gives him worth. And truly, he and Ranulph are perfect for each other. Ranulph is very skilled but Angus is *gifted*, and they each enjoy the benefit of that—teaching and learning."

One of the kitchen girls approached the front of the table, looking slightly harried. "Milady," she said desperately to Tess. "Cook is wanting you to decide what he might do with Renny. He just returned."

Conall had no idea who Renny was.

Tess set down her knife. "Oh, Moira, I'd forgotten to tell Eagan—please inform him that I spoke with Renny. You can tell Eagan it's all settled and Renny should resume his duties." The girl bobbed her head, and turned to leave but Tess added, her tone hushed now, "Moira, please remind Renny to apologize to Eagan. Oh, and tell him to make it flowery. That should soften him."

Moira bobbed again and grinned at this last bit before returning to the kitchen.

And Conall wondered if he'd perhaps returned to the wrong keep. He didn't bother to ask about Renny or what he might have done to have need of Tess's intercession. But damn, if she didn't look so...happy. He considered that he'd left her, all those months ago, a frightened girl, nearly broken by these very people she now called friends, who deferred to her and laughed when they never had before, while she conspired all these little arrangements so that everyone else was happy, too.

Was it really that easy? To have them eating out of your hand, did you just cater to them, see to their well-being, indifferent to your own? He didn't think life worked that way. But here she was, one of them now, sought after and adored.

"You're stewing," she observed, while she continued eating.

"I dinna like change." Actually, he didn't dislike it. Mayhap, it was merely the unexpected he struggled with, and time would settle that.

But Tess had set aside her knife and turned to him. "Conall, Inesfree is your home. If—if you don't like something or would rather some change be undone...."

He shook his head. There was no change that wasn't good or didn't make better sense. "But I don't have to like it." His eyes again found Ranulph. "And if you think to sway me with your very delectable body, you should ken—"

"Can I do that?" He could very well see the intrigues turning around in her pretty head. "Is that possible?"

Best she didn't know the truth then. "Nae, lass, 'tis only for weak men, that." He almost laughed out loud at her crestfallen expression and was thankful she'd hadn't any idea how she did indeed weaken him.

LATER THAT EVENING, when Conall was finally finished in the hall, when all items requiring the laird's attention had been addressed, when Tess herself had been gone more than an hour, having carried a sleepy Bethany away, he entered his chamber to find it empty. He wasn't sure why this surprised him—he'd just expected Tess to be there, waiting.

But he wasn't about to sleep the night through without her. He closed the door to his chamber and climbed one more flight of stairs. In the tower room, he found her already asleep, snuggled under the heavy furs, and with not one line marring her forehead.

He stared for a long while, enjoying the lengthy sweep of her hair across the furs and pillows. It was, in some places, very near to the color of those furs and matched perfectly that soft blanket of smooth wool, and still other parts were highlighted to perfection by the low fire, streaking the silky tresses with gold.

He passed a glance over Bethany, found the child sleeping with her arms and legs tucked underneath, pushing her bum into the air. Quietly, he doffed his belt and sword, laying them at the side of the bed. His plaid followed, though the proper wearing of it did require some time to remove. He didn't worry about anything else but pulled back the furs and joined her, folding himself around her, his arm slowly and smoothly pulling her close.

She woke, just a bit, and smiled at him.

"I don't want you in the tower, lass. I want you next to me."

Tess nestled against him. Her response was a long time coming and uttered rather sleepily. "But then I would ask, 'what of Bethany?', and you would say, 'she can come too,'" —she paused to let out a very vocal yawn— "and then I would say, 'you might as well just sleep here then.'"

Conall smiled at this and fell asleep with Tess in his arms.

CHAPTER 29

"I need to discuss something with you." Conall said to John the next evening.

John's bushy brows crunched over his blue eyes, considering Conall's intense expression. "Will it require ale?'

Conall shrugged. "Aye, it might."

"C'mon, then."

John stood and slid his fingers into two cups, taking them up from where they'd sat on the table, and grabbed up the crock of ale with his other hand. Conall followed him outside, across the yard and up the steps to the gatehouse. They acknowledged the watchmen and strode further down the elevated walkway. John stopped some distance away from the guards and poured out two cups from the jug. He handed one to Conall.

"I get three guesses who we might need to discuss?"

Conall considered the view before him, out over the yard and beyond. There wasn't much to see, save the fields and line of trees, shown by the light of the moon.

He took a long sip of the ale.

"That night, at Marlefield, and then after, why did you no let me seek revenge? You of all people?"

John nodded and there was something in his demeanor which suggested he'd expected this question, maybe even long before now.

He bent at the waist and leaned his thick arms on the stone embrasures. "Is true what I'd said then—before your dear mother passed, she bade me promise to keep you safe. Your da were an honorable man, a guid man, but he were a hothead, and dinna your mam know it." He was quiet then, memories teasing him. His lips pursed and quirked. He stared now into his cup, the ale half gone, giving the impression of being very far away. "Belle died first, with our third. Your mam were gone the following year. Then me boys were gone, and you were all we had left. Your da dinna dote on you, that's no what you needed. But he was fearful all the time, that's what made him underestimate Munro. He wasn't thinking straight, kept looking on the English, as if they were the only threat." He waved a burly hand. "Dinna matter now. That's why I grabbed you out of there. I vowed to your ma. But I tell you, the thought of you being eaten up with vengeance, or dying too soon for it, I could no bear it. Muriel would've haunted me dead, I ken."

He looked sideways at Conall, two hands around the cup now. "Anger, regret, vengeance—they've no place with the living, boy." He sighed deeply, suddenly much older than even his advanced years. "When you came to me with the idea about marrying the lass, I dinna like it, but I thought, 'let him have it'. No fighting, no violence, just a wedding."

He stopped talking though his gaze and his thoughts were perhaps still in the past.

Conall stood beside him, considering John's words.

After a while, when Conall hadn't asked one question or uttered one word, John said, "So here I am, guessing you're fretting about the lass now, and wondering what you're really about, 'cause it sure as shite is no about Marlefield anymore."

"But it should be," Conall finally said.

"Why? Why, boy?" John stood straight now, while Conall stared out over the battlements now. "Why? For all the dead gone before you? What's it got you? Let it die."

Conall's gaze swung sharply to John. "Let it die? I owe my father—"

"You owe him nothin' boy! You owe yourself, tha's all. You planning on spending the rest of your bluidy life correcting his mistakes? He made a mistake! It got him killed. Munro is a monster! It'll get him killed one day. But you're young, you got the lass—why is that no enough? Happy no good enough for you?"

"I can no be happy if I abandon this."

"Then you dinna deserve to be!" he roared. He sighed then, rubbing his hand over his thick beard. "You want permission, is that it? You think your da's up there saying 'avenge me, boy'? Aye, he's no. He's with your sweet mam and believe me, they dinna want this for you."

Another pause, while he stared hard at Conall. "Wed the lass, boy. No for Marlefield. No for your da. Marry her 'cause you love her, 'cause she loves you back. Have bairns and grow old. Life is hard enough." He slid his huge paw around the jug but didn't refill his cup. "If you dinna wed her, then send her home. Dinna be making your sweet ma weep no more." And with that, he stepped around Conall and walked away, the crock of ale swinging near his thigh.

INSIDE THE STABLES the next day, Conall and the farrier and the stablemaster discussed the state of the army's stock of horses. Their time with Wallace had diminished the number of MacGregor war horses significantly; in truth, they'd lost more mounts than men. Presently, the number of mares who would foal in the spring was not enough to replenish their stock. And while most of Conall's knights were responsible for securing and caring for their own steeds, he would still need to purchase dozens himself to outfit the rest of his army properly.

"If the army needs to move before spring," his stablemaster, Davidh, was saying, "you'll need to do so with smaller numbers."

Conall shook his head, "We won't march again before then," he assured him, and hoped that was actually the case. But he knew he could at any time receive a call to arms from any of the Scottish loyalists fighting for freedom.

They wrapped up their discussion and agreed they would need to travel in the spring to Glasgow to replace the lost war horses.

Conall turned and spied Tess exiting the keep. As he was within the shadows of the stable still, she did not notice him as her eyes wandered the courtyard. She was greeted by several peasants in the yard and smiled prettily at them. She ducked down into the cellar near her garden, emerging after only a moment with the wooden bucket she regularly used to fill her water barrel. She hadn't stepped more than a few feet when she was approached by Rodric, who kept the livestock pens inside the bailey. Rodric, a robust man more than twice Tess's age who'd fathered no less than eight or nine bairns, reached for the bucket. Tess resisted but Rodric was insistent. Tess handed the bucket to him with a gracious smile and the pair of them walked side by side across the yard to the well. Rodric said something that made Tess laugh. She replied with something that had Rodric chortling as well. Conall watched this without a shred of jealousy, not even for the smiles she bestowed upon another, but with a deep satisfaction for the happy place she had made for herself here. It hadn't anything to do with him, he knew. He'd done nothing to pave the way to her general and favorable acceptance here at Inesfree. That was all Tess, he thought, watching her and Rodric now at the well, the older man reeling in the filled bucket.

The smithy approached the well now, his own bucket in hand. The three now talked conversationally for several minutes. At one point, Bran, the smithy, pointed off over the roof of the keep, and Tess and Rodric's eyes followed and nodded at whatever Bran was saying. Tess and Rodric moved away from the well, Tess smiling and waving at Bran, who seemed to watch the pair for several extra seconds, his own smile kindly.

Conall could only stand by and watch for so long. The very familiar feeling of wanting to be near her, to be the recipient of that glorious smile, reminiscent of those very first few weeks after Tess had been stolen and brought to Inesfree. He needn't invent reasons to be near her now. Those days were gone.

On a normal day, Conall and Tess, both quite busy in and around the castle, only happened upon one another throughout the day—sometimes by design, Conall didn't mind acknowledging. Today, he had planned to seek her out, with the intent to speak to her once again of wedding. He had no plan to demand, but instead thought to ask if she might—*good God*! He stopped his own considerations, his palms suddenly sweaty, realizing he hadn't put together any words he might say to her. He wanted to ask her properly, let her know it hadn't anything to do with Marlefield now. He just needed her to know he wanted her with him. Always.

Would you do me the honor...?

I think we should wed now, lass.

It would give me great satisfaction.... Immense pleasure?

Conall threw his head back, considering the timbered ceiling inside the stables. Jesu, why did these all sound so bloody awful?

It had to be right. She had to know—

"Laird?"

He started and turned to find Davidh considering him with a worried frown. Davidh raised his eyes to the ceiling as well, though his head never moved.

"Aye," Conall said lamely, and mumbled something unintelligible as he stalked out of the stables finally.

He couldn't remember a time, not in his entire life, when he'd been nervous. Scared? Yes. Angry, annoyed, frustrated? Regularly.

He could easily list a dozen emotions he'd felt, the greatest range admittedly coming *after* he'd met Tess of Marlefield, but he would vow he'd never experienced this chest-pounding anxiety before, not ever.

He began walking toward her and she turned, catching sight of him, shielding her eyes against the afternoon sun. And he witnessed, not for the first time, one of the reasons he very much thought they should wed: the smile she now offered him. It wasn't the same one she'd give to Eagan or the smithy or even Angus or John, and it was even different from one he could scarce recall but was sure his own mam had shown him when she'd been pleased with him; this smile was for him alone, he knew, a lover's smile without calculated enticement, an intimate smile that warmed and mesmerized him.

Conall stopped but a few feet away from her, a fleeting thought teasing him that if they were wed, he would keep right on walking, and he would kiss her.

He was still staring at her, at those green eyes that so rarely showed fear these days and her indescribable hair, shining and bright under the kerchief of soft pink, streaming down across her shoulders. He should probably suggest to her that she wear a brimmed hat to keep the sun off her perfect skin, but he found he much appreciated the golden color she'd earned all summer. Her small hand lowered from her forehead. And then sadly, her smile disappeared.

"Conall?" Worry tinted her voice.

Well, yes, he had forgotten to speak.

"Will you walk with me, lass?" His silent approach and pained expression had surely unnerved her, but he feared his attempt to smile now resulted only in a grimace, for she appeared concerned still. When she turned to hang her garden gloves over the rim of her water barrel, Conall exhaled deeply, trying to steady himself.

Tess faced him again and slid her hand into his. And now Conall relaxed. He led her away, out of the courtyard and through first one gate and then the next. Outside the castle walls, he turned toward the loch.

"Conall, is aught amiss?" She asked as they reached the water's edge.

He considered a place for them to sit.

"You have me fairly anxious," she added, "looking so glum and—"

He shook his head and faced her, cutting off her words. "Aye, 'tis me that's nervous, lass." He should have brought a blanket, something for her to sit on.

Tess tilted her head at this. "You? Nervous?"

Conall looked into her pretty green eyes, a hint of disbelief, a hint of excitement given equal space.

"You might want to kiss me then," she said boldly.

His lips tilted upward. "That will no relax me, lass."

"But it will remove all worry from your mind, if only for a while."

This was true.

Still holding her hand, Conall removed his sword and set it upon the ground then sat on the dry coarse grass. He reached up and put his hands on her hips to guide her to come atop him, her legs straddling his. Her eyes widened at this, but he thought she might be more intrigued than scandalized. She settled onto him and arranged her skirts about her thighs and Conall began to think of other things.

Their faces were only inches apart. Tess wrapped her arms around his neck while his hands remained at her hips. She moved her face closer. Conall didn't move, wanting her to pursue even more. She did so, slowly, her eyes holding his gaze even as she touched her lips to his. When he tightened his arms about her, she closed her eyes and opened her mouth to him. He let her keep the lead, let her be the first to involve tongue, let her press herself beguilingly against him.

They kissed and Conall forced himself to keep his hands still. They could do no more, as he knew they were nearly visible to the guards atop the gatehouse. And, too, he had a question to put to her. But, aye, didn't she feel so damn good, and didn't he just want so much more?

"Argh, lass," he growled against her soft lips, his hands again at her hips. "You'll no want an audience, I think." He tipped his head back toward Inesfree. Tess's gaze followed and he smiled inside at her deflated expression.

TESS SCRAMBLED OFF his lap then and sat just beside him.

They rested side by side at the shore of the loch, loathe to give up this moment. Shoulders pressed together with Tess's head tilted toward Conall. It was peaceful and comfortable, and she didn't want to ever leave.

"You have your garden all settled for winter?"

Tess nodded. "All but the fencing. I never did quite get that properly repaired or installed, but there's time yet. I've started the seedlings down in the cellar—would be nice to have a door thereabouts, might keep it just a bit warmer over the winter."

"Aye, that can be arranged."

"Actually, if there's to be a wedding soon—" she felt the muscles of his arm tighten against her shoulder "—the entire courtyard and hall will need some attention. Has Fynn yet asked for your permission?" His hard arm relaxed.

Conall nodded. "Aye, no sooner was I returned when he pounced on me."

Tess laughed at this. "He's a good man, Conall. You should be happy Serena has found someone who loves her so."

"And I am. Her life hasn't always been easy, either."

Tess agreed wholeheartedly that Serena deserved such bliss. But then she used this as a weak transition to introduce a topic she dreaded having to discuss, though knew they must.

"At least her sire didn't massacre her lover's clan," she said softly, and now knew she did not just imagine the tensing of his entire body.

He turned his head so that his chin rested on his shoulder. He considered her, giving a little nod, though this seemed only to be acceptance that she knew of this, and that it needed some recognition.

"You should have told me, Conall," she insisted, her voice still calm and low, "at the very beginning."

"Would you have married me then, lass? Would it have changed anything?'

She had given this some thought, had wondered this same thing so many times over the last few days. She believed she spoke truth when she answered, "I'd like to think I would have." She shrugged though. "But I really don't know. Maybe I wouldn't have believed you. I was plenty terrified then."

"You weren't," he insisted. And then, with a bit of humor, "You were annoyingly brave." Did she detect pride there as well?

"I am sorry, more than you can know, for what my father did to you."

Conall only nodded.

"Do you think we should talk about it?"

This made him frown. "I ought no to relive it... no anymore. And what purpose would it serve to talk it out?"

"It stands between us."

"Nae, it doesn't. Truth be told, it hasn't for some time."

This was, if she understood him correctly, both very revealing and especially perplexing. Her present circumstance, while much preferred to her original situation at Inesfree, had her in a rather awkward role. It was possibly no secret what their relationship actually was now—"there'll never be secrets where there be servants", her mother had often cautioned—and she enjoyed Inesfree very much, far more than she ever had Marlefield. But she was his leman, and nothing more.

For allowing her Bethany, for bringing Angus to Inesfree, she'd promised she'd no more try to escape. She'd essentially given her life to Inesfree. She would never leave, not so long as Conall lived. But to have this, and nothing more—would it be enough?

Conall turned fully sideways and took her hand in his.

"You and I were betrothed once."

He watched her face for a reaction, but she gave him only but a blank stare.

"Pardon me?"

"Actually, almost betrothed," he said. "That's why the Munros had come to Marlefield that night. We were to be betrothed."

Her mouth formed a small o. "But for my father and his brutal crime."

Conall nodded.

"Did he—oh, he planned it for a while then." It only made it worse.

"Or," Conall allowed, "it started true enough, but he found a plan better suited to his greed and acted on that."

Tess looked into his blue eyes and wondered what might have been different if her father had gone forward with the betrothal rather than what atrocity he had carried out. Would she have loved Conall still? She would have, she was sure.

"Lass, I haven't asked in a while, because I needed to ken, or needed you to ken it dinna have anything to do with—"

A noise, just the snapping of a twig, but rather unnatural in the quiet of the wood behind them, sent Conall diving for his sword, only a few feet away. Just as his hand might have closed around its hilt, a foot slammed down upon it. Conall lifted his head to find himself surrounded by several dozen soldiers, all bearing the blood red crest of the Munro upon their chests. He stood straight, contemplating quickly his odds without a weapon until the point of a blade was aimed at his own chest, staying any further movement.

Tess startled and turned. Atop the hill above the loch, silhouetted by the late afternoon sun, stood her father. She paled, her fear for Conall immediate and overwhelming.

CHAPTER 30

"My daughter, Tess!" Arthur Munro boomed as he descended and drew to within a few feet of her. "I see I have come too late, my dear."

"I have been here for half a year," Tess challenged.

"Long enough, it seems, to have grown to like rape."

Tess colored a bit, suspecting that her own father may have spied upon Conall and her for some time. But she defended, "It is not—it has never been rape."

Raising a brow, Arthur said, "But sinful. And treacherous. Tell me, has he married you?"

Tess shook her head slowly.

"And then he stopped demanding the marriage, did he not? Perhaps when he learned that Marlefield was no longer connected to your dowry. This, of course, makes you nothing more than a whore, as well as traitor to your clan."

But Tess ignored the purposeful insults. Conall had not mentioned marriage to Tess in months. A question in her eyes, she turned to Conall, but found his burning gaze upon her father.

Arthur motioned to the soldiers surrounding Conall. "Let us find this Inesfree. I'd like to unseat another MacGregor and claim it as my own."

Six men, allowing for no mercy, prodded Conall with the tips of their swords, not daring closer contact. As it was, Conall rose head and shoulders above Munro's men, and likely his legend even higher.

As they passed Arthur, the older man baited, "I do hope, MacGregor, that this manse is in as fine a condition as the last one I took from you."

To his credit, Conall ignored the barb, meant only to rile him and scatter his thoughts. Refusing to rise to such pointed provocation, he offered Sir Arthur an infuriatingly untroubled grin.

They marched up the hill and through the wood, toward Inesfree.

"Father? Father!" Tess cried, stretching her legs to catch up with her sire. "What do you plan to do with him?"

Arthur continued walking. "Do with him? Why, nothing at all, daughter." And just as her relief expelled itself in a sigh, he added dangerously, "I only mean to kill him."

Tess cried out and from the middle of the moving line of soldiers, Conall turned at this sound, toward the rear where walked Arthur and Tess, to ascertain the reason for her cry. For his attention, he was summarily knocked to his knees by the flat side of a sword swung sharply against his head.

Tess screamed again at this and made to race forward.

Arthur grabbed her by the arm, spinning her around.

"I am prepared to spare you, daughter, though your betrayal be great. Plead not for MacGregor or it will go the worse for you."

"For what reason do you seek to kill him?" Tess demanded hotly. "Surely not for me—"

"Reason? I need no reason," Arthur hissed in her face. "But let it serve as a warning that none should dare to take what is mine."

"I am—"

"I refer—" her father cut in bitingly "—to Marlefield."

"Of course," Tess murmured as Arthur dragged her forward. "I'm guessing you will justify this with the same reasoning behind your slaughter at Marlefield all those years ago?"

He seemed not at all surprised that she knew of his perfidy of more than a decade ago. "It remains true that those disloyal to our overlord will be punished."

"That is only what you tell yourself to shroud your true motives."

He did not demur. "Of course. And that is what I will tell the nobles and our king, if they should even care, though I much doubt it."

Tess was disgusted and disheartened by his complete lack of honor. She must think of a way to save Conall. Begging would gain her naught. Likewise, offering her own life instead would likely serve only to have them both killed.

But what were her father's plans? Inside Inesfree, his pitiful force of three dozen or so soldiers would face a massive MacGregor army, primed and eager, no doubt, for battle.

What little hope this calculation fostered inside her was demolished as they exited the wood and approached Godit's Rise. There, to Tess's utter dismay and rising fear, waited the remainder of her father's army. Nearly three hundred strong, armed, poised.

Tess's heart sank to her knees with the loss of hope.

In the distance, she saw Inesfree, its walls lined with soldiers, surely unnerved by the growing party gathering at its door, and likely fearful for Conall, outside and outnumbered.

Arthur shoved her off as the two parts of his force met. Tess followed frantically as her father approached Conall.

"Open that gate."

Conall shook his head, his eyes quickly taking in the whole of Tess and then turning back to Munro.

Munro grinned—a grimace really—and roughly grabbed Tess near again, surprising even his own men with a knife pressed to her throat. "Open that gate," he insisted again.

"Do not!" Tess cried, her eyes upon Conall, whose own eyes were tortured, his jaw tight, lips pursed. "Do not, Conall!" She repeated angrily, knowing that he would do it anyway. She could see it in his eyes as they focused on her. "Oh, Conall," she sobbed when he then lifted his gaze and nodded to her father.

Tess was released at once. She ran to Conall, pushing through two Munro soldiers, flinging herself upon Conall. "Oh, Conall. Why? Bethany, Angus, Serena—everyone! They will all be killed."

Conall ignored her, even as she clung to his chest, arms around his neck. He wouldn't look at her, his hard gaze fixed on her father. "Tess remains here. She does not come within," Conall insisted.

"But she must," Arthur laughed, "She'll want to plead till the end for your life."

At this, Tess spun away from Conall to lunge at her father, hands raised to claw at his eyes. With one effortless swipe of his gloved hand, Arthur knocked her to the ground. Conall growled and jerked forward. Once again, the swift appearance of several swords at his chest halted him. Angrily, he grabbed the tip of one in his fist, squeezing until he bled, forcing the blade to lower, quite easily against the lesser strength of the young man who held it. But then those other blades pressed closer, two at his neck, just piercing the skin. Infuriated, he flung the blade away, the force sending the soldier into the dirt.

"Bring her," Arthur said, adjusting his gloves as he led the party closer to Inesfree. A man, barely more than a child, helped Tess from the ground.

As the army, now moving forward as one, reached long bow range, Conall was led to the front to walk side by side with Arthur.

"Pray do not disappoint me, MacGregor," Arthur said out of the side of his mouth, eyes upon Inesfree. "You father, you know, whimpered at the end."

Again, Conall did not deign to respond.

"Now give the call," ordered Arthur.

Conall stepped forward. He walked quite a few paces ahead of Munro to be seen and heard. His eyes scanned the wall, then found and stayed with John Cardmore.

"Raise the gate!" He called.

"Conall, no!" Tess cried from behind him.

John Cardmore did not move but studied Conall's face.

"And get those men off the wall," Arthur said.

"Captain!" Conall called. "Get them down from the wall."

John Cardmore's huge form disappeared from view as he walked along the wall, toward the outer gatehouse, behind the other Mac-Gregor men. One by one, the MacGregor soldiers filed down into the bailey. After a moment, the walls were clear, and the portcullis began its slow rise.

When the gate was fully open, Munro soldiers swarmed the entrance, but they found only MacGregor soldiers, those within the courtyard, throwing down their swords.

Tess's dismay increased as she was dragged inside by her father. He'd waited outside until a sizable number of his troops were inside the yard. Arthur released her arm again and pulled forth his own sword, turning and waiting for Conall to be brought to him. With an ugly grimace and a mocking tilt of his head and sword, he said to Conall, "After you."

Conall walked, unarmed, across the bridge and into the bailey, with Arthur Munro spurring him forward with his sword at the back of his neck. Someone grabbed Tess's arm and bade her enter as well.

Inside now, enough Munro soldiers had entered to show their numbers greater already, though still the bulk of them remained outside the gate. They kept their drawn weapons trained on the empty-handed MacGregors and kept a distance of several feet between the two armies.

Tess looked around frantically. She was grateful she saw only soldiers in the yard, no innocents and thankfully not Serena or Fynn or dear Lord, not Bethany or Angus. But anguish tore at her when she considered the very small number of MacGregor soldiers. Even if they had retained their arms, they hadn't the numbers even to manage the quarter of her father's guards inside the castle. She sought out the figure of John Cardmore. With Conall unarmed and under the sword, John was their only hope. She couldn't believe they would surrender, just hand over the castle to her father. But hope was nebulous, and Tess was actually fearful that surrender or no, all of Inesfree was bound to die today.

John's eyes, narrowed and trained on Arthur Munro, strengthened Tess's tenuous optimism. She knew him well enough to recognize the resolve behind his hard gaze. While her father surveyed the yard, taking stock, Tess watched John's eyes dart ever so briefly to the ramparts now emptied of soldiers. She hadn't any idea that any plan or strategy was in place, but something tingled inside her. Her own eyes scanned the ramparts and then many other parts of the castle, but she saw nothing to give her hope. Yet, still she clung to that resolve she'd spied in the captain's eyes.

"This is disappointing in the extreme," her father said, while Conall stood still before him, near the middle of the yard, with all the MacGregor soldiers forced back, near to Tess's garden and the keep. "I don't mind a good scrum, MacGregor, but your pitiful army just dropped their weapons like they were on fire. At least your father's army fought back."

Conall turned and faced Arthur Munro, standing a good many inches above the height of the older man. But his eyes slid past Munro and met with Tess's, who stood a good distance behind her father.

She met his gaze, trying very hard to appear brave. But his eye had only settled on her for an instant before steadying harshly upon her sire.

"You will fall today," Conall said. "You will drop to the ground and it will be done."

Conall's eyes shifted one more time to meet Tess's for the briefest of seconds. And Tess understood with this second glance and with these words, he was giving her instruction.

"A bold claim to make, MacGregor," Arthur Munro said with an over-confident laugh. The snicker ended abruptly. "Kill them all," he ordered his soldiers. And he raised his sword to begin with Conall.

Tess's eyes widened. Conall did nothing to defend himself, only shouted brutally, "Loose," as his expression twisted into a menacing mien.

Just as a scream built in her chest, Tess was aware of a strange whooshing noise that rent the still silent air, in just that split second after Conall had roared. Yet even before her scream met air, she watched as a dozen arrows pierced and struck her father's body, coming from so many directions all at once. The force of the assault spun him around, so that he faced Tess now. He went immediately to his knees and then fell over, face first into the dirt of the courtyard, shafts breaking off underneath him. The last thing he saw was Tess.

The ramparts came alive then, with so many MacGregor soldiers rising from their crouched positions to rain more arrows down upon the Munros within the bailey, and even more upon the front side of the wall, catching the Munros outside the gate unawares and felling dozens with the first wave of sent missiles.

The MacGregors in the yard reached for the swords they'd dropped conveniently close to their own feet. Left with little choice, though their laird be dead, the Munros met them head on. Tess was surrounded by swords swishing through the air and ducked and scurried to the wall near the gate, recalling Conall's instruction. Crouching there, she watched with panicked eyes as peasants even poured from the hall, knives and daggers raised to lend aid. Conall had taken on the closest Munro, feinting as the man lunged, and rebounding to punch the man square in the face, grabbing the Munro's sword as he stumbled. John Cardmore dispatched two men who'd charged him, thrusting his right hand and sword to one assailant and impaling the next with the dagger in his left.

Tess heard the sound of the portcullis being lowered, and she knew they planned to trap the Munros inside, now definitely outnumbered. The soldiers on the ramparts stopped sending arrows down, now that close combat was established. Tess shrieked and bent her head as a Munro sword swiped very near, landing in the stone she clung to, only inches from her hand. The MacGregor soldier he'd been aiming for dodged but didn't turn fast enough and was then skewered by the same blade, falling near to Tess's feet. Without thinking, Tess fell to her knees beside the wounded man, recognizing Donald. Instinctively, she slapped her hand over the blood oozing from his chest, having no idea that she was now under the blade until a shadow fell over her. That same Munro aggressor raised his sword above his head to deliver a killing blow. Tess had no response but to squeeze her eyes shut, but the blow never came. She opened her eyes and gasped, as a flat blade emerged from the man's chest. The Munro soldier looked down at the protruding tip before he met Tess's surprised gaze. He fell before her eyes and there stood Ranulph behind him, his dagger now dislodged from the fallen man. Ranulph appeared just as shocked as Tess, his hand shaking, but he recovered first and grabbed her hand. He pulled her away from Donald, now dead, and headed toward the doors to the hall, his long dagger poised before him, his head and hand jerking left to right, considering all points of attack, clearly ill at ease with this role.

Carnage was all around, the Munros and MacGregors fighting fiercely and to the death. Tess stumbled and swung her gaze around to find Conall, barely visible through the heaving and shoving bodies and the cloud of dry dirt raised and hovering about them. But she found him, watched him destroy with ease first one and then another attacker. He was quick and sure, his movements economical and extremely swift despite his enormous size. And then she heard his voice and knew that he was aware of her present unharmed condition and flight to safety.

"Archers!" Conall's voice rang loudly above the guttural and strident noises of the battle. "To Tess! To Tess!"

Her attention was returned to their flight now as Ranulph stopped so suddenly before her, she crashed into his back. They were just near Tess's garden, very close to the doors of the hall but were confronted by a Munro warrior. Tess saw little more than his black eyes and horrid smirk as his helm covered most of his upper face. He was large and tossed his sword about, hand to hand, with obvious finesse and with the effective intention of terrifying Ranulph. Ranulph pushed Tess further behind him, holding the long dagger with his left hand. The Munro gave a twisted smile, lunging without striking in a great tease, which had Tess crying out. But then the big man's chest was littered with perhaps a half dozen arrows, all at once, and so unexpectedly that Ranulph and Tess both turned toward the ramparts near the gate. The MacGregors up there, those watching the inside of the gate, had their bows nocked again already, aimed in front of Tess and Ranulph.

"Get her inside!" One yelled. Ranulph wasted no time but took up her hand again and pulled her along the edge of her garden. Twice more, Munro men fell in front of them as the warriors on the battlements led them safely to the keep. Ranulph and Tess stood back to back at the large arched doors, as Ranulph banged for entrance while Tess watched the melee they'd barely escaped. Yet another Munro came charging and screaming at her, sword raised, and he, too, fell, as had the others, though this time because his head had been lopped off his body.

Tess's shock and fear would not even allow the scream within to come out. Standing now over the headless man was Ezra, without any helm. He nodded curtly, his face still as ugly and unhappy as ever, no softening at all for the life-saving deed he'd just executed. He turned and staved off several more attacks while Tess watched in horror and Ranulph continued to call out for entrance at the door.

Finally, the door opened and Ranulph and Tess dived within before the door was slammed shut and the brace dropped again. Both crashed immediately to the floor, quivering and crying.

The first thing Tess heard, before the door shut out so much of the noise was Angus, his voice louder and more ferocious than she had ever imagined, "Goddammit, where is she?" He banged his fist on the table.

"She's here now, Angus." Serena's voice. "She's safe."

Serena knelt before Tess just as Bridie fell before Ranulph.

Tess's palms were upon the floor, trying to steady herself, to stop the trembling. Serena's hand came under her arm. "Come Tess, away from the door."

She felt another hand beneath her other arm. Tess was pulled to her feet by Leslie and Serena. She looked from one frightened face to another as they led her to the table with Angus. She noticed Leslie had two daggers in his normally unadorned belt.

"Bethany?"

"The children are safe in the chapel with Dorcas and Moira," Serena informed her and pushed Tess down at the table across from Angus. Tess reached out her hand to cover his and saw and heard his whimpered relief.

Ranulph was pressed onto the bench next to her, still shuddering as Tess did. She turned and threw her arms around him, while Bridie, standing, hugged them both and cried.

And then there was no noise. Suddenly, only a moment later, the clanging of swords, the cries of those speared or gouged or hacked, the gruff and frenzied clamor of battle faded to near silence.

Everyone inside the hall, only a dozen or so who hadn't sought refuge somewhere deeper within the keep, stilled and cast anxious eyes toward the doors. All exchanged fretful glances, for what seemed like many long minutes until Tess could stand it no more. She stood and ran to the door, hobbling as her legs wobbled.

"Lass, no!" Leslie called, at her side, his hand upon the face of the door while Tess fumbled with the heavy brace.

"But Conall," she said, turning her worried eyes upon the hapless steward.

"We wait," he insisted, trying to be stern, to not be affected by her beseeching gaze. He failed and pushed her gently out of the way, pulling forth a dagger with one hand while lifting the brace with the other.

"Ranulph, no!" Bridie cried as her husband came to Leslie's side. The two men nodded at each other, each awkwardly armed, and Leslie opened the door. Ranulph presented his dagger first, then he and Leslie led Tess out.

The yard was nearly still, but Tess recognized instantly that the only ones standing were MacGregors. Some Munros did survive, but they were on their knees, their hands linked on top of their helmets, grouped together and under guard of several unwounded MacGregor men. Leslie and Ranulph relaxed but kept their daggers ready.

Dozens of bodies spotted the yard, mostly dead, but some moaning low. Tess was sorry to see so many lives extinguished, and more so because it was her own sire who instigated this travesty. Sadly, she recognized a few more MacGregor soldiers among the dead, though their numbers were not one tenth of the Munros' losses.

Still a cloud of dust hung low in the air in certain sections of the courtyard. The earth which had settled coated all those fighting men with a fawn colored powder, settling in their hair and upon their faces and over their persons so that from a distance they appeared but one color.

But Tess recognized Conall still, by the sheer size of him, and forced out a relieved breath. He was coming down from the wall, his sword re-sheathed. He did not see Tess as he made his way directly to a fallen MacGregor. He went to one knee beside the man, almost exactly in the center of the yard. Tess approached from behind without a word.

The man upon the ground was larger even than Conall, stretched out on his back, with one knee bent. Blood covered his chest and his shoulder. His eyes were closed, his face covered in that fine dusting of buff grime. Tess cried out, recognizing the unmoving body as belonging to John Cardmore.

"No!" She sobbed and fell to her knees beside Conall, her hands going to John's chest, searching for the source of the wound. She felt Conall's hand at her back as she bent over John.

"Tess."

"We have to get him inside," she insisted. "We have to—"

"Tess," this now, with greater firmness, from Conall.

Tess turned to Conall, distraught at his lack of emotion. "Conall, why aren't you doing something? We cannot just let him... oh, John," she wailed, turning back to the captain.

"Ach, now, lass," John said, opening his eyes, bright blue within that monotone face of dirt. "I think we're only waiting on a litter."

Her relief was so strong it pained her. Traumatic laughter erupted and she leaned to shower his face with kisses, her tears leaving streaks upon his leathery cheeks.

"'Tis his shoulder, is all," Conall said.

"No like they can carry me, aye, lass?"

She sat back on her heels, her hand at her chest, leaning into Conall's shoulder.

"The Munros outside the wall turned and ran once the gates were closed," Conall informed her. After a moment, while they both gazed upon the useless killing, Conall said, "I am sorry about your sire, Tess."

She looked for and found her father's body and wondered only briefly at her own lack of sorrow. "I am sad that I am an orphan, now completely," she said somberly, "but, truth be told, I never really had a father. I should be sorry as well, I suppose, but he... he deserved to die."

EPILOGUE

Angus sat in a chair near Tess's garden. In his hands, he held one section of the wattle fence and at his side sat a basket filled with the thin, pliable branches and twigs used to make them. He didn't need sight for a chore such as this. Weaving and braiding came easily to him. The lass's hands were too soft for this; his were hardened and callused, and proudly so. She wanted her garden 'pretty', she'd said, for Serena and Fynn's wedding. He had some idea that she planned to festoon it with some ribbons and girlish fripperies that surely only she and Serena might notice. But he was happy to oblige her.

While he wove the twigs into a small section of fencing, he thought as he often did of his circumstance here at Inesfree, and how it all began. Before Tess had come to his cottage, he'd not been visited by another soul, excepting his own son, for more than twenty years. It wasn't living, he'd known, but he'd accepted it, same as he'd accepted his blindness so many years ago, same as he'd endured the death of other tiny bairns after Fynn, and then the passing of his Nan. Angus could still clearly recall how he'd enjoyed the lass's company that evening, and his lips tilted with the memory. When he'd heard riders coming, though they'd been intent upon stealth, he'd scrambled around and found his only available weapon, an aged and rusty sword. He'd brandished it bravely, imagining this was as good a way to go out as any, protecting a lass.

He'd stepped outside the cabin while the lass had continued to sleep and walked carefully away from the door just as the riders neared. It had been decades since he'd heard the sounds of an approaching army, but he'd reckoned there to be around fifty mounted men.

He'd raised his sword, unafraid. "Turn yourselves 'round,'" he'd called out.

The horses stopped moving, and a set of heavy feet thumped to the ground. He hadn't moved, and not one ounce of fear had shaken his sword hand. Even without sight, he had sensed the urgency and simmering disquiet which came, rolling off the man who had approached him, well before his deep and uncompromising voice boomed from only a few feet away.

"We're looking for a lass."

"Ain't seen none," Angus had said.

"Aye, but I'm thinking you have," the man had replied. "For yourself, I think you'd no bother to stand against us. But for a lass, you might." He'd stepped closer and lowered his voice. "She does that, makes you want to keep her safe. She dinna even ask, you just want to do it."

Angus had hesitated, maybe too long. "Ain't seen a lass."

"Aye, old man," the mighty soldier had said. "Then you will no mind if I have a look around."

It had been pointless to resist or keep up the charade. There had been nothing in this man's voice that spoke of ill-intent, toward him or the lass.

"Now what would you be wanting with her? And I'll be knowing—before you take her away—why she felt she had to run from you."

The warrior had not spoken immediately but had stepped still closer to Angus. When he'd answered, it was less the words that came and more the sound, leveled with so much anguish as to be physical as he'd said, for Angus's ears alone, "I canna breathe without her," that had convinced Angus to lower his worthless weapon.

"Are you alone here then?" The big man had asked.

"Aye, but I'd hoped I might convince her to stay."

"As did I." This had come not without some critical humor.

"Then you'd best take me with you," Angus had said. "I'll not be just handing her over to you without making sure I'd done right."

He'd heard then a slight consenting chuckle and another set of feet hit the ground. His arm had been touched, and he'd been led away and sat upon the back of a cart.

Now, he tilted his head, taking in all the sounds around him, the yard busy today. It had been well scraped of the battle that had been waged here only a week ago. Angus could still sense it, but he doubted most others could. He heard the pounding of the smithy, hammering out some forged item; he could pick out the voice of Davidh in the stables, lightly upbraiding a young stable hand, who'd forgotten to secure a stall; in the far corner, he perceived the swish of water sloshing as someone hoisted up a vessel from the well.

John sat beside him, wounded but well, employed with the same task as Angus. He grumbled about the twigs not listening to his hands. Angus heard the lass, in some conversation with Bethany as the two sat inside the garden to the left, where the vegetables had been this summer.

"We have to make sure the fence is secure within the ground," Tess was saying.

"Fence," said Bethany.

"Yes, darling. It's called wattle. And this here is the tool that Conall has given me," this, with some soft exasperation, followed by a tapping noise, "and why he thinks this will work is beyond me. I couldn't pound butter with this thing."

Laughter came close then, followed by Ranulph's voice, "Here, milady. I've a better hammer for the job."

Tess's tapping stopped, and then Angus heard a more robust drumming, followed by Tess's happy exclamation, "Much better. Thank you, Ranulph. Conall should focus on soldiering, I think."

Angus laughed. "He can hear you, lass." Angus felt her turn her head, looking around guiltily, he was sure. Of course, Angus had known he was close. He always knew and was continuously surprised that no one else could sense his presence. It didn't always silence a room or an area, but there was ever an air of heightened sensation that hovered about when the laird was near the lass.

"Aye, he can," Conall said, without any reproach in his tone. He greeted Ranulph, and Angus was pleased to hear no thread of hostility toward the man. A sharper and stronger pounding of the fence into the ground followed and Angus knew that Conall had taken the hammer from Tess.

Tess came to stand near Angus, reaching for the finished sections propped against his chair. But she was stopped. Angus realized by the way her breath caught, that the laird had touched her, maybe moving her out of the way to tackle the wattle fence himself. No, they were still, and close to each other, as told by their short breaths.

Next to Angus, John stopped fiddling so unsuccessfully with the branches; Angus was sure he watched the pair closely.

Little by little, movement around the yard ceased. But Conall and Tess hadn't any idea.

Bethany came to stand next to him, her hand idly upon Angus's leg. He imagined her curious little eyes were on the laird and the lass as well.

"You should wed me now, lass," Conall said. Angus scrutinized his tone, which suggested he'd been thinking on it, had been planning to say as much, though this now seemed to have just spilled out. As far as proposals went, this one needed work.

Angus could well feel Tess's surprise. "Why would you want to wed me...now?"

"Lass, I dinna think you were as daft as John is convinced I am," he said, with no small amount of humor, embracing his own carelessly spurted words and even their poor timing and delivery. "Dinna you ken I love you?"

The lass likely couldn't discern it, but Angus heard well the anxiousness in the laird's voice. She didn't though, not over the thundering of her own heart.

She tried to speak. Only breath came forth. Finally, a bit exasperated, she announced, "No. I *dinna ken*."

John let out a soft chortle beside Angus.

"Aye, you do," Conall said patiently and kissed her briefly. "You feel it in my hands when they touch you. You must see it in my eyes when they find you. You seek it in my kiss, and you ken it's been with us for longer than even I dare to admit." The lass caught a startled and happy cry, subduing it. "No more tears, lass. Just say the words back to me and give me your promise it'll always be so."

It took a moment for her to gather herself to speak coherently. Aye, but the lass was ever one for blatting and bawling, Angus thought fondly, never having known a person so filled to the brim with such wayward emotions.

"I am—I have been—so in love with you, for such a very long time."

Angus tipped his head, aware that his own eyes misted.

"Promise him!" Came a shout, from somewhere across the yard.

Tess gasped and Conall laughed. Angus sensed dozens of people watching them, on the wall, some gathered in the yard, their faces wreathed in smiles, he imagined, some women dabbing at their eyes with the corners of their aprons perhaps.

And now Tess laughed while Conall waited.

"Promise him!" More calls came. Angus could pick out Serena's tearful call and Fynn's happy shout.

Bethany joined the ruckus, with a cry of "Pomis him!" sounding above them all. Angus chuckled when he heard John's voice, "Aye, get on with it, already!"

"I promise! I promise!" She finally answered and Conall locked his lips to hers as the growing cheers and whistles became thunderous.

———— ∾ ————

The End

Thank you for reading **The Touch of Her Hand**.
Gaining exposure as an independent author relies mostly on
word-of-mouth, so if you have the time and inclination, please
consider leaving a short review wherever you can. Thanks!

Other Books by Rebecca Ruger
The Highlander Heroes Series
The Touch of Her Hand
The Memory of Her Kiss
The Shadow of Her Smile
The Depths of Her Soul
And Then He Loved Me (A Highlander Novella, Book 1)

Coming September 2020
Highlander Heroes Book 5: The Truth of Her Heart

Coming February 2021
Highlander Heroes Book 6: The Love of Her Life

Coming Fall 2020
Mountains To Move, A Highlander Novella, Book 2

Other Books...
The Regency Rogues:Redemption Series
When She Loved Me
If I Loved You
She Will be Loved

Made in the USA
Monee, IL
17 April 2021